Ian Gouge

An Infinity of Mirrors

Coverstory books

First published as "Mirrors" in ebook format, 2015;
"Mirrors" paperback published in 2017.
"Mirrors" is no longer available.

This edition published by Coverstory books 2018;

ISBN 978-1-9997840-4-1

Copyright © Author 2018

www.coverstorybooks.com

Other Books by Ian Gouge

Novels and Novellas

Losing Moby Dick and Other Stories - Coverstory books, 2017

Losing Moby Dick - Kindle 2015

Writing to Gisella - Kindle 2015

Riding the Escalators - Kindle 2015

The Big Frog Theory - Paperback, 2017; Kindle, 2012

Short Stories

Degrees of Separation - Coverstory books, 2018

Secrets & Wisdom - Coverstory books, 2017

Poetry

After the Rehearsals - Coverstory books, 2018

Punctuations from History - Coverstory books, 2018

Human Archaeology - Paperback, 2017

Collected Poems (1979-2016) - Paperback, 2017; Kindle, 2018

Chapter One

At first he was unsure of what he was actually seeing.

The sun that now shone brightly through the large shop window - and which, to make matters worse, was further enhanced by its reflection off the recently rain-soaked pavement outside - could surely only generate a light that would be prone to playing tricks. Unleashed in an environment of gilt and glass - not to mention the myriad of mirrors! - he was certain of one thing only: namely, that it could not be trusted.

He preferred an even light. Undoubtedly that of a few minutes earlier - the post-shower illumination, still subdued by the remnants of grey cloud that endeavoured to keep it at bay - offered the kind of gentle suffusion that would have been ideal in his present environment. Strangely enough, as they had entered the shop (he following Julia, of course), he distinctly recalled a brief glance towards the heavens. There had been no purpose in the gesture apart from the automatic Englishness of it; the preoccupation with the somehow random mechanics of the atmosphere and its influence on the general state of any sane individual's mind.

Not that there was anything untoward in his own psyche at that precise moment: he had been a little bored, yes, but would admit to no more than that. Julia, sensitive to his general demeanour and aware that he was unfamiliar with their precise destination, had taken the trouble to offer him directions to the shop (some tortuous navigation based on other, equally unfamiliar shops), and had promised him, by way of compensation, that it was no more than a few minutes walk from the car. Depending on one's definition of 'few', he supposed that she might indeed feel her description to be accurate - but had he been pressured, he would have needed to beg to differ. Regent Street was, indeed, not that far from where they had left the car - and that had been a trial, finding a parking meter! - but it was also, as any leg-weary tourist would immediately testify, by no means the briefest of thoroughfares in the capital. The consequence of them parking beyond the Oxford Circus end, rather than close to Piccadilly, was measurable in minutes: had they been in transit a little earlier, it might also have been measured in the weight of water that would have fallen on them from the previously leaden sky.

As far as excursions were concerned, this was not one he had been particularly looking forward to; not that there was anything sinister in that, of course. Shopping, in almost any form, failed to stimulate him; and shopping with Julia - who seemed to operate according to a completely different set of rules under such occasions - invariably left him bored. She would have been aware that the combination of both his sense of duty and a subservience to the feelings he held for her would not permit him to allow her the expedition as a solo affair - though that might well have been the most satisfactory arrangement all round, as demonstrated in her attempt to encourage some enthusiasm in him earlier that morning.

"But it's what she wants!" she had said playfully, hoping to draw him into the undertaking.

He remained unconvinced. A mirror seemed to him such a strange wedding gift - even for someone as 'unusual' as Julia's sister - that he failed to warm to the idea any more than if she had been enthusing over the potential purchase of a doormat.

"It has to be a bit special, of course. I mean, not just any old mirror - which is why I want us to go into town. And why I want *you* to help me choose it!"

The last comment - added as an afterthought in a desperate attempt to hang on to him in some sense - was so transparent that it died the instant it was uttered. Julia would choose; he might be asked to nod or to comment, but he would *not* be asked to choose. He might be asked to carry - and there his presence would certainly be something more significant, if not indispensable - but, as always, Julia would drive them forwards, pushing on through the morass of daily transactions which, by and large, passed him by in something of an anonymous blur. He might have feigned an interest (his failure to dissemble when it was politically correct to do so was a complaint she had often laid at his door), but his attitude was dominated by the phenomenal sense of unimportance he attached to the whole venture - even if it was what Laura said she wanted.

On their arrival - an arrival heralded by the ferocious blast from a heater suspended above the door - he had taken little interest in the initial proceedings, willingly divesting himself of the responsibility of being Julia's chaperone once the smart Assistant had hove towards them from the depths of the shop. As soon as it seemed prudent - that is, as soon as his sensibility told him that Julia was happy to release him - he had slipped away from her side and strolled, arms behind his back, the fingers of his right hand tapping on the reverse of his left.

There was not far he could go, of course. The shop, which was not enormous, was arranged as two aisles, with a partition down the centre dividing the floor space. This singular construction - like its more solid brethren that, on either side, kept a Travel Agents and a Gentlemen's Outfitters at bay - was hung with numerous paintings, photographs and posters, all elaborately framed and each bearing a small, if not discrete, price tag. Out of habit, he always checked the prices of things first; not because of any intrinsic need to worry about what he could afford to spend (there was no problem there!) but in order to establish the place these objects should occupy within his personal scale of quality and respectability.

The prices were, he had confessed quietly to himself (though without surprise) a little on the steep side; not, he might have added as a caveat, that he had any major expertise in the value of 'Art'. For what they were - and he recognised many of the posters, so they could not have been *that* exclusive - he suspected that the asking price had been slightly inflated, presumably to allow for the not inconsiderable rental of the premises and the legendary - if potentially inaccurate - notion that tourists (and Americans especially) would pay anything for trash. Indeed, having recognised that by and large the artwork was over-priced, he had then realised, in some obscure and intuitive sense, that there was also too much of it. Class, something told him, would not have permitted quite so many things on display; there would have been a little more space around the paintings - a little more 'wall' - giving, in some odd way, a sense of respect to what was being sold. Lots of space - as he knew from his infrequent visits to the City's galleries - implied reverence, though there was, he was sure, nothing here to be revered.

This vague dissatisfaction with the establishment, and the sense that somehow Julia had been sold short by whoever recommended the place to her in the first place, had led him to cast a brief glance in her direction. The smart Assistant - who seemed to be dressed in relation to the prices of the objects and not their quality or quantity - had taken Julia in hand, and was leading her towards the small section near the front of the shop where the mirrors - in equal abundance to everything else it seemed - were ranged. He had thought for a moment of returning to her side; of even trying to rescue her - striding over cavalry-like, taking her by the arm, and leading her out of the ambush and into safety. However fanciful and appealing this might have been (and make no mistake, to some part of him it *was* appealing) any such attempt would have been doomed: firstly, it would not have been what Julia wanted - after all, she had given herself up willingly to the trap - and secondly, it was simply not the sort of thing he did. So, with some sense of resignation, he had resumed his perambulation around the shop.

When Julia had called - that inevitable cry of 'Mark!' delivered in such a way that, despite its soft sound and its feminine origins, it bore for him all the hallmarks of an order and none of a request - he had already turned at the end of the shop and was actually heading her way. Two days before he had stayed up late (despite the protests this time!) to watch - again! - a showing of 'Ben Hur' on one of the satellite channels. As he moved towards Julia - walking now, though still attempting to imitate a stroll - he was reminded how the shop layout, the long and thin circuit, was akin to the circus where the great chariot race was held. With the finish in sight, was he to be Charlton Heston, victorious with his white Arabian steeds, or Ben Hur's old adversary, Messala, vanquished at the last?

The smart Assistant was, with some difficulty, holding a large mirror; Julia, standing proudly at her side, as if making the choice was a cause for celebration. Mark, still some feet away, already knew that in this particular tournament Julia would be victorious, and suspected that the part so ably played by Stephen Boyd had been reserved for him.

"Here it is!", Julia said triumphantly, "What do you think?"

Mark - aware that his contribution to the choosing had indeed been mythical rather than real - tried to suppress the sense of 'I told you so' that was rattling around inside his head; the superiority of sub-conscious over conscious and the certainty that, in the end, it would indeed be Julia's choice of gift. He could not have voiced the thought; with whom would he have shared it?

The mirror itself - now pointing directly at him and in such a fashion as to give the smart Assistant the head and legs of a woman but the slightly larger torso of a man - seemed a little uninspiring. Mark had taken a quick glance at a number of the others that were strewn around Julia in such a manner as to suggest examination and rejection, then struggled to spot any immediately significant difference in 'the chosen one'. The frame was gilt - but then so were the frames of those discarded, with the exception of two or three wooden ones. One of these, a handsome mahogany offering, was instantly his own preference and had he indeed been allowed to contribute to the debate, then this item would have captured his vote. That of course would have led to all sorts of complications - he and Julia nominating different champions - though he had no doubt that the end result would still have been the same. Perhaps - and this as he had come to a standstill some three feet from the smiling duo - it was best that he had been given no choice at all: to find out *for certain* that his vote was actually worth less than his partner's might have been a little too much to take.

It was just at this moment, as he wrestled limply with his theme, that he was suddenly quite unnerved by what he was seeing - by what the mirror showed him, in fact.

"Well?" After her initial 'Mark!', it seemed not impossible that this second word might constitute the entirety of Julia's correspondence with him on these premises. She was anxious for confirmation, for his approval, poised like a cat ready to pounce on anything contrary; even the slightest of indications would have been enough for that hair trigger of hers.

He had heard the word, but was too busy concentrating on what he could see in the mirror to immediately respond. A little above the right hand pocket of his jacket - a brown tweed jacket that he had picked up on a golfing and fishing holiday in Scotland some years before, and which, he might add, had been unquestionably his *favourite* jacket of all time - he noticed what could only be described as a blemish. He leant slightly forwards (Julia could only assume that he was examining the frame) to confirm his initial diagnosis. It was indeed a blemish, a fault in the cloth, a small patch were the pattern seemed to be broken, out of kilter; as he looked in the mirror - in the bright, playful light - it appeared not as a minor flaw, but as an ugly and unsightly mark.

He brought his right hand from behind his back (where it had maintained its post, fingers tapping throughout) and lifted the edge of the cloth. Taking his eyes away from the mirror for a second, he glanced down, needing to confirm the reality of what he had been shown; indeed, the weave was flawed.

"Remarkable", he said, looking back towards the mirror.

It had been intended as no more than an aside to himself - some form of internal confirmation that there was something he had lived with for years and of which he had never been aware - but he had evidently spoken it a little too loudly (or perhaps that it had escaped at all was enough) for the mirror to be suddenly whisked out of his line of sight by the Assistant whose triumphant action had been prompted by Julia's "We'll take it!" uttered but an instant after his own, more private, contribution.

He remained motionless for a few seconds, watching the pantomime being played out by Julia and the Assistant with the air of someone on the outside; an observer, distanced and with no stake in the game. Once the mirror had been deposited on the counter and a large sheet of brown paper produced and thrown over it - Julia casting a quick, smiling glance in his direction at his point - Mark felt able to move again, freed from the strange paralysis that had descended upon him.

He wanted to confirm still further - as if what he had seen already was not enough! - that there was indeed something wrong in the material of his jacket; he could not comprehend how, after all this time (and perhaps the passing of time was the key) he could suddenly recognise something that had been blatantly obvious for years. To his left several mirrors - obviously not getting on Julia's shortlist - still hung, huddled together on the wall. Turning, he shuffled almost imperceptibly until he was able to get a clear sight - without appearing to be looking of course, and this was the trick - of his right-hand pocket. A glance towards the door (to check, guiltily perhaps, on the progress of the wrapping; or beyond the counter, to the source of the light) confirmed that his actions had not been interpreted as suspect and that he could pursue his enquiry.

Whether he expected to find that the cloth was actually perfect he could not say. Indeed, had he done so he would have found himself embroiled in another, rather troublesome debate over how he had managed to imagine the blemish in the first instance. However, the mirror he was now concentrating on - this second looking glass - could do no more than confirm the story already told both by its contemporary and, more importantly, by his own eyes without the assistance of any intervening medium. The question he now faced (this as he straightened slightly, trying to come to terms with a rather strange sensation that the revelation had planted in his consciousness) was why - or indeed how! - no-one had said anything to him about the jacket before now. Why was it that after some twelve years of wearing the thing, of being seen in it so much that people even commented on the fact that it seemed a part of him, why was it that no-one had mentioned the flaw?

A noise from the counter roused Mark from the brief trance in which he found himself (standing stationary, staring at something but seeing nothing), and when he refocused, he saw the Assistant supporting a relatively thin oblong brown paper package on its side. Again both sets of eyes were focused in his direction, and the smile from Julia told him not only that she was unquestionably pleased with the result of their visit, but also that it was time to leave and that his assistance was required.

She squeezed his arm gently as he reached her side. It was a gesture she often used to convey a million and one things; but whichever of these, it seemed they were always benevolent and Mark had learned to respond with a certain smile of his own.

"Ready?" It seemed a strange question from her given the minor role he had played in the drama thus far and how, in his own mind at least, the proposition could be more accurately posed the other way round.

"Ready" he said, offering the parallel.

Julia looked at the parcel and Mark, interpreting the gesture, extended his arms towards it.

"I'll get the door," said the Assistant definitely, and moving away from the counter left Mark balancing the package on his own.

"Can you manage?" Julia's smile had now been replaced by a study of more practical concern, though not rising to any great extent of being worried. It was, Mark knew, the sort of thing one ought to say at times like this, just as responsibility were about to be handed over.

"Fine."

He pulled the mirror to his chest and endeavoured to get his right hand underneath it as his left steadied the side. It was larger than he had imagined - larger than it looked, in some strange way - and it seemed as if the grip he had planned for it (a 'natural' grip, to all intents and purposes) might be insufficient here. Allowing his fingers to find a degree of comfort in their new, tensed state, he went to lift the parcel from the counter. It slipped instantly - just an inch or so - and landed with a reasonably soft 'thud' back on the surface. A breath escaped from Julia. Mark looked quickly at her. It should have been a word, or even a number of words, but knowing what the words might have been - "Careful!" for one - the breath was sufficient admonition for him to take stock of the position and readjust his grip.

At the second attempt - Julia all the while nearby, but without laying a finger on the brown paper - Mark and the parcel moved as one away from the counter and towards the door. Not only was his burden larger than he had imagined, but it was also heavier too, and passing out into the street - being hit by the noise and the smell of the city - he was suddenly concerned about the distance they had to travel to the car and his ability to make it in one piece. Not known for her lucid thought or incisiveness - not in his mind at any rate - Julia, who must have picked up his concern telepathically, was already away from his side and out at the kerb hailing a taxi.

"I know it's not far," she said, returning to lead him towards the black cab that was now squealing to a halt in front of them, "but if he doesn't like it then that's his problem. And he was going that way anyhow, so I don't see what he's got to complain about!"

She was condemning the Cabby before they had even told him where they were going; deciding, in advance almost, that whatever happened she was going to give him a piece of her mind just to let him know where he stood. In the event - as Mark struggled stiffly across the pavement - the Cabby turned out to be more of a White Knight than a Black one, and, seeing his passengers struggling, he actually got out of the cab to give Mark a hand into it. The sudden easing of his burden (surprisingly significant since he had travelled but a few feet with it) came as welcome relief to Mark who nodded his thanks to the driver. Julia - now facing a completely different situation to the one she had envisaged being in - went over the top in her effusive thanks to the man, not only as they climbed into the taxi, but as they set off too, regaling him with the details of their expedition with such enthusiasm that it was almost impossible for him to get a word in edgeways.

Mark, hands clasped together and adjusting to the sensation the sudden effort had left in his fingers (the string round the paper was abrasive too), rested for the brief duration of their journey and watched the other shoppers marching the street, all seemingly carrying smaller burdens than his own. As a backdrop, he could hear Julia's version of the purchase, and a somewhat gruff voice punctuate her sentences with "Yes, love" and "I know what you mean".

To a certain extent, Mark imagined - once they were settling within their own vehicle, the gift laying flat, out of sight - that Julia might have felt the taxi ride the most enjoyable part of the whole episode. Not only had the driver - Frank, apparently - turned out not to be an ogre, he also proved to be doubly considerate to the extent of again leaving his cab at the end of their brief journey - "I know it's not far, love, but I'd 'ave done the same thing" - to help Mark get he parcel into the boot of his Audi. Julia had paid him twice what he had asked as a fare on the basis, she said, that had he not done so they might have lost a great deal more money. Her statement, uttered as they pulled out into the mainstream of traffic and began to head north, brought two things to Mark's mind that he had not as yet considered: would he have lost control of the parcel, and how much had it cost anyway? The second question was of little importance, though given some of the prices he had seen displayed in the shop - and if size and weight were anything to go by - then the package now resting in the boot of his car had certainly not been given away! As to his ability to keep a hold of it while they walked Regent Street, there he was a little more concerned. He could not - and this he knew despite any internal bluff - have made it all the way without stopping; indeed, without assistance of some kind. Whether he might actually have dropped it, had lost his grip on the string - which would have been gnawing into his fingers remember - and been witness to, if not responsible for, an almighty 'crash', was difficult to say; but as they pulled away from a set of lights, Julia once again offering a brief squeeze of his arm, he too was thankful for Frank.

Chapter Two

Belsize Park was reached after twenty minutes or so, Camden Town giving way to something a little more refined as Mark steered the Audi along his favourite route across town. He used to wonder where the name had originated: was it, perhaps, some form of combination of 'Belle' and 'Size', indicating that its earliest inhabitants were comfortable with the general geography of the place and its relaxed surroundings?

He wondered - as he pulled off the main road from the city - whether Belsize Park might not be some form of resting place for those who had been unable to make it all the way up to the top of the hill and the haven of Hampstead; not that Hampstead was truly much of a haven any more, of that he was regretfully certain. Its large, grand houses had been turned, one by one, into flats and bedsits; small, squat little rooms where people festered in the forlorn hope that one day they would be rescued - or such was how he imagined it must be. He had been lucky, of course, in that he had never needed to resort to living in such a place; his own residences had been more or less provided for him, and with all prerequisite elements to ensure comfort.

There was - at least from his own point of view - no longer any concern about "making it" to the top of the hill. Thanks to his Father's judicious investments and the little he himself had been able to input once he was out of college and working, he was now residing on the borders of Hampstead Garden Suburb in a rather pleasant, if unostentatious, detached house with its own small swimming pool in the garden. He did not like to think that he took his good fortune for granted; after all, he had driven through Camden often enough to know that there were people less fortunate than himself; people who had not been lucky enough to have the 'start' that he had. The words of his Father - something about 'making your own luck' - had been drummed into him at an early age, however, and even tough he could *see* the environment around him (in social and political terms) he was unable to *appreciate* it.

Julia did little to disturb this balance - and though the balance was paradoxically a little one-sided, there was enough on the lesser side for Mark to maintain a degree of equilibrium with which he was comfortable. She had moved to London from Hertfordshire in pursuit of a rather vacuous career in advertising which, when it came down to it, was not as she had imagined it would be and which left her, in consequence, at something of a loss. Her meeting Mark - a blind date of sorts, organised by some mutual acquaintances - had turned out to be just the thing to interrupt the thoughts she was having about returning home and in some way, shape or form, 'starting again'. Belsize Park, in her terms at any rate, was already something of a 'step up'; which meant, of course, that attaching herself to Mark's own establishment further up the hill was a *real* achievement.

For his part, Mark was aware of all of this. He had been aware of it the first time he had introduced Julia to Simon and Beatrice (which had been, for some obscure reason, before she had actually seen his own house). They had purred up from the tube station (much as they did now, Laura's gift in the trunk of the car) and Julia, almost without reservation, had extolled the virtues of the tree-lined streets and the large hedges that kept the roads separated from the houses. She had been complementary - a little over-enthusiastic possibly - in the praise she lavished on the bricks and mortar in which Mark's Aunt and Uncle lived, but had, as a reward, been given the standard tour of the house and garden by Beatrice, allowing Mark a quick mid-afternoon Whisky with his Uncle.

"Fine girl," Simon had said, after a manly pause in their sipping of Scotch, watching both Julia and Beatrice walking past the window outside and heading for the small pond at the bottom of the garden.

Mark, recalling the conversation as they approached once more that same house - and glancing to Julia as if to refresh his memory - had made some comment broadly in agreement with Simon's judgement, but (and here he had been careful) without going over the top. Since the death of his Father, Simon and Beatrice had taken the role of parents upon themselves (his Mother having been dead for many years) and had made it fairly evident that one of their prime duties was to see the young man settled down. They tried to probe little into his personal life - though Beatrice, as his Father's Sister, evidently felt that she had a little more right in this area, and was, in consequence, slightly more direct in her inquisition. Mark had mentioned the odd name, but had rarely gone beyond that. Indeed, there seemed - with perhaps one exception - to be little justification in going any further. As a result of this previously unbroken tack, his arrival with Julia caused something of a stir, as evidenced by Simon's "Fine girl' - which was as near to close questioning as his Uncle came.

The Audi turned off the road and through the gap in a tall hedge delimited by two stone pillars. The trees which overhung the entrance seemed to have grown since Mark's last visit and drooped low over the car, providing a short tunnel for them to navigate before breaking out and into the sunlight again. He had always liked the approach to their house, especially when, as a child, he imagined himself leaving behind his normal life and venturing through a forest before coming out into a new world. There was nothing remarkable about the house he knew (something that maturity and a little experience of the world gave him), but it did have the rather singular quality of being remarkably detached from the road, almost as if it were in a land of its own. He could see why the place had appealed to him as a child because of this; but he was certain too that there was something about its inhabitants which made it a little bit special.

He grew up with the notion that Beatrice (who had seen them arrive and was now standing at the front door, offering a little wave) was a little 'odd'; that there was something about Daddy's Sister that - to an eight year old, at least - was not quite 'right'. Perhaps it was simply that she represented the sort of person he should have been growing up with, and that living alone with his Father had robbed him of the sensibility of a whole generation of womanhood. He used to be amazed at the different cakes Beatrice used to be able to conjure up from her kitchen (and from the larder that seemed more like an Aladdin's cave than a food store), and the intense variety of voices she seemed to have at her command. She made fewer cakes now than she used to, partly, he knew, because he was no longer a child and there was little outstanding need to pamper or please him. Her voice, beginning to wear with age too, had lost much of its resonance, and even though there were occasional traces of it (he wondered if she had ever sung Opera, but had never asked), her range had slipped away.

The car drew to a halt with the sound of tyres on gravel which brought back its own memory of earlier days as seemed to be his mood at present. He had maintained an old bicycle at the house (secured in his Uncle's shed amongst the various gardening utensils) which, from time to time, they would take out with the pretence of restoring to its former glory. They would tinker for a short while - Simon endeavouring to explain the mechanics of the gear change or the roll ball bearings had to play in modern machinery in general - and then give way (Mark was sure under strenuous pleading from himself) to a little oiling and no more. He would ride the bike around the house (there was a path either side, that connected front and back) on the strict instruction that he was to go no where near the main road. It was a rule he was happy keeping to: there was enough excitement in peddling as close as he could to the pond without falling in or skidding across the drive and sending the gravel flying (hence the memory) for the prospect of the road - the outside world, no less - to be low on his list of diversions.

Julia left the car with a promise to "Fetch Simon", and walked straight into the welcoming embrace of Beatrice. They had got on well together after that initial meeting (Mark wondered how much that early enthusiasm of Julia's had helped) and she appeared more kin with his Aunt than he himself did. As he closed his door and walked round to the back of the car - accompanied by the more sedate sound of his footsteps on the gravel - he watched the two of them, Julia's arm round Beatrice's waist, disappear into the house. There was more than a suspicion, as he stood staring down at the brown paper oblong, that it would be a little while before Simon would appear, suspecting that the women would go into secret session to talk about whatever women talked about (one of Life's mysteries!) without paying any heed to the demands to be made upon the men folk - and Simon in particular - at this precise moment. Resigned, because of this, to another Herculean effort on his own, he had manoeuvred the parcel into something like an accessible position when he was surprised by an arm on his shoulder and Simon's familiar "My Boy!" greeting.

Mark straightened, turned, and shook his Uncle's hand.

"So that's the beast, is it?" Simon looked down into the boot and at the brown square with one edge now raised upon the cill and pointing directly towards him. "Julia said it was a bit of a monster."

"It's just a little heavy, that's all."

"Awkward too, I'll bet."

"And awkward; yes."

There was a brief silence was the two men contemplated the task ahead, then, with a typical tap on the shoulder, Simon indicated to Mark that the time for contemplation was over, and that there was work to be done.

After a moment, the mirror hung suspended between the two men, Mark walking backwards towards the house under Simon's guidance, glancing occasionally over his shoulder to check his footing. They gained the hallway without incident, and without the need to pause. With the two of them (four hands supporting their burden, one at each corner) the weight was so evenly distributed that it seemed much less of a chore to carry. There was a slightly awkward moment when, approaching the door, they observed (unspoken, of course!) the need to tilt the package to get it through the arch, but this little trick was accomplished with reasonable ease and a little extra strain upon the fingers.

Now they were inside, Mark paused. Only the first stage of their journey was over.

"Where are we putting it?" He looked at Simon who, though a little redder in the face than a few minutes previously, was smiling at him.

"Upstairs," came the reply, but not from Simon. Beatrice, having heard their footfall in the house, appeared from the kitchen. "My goodness! It is quite a big one, isn't it?" She turned in the doorway and looked back to where Julia must have been sitting. "You were right, my dear; it is quite enormous!"

Mark, not waiting for any reply of Julia's (which he might not have heard in any event) was beginning to feel some discomfort in his fingers, and even though Simon was still smiling, he suspected that he was not alone in this.

"Aunt!" He tried to sound a little impatient.

"Sorry Dear, yes." She returned to him. "We've made a little space against the wall in your room."

"My room?"

"By the bookcase. Are you all right, dear?"

The last remark was plainly addressed to Simon who, with a brief reply, indicated that all was well - and that things would be even better as soon as they had deposited the mirror in its final resting place. Mark, alive to the innuendo flooding through the exchange, adjusted his grip again, and began to journey up the stairs.

They still called it his room, even though part of him felt that he should have outgrown such territory years previously. There was a time in his life - as perhaps there is a time in every child's life - where he came upon the notion of privacy, of space; where he felt the need to have somewhere to retreat to (or emerge from) which *belonged* to him. He had his own room at his Father's house of course; indeed, it felt at times as if the whole house belonged to him, and that it was his Father who was the minor partner in the building. Yet Simon and Beatrice, as they saw him so frequently - and as they had plenty of rooms to spare - had decided at an early stage that Mark should have 'a room' there too. They did not go quite as far as his Father had in terms of indulging his spasmodic peccadilloes for posters and other decorative styles (he had painted a five foot face on his bedroom wall one year) but they were happy to accommodate him as best they could without compromising their own sense of taste and the general tenor of the house.

Despite his maturity, his 'growing up', somehow it seemed natural to him that they should still regard it as 'his room' even now. Those four walls had developed with him, survived impassively the various fads he had gone through - even out-lasting the rather bleak period when, as a teenager, rebellion was the thing and he hardly saw his Aunt and Uncle at all - and had now become his study; the place where he worked when he was researching the biography of his Father.

Simon had been insistent. Once he had been approached by his partners (he had a small but influential stake in a publishing company) for a definitive biography of his brother-in-law, it was self-evident that Mark - who had shown a degree of talent in the things he had written thus far: articles for the magazine he worked for part-time; freelance pieces in the National press; even short stories - should be given first refusal to author it. Mark had been immediately reluctant. He used his lack of experience and his closeness to the subject (this, as if his Father were some abstract third party) as sound reasons for not being involved at all. The general forces were ranged against him however, and when Beatrice (whether or not spurred on by Simon, he was unable to say) joined the fray, laden with arguments which supported Simon's instinct that Mark was indeed the man for the job, he knew the die was cast. Knowing Beatrice was not to be engaged in combat lightly - and, if he was honest, he had been warming to the idea in any event - Mark gradually relented, allowing his own arguments to be weakened until they simply evaporated. Thus his room became his study, and, when he was working on the book, by and large he worked from there.

By the time they turned into the room, the package - thanks, no doubt, to the climbing of the stairs - seemed to have increased in weight by a significant factor. Mark noticed how Simon's smile had vanished under the strain, and - more immediately - how his own fingers were beginning to feel numb. In the room there was indeed space along the wall by the bookcase which, as Beatrice had forecast, had been created by moving a small chair and side table out into the centre. As they rested the mirror on the floor (Mark managing to resist the urge to actually drop it from an injudicious height) he noticed how it seemed now to be occupying pride of place, and how the rest of the room - in becoming more cramped and cluttered - appeared almost subservient to it. As he stared at the still-covered mirror (and as Simon, hands on hips, straightened his back with a telling sigh) it gave him an uneasy feeling to have it there as if its intrusion into his life (he glanced again at his jacket) had already been too much to bear.

"Thankfully we won't have to move that again in a hurry," said Simon, endeavouring to restore his perennial smile. "When does Laura tie the knot?"

"In a few weeks."

Mark tired to balanced the notion of knot tying and marriage in his mind for a moment, attempting to establish the accuracy of the image - bondage, fixity - with what was, to him at any rate, a rather obscure and notional social status. He wondered too (this as he followed Simon out of the room, attempting - in some telepathic way - to see through the floor and to the rooms downstairs) how much a potential marriage to Julia might involve the tying of knots. They had not talked about it - except to joke with friends (especially Peter and Claire) - and, in his own mind at least, the time was not yet right to do so. He could not have made any attempt to guess Julia's opinion on the subject even though he had his suspicions, and even though these suspicions led him to believe that her viewpoint diverged considerably from his own.

Downstairs, Beatrice and Julia were still ensconced in the kitchen, sitting at the large kitchen table, empty coffee mugs before them. By the time he followed Simon into the room they had already looked up, and Beatrice was in the process of rising and making for the kettle. Despite Julia's smile, displayed solely as greeting, Mark could not help but feel that their arrival had forced the conclusion of something private and secret to which he (and, to a lesser extent, Simon) could not be privy.

"All right?" Julia's question - obviously aimed at their recent activity - was general enough to allow interpretation. Mark wondered if she was asking after their health - the degree of feeling in the fingers; the getting back of breath after their labours - or after the well-being of the brown oblong that now pressed heavy against the joists above their head.

"Yes, my dear," said Simon, relieving Mark of the need to answer. "Mind you, it is a monster, isn't it?"

It seemed not the first time that Simon had used that image. Mark, now that he was seriously embroiled in his Father's biography - and all that entailed in terms of literary style - seemed to be quicker in picking up such things, more readily noticing where people were being lazy with language. His Father would have approved of this as a turn for the better, even though his son felt slightly uncomfortable that what was becoming something of an automatic reaction to others' speech might eventually colour his response to the simplest of conversations.

Julia looked at him - still with that smile - as if needing his confirmation of Simon's words. He sat on the stool next to her, and she squeezed his arm lightly.

"Fine, yes."

"Coffee?" Beatrice rescued him from the other side of the kitchen.

"Please."

"Simon?"

Mark wondered how Beatrice addressed his Uncle in private. 'Simon' seemed so unnatural from her; a false, public name. He gave them both credit for a degree of intelligence and imagination (certainly far in excess of the 'average' citizen) which would, almost by necessity, insist on something other than a given name to register their intimate familiarity. As a youth, he had noticed the advertisements in newspapers around Valentine's Day, and wondered what kinds of people lurked behind 'Poodle', 'Wumpkins' and 'Flossy'; it intrigued him to consider the reasons for such alternatives, as if people were trying to get away from - or, heaven forbid, get closer to! - their 'real' selves. He could only imagine warm intimacies between Simon and Beatrice; something commensurate with their age, their personalities, their love for each other. Julia - and for this he was thankful - had given no indication that she wished to additionally christen him with a private name. Having grown up with 'Mark' - and having gone through that period (as he assumed all did) of hating the name and wishing for anything but - he liked to think that, in some way, he might have grown into it, that it fitted him, and that - in some obscure sense - it was 'right'.

"Will you stay for dinner?" Beatrice's question - delivered as she returned to the table with a fresh pot of coffee and two clean mugs - had been foreseen and debated during the journey from Regent Street. "Beatrice will ask us to stay for dinner" Julia had said with certainty, demonstrating the closeness she now enjoyed with the two of them, and displaying her spasmodic talent for reading his mind. He had not been in the mood for a long stay, preferring, he said, to go back home, perhaps with a view to going out later. This had been countered by Julia who suspected that they would simply go home and stay home and that Mark would collapse into inertia. She had favoured acceptance, but had given way in the end, preferring preservation of Mark's good humour (which seemed to be on the wane since they left the shop) to commitment to an evening which, in the past, had by no means proven to be a guaranteed success.

"Thanks, Beatrice, but we ought to be making tracks soon. I've got to get a letter off by the last post and I'm only just half way through it." Mark was grateful that Julia had taken on the apology herself, though a little surprised that she had chosen such a detailed fabrication as means of refusal (at least he *assumed* it was fabrication, though this was not necessarily the case). "Maybe next week would be nice."

Mark had not expected the follow-up, despite the political correctness of it.

"Of course, dear; that's fine. Perhaps you should call us on Monday, and we'll sort something out."

"I'll probably be over tomorrow, to work on the book. We could arrange something then."

This had not been in the script, and had slipped out from Mark before he had time to check it. The proposition hung a little heavy in the room (especially he sensed, with Julia) before coming down to settle on them all. There was no protest.

Julia had waited until they were half-way towards Hampstead before letting Mark know how she felt about his recent announcement. They had all finished their coffee in a light enough mood, with Beatrice asking about Laura's preparations for her 'big day', and about the honeymoon. Perhaps less bothered with these 'romantic' issues, and with his mind on the 'once bitten' adage, Simon seemed more concerned in obtaining a cast iron guarantee that - from the point of view of his health - he would not be required to lay hands on the mirror ever again. He was aware that Laura and Tim were moving to Oxford - Julia had informed them that all the arrangements were well in hand, and that the house would be ready for them on their return from the Caribbean - but Simon wanted to know how the mirror was to make its way there: *when* would it leave the house, and *who* would be responsible for its transportation? Mark, who had been talking with his Aunt about the virtues of Barbados at this time of year (something, coincidentally, that they had both experienced), paused to catch Julia's reply to his Uncle's question.

"Well, Laura will be getting most of her presents at the reception of course, but I suspect that it may not be really feasible to take the mirror over there and then to lug it all the way to Oxford." She paused, as if to allow the logic of her argument (undoubtedly freshly made) to sink in. "So what I may do, is suggest to Laura that we simply take it straight to Oxford and hang it for her, so that it's ready for when she gets back."

Mark was struck by Julia's reference to 'her' throughout this passage, rather than to 'them'; after all, it was a marriage, and they - Laura and Tim - would be returning as a couple. It was not this however (despite the vague sense of alarm it held for him) that he chose to pick up on.

"We?"

"Sorry, darling?"

"We? You said that *we* would take it to Oxford."

She laughed, apparently amused at Mark's desire to clarify what seemed perfectly obvious.

"Of course! You don't suppose I'm going to pay some removal firm or other just to carry a silly little mirror from here to Oxford!"

Mark looked at his Uncle, who seemed less than reassured by this reply - especially as it was one neither of them was looking for.

"But I'm not sure that it's fair for us to ask Simon to help carry it again; after all, it is really very heavy - and awkward."

It was, he knew - indeed, as Simon immediately recognised himself - something of a weak plea, but it was all he could muster, and even though it had been drafted in his Uncle's name, it carried more than a little concern for himself within it.

Julia smiled at Simon and tapped his hand.

"Don't worry. We can always get Peter or someone to help us."

That was how they had left it; loosely arranged, but with Mark certain that he would be required to man-handle the glass at least twice more - for he was only too acutely aware that there was the Oxford end of the journey to contend with too.

If Julia had been unhappy with his attitude towards what was, after all, *their* gift to her Sister - and on the most important day of her life, to boot - then it was not this (he soon discovered) that had been playing on her mind since they left the house. She had become quiet the instant they began to drive away, and had given only perfunctory replies to any attempt Mark made at light conversation thereafter. He knew - in as much as months of experience with her, and years of experience in general, told him - that there was a storm coming, though it was impossible just yet to say whether it was going to be a squall or a gale. Mentally he prepared himself, battening down whichever of his internal hatches appeared open and liable to succumb to the flood. By the time Julia eventually broke, he was reasonably prepared.

"I don't believe you just did that!" The first wave broke over him from a quarter he had not expected.

"Did what?" In real terms - that is, in the immediate past - he had just turned right at a roundabout. It had not been a particularly clean execution; his signal was perhaps a little late, and possibly he had been a touch sharp at the exit, but it was obviously not enough to warrant a literal translation of Julia's words.

"What you said to Simon. About tomorrow."

He trawled back to the scene in the kitchen, attempting to reconstruct events in as realistic a way as possible in order for him to enter the debate on something approaching an equal footing. He could remember his words - or an approximation of them - but would not have liked to have been pressed on where others were at the moment of their delivery, their relation to him - was Simon standing or sitting? had Beatrice finished making the coffee or not? - or, more importantly, their reaction. Nothing significant stood out in his memory.

"Do you mean about working on the book? That's all I can remember, anyway. What's so significant about that?"

The significance was hidden for a few moments in the silence that Julia chose to impose on them. Mark, still trying to concentrate on his driving, was pleased that they were nearing home; soon his automatic pilot would cut in and he could try to give Julia a little more attention, something he was sure - this general air of disinterest engendered by his driving - that was simply fuelling her particular fire.

"Nothing really. Nothing at all. Just that tomorrow's Sunday and we had talked about going down to Hampton Court for the day. That's all."

Another conversation - albeit a much older one - drifted back into his consciousness. All he could recall - and he hoped he was not being selective here - was a brief discussion about the sorts of things they could do at weekends, now that the weather was beginning to brighten up. OK it was still early spring, but the signs were there that summer might not be too far away, and Julia had expressed a determination to 'make the best of it'. Mark might have applied this statement to a myriad of things, but just at the moment only the next day was relevant.

"We talked about all sorts of things we *might* do, yes. But I can't say I recall any definite arrangement for tomorrow. Hampton Court was on our list, sure; but so were lots of places."

He used to word 'list' as if there were some tangible evidence of the conversation; some form of contract to which one might append one's name, or sign in blood. To him they were just vague arrangements, but he now suspected Julia had the thing already mapped out; and to such an extent that there might well have been a real, physical itinerary somewhere.

As they pulled into the driveway of his house, a number of large spots of water suddenly crashed against the windscreen. These were simply heralds for the downpour that instantly followed. As he turned the engine off, he looked vaguely skywards.

"It will probably be terrible weather tomorrow, anyway."

Julia (who was in the process of unbuckling her seat belt) ignored this last remark. He had delivered it with the air of a man who was hoping that divine intervention might, at the death, get him off the hook; but Julia, already out of the car and dashing up to the house, showed no inclination to countenance that Divine Will might have precedence over her leisure plans.

Chapter Three

Mark worked through the remainder of the day secretly hoping Sunday, when it dawned, would not let him down, and the weather would indeed be foul. Julia made her general disappointment with Mark's selfish plans further evident when they got home by engaging in general domestic activities which, in that they were tasks for her alone and in which Mark could not contribute, effectively cut her off from him for large portions of time. They came together for dinner, of course, and although the atmosphere was far from icy - they were still talking, indeed! - it bore enough of a chill for Mark to be only too aware of her feelings. Even a glass of wine, pressed upon her at his insistence, did little to relieve a generally overcast nature.

Faced with such a situation - a situation of his own making, Julia would undoubtedly argue, thereby relieving herself of any of the responsibility for it - Mark found himself with a little too much time requiring self-amusement. The present day's rain - which had been sporadic, but less in evidence since Regent Street - had abated sufficiently for him to consider washing his car before dinner; something that seemed in keeping with the tone already set by Julia, even though doing so would be in conflict with its traditional place as an occupation reserved for sunny Sunday mornings.

He had helped his Father often enough in such pursuits, revelling in the fetching and carrying; rejoicing in the trust imparted in him when, for the first time, he was allowed to carry the bucket - brim-full of soapy water - from the kitchen and through the house to the car outside. There had been some form of ritual associated with the process, and although observed at an early age - and, *as ritual*, understood soon after - he was kept from active participation for a number of years. In consequence, the business of those early sunny Sundays soon lost interest for him, and, in an attempt to busy himself, he would often let other, less appropriate things, divert him. Upsetting his father - which was often the result - was seldom his true motivation, although later, when he had matured enough to begin to realise the power he held - this ability to manipulate - he used it with the objective of being *included* in what appeared to be this most significant of activities. Washing the lights had been the first task to be allocated to him, and although this failed to involve much responsibility (as he realised later), at the time the cleaning of those very instruments upon which his father was dependant for seeing in the dark seemed to be such an important task that he would spend as much time on them as his Father took for the remainder of the vehicle, just to get it right. Later, when he moved on to become responsible for the wing mirrors as well, he knew that, in his Father's eyes, he had attained some kind of status which, although he might not yet understand it, he was determined not to abuse.

Since then of course - though exactly when the transition might have occurred he could not say; perhaps with the ownership of his own car - the mystique had vanished, and now, as he addressed the Audi with his own bucket and sponge, his primary concern was in getting the job done as efficiently as possible. Indeed, there was no thought involved in the process any more. If anything, it was an excuse to switch off and think about other things; a quiet time when activity and solitude went hand in hand and offered a kind of freedom difficult to achieve in many other ways.

As it turned out, the heavens were kind to Mark in more ways than one. Sunday dawned dark and overcast, with the depressing nature of the threatening sky complimented by a chill wind that had sprung up overnight. This was sufficient for Julia to concede - still in bed, propped up on one arm, and looking out of the curtain opened by Mark specifically for the purpose - that it appeared not to be the day for external adventures. Given such a statement, Mark could of course appear to be magnanimous, and, with one arm around her, affirm that, had the sun indeed been shining, he would have forsaken his planned time with the book for a visit to Hampton Court.

Whether or not Julia bought this last statement as an absolute truth or not was difficult to say; it had been, however, an essential move in the game they were playing which allowed neither to be the loser and to have equilibrium restored. Cessation of hostilities was signalled with Mark - who had got up to make the tea, and who had been ready to perform his morning ablutions in the bathroom - being dragged back into bed from which he eventually emerged around three quarters of an hour later, the peace treaty having been sealed. Julia, as was her wont after any early morning love-making, remained in bed later than she would normally, reading the latest block-buster she had on the go, and drinking coffee from the cafetiere Mark tended to make for her before he disappeared about his own business.

The second reason the weather had been kind (and this as Mark pulled out of the drive heading south) was that his car still looked as bright and clean as it had after the attention he had given it the previous day. It seemed - this performance of washing one's car - one of life's most pointless duties: however well the task was carried out, however much love and care was taken, the effort could - and would! - be quickly and simply wiped out by the first shower. Within minutes the old status quo would be restored, and the plan for the next sunny Sunday begin to shape itself. Pausing at a red traffic light, he reflected how - if he wished to be a little unfeeling, if not to say brutal - love-making might be argued to fall into the same category. He had left Julia with their relationship bright and shiny once again, but soon along would come some shower or other (of whose making was irrelevant) and things would begin to look a little dull and dreary again. As the lights changed to green and the car began to pull away, he thought - with the first spots of that morning's rain falling onto his windscreen - that the parallel might lack sophistication to stand up well to any scrutiny.

When he arrived at his Uncle's house some fifteen minutes later, he was greeted by Beatrice who, despite his statement of the previous afternoon, seemed a little surprised to see him.

"Simon's out", she said, as if that fact might have such a significant bearing on his presence that he would retrace his steps through the house, jump back in his car, and disappear in a cloud of exhaust fumes.

The news was, however, of little relevance to Mark given that Simon's attendance (having he remarked to himself how, not too many years ago, Beatrice would have opened with "Your Uncle's out") was not necessary for him to continue with the book. His Aunt's statement did, however, beg to be followed up, and out of little more than courtesy and idle chit-chat, he asked after his whereabouts.

"Oh, he's just walked round to get a newspaper, Dear" - this as she waited for their ancient kettle to boil, adopting the kind of semi-professional pose some women manage so successfully in the kitchen. "The Paper Boy got it wrong again, and so he's had to go chasing round to the Newsagent's. I don't know why we pay these people sometimes, I really don't."

As she poured his coffee, Mark caught in her profile a trace of his Father's face, and - were he disposed to continue the analysis - something of his own visage too. The family's features were not, by and large, that exceptional; a slightly elongated face which, being also a touch on the thin side, lent itself to austerity rather than generous bonhomie. The 'Packard nose' - often a source of amusement during quiet family get-togethers - was its most striking feature: this too was a little longer and thinner than the norm, and carried with it the very slightest (though undeniable) 'hook' just above the tip, which, on female members of the lineage, offered the unflattering parallel with the black-clad, broomstick-flying crones from children's legends. Beatrice may have been many things - indeed, Mark suspected that he and Simon might, between them, be able to generate a significant list - but a witch was not one of them.

"I'll tell him you're here when he gets back."

She had said this as if it were the last word on the subject, closing their conversation, and giving him permission (rather than simply allowing him leave) to vacate the kitchen for his study. Turning, he left her, allowing himself a quick glance over his shoulder when he reached the door. It appeared that she had forgotten his presence already, and was addressing herself to an open book by the cooker, alongside which stood a couple of bowls and a plate with meat on it. There was still that air of professionalism about her, and Mark wondered, as he ascended the stairs, if, once he had left the kitchen, this look might have been replaced by another.

The door to his room was open and, having turned at the top of the stairs, the first thing that caught his eye was the brown paper parcel standing against the wall. He noticed it immediately because it was new and had changed the whole aspect of the room - a feeling further enhanced when, after placing his coffee on the desk, he took off his jacket and found the chair on which he normally laid it to be a degree closer than formerly, it having been moved to allow for the package. For a few seconds, he stood and eyed the large square suspiciously. It was quite enormous; certainly larger than he recalled, and much too big to again enlist the assistance of Simon in its final removal from the house.

From downstairs came the noise of the front door opening and Simon's voice - "It's only me" - calling through the hallway on its way to the kitchen. Mark turned back to the desk and sat down. Apart from the word processor and a small ornamental jar containing a few pens and pencils, the surface of the desk was clear. Noticing a small mark in the leather surface which - he was ashamed to say - he had been responsible for a few years previously, Mark suddenly found himself trying to remember what the surfaces of his other desks had been like. At home, everything was new and clinical, as was all the furniture at any office he could ever remember being associated with. In order to identify something other than an unblemished surface, he found himself travelling back to his school days, where desks were more trophies than items of furniture; where one made one's mark - quite literally! - and etched out a history of tenancy. There had been a number of deeply cut messages from previous incumbents at one such desk he had occupied, but neither of the girls concerned were known to him. Had he added anything of his own there? He tried to remember, seeing if he could envisage himself, compass in hand, poised to bury it into the hard surface.

Simon's footfall on the stairs roused him from his unfinished reverie, and, switching automatically into his working mode, he flicked on the computer and pulled open the top drawer of the pedestal at his side. He had the files containing his working notes and the first draft in front of him when his Uncle entered.

"My Boy!" the elder man said, walking into the room and placing his hand on his Nephew's shoulder, "Beatty said you were here".

"Hello, Uncle. Sorted the Newsagent out?"

"Incompetent idiot!" he said impatiently. "I don't mean to be a bigot or anything, but - well, you wouldn't have had some much trouble and misunderstanding a few years ago, that's all. I've got nothing against these people, mind; I mean they work like the devil, some of them, and good luck to them too! - but, sometimes; well, I don't think they quite *understand*. Do you know what I mean?"

Mark smiled at his Uncle's attempt to avoid racism; it was a genteel form of bigotry, borne from a belief in the days of the Raj but tempered with a strong dose of being a gentleman and a 'decent chap'.

"Anyway, that's that! Now I'll leave you to it. If you need anything, I'll be downstairs. Beatty said she'd found a few more old photos, and was going to look them out for you. Don't suppose you need them just yet?"

"Not really."

"Fine, fine. I'll leave them on the desk for you - when she eventually gets round to sorting them out."

There was a brief pause while Simon weighed up if this were a suitable way to close the conversation and leave the room. With nothing else forthcoming from Mark and the computer humming quietly in readiness, he smiled, tapped his Nephew on the shoulder again, and then was gone.

Mark lay the two folders alongside each other, then opened both in turn. The first - the bulkier of the two - contained numerous sheets of hand-written notes, some stapled or clipped to other documents or photographs. On the top of this pile lay a single sheet which Mark had used as an outline plan of the work ahead. When he had started, it seemed as if his Father's life would be a simple thing to document; after all, he had lived much of it with him and knew many of the significant milestones. However, even the first days of research had shown that there was much more to be discovered, layers of his Father's history which were new to him - either because they pre-dated his own existence or, and this seemed the more obscure, because he was simply ignorant of them. It had never occurred to him - not in any *real* sense - that his Father had a life of his own, outside of that joint experience they shared together.

Because of this, there came a strange new sensation that here was a man - the person he had been closest to since he could remember - who, in some unfathomable way, he did not know. There were questions which, although they seemed innocent enough when applied to others, he now found himself needing to ask about his own Father, and, because of this - because of the damage the answers might actually do to the reality of his world and their relationship as he currently perceived it - they seemed dangerous and ominous. At one point, he had been sufficiently taken aback for him to ask Simon to reconsider his position as author of the biography. Of course, he did not go in to any detail regarding his concerns, but rather formulated some general theory around his own competence, experience and closeness to the subject. It was, fundamentally, the same argument he had originally used to excuse himself from the work, and, as before, Simon was still confident that he was the man from the job.

Whether or not his Aunt had an inkling as to his deeper reasoning was difficult to say, but Mark did catch a sense that *she* might not be as certain as before, and often, during their early exchanges, he wondered if Beatrice - who, after all, was his star witness in much of this - might not be a little unwilling to divulge all she knew. In order to overcome the general reluctance - both his own and Beatrice's apparent, though unspoken, reserve - he decided to play himself in gently. He had wanted to plunge into his Father's life at the time of his own birth; it seemed to him that the most significant events were those that followed on from there: they were certainly the events about which Mark - as both Author *and* participant - could contribute the greatest degree of insight. However, he was persuaded to start with something less tangible, about which only research and - from his own point of view - an impersonal perspective could furnish the story. It would play him into the task, allow him to get a feel for the book and - this was his Aunt's argument - to get a feel for the *man* too. There was, she suggested (Mark remembered a late night conversation with Beatrice, Simon and a bottle of twelve year old Macallan) a need for Mark to look upon his Father afresh, to try and remove all the preconceptions that the years of closeness had given him; he needed, above all - and this, with feeling - to get some 'distance' from him.

- * -

It was an unexceptional rather than inauspicious entry into the world. Charles Michael Packard was born at home on 21st May 1932, the second child of Albert Henry Packard and his wife Louisa May. The labour had been without complication and of reasonably short duration, and Charles was delivered without difficulty five hours after Louisa's waters broke. Albert, who had been at work in Mason's Steel Mill, received the news on at the end of his shift, and, with his daughter Beatrice in the care of neighbours, reached his wife's bedside with Charles already two hours old.

The boy was named within a few minutes of that first visit: Charles because the Packards had a liking for solid, traditional names; Michael, because they also had an eye for the future, and this latter was something of a popular name at that time and seemed to promise much...

-*-

Mark re-read his beginning as he always did, skipping on after the first chapter or so through the draft towards his most recent addition. He was, by and large, pleased with the job thus far - if only from a technical point of view. There seemed to be a certain style amidst the matter-of-factness he was trying to instil, his practice as a journalist standing him in good stead for the general task. Indeed, he had been confident enough to show the initial chapter (which covered the first few years of his Father's life) to both Simon and Beatrice when it was completed.

There had been some debate in his own mind at the need to do this, but he felt that it was justified on at least two grounds: firstly, to prove to Beatrice that their one-to-one conversations regarding her memory of those early years was in fact bearing fruit and that something tangible had been born from them; and second, to gain confirmation from Simon that the work he was likely to produce was of sufficient standard to warrant continuation. The news that he most certainly was *not* wasting his time was welcomed by Mark, and provided the necessary impetus for him to push on. Simon's reaction - an affirmation that he had made the right choice of Author - was superseded only by Beatrice whose enthusiasm for Chapter One seemed (to Mark at any rate) to come as much from relief as anything else.

Charles and Beatrice Packard had been beset by problems as children which, to all intents and purposes, passed them by with the blissful ignorance that is any child's initial inheritance. There was much uncovered by Mark which was new to him. His Grandfather - who had died well before he himself had been born - was an alcoholic who, in times of extreme inebriation, would beat his wife almost senseless. Several times she had made to leave him - even to the extent of hauling her children to her Sister's house in Leeds, though always to return a few days later. To the young Charles, these events - probably because of their irregularity - were, according to Beatrice, much more of an adventure than a trial; however (and this she had added almost as an afterthought) although she had been the first to perceive that there was something quite sinister going on, she was sure that, before the old man's death, Charles had absorbed much.

Mark, when he had come to cover this slightly darker passage in his Father's life, had been able to draw for himself (though at this stage only in his own mind and not on paper) influences in the mature Charles Packard which might conceivably be traced back to those earlier incidents. He had, for example, ridden something of a roller-coaster in terms of alcohol abuse himself. The popular press (in as much as Literary Critics ever attained such a status) had, at the time of his greatest acclaim, made great play on his Father's liking for the bottle - and then his periods of purgatory on the wagon. Mark could not recall any significant influence on his own upbringing relating to this, the exception being the first time he returned home drunk from a party and his Father had lectured him long and hard about the 'demon drink'.

In his work, his characters would sometimes struggle too. Charles Packard had something of a reputation as a 'moralist', which, considering his own philosophy on life, seemed to be a contradiction in terms. His heroes - or, in one famous exception, his heroine - would often be struggling against a single force throughout their existence. Often the foes were manifest in faceless organisations or political hierarchies, but occasionally - and these were the most celebrated - they would be struggling against themselves. There was not, however, a single character who struggled against drink; perhaps - and this was pure supposition on Mark's part - the fact that his Father was living that battle for real, was enough.

"Coffee?"

A call from Simon drew Mark out of the pages spread before him, and he felt suddenly tired. Working on the book had a numbing effect on him, as if in doing so, he were giving up to it more than just the mechanical effort to type at the keyboard, even to the extent of undergoing some kind of exhausting self-examination in the process.

"I'll be down in a minute."

He looked at the desk. He had made a few fresh notes - thoughts for later chapters - and, checking the word count on the screen - had translated some of the notes he had already made into several hundred words. Working - in terms of producing sentences - had never been a problem to him (certainly not as much of a problem as it had come to be for his Father in his last years) and, in printing and saving his latest effort, he felt one step advanced on the ladder that had seemed just recently to be extending faster than he was climbing it.

"Julia phoned." Simon was alone in the kitchen when he finally made his way downstairs. Mark compared his Uncle's presence there - in terms of its 'professional' appearance - with his Aunt's, and wondered if all men were as uncomfortable in such an environment. Even the way Simon poured the coffee seemed to embody all the unlearned lessons of successive generations of men, as if the very act of tipping the kettle were a travesty of what the appliance was actually intended for. "She said that as the weather's picked up, she'll be over around half twelve. Something about Hampton Court."

Mark glanced out of the window. The weather had indeed brightened considerably; it was something which - to him at any rate - had gone unnoticed, along with the two hours he had spent in the study.

Beatrice was sitting, legs up, on the sofa in the lounge reading the Sunday newspaper that Simon had brought back from the shop. She glanced up on the entry of the two men, smiling generally at them.

"Hello, Dear." Her first words were specifically addressed to Mark. "Get much done?"

The enquiry regarding progress on the book always came from Beatrice in this format. Mark wondered why she never asked about specifics relating to the work - like the number of chapters, or the number of words - instead preferring to log his progress by his own sense of having *done* something. He thought about the two hours he had spent, the notes, and the several hundred words, yet despite these (which would have proven to be admirable measures had she requested them: 'I wrote three hundred words' he might have said) Mark felt a little unsatisfied with the morning's effort.

"Yes; it's coming along nicely."

He could have chosen a specific response of course, but preferred to keep the exchange at the level chosen by his Aunt. This was especially necessary when he felt himself to be lying. After the headlong rush of the early chapters, the nearness to his own time - and his own contribution to the story - was beginning to loom, and the effort the book was beginning to require from him seemed to be growing disproportionately.

"You look a little tired, Mark."

Perhaps she could read minds too. Mark always suspected great things of Beatrice; mostly instinctive, genuine things over which she had no control but which - to her at least - were natural.

"Do I? I didn't sleep so well last night. I expect that's it."

The lie floated across the room.

"Julia phoned. Apparently you're going to Hampton Court."

Simon looked up from the colour supplement.

"Mark knows; I told him."

"Did you, Dear. Well done." It came out almost the way one might praise a dog, Mark thought, though he knew that there was nothing patronising intended. "Will you go to the Maze? It can get very muddy in there when the weather's been bad. In fact, I'd be surprised if they opened it today."

"I don't know what Julia's got planned. Just a late lunch and a walk along the river, I expect."

Julia, with Mark already in Belsize Park, arrived at Simon and Beatrice's house in a taxi. Mark, who had given up on the colour supplement and had retreated into Simon's old coffee table book on Greek mythology, glanced up at the sound of footfall outside just in time to see Julia walking past the lounge window. With Beatrice having returned to Sunday duties in the kitchen and Simon pursing his favourite habit of 'pottering about', Mark had the room to himself. It was nearly twelve thirty.

As the doorbell rang, from somewhere else in the house came Simon's call of "I'll get it"; Mark thought of offering "It's Julia!", but decided against it. He flicked through a couple more pages on the goddess Diana, hearing, as he did so, Simon's footfall through the hall and then his greeting of Julia. From the kitchen Beatrice called her own welcome. Mark, wondering if Julia would come immediately in search of him, placed the book at his side and waited, looking expectantly towards the doorway. There was a glimpse of Julia's blue coat as she went by, and then nothing. Ten minutes later he joined her in the kitchen.

"You don't want another coffee, do you Dear", said Beatrice, standing almost exactly where she had the previous day, "Julia says you're just about off."

Julia looked up from the table where she cradled her own coffee.

"How long will it take us, do you think? About an hour?"

It was a question he had not yet confronted, but, as all journeys across London seemed to take at least that, he supposed Julia's estimate might not be that far off.

"Something like that."

She downed the remains of her coffee and rose.

"There's a little place Laura told me about - an antique shop actually, but they serve the most delightful Sunday lunches apparently. Anyway, they close at three, so we'd better get a move on."

Mark considered protesting that they would not have time, that the journey was bound to take too long, that they would have difficulty parking, and that - in the end - they would miss the restaurant and Julia would become irate and the day would be ruined; but he was carried along by her irresistible force, and soon found himself outside on the gravel, unlocking the Audi and waving farewell to Beatrice, who had sacrificed the kitchen for the lobby.

Chapter Four

Luckily the same thought occurred to Julia after about half an hour's driving. She suggested to Mark - this as they neared Brentford (Mark's preferred though not particularly direct route through the city led them this way) - that they might not manage to get to Laura's antique shop before it closed. Consequently, a brief debate had led to the conclusion that they should stop en route for lunch, and, considering where they were at the time, chose Chiswick as a likely spot.

There were a couple of pubs by the river from which, on sunny summer days, one could watch crews rowing in the early evening. Later, those same men would be ashore, drinking pints in the very hostelries from which they had earlier been observed. It was still too early in the year for many rowers. One or two dedicated souls braved the present rawness of early spring, and these at least gave Mark and Julia one topic of conversation over lunch.

It was well after two when they left the pub, and, by the time they had negotiated Richmond, they arrived in Hampton Court close to three. Julia, pleased that they had stopped for lunch, was not - as Mark had feared earlier - depressed by such a late arrival. Indeed, having dispensed with the somewhat mundane chore of eating and drinking (as opposed to the rather exciting treat such a meal had promised to be a little earlier in the day) she seemed pleasantly relaxed. As she slipped her hand into his - this after they had parked the car and were walking towards the big house - Mark, with some lack of charity, found himself wondering if it might not have been the two gins she'd had in Chiswick which had loosened her general demeanour.

Finding the Maze to be open (it was, a luck would have it, the first day of opening that year) they stood for a full three minutes outside the entrance weighing up Beatrice's advice with regard to the conditions underfoot and trying to decided whether or not they should go in. The decision was swung by the fact that neither of them had been there since they were at school - indeed it was the only maze Mark had ever tackled - and that, as adults, they owed it to themselves to take the challenge which, they both admitted, had seemed to be so relatively simple as children.

Memory, at least in Mark's case, was immediately proven to be something of a hostage to fortune as - with a rapidity that surprised them both - they found themselves retracing their steps through junctions in the tall dark hedges. They took turns in leading not through any pre-arranged plan, but simply because unspoken common sense told them it was the easiest way to avoid any recriminations later for being the one responsible for the disaster. For his part, Mark would as gladly have led as follow, as long as the end result was acceptable, and - as far as he could see - whatever happened, that was fixed: they would find their way to the centre, then they would find their way out. The only variable was time.

Although it was early in the season and as yet few people had been given the opportunity to take on the challenge, it was surprisingly heavy under foot, and - as they revisited one particular spot for at least the fourth time - Mark felt conditions might be prone to rapid deterioration. At one stage he stopped to examine the state of his trouser hems, certain that they would already have suffered. He paused, pulling his hands from his jacket pockets (an in doing so remembering the blemish in the material which, of course, he was obliged to check once more) then bent down. The corduroy revealed that he had already managed to gather some mud on them and with that knowledge came a growing feeling that he wished they had taken Beatrice's advice.

Julia's voice roused him from the state of his clothes. He straightened. She had been leading and, evidently unaware of his need to stop, had pushed on.

"Mark?" He voice, somewhere between concerned and angry, floated across a hedge towards him.

"OK, coming."

His statement had carried with it a degree of matter-of-factness - the confidence he might display as if he were simply crossing the road - that was intended to reassure her that all was well. After all, he had merely paused to examine his turn-ups, nothing more nor less than that. Evidently with a greater awareness of their general situation than he, Julia sounded a warning that he should 'stand still!' and that she would retrace her steps; but by the time Mark heard it he had already passed through one junction (confident that Julia had gone left) and then pursued her voice towards his right. By the time Julia had regained the spot at which he had paused, he had gone.

"Mark. This isn't funny."

When the words reached his ears, Mark sensed that the anger now played the major role in her tone, and that the concern - although lessened - was a degree more profound. He tried to sound relaxed and offered a light laugh to the hedges in general, turning as he did so to ensure a fair spread of his voice. This inflamed Julia even more who, not unreasonably (as she would argue later) had by this time assumed that he was playing some sort of game with her.

He remained stationary, endeavouring as he did so, to reassure her that there had been a simple accident and they had become separated. She had echoed his word 'accident' in a sentence all of its own. The upshot of the dilemma was that Mark found himself conversing with a succession of hedges as they tried to navigate back towards each other, the general instructions based on their perceived relationships to other things - like the tower in the centre, or the palace itself. Mark, pausing again to examine his trousers (which were growing ever grubbier in spite of his relative lack of movement) and to light one of the small cigars from the limited supply he carried in his inside jacket pocket, wondered how much of life was like that, getting one's bearings and directions through relationships to other things. Reported relationships come to that, too. He had navigated often enough in the wake his Father left as he had ploughed his own way through life intent on reaching his own harbours and, in consequence, dragging Mark along much as a yacht might tow a dinghy. It had been an uncertain kind of passage at times, and one which he was coming to re-appraise.

"Mark," Julia's voice - which seemed so deceptively close that Mark assumed she must be just feet away - broke into his thoughts, "why don't we try and make it to the centre, on our own. We could meet there. We're getting nowhere like this."

Sounding his agreement, Mark looked towards the target - for now there appeared to be one, real and physical - and adjusted his plan accordingly. The notion of a race to the centre (even though Julia had made no mention of a 'race') appealed to that part of him which relished a challenge and the desire of being first at something; the other part of him - that which liked being led, and which had insisted on the cigar - told him to relax and take a long drag on the tobacco. The latter, victorious, retained him a few moments longer before he set off. Less than two minutes later - and with the tower almost within touching distance - he turned a corner and ran straight into Julia. Their laugher had been spontaneous and carried with it more relief than either would have been prepared to admit. It also carried a degree of victory for, having approached a three-pointed junction from separate directions, the way to the tower (which they gained less than a minute later) became self-evident in that it had to be the third option. The 'race' (had Mark been tempted to contemplate some form of 'action replay' in his mind) had resulted in a tie.

Looking out over the maze (which was deserted apart from one other couple near the entrance) Mark was surprised that, from here at any rate, it should look so easy. He had expected to be greeted by a sight which, considering their recent trials, rendered their reaching the centre something of a victory; instead, in taking so long, they had actually failed to achieve that, which twenty years earlier, had been monumentally easier.

There was, they were both relieved to find, a quick way out of the maze, plainly signposted in order to remove any impending stress that might be associated with having to undertake the reverse of the journey already experienced. Mark, partly out of some sense of manhood, joked about plunging back into the maze and finding their way out the 'hard way'. But it was a proposal offered in the certain knowledge that Julia (who was beginning to relax once again) would veto the suggestion, insisting that they had had quite enough of being lost for one day. Consequently, they soon emerged onto the broad pathways that surrounded the palace, and Julia's restored sense of well-being was demonstrated with her taking, once again, Mark's hand.

Ignoring Hampton Court itself - in as much as one could ignore it - they wandered down to the river. It was, Julia said, too late in the day to contemplate actually going inside the palace: they would need so much time after all, and, in any event, she was not in the mood. The decision gave Mark no problems at all, though he did wonder (and this was unspoken of course) if the argument about having enough time was particularly sound. In his experience, one always imagined that vast acres of time would be required to look over such a place - as if one were going to pore over every artefact, and drool over every picture and tapestry - but it seemed never to quite work out that way, and boredom (which had a threshold all its own) would take over, and any visit longer than an hour or so might be regarded by some as a triumph.

The river, to Mark's eyes at any rate, was not particularly attractive here. Despite the presence of Hampton Court - which added something of an imposing vista when viewed from the correct angle - they seemed always to be too near a road or too close to other buildings to permit any form of carefree meandering. As he stopped to light a second cigar (Julia had loosed his hand and was now walking on a few paces ahead) he wondered how things might have looked before the roads and the buildings, when there was just the palace. Under those circumstances -

simple rather then primitive, he would say - Mark was certain that the difference would have been quite startling, and he wondered how fine the dividing line was between what history created and what it destroyed, and who was to judge which was which in any case.

Having stopped, then turned back, Julia was at his side before he could move on.

"Why don't we go and see Claire and Peter? Just for a drink or something?"

Mark could tell, although she would not admit it, Julia was also bored, and that the prospect of a visit to their friends - which might have suddenly popped into her mind (for that was the way things usually seemed to happen) - was her means of saying that she wanted to leave, that the experience of Hampton Court was over. As he had no special attachment to the place - and, after all, he had been feeling vaguely dissatisfied himself - he agreed, and they made their way back to the Audi from where he called Peter.

"They're just going out," he reported, Julia now sitting in the passenger seat while he stood by her open door, "Something about his Aunt. I didn't really understand."

"Oh. And they'll be out for the rest of the day?" She was evidently disappointed, as if her attempt to redeem the expedition had failed.

"So he said. He did suggest Tuesday evening, though."

"Tuesday?" Julia's voice raised slightly, giving a sense that perhaps she felt that there was hope after all, even though Tuesday seemed an age away.

"He's got some meeting after work - cheese and wine something-or-other - but suggested we met at 'The Merlot', about eight."

That particular wine bar was not one of Julia's favourites he knew, but given the circumstances - her sudden desire to see Claire and Peter, and Peter's apparent work commitments - Mark was certain that she would, on this occasion, not object to the venue. He was proved right, and, as they drove away from Hampton Court, found himself relieved that they did not have to go through the rather tedious - and ultimately redundant - exercise of finding a mutually acceptable place to meet from the list of the several dozen they all knew.

'The Merlot' was a small establishment - professing both French connections and pretensions - that was tucked away in Highgate. It had been a discovery of Julia's when she had lived in Tufnell Park, and -

during the previous couple of years - had been something of a regular haunt. Indeed, it had been one of the first places she had suggested she and Mark went during their early days together. As far as wine bars were concerned, Mark - who had no strong opinion on them for the most part - found the place perfectly acceptable; for him it had none of the offensive character that Julia had begun to tag upon it. He wondered if, since their relationship had become more established (since she had moved in with him, in fact) Julia had begun to feel that she had graduated from 'The Merlot', and that the small, vaguely shabby, and - to be blunt - the less chic establishments (in which category it undoubtedly belonged) were no longer worthy of her patronage.

There was another possibility which, though he did not query her about it, also was resident in his mind; namely, that she had a more specific reason for not wishing to go back there: perhaps the place held bad memories for her, or there was someone there - another regular - who she wished to avoid. He had kept reasonably clear of Julia's past, not wishing to be seen to pry. Part of him might have liked to delve into her history (much as he was now engaged with his Father's) but the fact that his lack of inquisitiveness was largely reciprocated by her was sufficient to keep curiosity at bay. It was not that he had anything to hide; far from it. It was rather that part of his philosophy (in as much as he had one!) declared that what was past was past and should remain so.

As far as philosophies went, this seemed reasonable enough; indeed, had he given it a great deal of thought, it might have appeared to him less a philosophy and more simply behaving as an adult. For the most part his own style of personal isolationism kept him immune from the baggage that other people carried around with them, and though he did not feel particularly encumbered with what might have been regarded as his own psychological portmanteau, he had no desire to be tied to - nor responsible for - anyone else's.

The intervening time passed off unremarkably enough - Julia, along with the vast majority of the masses, returning to work on Monday; Mark spending a little more time working on the book - and as they drove down the small side street towards the wine bar, Mark felt as if *nothing* had happened in the interim, and their arrival at 'The Merlot' almost directly followed on their departure from Hampton Court.

"Peter must have come straight from work," Julia said, as she spotted his Porsche parked behind Claire's white Golf.

"He said he would; he had that buffet thing, remember?"

Julia chose not to respond, as she was now concentrating on Mark's efforts to park between two almost identical Cavaliers. It was a habit of hers - this taking his driving seriously - to which he inwardly objected. He was certain that it was not intended to be critical - indeed, very rarely did Julia pass any comment, positive or negative, on the way he drove - but it did put a little pressure on him at times (like now) when, to be frank, there might not normally be any pressure at all. Consequently, when he managed to reverse the Audi into the gap first time, he felt comfortable enough to offer Julia a smile as an accompaniment to him pulling on the handbrake. She tapped his hand, then turned and opened the door.

As he watched her walking round the front of the car and on towards the door of the wine bar (as he, meanwhile, fiddled in the glove compartment for his wallet) Mark wondered how much Julia had changed over recent months. There would have been a time when she would have waited for him, not got out of the car until he did, not walked into anywhere without him, and seldom have been satisfied with just a brush of the hand. He accepted (he had found his wallet now, and was out of the car and closing the door behind him) that things changed as relationships grew, but Julia seemed to have taken on a whole new personality. It was difficult for him to come to terms with it as, in many instances, she offered him remarkable freedom; yet at other times he felt overpowered, as if he was juggling with something indefinable, trying to keep not only their relationship in the air, but other things too. The book had been bothering him a little on this score recently, and he was also under some pressure from his magazine editor to deliver on an article he had promised some months previously. With one foot on the front step of 'The Merlot' he suddenly wished that he might be able to simply drop all those things he was keeping in the air - and, as he stepped inside, the smile from the car had evaporated and he felt suddenly tired.

Once over the threshold he paused. Tuesday was not a renowned drinking night, and 'the Merlot' was about half full. Despite this, however, it took him a little time to adjust to the light (which was surprisingly dingy, and seemed, if anything, even darker than the street outside) and then, once in tune with his new environment, a few seconds more to spot Julia and Claire in the far corner. Julia - who was already sitting - must have picked Claire out with the instinct of a homing missile. Mark could imagine her striding across the wine bar in a straight line, right to Claire's table. Within seconds of her entrance, she looked as if she had been there for hours.

Mark guessed that at some stage on her journey she must also have made contact with Peter who, still in his working suit, was standing at the bar looking in the same direction. Peter had returned his attention to the waitress, turning just as Mark placed a hand on his shoulder.

"Hello, old Chap!" Peter feigned to land a punch in Mark's midriff.

"Doesn't still hurt, does it?" The two of them had played squash a few days previously and, over-stretching during one exhausting rally, Mark had managed to smack his racket into Peter's shoulder.

"What? No, it's fine. Played yesterday, actually; young chap at work."

"Give you the run around, did he?"

Peter smiled broadly.

"Piss off!"

Mark could tell that Peter's day had been a successful one. He was one of those men whose job was of almost supreme importance - even though they might deny it - and a successful day (which, in Peter's terms, meant closing a deal and earning a significant amount of commission) would stand him in good stead for at least a week.

"Better make that two bottles, please love." Peter picked a bottle of red wine from the counter and two of the glasses that had been resting in front of him. "Bring the rest over, there's a good chap."

His seeing Peter had succeeded in lifting Mark's spirits a little, and when he reached the table a couple of minutes later, he was in sufficient humour for his smile to have been restored. He wondered if Julia would ever have been able to guess that between the car and here - and in such a very short space of time too - he had experienced something of a 'dark' moment.

Claire smiled up at him.

"Hello, Tiger", she said, offering him her cheek which he pecked dutifully. Julia patted the seat next to hers, and he sat down.

The conversation took off as it always did with the sorts of 'catching up' news that people seemed comfortable with in order to get things going. Peter - as Mark had already suspected - was in a position to dominate the early exchanges, especially as he had the prospect (and the meeting was next week) of closing his biggest deal of the year, which, Claire immediately pointed out, would also mean a trip to the Bahamas.

Julia tried to keep up their side of the conversation with relatively trivial bits of information, but, as usual the balance was only there in terms of words rather than substance. Mark - who was chipping in on autopilot - had already been distracted by the fact that the top three buttons of Claire's blouse were undone and, being bra-less, when she leant forwards the nipple on her left breast was clearly visible. He had always suspected that Claire's figure would be something to behold, and here, for the first time he could remember, was a glimpse of hard evidence.

He tried to combat his desire to stare by suddenly bursting into laughter and throwing back his head in what was, to be truthful, a style not entirely natural to him. When Claire rocked forwards for her glass, he tried casting his eyes around the bar, making a show of examining the other clientele.

"And how's the book going?"

There was no avoiding Claire when she asked a direct question however, and Mark, returning her gaze, fought to concentrate on her eyes as he replied.

"Fine. Another few hundred words, you know. Chipping away."

"Julia says it will be a masterpiece."

Mark looked at Julia then back around the table generally.

"Of course," he offered, and the others laughed.

"More wine?" Peter had raised the half empty bottle in a gesture of plenty which, coincidentally, had been accompanied by both Julia and Claire standing up.

"Little girls' room," Julia said as she squeezed passed Mark, leaning on him as she did so.

"Is it going OK?" Peter, having poured the wine and waited for the women to depart, broke into the short silence with something that sounded more serious.

"What?"

"The book?"

Mark paused and took another sip, allowing a little more silence to enter into the conversation almost as if it were a third party making its own, important, contribution. He looked at this glass. When driving, he was always cautious about his alcohol intake. He looked back at Peter and offered him a smile which was intended to be both reassuring and inscrutable; the mirror behind Peter's seat gave no real indication whether or not he had been successful.

"Uncle likes it; and, I guess he's the best judge." Mark's answer left more than one question begging, but before Peter could probe and further he was rushing on. "So how about squash then? Thursday's usually good for you isn't it?"

"Usually; but I've got a meeting in Windsor all day - preparation for the big one next week," Peter too paused for wine. "What about Claire?"

"Claire?"

"Yes. I'm sure she'd play. She's really quite good now, you know. I mean we've played a lot recently and, OK you'll beat her easily, but it might be fun."

Playing squash with Claire was not something to be taken lightly under the present circumstances and - in his present frame of mind - not a prospect to be toyed with. Before Mark had the chance to reply, she and Julia reappeared.

"Squash on Thursday?" Peter said, standing to let Claire into her seat.

"I thought you were in Windsor?"

"I am. But old Mark here will give you a good thrashing!" Peter, being deliberately suggestive, broke into a loud laugh at his own joke, which - despite its underlying innocence - Mark was surprised to find just a little uncomfortable.

"If he's man enough..." said Claire, keeping the banter going, and, as Mark thumped the table in a mock gesture of challenge, he noticed that all buttons on her shirt - bar the top one - was now fastened.

Later, as they drove home, the Audi picking its way through north London streets in stealthy quiet, Julia broke into the silence.

"Are you OK?"

Mark, surprised by the suddenness of the question as much as its content, glanced involuntarily at her before returning his eyes to the road. The streets were surprisingly quiet, and they had made good progress since leaving Highgate. Having finished the two bottles of wine, they had all moved on to coffee and, although the general spirit of the evening did not fade, their reliance on alcohol as its catalyst did.

He tried to think of some specific incident which might have triggered Julia's question, but none came back to him.

"Why?"

"Oh, I don't know," she had returned her eyes to the road ahead, and was watching the break lights of the car ahead as it slowed for traffic lights. "Nothing specific, I guess. You just seemed a bit strange, that's all."

"Strange?" Mark looked at her again.

"No, not strange. But, well, preoccupied." Silence for a moment. "Like there's something bothering you; as if you're worried. I don't know."

Mark let her words sink in, trying to weigh up the concept of being worried and balance it against his present existence which he felt, in general terms, to be pretty good. There had been Claire's breasts of course - and then the prospect of the game of squash - but he was hardly going to mention those! And in any event, he was certain that such a preoccupation could hardly translate itself into any form of external expression that might be open to interpretation as worry!

He wondered how he might reassure Julia that he was actually perfectly fine, and that she was imagining things. Or even if she was not imagining things, that he was still okay. Perhaps he had been feeling a little tired, perhaps not; but whatever it might be - assuming that there might *be* anything anyway! - it would surely be too complex for him to try and convey.

"I'm fine", he said, and pulled away from the lights.

Chapter Five

There was one other thing that had slightly thrown Mark during the early exchanges in the wine bar. He was standing in their bathroom, examining his face as he brushed his teeth, and allowing his mind to wander back to the concern Julia had expressed in the car.

She had been in friendly combat with Peter, trading opening blows regarding who had done what and who had been the most busy, valiantly fighting a rearguard action against an adversary whose weapons seemed significantly loaded with pound signs. Despite this back-foot stance, Julia's tenacity would not allow her to give in, and perhaps her boldest challenge was to announce that she had bought Laura's wedding present.

Claire, Mark noticed (despite his attempts *not* to notice) was more interested in this new conversational twist than Peter, who - comfortable in his certain victory - eased himself back into his chair and sipped at his wine.

"What did you get her?"

Mark would have liked to have been excused from this particular exchange, preferring instead to engage Peter in discussions that were more appropriate to their sexual heredity; but Peter showed no signs of wishing to comply at this precise moment, and Mark - in spite of himself - felt drawn in.

"A mirror. For her hall, I think." Julia replied.

"A mirror?"

"That's exactly what Mark said," Julia looked at him to make sure that he was involved, "but Laura was quite adamant. I got the name of this rather swish place in Regent Street and we went down there on Saturday."

"Regent Street? Wasn't that a bit pricey?" Claire cast Mark a look, expecting to receive confirmation from him, but Julia was in full command from their side.

"A little, perhaps. But it is a really fine mirror, isn't it?"

Now he was in, and unavoidably so; any response relating to the forthcoming cricket season or Tottenham's chances in the Cup replay would have been simply unacceptable. Mark felt all eyes upon him, even Peter's who had evidently rested enough.

"It's big, and it's heavy."

Claire laughed.

"Poor love had to carry it, too," Julia, stepping in again, tried to prevent Mark's interception from ruining her thread. "And we've got to take it to Oxford before the wedding. I thought we'd hang it for her in the new house; you know, the one she moves in to when she gets back."

"So you'll have to carry it again! Poor thing!" Claire leant forwards, offering mock sympathy, and Mark tried some kind of 'here-we-go-again' gesture to Peter, who smiled.

"Actually Peter, we thought you might be able to help." Julia pounced on Peter's smile.

"Oh. When is it?" Mark wondered if Peter might carry round his diary in his head, memorised for occasions such as this. He sensed him waiting for a date to which he would be able to respond in the full and certain knowledge that he was actually busy. Julia would have none of it.

"When are you free?"

Back into the general melee, Peter had been off again, and the evening had progressed.

Placing his toothbrush in its holder and pulling back his lips to check his teeth one last time, Mark wished he had been able to make some definite arrangement with Peter; the squash match would have been ideal - just so that the two of them could have had a quiet chat. With a sigh, he switched off the light.

The next day, the mirror - still sheathed - was awaiting him as he entered his study. Julia had left for work early, planning to take a half-day and spend the afternoon looking (for the umpteenth time, as far as he could see) for something suitable to wear for Laura and Tim's wedding. In consequence, Mark's day had stretched before him as he sat at breakfast, combining Wheetabix with the Times. With Julia providing the bookends to his waking hours, he was free to order the remainder of them after whichever fashion - and in whichever order - he chose. That he would, at some stage, visit his Aunt's house was never in question, the only issue - and this he wrestled with briefly as he folded his newspaper at the end of breakfast - was when he would do so and for how long.

It seemed sensible - and the most attractive option come to that - to go there first and get the difficult part of the day over with. He wondered, as he finished his coffee and looked out of the dining room window, why he should automatically consider working on the book to be the most difficult. There had been days when knowing what to do with the 'other' time - that large, unallocated portion - proved far more problematical;

there was a temporal space which required filling, and along with a decision on how to fill it came - as an unavoidable bundle - questions regarding the 'usefulness', purpose, and otherwise of those activities chosen to stop up the gap. He had never considered himself to be that good a time waster - though, being honest with himself, he had not contemplated this in relation to any overall scale of effectiveness. Certainly there were things he did which 'passed' time: watching the television was, for instance, a fundamentally fruitless exercise which, by and large, allowed time to pass. The notion of actually doing something to *waste* time was a different proposition all together, and one which he seemed to have only recently begun to comprehend as such.

It was a difficult question he had not been able to resolve between leaving the breakfast things in the sink and getting ready to go out. The satisfying 'thud' of the Audi's door closing him in accompanied the resolution that he would deal with one part of the day at a time, and that the book should be his first task; whatever was to follow he would consider later. Thus it was he arrived at Beatrice and Simon's prepared for probably half a day, yet uncertain about the remainder. Not finding them in was something of a surprise, but, as he had his own key - a precaution of his Uncle's for just such an occasion - it was no more than that. They had not been gone long: the kettle was still fairly warm when he walked into the kitchen to make coffee to take to his desk.

Having eyed the mirror with some degree of mistrust, he walked towards the desk where his attention was drawn to a simple brown envelope laying flat on its surface. Considering its position, its relation to the other items and its distance from them, it was evident that the envelope - which bore no salutation - had been deliberately placed there. He put his coffee on a coaster (thereby destroying a certain symmetry that the envelope had created) and sat down. It was obviously for him and, once he had sat down, he picked it cautiously from the table.

It surprised him immediately with its weight, and he found himself feeling through its skin to try and gauge what it contained, much as one might presents at Christmas. Turning it over, he found it to be unsealed, the flap simply tucked in, and with a simple flick of his fingers it was open. He pulled the envelope slightly and peered in, then, satisfied with the contents, tipped them out onto the table. A small pile of photographs lay before him.

He resisted the temptation to immediately delve into the images, preferring to ease himself back in his chair and raise his coffee from the desk. As he took his first mouthful, he tried to assemble a small mental album of the photos that lay before him, expanding them from the fragments he could make out as individual corners of a few were exposed peeping from beneath those that lay on top of them. He had no doubt these were the photographs Beatrice had promised him, especially as the only one he could presently see whole - that on the top of the pile - was one of Beatrice and Simon standing with his Father near a river bank. It was a small black and white image (indeed, he had seen nothing from the fragments to suggest that any were in colour) and the central characters had been badly framed; there was too much sky above them, and too much field to their right. On the far side, the nose of a cow poked cheekily into shot, and Mark - who had, of course, seen the photo before - realised that had he been a little further off centre when he had held the camera and thus managed to get a little more of the bovine intruder into the frame, the result might have been hailed as a masterpiece!

He put down his coffee and separated each item, trying as he did so, not to become involved in its content, but rather adopting a detached, intellectual view of them, grouping them into small areas of the desk each in their own particular category. By the time he had finished (the whole process taking no more than a minute or so) the desk was fairly littered with photographs - this, despite the considerable size of the desk and the limited number of images he had to sort. There appeared to be numerous potential groupings too, but Mark had settled on just five: his Father alone; his Father with other people (the photograph with the cow had been the first one to qualify here); any with his Mother in; any with himself; and the rest. This division - which yielded the most photographs in the first two groupings (but as Beatrice had, presumably, already gone through some form of selection process, he guessed that was only to be expected) - had not been premeditated, but had fallen from his mind much as the photographs themselves had fallen from the envelope and been subject to a degree of random force outside of his control. That he had insisted on a pile for those in which he himself featured was, on reflection, something of a surprise to him. After all, the book was about his Father, and, however he chose to cut it, he was no more than a bit player in the overall scheme of things.

He was also surprised by the size of his Mother's collection; indeed, there was but a single photograph. Mark wondered if this was anything to do with Beatrice; perhaps she had edited out the vast majority of the pictures containing her. But if she had - and here Mark could only speculate, especially as he was highly dubious as to this line of thinking in any event - was it because Beatrice did not (and after all this time too!) actually like his Mother, or was she trying to protect him from something, perhaps the harbinger of a painful memory? Neither seemed to yield anything in the way of insight as far as Mark could see (though he did make a mental note to ask Beatrice again exactly where she stood with regard his Mother - there had been stories after all!) and he decided that the simple reason for the paucity was that Beatrice just didn't have very many photographs of her.

The one that now confronted him showed her alone, standing against some large building built from huge stone slabs. It was a full length photograph, taken at an angle so that, as she leant her head and shoulder against the wall, the gap between her and the stone was clearly visible, and the sun - which was behind her - shone brightly through the gap. She was wearing a soft white dress, which, given the direction of the light, was almost diaphanous, and (here Mark could imaging the sheen of her auburn hair) gave her the air of a model who had stepped straight out of a Pre-Raphaelite painting. Which, in some respects, was exactly what she was.

-*-

Charles Packard met Mary Elizabeth Browning in the middle of the long summer of 1955. Charles - with the unhappy episode in the Army now behind him - had settled into his work at the wallpaper factory with a degree of mechanistic lack of flair his immediate superiors had taken as a natural aptitude for the job. Despite the numbing monotony of his labour -

> 'the Devil rides the vast machines
>
> and whips us, day-long, into our
>
> silent and humble submission'

(The Factory Gates, 1956)

- he was able to maintain his commitment to the job by occupying his mind elsewhere. Later, in 1975 during an interview with Michael Parkinson, Charles confessed that many of his ideas - especially those which involved 'those crusading for their freedom' - came to him during those long days at the factory.

With an almost antiseptic view of his weekdays' labours, Charles became determined to live his life elsewhere, and much of the early part of 1955 was taken up with extra-curricular experimentation. Having left school too early (a sacrifice which he never publicly regretted) he found himself with an unsatisfied sense of longing for some form of mental stimulus. In

May of that year (a little after his 23rd birthday) he joined a pottery group in the centre of Warwick. This was his first sortie into the creative world and, although ultimately a failure in terms of personal satisfaction, he had gone into the venture with a commendable degree of enthusiasm.

Before the end of June he had left and taken up woodworking. In the same Castle Street craft centre (something of a new venture for 1955) courses were offered in 'Woodworking and Turning'. Charles confessed later to a recollection of his Grandfather as Cabinet Marker (though subsequently discovering this to be inaccurate) and had decided to follow this new course on the basis that the talent might have been passed down through the generations. After three weeks and numerous plasters, he took the advice of his tutor - who described him as 'the most inept man with a plane I have ever seen in my life' - and withdrew from the programme. The move coincided with the first week in July, which was also his scheduled annual holiday, and he retreated to his parents' house in Sheffield ostensibly to recuperate.

In terms of domestic accord, things in Sheffield were still as tense and unsatisfying as they had been prior to his departure two years previously. His Father, now ageing rapidly, still promoted the virtues of a career in mining and offered to get Charles an interview with his pit boss. Charles declined. He had seen his Father dig his way out of underground working and into pit management, but at a price which only now was the sickening man beginning to pay. His Mother, whose own decline seemed to keep pace with that of her husband's, endeavoured to keep the peace between the two, but by the end of the week and Charles' departure, all were beginning to show the effects of his visit. Later he would write:

'Despite the smiles, despite the waving,

the back slapping, the hand shaking;

despite the promises, despite the tears,

there comes a weariness with years.

Time is not for mending here,

decay boasts but a single path;

and life is not for blessing here,

this my Sheffield epitaph.'

(Sheffield Song, 1960)

Charles returned to Warwick even more determined to find his way. His job, he knew, was not his life. On July 6th he saw an advertisement for 'Drawing and Painting Classes' in the Warwick Echo and decided that if his hands were not made to plane wood then perhaps they were made to wield pencils. The next class was scheduled for the following week and, in the intervening weekend, Charles took a bus to Birmingham to visit to city's Museum and Art Gallery.

He had never been particularly interested in Art as a child; his environment had never encouraged interest in it as an acceptable pursuit. His friends from school - most of whom went on to work in the pits or the mills - spent their weekends either playing football or talking about it. Charles could just about hold his own in these conversations - siding with the Wednesday whenever required to show allegiance - but without passion. Since his removal from Sheffield, his burgeoning sense of self had told him that there were other things in life besides football. It was against this background that he had begun to feel what he later described as 'a gnawing ache, that seemed to be slowly chewing at my consciousness'. His trip to the Birmingham gallery was his first attempt to satisfy that ache.

> "I stood on the threshold of the gallery not quite knowing what to do. There were lots of other people around, of course, mostly going about their typical Saturday morning stuff - shopping and the like - and because of these two factors I felt strangely alone. However, after a couple of minutes, a tall and rather elderly Gentleman passed me on the steps and went inside. I took my lead from him."

> (Interview with David Frost, 1984)

Charles' first experience of Art (in the domestic and formalised surroundings of the Birmingham gallery) was, as he admitted later, a little confusing. He had lost his elderly guide quite early on, and found himself confronted by rooms and passages each promising differing delights. Having decided that he had come to see 'Art', he fought the desire to concentrate on more tangible things - like the Natural history collection - and followed signs to "19th Century Art" which seemed, on the whole, to be a reasonable starting point. Having observed others in the gallery who stood quietly in front of the various paintings hung on the walls, moving from one to the other after a few seconds, Charles had discerned what it was he actually had to *do*; knowing what exactly he was supposed to be looking *at* was another matter.

> "I left in what I can only describe as a state of extreme confusion! I mean, I had stared at these things - image after image - in the rather stupid expectation that something was supposed to happen! Maybe that's not unnatural; I expect people still do it. I suppose I

had some inflated idea of my own intellect or something, and the notion of simply seeing if I actually liked anything never really occurred to me!"

(Interview with David Frost, 1984)

The one thing that did make an impression on Charles was, however, the gallery's collection of Pre-Raphaelite paintings, and particularly the work of Burne-Jones and Rossetti. That he should have left that Saturday with those images engraved in his mind was, he confessed later, 'a little more than fortunate'.

Three days later, he attended his first 'Drawing and Painting' class. The group had been together for some three weeks, and because of this, Charles' late arrival immediately cast him as something of an outsider; a general stance with which, however inaccurate, he continued to struggle for the remainder of his life. Small cliques had already begun to form and, although he had been allocated a space sufficiently close to a number of other people, their apparent mastery of the craft - compared to those first, hesitant strokes of his own - only enhanced his feeling of isolation.

Despite the extra attention given to him by the class leader - a retired teacher from Coventry, Hermione Swift - the brushes felt clumsy in his hands and he struggled when trying to ensure that the correct amount of paint attached itself to either the brush or the paper. This rather unsatisfactory attempt at water-colours - which he carried on with well into later life - left him more impressed with those who could master the medium, but cold with regard to their results. The additional reason for his lack of success during that first visit was the distracting presence of Mary Elizabeth Browning.

Born in Ashford, Kent, in 1935, Mary had moved to Warwick in 1946 with her Mother. Her Father, who had been called up at the beginning of the war, was killed in Normandy during the first day of the 1944 landings. Her Mother, who was a Governess, had - thanks to an excellent reputation established in a short period in both Ashford and Canterbury - found herself engaged in a large house on the outskirts of the town working for a Member of Parliament, William Henry Watson. Mary, who was a little older than either of the Watsons' children, enjoyed many of the advantages that went with both the title and property of the house's owner, and, in consequence, completed a reasonably full education to eventually leave her Mothers' side late in 1954 to take up a post as Infant Teacher in a small school in Warwick.

Like himself, Mary had been a late starter in the Art class, though she did have one week's advantage over him. She had decided that, despite the temptation to return to the Watsons' house for the summer holidays, she should remain independent and had taken a part-time job to fill the gap between the school's academic years. She had also decided that some form of hobby was in order and had joined the drawing class with the comforting knowledge that she knew she already possessed a degree of talent in that area. It was not her talent which distracted the young Charles during that first evening however; rather, he was struck by her mass of auburn tresses and the image of Pre-Raphaelite woman she conjured up for him.

> "She was, if you like, my Muse. Had I been asked to conjure an image of her in advance, of someone who would inspire me to live, then I could only have pictured an image of Rossetti, and I could only have drawn Mary."

> (Scenes From A Life, 1988)

It was several weeks before Charles - who was still a relatively shy young man - and Mary spoke. They had come together at one of the materials' tables (whether by his contrivance or not, he would never say) and had both attempted to pick up the same water-colour set. The die was cast.

Within two weeks, Charles had changed his position in the class to become resident alongside Mary. Like him, she had not found a natural inroad into any of the established cliques, and, quietly, they formed a small group of their own. Hermione was pleased with this development as she was finding Charles difficult to handle - 'Something of a slow learner' - and having Mary take him off her hands allowed her to revert the bulk of her attention to the main body of her class. Mary, who was under no illusions as to her own ability or ambition, was happy enough to belong to something that allowed her to relax - and she was only too pleased to help the quiet young man whose sense of perspective (amongst other things) seemed faintly ludicrous.

Charles, even with the assistance of Mary's marginally more professional eye, failed to blossom as an artist, despite his very best endeavours to do so:

> "It was like asking a blind man to see, or a dumb man to speak: however hard I tried, I communicated nothing. Every pore cried out to be free of the torment - but at the same time, those very same pores cried to be thrown deeper and deeper into the torment, just so I might be rescued by Mary."

(Scenes From A Life, 1988)

Despite his obvious lack of ability - and lack of progress - Charles stayed in the class; and Mary - whose own output suffered because of this - stayed as well. His immediate Pre-Raphaelite image of her, which was to remain with him for the rest of his days, was soon supplemented by an appreciation of her qualities in other areas: the consideration she showed, her patience, her talent, even her level-headedness. He was not overwhelmed by some boyish crush as he had been just the previous year, but 'intoxicated'. Soon, Wednesday evenings became the most important part of his week, and that which he looked forward to as soon as the previous one was over.

His problem, he soon realised, was the need to be able to communicate how he felt to Mary herself. The summer was rapidly drawing to a close and Mary was due to return to her teaching, something which she suspected might prevent her further attendance at the class. The prospect of 'losing' her was something that Charles felt unable to endure, and on more than one occasion brought himself to the brink of declaring himself, only to retreat at the very last moment.

The turning point came after class early in August. Charles had returned home:

> "I recall it distinctly. I was sitting at the kitchen table. I had just written a letter to Mother (I liked to write frequently; she worried so) and had left the table to fetch an envelope. When I returned, the writing pad lay open on the table with my pen alongside it. I simply sat down and wrote 'Mary' at the top of the page."

(Interview with David Frost, 1984)

What then followed was the first piece of creative writing from the pen of Charles Packard. It was not, as he admitted later, a thing of any particular beauty nor built to stand the test of time (indeed, no copy remains), but it did enable him to push a little harder at the door he had been trying to open for so long; and hard enough to allow a little light to shine through.

The next week Charles carried the neatly folded sheet of paper to the drawing class. Mary was a little late, and, for a while, he thought she might not be coming at all. His work was particularly bad that evening as he was unable to concentrate, his mind struggling with the decision on when to give her the poem - and then fretting over the possible outcome. Then, half way through the evening, 'in a feat of clumsy incompetence', he spilt a small pot of blue wash over the picture he was half way through painting:

57

"She laughed. It was a free and magical kind of laugh, and
something in it seemed to unlock something in me. I pulled the
paper from my pocket and just handed it to her. She unfolded it,
and then I watched her smile disappear. Her cheeks became a
little red, and I suddenly knew that I had ruined everything and I
would never see her again. It seemed like an age, but eventually
she looked up. I will never forget that look in her eyes: so open;
so candid. Her gaze never faltered. "It's beautiful" she said, and
she smiled, softly, nervously. It was the most sublime moment of
my life."

(Scenes From A Life, 1988)

Three months later, Charles Packard and Mary Browning were engaged.

Chapter Six

Julia awoke in something of a diabolical mood on the Thursday. Mark - who had, over the months, become sensitive to Julia's regular and not unnatural mood swings - was aware that he might be in for a difficult morning when he woke to find that she had already left their bed, showered, and was downstairs in the kitchen. He could hear the faint 'clinking' of crockery and cutlery without the accompaniment of any other background noise. He lay still for a few moments, debating whether or not to immediately get up himself, and hoping that he might suddenly hear strains of Vivaldi or Handel emanating from the stereo which would signify that everything was all right after all.

By the time he reached the shower (and he had taken a fair degree of time to rouse himself, pull on his dressing gown, pick out his clothes from the wardrobe, and generally fuss about) there was still no respite from the silence from below. Even the clinking had stopped, and Mark could only assume that Julia had left the kitchen for either the dining room or lounge. As the jet of hot water pulsed onto him, he remembered - and with a degree of conscious recognition this time - it was Thursday and that he was scheduled to play squash with Claire at eleven-forty. He paused, soap in hand, then, as if to scrub the sleep from his body, set about creating a fresh layer of lather to replace that just washed away.

He had made sufficient time to consider the day's prospects - and to find himself still (to his surprise) regretting that it was not Peter with whom he would be playing squash - when he eventually left the bedroom. On reaching the bottom of the stairs he had sensed (without visual confirmation) that Julia was in the lounge, and, choosing to ignore her for the moment, went into the kitchen. There was a half-pot of coffee on the table and an empty cup beside it. Things might not be that bad after all.

By the time he joined her - his coffee augmented by a small plate bearing two slices of toast - Julia, who was sitting feet-up on the sofa, had already managed to spread the majority of the day's newspapers about her. Mark, because of his erstwhile 'profession', took five daily papers. It was possible he might have something in any of them, though as such an event - publication - was hardly a regular occurrence, to keep his local Newsagent so busy might have been said to be a little 'over the top'; but Mark could afford it and, in any event, it created the right kind of impression. The impression that Julia was currently creating - this solitary figure in the midst of broadsheets and tabloids - was not especially healthy. Mark recognised it as general discomfort and boredom, though in doing so also observed within himself a degree of trepidation in case any of her apparent malaise were down to him. He debated for a second over the kind of greeting he should give, then, deciding on none at all, planted himself in an armchair and picked up the nearest broadsheet.

"I haven't seen that one yet", said Julia immediately, almost as if Mark should have been able to divine as much from its position on the carpet. Mark tossed it back roughly to where he had found it and leant across to take the paper Julia was now offering him.

"Thanks."

"Are you OK?" Her next words came to him a few minutes later, just as he had begun reading an article relating to Social Services' child care schemes. Julia's voice sounded odd, even a little hesitant; but, for once, it was her words rather than their mode of delivery that surprised him.

"Me?" It seemed strange that he should have risen wondering what might be wrong with Julia and yet here she was being concerned about him! He had not considered whether or not *he* might be offering some hint or semblance of discomfort or unhappiness, and, for the present, dismissed any immediate intention of doing so. His reply had been delivered with the natural surprise that her question had generated; there was none of the inflection that might have suggested that Julia should look to herself before casting aspersions elsewhere. Even though it followed rapidly on from his last, his next word was a little more measured.

"Why?"

He met her gaze for a moment then searched for his coffee, waiting for some kind of response.

"Oh, I don't know," with this as her opening, he felt safe enough to be able to engage her head-on, and looked up again, "you just seem a bit - well, different somehow."

"Different?" He had, since beginning the book - if not since the beginning of his journalistic career - occasionally insisted on the correct word; the *mot juste*. As it seemed that he might be, in some obscure way, under attack, then he was determined that he should understand as fully and completely as possible the nature of that attack. Julia's initial volley had been less accurate than a shotgun.

"I don't know," she floundered a little, "just the last few days really. As if something's bothering you. Is it? I mean, maybe it isn't. Maybe it's me. I thought it might be the book. Possibly."

"The book?"

She looked away, a little guiltily. Mark waited for her to continue, sensing a reluctance to carry the thing through.

"What about the book?" She had offered him something tangible.

"Well," she looked up again, "you seem so preoccupied with it. And working too hard, maybe. Like Sunday..."

She let her sentence fade and Mark recalled the disappointment - not to say anger - she had displayed on Saturday about him planning to work the following day. He vaguely remembered wondering - even then - if there had been something amiss with *her*. His silence seemed to weaken her case.

"Look, I know it's important to you, and that you've got to get it finished..."

Again her words trailed off, but this time with the air of defeat about them. Mark - who had been contemplating the counter-attacking 'and what's wrong with you then!' - chose to remain silent, preferring to let the subject slip. He returned to his article more certain then ever that Julia was a little under the weather and that it would be best to simply ignore her outburst.

He finished reading. Julia was still in more or less the same pose, and giving out roughly the same message. He checked his watch.

"What are you up to today?" It seemed prudent for him to make some kind of effort. After all, his own day was pretty much defined - squash, lunch, work - and under the circumstances he felt a little churlish not making himself aware of what Julia had planned, especially as Thursday was one day when she tended not to go into work herself.

She threw the paper she was reading to the floor with an air of relief.

"I need to go and see Laura. She wants my advice about some material or other. She rang yesterday, before you got home. I said I'd pop over around lunch time." Despite her apparent lightness, she seemed a little less than confident of her ground, and offered her own movements a shade defensively. Mark smiled, attempting to restore a little sanity to the morning - an action which allowed Julia a bold continuation under the circumstances. "Are you going over to Simon's?"

Mark, though winding down from his **mot juste** frame of mind, noticed how she had avoided asking him if he were going to 'work on the book'.

"Later. I've got that game of squash first."

"Squash?"

"We arranged it in The Merlot the other night. You might not have been listening."

"I thought Peter was busy," she had allowed herself a brief moment to reassemble her memories of that evening before continuing.

"He is. I'm playing Claire. Don't you remember the conversation?"

Julia reddened a little but said nothing. Mark, confident that she was indeed confused at present did nothing further to elaborate on the arrangements. He retrieved his coffee cup, drained it, then, discarding the paper, stood up.

"Shall I take that out?"

Julia followed his eyes to her own empty mug, raised it from the floor, and handed it to him.

Back in the bedroom, Mark looked for his sports bag which he usually kept on top of the wardrobe. It was only after he had failed to find it there that he remembered he had packed it late the previous evening in preparation and left it just inside the spare room. He wondered if Julia had seen him packing it; if she had, then surely she would not have shown any surprise at his recent announcement. He tried to reconstruct half an hour from the previous day - locating both himself and Julia in the house - and rebuild those few minutes during which his green Jaguar sports bag had been transformed from empty vessel to fully prepared luggage. The effort was wasted however; it was not simply the exact location of Julia during the operation that flawed him, but the exact time of it too. He sat down on the bed with a low sigh and flicked off his slippers.

There were nearly two hours to go before he was due to meet Claire. They had decided that it would be best to see each other 'on court', thus avoiding any unnecessary hold-ups elsewhere. It would take him about half an hour to get to the club and get changed, which left him insufficient time to do anything particularly meaningful. He had no intention of hanging about the house - even though the idea of beginning to rough something out for the piece for which his editor was waiting held some merit - and had decided to drive up to Hampstead.

When he appeared downstairs, bag in hand and sporting his jacket, Julia was in the kitchen.

"Off already?" She glanced at the clock on the wall. "I didn't think you were supposed to be playing until eleven something."

"I'm not. I just thought I'd pop up to the shops. I need to get a couple of new squash balls; and that book I'm reading - the one about Chamberlain - is just awful, so I thought I'd get something else."

"Aren't you supposed to be reviewing that one?"

"The Chamberlain?" Mark paused long enough to allow Julia to nod. His sports bag was growing heavy in his hand. "I was. I mean, I am. But there's no urgency. I'll do it later; it just seems so cumbersome, that's all. And dry too. I don't understand why people make history so antiseptic."

He heard the words leave him and wondered exactly what they meant. Perhaps it would have been useful to have been on the receiving end of them; to have had an alternative view, another perspective. As it was, Julia was advancing on him and, leaning slightly on his arm, gave him a peck on the cheek.

"Play well."

"I'll probably get there early anyway," he said, turning, "I've booked the court for long enough, and a warm-up might do me good."

"Give my love to Claire."

Throwing his bag in the back of the Audi, he thought what a strange exchange that had been: the discussion of his itinerary, and his justification of it. He was also a little surprised at the stance he had taken; there was much of the defensive about it. The story about the biography had been true, but little else. Squash balls he did not need (and if he had, the club would have them by the dozen) and the idea of getting to the court early to warm-up was something that had come to him on the spur of the moment.

Despite difficulties with parking, Mark had completed his rather superficial shopping within three quarters of an hour. He had dallied in the bookshop for a while, yet - despite finding nothing that took his fancy in either the history or biography sections, and in the end choosing something that was nothing more than pulp science fiction - even this activity seemed to be over in minutes. Recognising it to be still too early to go to the club, he decided on a coffee and sat in Carwardines' window overlooking the pavement and thumbing through the first pages of his new acquisition. Despite his fondness for books, this particular paperback felt a little strange in his hands; and he felt oddly out of character embarking on a fictitious story about a fantastical future when his entire academic upbringing - not to mention his present labours - were firmly rooted in the concrete past.

Outside, a light but steady stream of mid-morning Hampstead shoppers went about their business. Most were well-dressed - 'well heeled' one might legitimately say in the true historical context of the phrase - and carried themselves as if the world was actually 'all right' and their place in it secure. It was a feeling Mark had occasionally recognised in himself, though he was certain that his demeanour would never give the game away quite so crudely as those he watched now.

It was - and he reflected on this as he stepped out of the Audi and on to the gravel car park at the club - an inevitability that he should, despite all his efforts, arrive there early. At the reception he showed the young woman his membership card and asked if he might be able to get on to court a little early.

"The people who booked it before you haven't turned up, Mr Packard," she said, checking the register in front of her, "So if it's free, go straight on."

"A warm-up might do me good," Mark said with light confidentiality, and she returned his smile with the impersonal professionalism with which receptionists are paid to endorse all their customers' comments.

It was a little after eleven twenty when he opened the door of the enclosed court and stepped inside. It felt cold and he shivered involuntarily as he unzipped his racket case, depositing it in the front right-hand corner of the court. Looking up at the four blank walls, he flexed his leg muscles, sub-consciously imagining that he might be on one of the courts with a public gallery and thus be obliged to try and imitate one of the better club players who had once given him both a game and a lesson; but the process - which was all too brief to be effectual - did little good, and when Mark drew back his arm to take his first swing he was still quite cold.

For a while he simply limbered up by knocking the ball relatively aimlessly against the wall. He was thinking about the various events of the morning (which, though minor, held some kind of fascination for him) and had already begun to bend his mind towards that afternoon's work. One or two slightly harder strikes - and the consequent stretching to retrieve the ball - eventually began to take his mind away from the status of his book, and relocated him firmly on the squash court. As if in recognition of this, he began a structured exercise along the right hand wall, banging the ball in hard and low - as tight to the wall as he could - and gradually building up the pace. After fifty or sixty strokes, he turned his attention to the other side (his backhand wing was by far his weaker) and tried to repeat the exercise, which he did with less fluency.

Back on his forehand, he carried on for a few further strokes then, pausing for breath, checked his watch. There were still a few minutes to go before their scheduled start time, but he was fairly confident that Claire would not be late. On this basis, the last thing he wanted to do was to appear to be idle when she arrived, so - despite already feeling the effects of the warm-up - he decided to press on with a programme of alternating forehand and backhand shots from either side of the court; something which not only involved practising strokes on either wing, but a considerable amount of lateral movement too.

Mark, entranced into the rhythm and trapped by the flow of adrenaline and energy that the exercise gave him, pushed on, attempting to stretch himself more and more with each shot. He began to count the number of strokes in the rally, and, in doing so, emptied his mind of all else apart from his movement and the concentration which allowed him to progress the count in his head. That internal beat of the ball's thump against his racket, then its crack against the wall and the count that followed - 'Nine', 'Ten' - became so hypnotic that when there came a tap on the door followed by the door's opening, Mark was initially oblivious to it.

Bending to retrieve the ball after a missed half volley on his backhand, he caught a glimpse of Claire's shoes, then, rising (and having let the ball slip past him) her whole body. In that brief moment it suddenly dawned on him that in almost every respect Claire was just a little outrageous. There was nothing that might cause offence (indeed, just the opposite, if the truth were told) but everything about her was a little 'too' something: her sports skirt was just a little too short; her top - plain white with just a splash of colour - boasted a neckline (a tasteful, curving neckline) that was just a little too low.

"My! Have you played a game already?" She smiled, showing her white teeth through her too-red lips, and Mark - pausing for the first time in a few minutes - suddenly felt the sting of sweat in his right eye.

"I was just warming up."

"Just warming up!" His attempt to make his exertions thus far appear normal rather than cavalier, failed. "You look exhausted! Are you sure you still want to play?"

"Play?" He did not allow himself the opportunity to think about his reply. Peter's words - 'you'll beat her easily' - along with his ego (which was at its misguided peak on a squash court) forced his reply. "I'm fine. Do you want to knock up first?"

"In a minute."

Claire left Mark to volley the ball gently against the front wall for a few minutes as she loosened up. It was evident as she did so, that the aerobics classes she took with Julia had done her the world of good, and her legs flexed impressively below her white skirt. Mark, paused as he sensed that she was about ready.

"OK?"

"Ready," she replied, smiling, though with a slightly more serious tone in her voice. "A gentle knock up first, then. OK?"

The first few minutes - as Mark struggled to regain his earlier sense of warmth and well-being, the wait having cooled him off a little - confirmed that Claire was indeed quite an accomplished player. There was a certain rhythm about her ground strokes which - although her volleying was weak - led him to suspect that she might not be the push-over he had expected. Mark spun his racket, Claire called 'rough', and the first game began.

Thanks to some fairly powerful serving, Mark was able to build up a quick lead which bade well for an early victory; however, once Claire had found his length and established her own game, the rallies became longer and points - after six-nil - were harder to come by. Mark, attempting to assert his supremacy by varying his serve, found himself undertaking shots of delicacy and finesse which (to be blunt) his level of skill could not deliver. Claire began to rein him in and, at seven-five, Mark began to fear the worst. Resorting to his initial tactic on serve - and raw power for everything else - he finally managed to take the game nine-six. As his last shot sped by Claire's outstretched racket against the left-hand wall, he allowed himself to relax.

The transformation was both sudden and subtle. He realised that he was, once again, hot and sweating heavily; he felt slightly tight in the chest and his legs were beginning to remind him that they were not as used to exercising as he might like to thing they were. In addition to all this however, his mind - freed from the tortuous concentration of rally after rally - was suddenly free to wander again, and did so just in time to catch Claire bending to retrieve the ball. Her knickers - as white as everything else - were, predictably, just a little too skimpy for the task in hand and, in consequence, Mark found himself staring (for the briefest instant) at a slightly larger portion of her buttocks than he might have expected.

"Good game," she said, straightening and walking towards him, her face now redder than before but still no match for her lipstick. "Do you want a rest?"

Mark, with his mind now doing vigorous exercises of its own in trying to piece together the newly enhanced image of his opponent - the breasts from 'The Merlot' with the legs, thighs and bottom of the squash court - forced himself to abandon the jigsaw by insisting that they carry right on.

"Your serve; OK?"

"OK, buster," she said, moving to the serving box, "you won't be so lucky this time!"

The damage had, from Mark's point of view, already been done. Not only did he find his concentration slipping, he became suspect to attempting drop shots into the front of the court; shots which forced Claire ahead of him and down low in order to retrieve them. On the majority of occasions her efforts were rewarded handsomely, and Mark found himself too often stranded in the middle of the court and slow to react to a ball passing him down the line. Before he knew it, Claire was announcing the score as five-one.

"How many?"

"Five-one," she said breathlessly at the end of the rally that had rewarded her with her fifth point. "Aren't you counting?"

Into the next rally, Mark tried to revert to his former tactic; but, catching Claire slightly out of position, he attempted a drop shot again and chased in to follow it up. Either the shot was not quite as good as he had hoped or he had been closing in a little too quickly, but the end result was that in their combined efforts to retrieve the ball, Mark found himself trapping Claire in the front corner.

There was a slight pause as Mark found himself half-pressed against her, his left leg brushing her thigh and her right breast gently pressing against his chest; he suddenly sensed the thumping of his pulse as his racket hung semi-limp at his side. For a moment his eyes, his mind, almost all his intelligent senses, lost their focus.

"Good shot," she said, and her words - resounding almost like the report form a gun - had him recoiling away from her and after the ball.

As he prepared to serve - redder than ever now - he was unconvinced that his last shot had been that hot. Indeed, had Claire claimed to have won the point herself he would have been in no position (and, more importantly, not in the frame of mind) to argue. He crashed the ball unstoppably against the front wall.

"Shot," she said. "Five-two."

For the next fifteen minutes, Mark found himself trying to play as hard as he could, attempting various tricks to convince himself that it was Peter or some other member of the club that he was playing. He ignored the complaints in both his lungs and his legs, the burning sensation on his face and the stinging sweat in his eyes, and drove himself forwards. He rescued the second game to take it nine-six, and ripped through the third nine-one. When they finished the last point, Claire conceded defeat.

"OK buster, you win! I need a drink."

Fifteen minutes later, Mark joined Claire in the small club bar. She was already half way through a pint of orange squash and, though still a little flushed, more like her out-door self.

"Beer?" She offered. "The spoils of victory!"

Mark threw his bag on the floor and pointed to her glass.

"One of those will be fine, thanks."

They sat at a table near the window, overlooking the small lawn outside. A squirrel skipped across the grass.

"Some game," Claire volunteered. "You played pretty mean in the end there, you know."

It was intended as much as a joke as anything else, and Mark - who had sufficiently recovered his composure - was able to accept to as such.

"I'll have to have a word with Peter."

"Peter? Why?"

"He said I'd beat you easily."

"The bastard!" She was smiling.

"Either you're much better than he thinks, or I'm much worse. And I wouldn't like to say which!"

They chatted for a while; Mark bought some more drinks, then Claire turned down his offer to buy her a late lunch, claiming another engagement.

"I'd rather have lunch with you of course, darling, but it's my Aunt you see, and I'm afraid I have to keep the old crow happy!" She flashed her teeth through newly painted lips, and Mark made a show of reluctantly accepting her excuse.

In the car park she pecked him on the cheek, leaving a small trace of herself there.

"That was fun. Maybe we should do that again."

He released her arm, which he had found himself holding lightly.

"I think I may need a little more practice first!"

It was a feeble joke, but seemed suitable enough to close the encounter. Throwing his bag onto the back seat of the Audi, Mark watched Claire as she slipped into her car, waved, then drove off. For a moment he remained inert, then, with a meaningful turn of the ignition, kicked his car's engine into life.

Chapter Seven

Mark found Beatrice alone in her kitchen a few days later. He had, since the afternoon of his squash game with Claire, been toiling at the book, attempting to wrestle with how to effect his own introduction into the story and - now that he was also dealing to a large extent with his Mother - trying to get some kind of balance between objective reporting and personal statement.

He had not reflected that much on the match itself, though would admit to his mind wandering a later that same afternoon as, struggling with the build-up to the depiction of his own birth (a rather eerie concept!) the image of Claire - a still fragmented though somewhat mesmeric image - intruded on his thoughts. When he arrived home, Julia - who had evidently received some news of the match from the defeated opponent - had greeted him with "Hail the conquering hero!" and made great play on the difficulty with which he had forced Claire into submission. It was flattering, he decided, that she and Claire should discuss the events - and his own performance - so soon after their conclusion. Drawn into the general banter, he found himself - in something of an unguarded moment and not without a little internal heat - reflecting on the collision in the corner of the court. In consequence, he had changed the subject completely, and steered Julia away with an interrogation of her afternoon with Laura.

Beatrice looked up from her cookery book as he walked through the door.

"More coffee?" she said inquisitively, eyeing the empty mug in his hand.

The kitchen was warm and inviting, filling gently with the smell of the bread now baking in the oven and suffused with an overall sense of wholesome well-being. Mark smiled and walked to the kettle.

"Can I make you one?"

"No thank you Dear, I've just finished a tea."

He filled the old kettle then returned it to its rightful place, plugged it in and switched it on; all the while, he felt his Aunt's eyes on him. He paused then turned.

"Not going so well?"

"It's gone better," he paused, trying to decide between sitting down and putting coffee and milk in his mug. He chose the latter. On the table, the small notebook he had brought down with him threatened like an alien form on the wooden table, catching his eye somewhat malevolently as he waited for the kettle.

He saw Beatrice glance towards it too.

"Aunt?" She looked back at him without replying. "Can we talk? I mean do you have a few minutes?"

She looked at the clock on the wall above his head.

"The bread won't need me for a little while, if that's what you mean."

"I think it might be good if you could just help me sort a few things out in my own mind."

Beatrice stood up, leaving her book open - an obvious indication that she intended to return to it, and as notice to Mark that there was indeed some form of limit to the time she had available, unstated though it may have been.

"Bring your coffee through to the lounge. Simon's out, and we'll be more comfy in there."

When he walked into the sitting room, Mark found himself comparing - though without any premeditated intention to do so - the way his Aunt sat on her sofa with Julia's pose just a few days previously. That image - Julia's impression of frustration, anger, or whatever it was - came to him involuntarily; it was surprising in that it was there at all, and even more so because Beatrice's relaxed attitude seemed so far divergent that the parallel was faintly ludicrous. His Aunt said nothing as he paused by the window, looking out on the front lawn.

Mark would have liked a little help here, and by delaying - by not sitting down - was fishing for Beatrice to offer him an easy introduction. None was forthcoming however, and after a brief pause, he was forced to turn again into the room and take the armchair alongside the settee.

"I have something of a problem, I think." It was not much of a beginning, but just about the best he felt he could manage.

"Writer's block?"

Mark could see the depth of experience in his Aunt's eyes as he glanced up at her. He almost suspected - just now, as she wriggled to get a little more comfortable (a gesture in itself as subtle as it could possibly be) - that she saw almost everything, and that her reply - 'Writer's block' indeed! - was simply a mechanism to ask him for more to go on.

"Of sorts, I guess." He paused. There appeared to be no easy way of approaching his subject or his problem - especially in the light of the fact that the latter seemed indefinable. "It feels odd writing about one's own birth. If you see what I mean?"

"Is that why you're stuck? Because you don't know about it?"

A car tooted outside, and Mark looked involuntarily to the window.

"Maybe. I mean, I really don't know. It's all been pretty easy up to now; just like doing research for some history essay. I'm used to research; what with the magazine and all. I have to do research for the articles I write."

He paused, conscious of his over-use of the word 'research', and how, despite his familiarity with it, there seemed an ill fit between the general concept and his strangely still-nebulous subject.

"But this isn't quite the same, surely?"

"Because it's family?"

"Because it's your Father you're writing about. That must make it harder, mustn't it?"

"You'd think so, wouldn't you," he smiled, pleased to be able to feel that he knew something - was aware of something - that Beatrice could not be. "But it really hasn't been an issue. I've approached him in much the same way as I would any other, and tried to distance myself from 'the protagonists' - if I can call them that! I think it's worked. Really."

Beatrice picked up on his uncertainty which, as he spoke, had gradually invaded his words until - chopping the sentences into smaller and smaller chunks and destroying their fluency - it was all-pervading.

"But now? What about now, Mark?" She let her phrase dangle in front of him rhetorically; then, before he had a chance to reply, raised the stakes dramatically. "If you're saying you don't think you want to carry on with the book then you'd better tell your Uncle."

"No. No, it's not that." Her suggestion had alarmed him and he called her bluff. "I can't. I mean, I'm too far in to it to quit; I'm too committed, don't you see? And I don't think anyone else could write it."

"Not the way you would write it?"

"Not the way I want it written."

This was a definite statement and, coming as it did from open and dynamic conversation, took him a little aback. He would have wanted to deliver such a sentiment in a much more measured and calculated way; but now it was out and he would have to stand by it. He waited; Beatrice would have to respond to that.

"I can see that." It was an unexceptional reply when it came, and Mark - who somehow had expected more - was deflated. "Of course. I mean, you're talking about your Father; *your* Father. Who else knew him better, more intimately? It has to be your story of him."

Not sure he entirely agreed, Mark took a long drink of his coffee which, thanks to the conversation, had begun to chill a little. He felt a little closer to the point, though it was still essentially invisible to him.

"I wonder if my problem - my 'present difficulty', can we call it that? - relates to the fact that I am just about to enter the story. OK, I know I'm not a major character in the general drama; after all, I'm pretty sure that my presence didn't have too much influence on Father's life plan - but I am there. I don't know if I can be that objective anymore, you see? Is that it?"

"Are you are worried that, while you can deny external influences whilst doing your 'research', you may not be able to deny yourself?"

Mark weighed his Aunt's words carefully. There seemed reason enough in them, but he was immediately struck by a hint of menace, of something darker.

"But why should you, Dear?" she carried on in her warming tones, and he allowed himself to be comforted by them. "After all, you are part of the story, like it or not; and however major a part you think you may or may not have in the overall scheme of things, you have a voice, an influence. Every drama has its minor characters. How would Othello be without Roderigo, for example? Or Hamlet without Rosencrantz and Guildenstern?"

She paused, aware that she was in danger of losing her thread. Mark watched an almost imperceptible adjustment of her legs which he imagined as being parallel with some other internal shifting.

"You just need to find the right tack, that's all. A way of being faithful to the truth and having your say - because, mark my words, people who read your book will *expect* you to have a say! You are writing from a position of unique power; and you can't deny it. You shouldn't deny it."

There was a brief lull. Mark felt vaguely as if he had just been chastised by his school teacher for doing something rather foolish. It was a tone he could only associate with school as he had never heard it from his Mother.

Beatrice was, he knew, more right than wrong. It was, of course, a question of balance, of striking the correct tone, but he was nervous about going too far - in either direction - and thus obscuring the truth. It was also a question of being fair; fair not only to his Father, but also to his Mother, and to the others he might write about. The sense of responsibility was suddenly daunting. He finished his coffee in two swallows.

He felt - looking again towards the window - as if he had tasted enough philosophy for the moment (it seemed suddenly bitter like the coffee): the obscure was difficult enough for him to handle at the best of times, and he knew that, as he progressed through the book, there would be much more to come. Dealing with his Father's version of 'Universal Truth' (or whatever he would eventually choose to call it) was one thing - he was remote enough, even now, from that - but dealing with something that attempted to peel away his own psyche seemed a little too daring to contemplate.

"When I was born, where were you?"

The shift of subject - Mark's endeavour to jerk the whole conversation back onto the rails - visibly surprised Beatrice, who signified her own reaction to the twist with an adjustment of her lower limbs. Mark wanted to be on territory where he felt a little more at home, and where he had a clear view of the field. Facts - real, tangible, historical facts - were his best weapon.

"Where was I? Well, let me see. Early fifty-eight - just into the New Year, wasn't it?" She knew his birthday well enough; Mark watched her stall as she allowed her memory to catch up. As he waited, he opened the notebook which had remained closed thus far. "Hong Kong, I think. Yes. It would have been when Simon had his first Far East posting. We'd gone out in fifty-five and came back after four years. So, we were there."

Mark felt he should have known that; indeed, he suspected that somewhere in his subconscious that very knowledge was buried. But he felt happier asking the question, ascertaining something solid again.

"But you came back in fifty-eight?"

"Yes, Dear. We came back twice a year, regular as clockwork. May or June it would have been, I expect. That's when I would have first seen you - not that you'd remember of course. You probably don't remember anything until you're about three or four, do you?"

"Was it a surprise?"

"Surprise?"

"That Father and Mother had chosen to - ", he hesitated over the correct phrase, wondering how he should describe the concept or idea which had led to his very being, "well, attempt procreation."

Beatrice laughed. It was a sudden, impulse-driven laugh, which led her to immediately cover her mouth with her hand. She reddened.

"I'm sorry, Dear. It's just that phrase..."

The lighter tone annoyed him and he chose not to respond, waiting for Beatrice to resume her composure and answer his question. The silence was suddenly a little difficult, and his Aunt, sensing his unease, became almost immediately serious.

"It depends on your point of view. I think I might say that."

"Point of view?" Mark refrained from laughing himself, but the notion seemed a ludicrous one.

"There were a number of theories; your Father was never particularly clear about the situation - not with me, at any rate. One time the story was that they had been trying for some time; another was - well - that they weren't really trying at all. I never knew when to believe him. Or rather," and this she added rapidly, "I had once known to believe him all the time, but he was beginning to be, well, less 'reliable'."

"And Mother?"

"Don't forget, Dear," Beatrice pursued her previous line of thought, ignoring his prompt, "they had just been through that rather difficult patch."

"After his first book?"

"Yes. And so, well, was it the right time for them? I don't know; your Father never asked me for my advice, so I kept out of it."

"You were away, anyway."

"Yes, as you say, we were away." Her last words slipped out almost in a sigh, as if they carried with them an unexpressed regret, or the fading memory of an unfulfilled wish.

"But what about Mother? Did she ever say?" Mark pulled her back.

"Mary? No, Mary never said. Well, she wouldn't; not to me. That wasn't her style. A little too much the martyr. Oh, she wanted children, all right. I mean you could see that. It was in her blood, her upbringing. I remember we saw them in October the previous year (she would have been nearly six months then) and I had never see her looking so proud or contented. Never before, and never since."

Beatrice stopped speaking and Mark looked up from his pad where he had been taking notes almost verbatim. His Aunt seemed to have slipped away somewhere, and Mark felt - not for the first time - that wherever she was, wherever her mind had taken her at that precise moment, *that* was where he wanted to be because that was where the story was; that was where the real truth lay. He looked down at his pad. There were notes there to be sure, but they were more like clues than anything else; he felt - somewhat obscurely - like an Archaeologist staring at an incomplete map and attempting to divine the entrance to the secret chamber of treasures. He put down his pen.

"Did you like her? Mother, I mean."

The question - the harshness of it - pulled Beatrice from her reverie and she set her feet firmly down on the carpet. She adjusted her cardigan sleeves for comfort, and Mark knew - though she had said nothing - that the interview was nearly over. She looked him straight in the eye.

"'Like her'? I don't know. I didn't dislike her, if that's what you're asking - though it's not the same thing at all. Perhaps I never really knew her as herself. She was always Charlie's girl; maybe that was the way I always looked at her - through your Father. Simon liked her, I know he did. And she liked him too. They used to get on famously. Sometimes I was a little jealous because I suspected that she didn't actually care for *me* very much." Beatrice, still looking at him, paused. Mark wondered if she wanted some kind of reassurance; there was a nervous vulnerability peeping through her words, which, no sooner had he caught a glimpse of it, was whisked away. "But that's no matter, is it? It's what your Father thought that counts the most," she rose, "and you're best placed to know that now."

-*-

On the thirty-first of January, 1958, Charles arrived at The Hen and Chicken a little after seven and began drinking. Since the disappointment of his first book and the argument with Harriman, he had taken to alcohol with an almost maniacal intensity, and what little money he still had was beginning to diminish with alarming rapidity.

George Walker, who remained supportive not only through the late fifties, but a steadfast friend well into later life, accompanied Charles on many of those evening binges.

"At first they were innocent nights out, but soon Charles started to let his bitterness get to him. What had once been creative and amusing lampoons at Harriman's expense, soon became little more than vile and obsessive invective. He felt persecuted, as if the publisher had deliberately sabotaged a great work of art, and seemed determined to act out his alcoholic revenge on no-one but himself."

Charles was later to describe <u>Pieces of Eight</u> as 'Pieces of Trash', saying that the Short Story had never been his strong suit, and that Harriman had been undoubtedly correct to express some reserve about it. This change of view never became public until the mid-seventies when his retraction came too late for Harriman, who died in 1966.

Packard and Walker were joined in The Hen and Chicken that night by John Lotterby and Max Smedley, the latter having now become the perfect foil to Charles' drunken rages, egging him on and sponging drinks in payment.

> "Max taught me a great deal - though of course, I was in no particular state to realise it at the time. When I eventually came to see him for what he was, I actually despised the man. And I despised myself for being suckered by him. About ten years ago I wrote him a letter, disowning him. It was, I suppose, a spiteful, vindictive letter - I don't have a copy now, and I know Max burnt the original - and he never spoke to me after that. When he died, some journalist quoted me as saying 'Thank God the Fucker's gone!' Maybe I did say that; and if I did, I guess I must have meant it."

> (Interview in Stand, 1982)

It was George Walker however, who, at around eleven fifteen, answered the Landlord's announcement that there was a telephone call for Charles Packard. When he returned to the table, he brought back the news that Mary had borne him a son. Charles - who was, by this stage, singing quietly to himself - was too drunk to respond.

Despite this somewhat inauspicious beginning, the birth of Mark Anthony Packard had a positive effect on Charles. Overnight he became transformed from a practising alcoholic into a doting father. With George Walker's assistance, Charles reached Mary's hospital just after three in the morning. Charles had slept a little and George (himself a father, though separated from his wife and child since the early Fifties) had plied his friend with coffee before driving him across Warwick.

"Perhaps I was more nervous than he was. I suspect that, until he got to the hospital, Charles didn't actually know what was going on. When we eventually found Mary and the baby, she had obviously had time to compose herself and relax after the trauma of giving birth; and though she looked tired, she seemed radiant. When Charles saw her, he simply knelt by the side of the bed and wept. That was how I left them."

Three days later, Mary and Mark left the hospital by taxi and arrived at their small house - funded in part by the small advance on <u>Pieces of Eight</u>, and on the promise of more - to find that Charles had not only decorated the spare bedroom, but also attempted to resurrect his imperfect woodworking skills and constructed a number of inappropriate wooden toys for the young baby.

The next day, the proud Father returned to his job at the factory, his pockets bulging with cigars. He was contrite with his employer, apologised about his recent behaviour, and set himself to the general task of being a responsible individual. It was a good time for Mary and Mark, and it was a good time for Charles too, in that he found a new vein of creative strength. Leaving the disappointment of his short story collection behind him and abandoning prose, he started writing poetry again and, most noticeably, a short series of sonnets. This work was not, in the main, exceptional, and Charles pursued it without outward ambition.

> "There was nothing at that stage that I wanted to write; not in any profound sense anyway. The 'Pieces of Eight' thing had taught me a lesson or two, and publication was the furthest thing from my mind. Turning my back on prose wasn't any kind of statement really - I mean I have never professed to be a great poet - but at the time it just seemed the sensible thing to do."

(Interview in The Sunday Times, 1973)

Despite his stated desire for poetic anonymity, some of his friends - including Walker - were highly complimentary about this latest work, and pushed Charles to see if he could get any of it published. Later that year, one of the pieces appeared in Orbit:

> 'And though these steps are hewn from rock,
>
> And though they hold their course,
>
> They feel the pace of Time's Great Clock;
>
> The weight of Man's remorse.'

(Sonnet Seven, 1958)

-*-

Mark looked up from his desk and back to the bookcase in the corner of the room. When he had taken up Simon's offer, he had asked for the top shelf to be cleared (it had contained mostly gardening books and back numbers of 'Country Living') in order that he could establish a collection of his Father's works there. Initially the shelf's contents had been somewhat meagre, and Mark had needed to supplement his own rather limited stock with new or second hand editions of the books he was missing. Beatrice had lent him one or two from her own collection to help out.

'It's only a loan, mind. And see that they don't leave the house!'

The entire exercise had not taken a great deal of time, and, once it was complete, Mark had felt ready to begin.

He rose from the chair. Against the wall, the brown package eyed him suspiciously as he moved past it. From the top shelf he pulled a thin volume, the words on its narrow white spine faded by time and handling, and opened it to the first page. In pencil was a brief inscription: "For M.A. July '61". The annotation felt like an old friend to him, and he ran his finger gently across its shallow indentations; then, delicately, he opened the book and re-read the whole of the sonnet.

It was, he remembered, one of his Father's favourite books; and one that he remained loyal to throughout his life. It held a special place for Mark too - this little offering - as one of the few precious things he could ever remember having in his possession.

Chapter Eight

The offices housing the publishing company to which Mark held a regular, if somewhat tenuous, attachment was located on the South Bank, which from Mark's perspective was on the 'wrong side' of Waterloo Bridge. Having made an appointment to see his editor (something that had been requested at short notice, which seemed a little out of keeping) he made his way along the river and past the National Theatre, leaving the edifice of the Royal Festival Hall, Shell Building and all, in his invisible wake.

He was not in the best of humours. Having spoken to Congreave only a couple of days earlier and assured him that his next article - a brief resume on the political history of Kuwait since Independence - was well in hand, he had been surprised that he should be called back (and then with what amounted to almost indecent haste!) to have the meeting arranged. He had spent a couple of days working on the piece (this, an internal and unspoken defence, rehearsed as he walked ever-closer to the ex-warehouse) and had managed to get it into a state where he would not be too unwilling for the editor to see it.

"We've had to bring the copy date forwards," Congreave had told him over the phone, "and I don't want to miss out on the chance to get the piece on Kuwait in, seeing as it's so topical at the moment and all."

Congreave's words came out in a rush, helter-skelter, without punctuation almost, and Mark often felt himself being dragged along, unable to dig his heels in and pause for breath. In this context - and, Mark was sure, because of his manner of delivery - Congreave was a man one did not say 'No' to particularly often; and even if there were an opportunity to break into the flow, there was still something about the man (his power, Mark guessed) that kept you down.

He nodded to the Receptionist in the lobby and walked to the lift. As he rose to the third floor, he checked his appearance. He noticed again the flaw in his jacket just as the 'ping' came announcing his arrival and forcing him to leave the lift and its mirrors behind.

"Hello, Mr Packard," said Congreave's Secretary as Mark walked into the outer office.

"Hello, Jackie. I think he's expecting me. I'm a couple of minutes early."

Jackie half-rose from her seat and craned her neck to peer round the open door of the office beyond.

"You should be fine," she said, resuming her seat, "just go right in."

Mark shifted his leather foolscap portfolio from his right hand to his left, allowing him the freedom to respond to the handshake Congreave always offered. He paused at the door, still uncertain as to his own mood. He would have much rather left this for another day or two, if only to give him a chance to hone the piece a little more, to knock off the rough edges. Congreave was a little fussy sometimes, and being here prematurely was not necessarily good news. Mark caught himself balancing items of self-doubt, and tried to banish them: after all, he had - when all was said and done - no real need to be here at all; it wasn't as if he needed the money. It was, he tried to assure himself, little more than a hobby, and perhaps he had been successful because this had always been his philosophy.

"Mark!" Congreave's voice - even managing at accelerate through that single word - bellowed from within and caught Mark's consciousness in mid-proposition, knocking him completely off-balance. When his hand met the firm grip of the younger man's he had still not fully regained his composure.

"Take a seat, take a seat!" Congreave threw himself energetically into the chair behind his desk and half spun towards his visitor. Mark slipped his folder onto the edge of the desk. "So how are you? How's it going? How's the lovely Julia? Going to make an honest woman of her before some shark comes along and steals her from right under your nose, eh?"

"Fine, Bruce; we're both fine."

Mark, delivering his short reply as slowly as he decently could, attempted to defuse Congreave's explosive introduction. It was a battle he was familiar with, and he had long since graduated from being awe-struck to progress - if it could be called that - to a level where he would either find himself irritated or swept along by it. This time, Mark felt that neither of these were an accurate assessment of his present state (that which he had been trying to establish just a few moments previously) and would have liked to have defined - for his own peace of mind, if nothing else - exactly how he was feeling. Bruce, however, was rushing ahead.

"So that's it, is it?" He nodded towards the leather pouch. "The latest piece of quality historical interpretation from the Master of Detail, eh? The next little piece in the overall jigsaw that, when it's complete, says something like 'The History of the Twentieth Century, by Mark Packard'. Something like that, eh, because you could you know? I mean, we've talked about it in the past haven't we - not that I'm making any promises mind; you understand, eh?"

It was an art, Mark had decided, knowing when Congreave was actually pausing from breath as opposed to allowing entry into the conversation. The trick - which, in many cases extended to becoming more a game than anything else - was to make any given pause last as long as possible before speaking. The inherent danger was that, in leaving it too long and letting the other think you had nothing to say, Congreave would pick up the cudgels and go headlong into another paragraph.

"One day, Bruce. And, yes, maybe you'll be the first to know. But not yet."

"Not yet, no indeed. I mean you've got that little job for your Uncle to finish haven't you? (How is old Simon by the way?) How's it going? Cracking on are we? Some task you've got there, I don't envy you; wouldn't like to have to write about my old man, know what I mean? Not that he did anything of note, that is!"

Congreave laughed - a brief, chased-through laugh that refused to allow anyone else to join in. Mark noted the pause: this time the other was waiting, evidently expecting one of his questions to be answered. Mark took a guess as to the significant one.

"Simon's fine."

"And the book?"

There should have been more: Mark was not expecting to be back in to the conversation quite so quickly.

"The book?" He felt a little unbalanced again. "The book's fine; you know? Coming along. It's a little - 'different' - writing about something like that."

"Family? I know. Tried it once. Not about my Dad (God rest his soul). Had an Uncle; did something marvellous in the war; killed some Jerries, saved a platoon or something. You know; real heroism-type stuff. Might have made a good story; might have made me rich enough not to be doing this sodding job!" Another express-train laugh. "But there it is, and here we are."

Mark looked out of the window. Two barges were making their way slowly down the river, their progress in direct contrast to the pace at which things in the office seemed to be going; so much so, indeed, that Mark found himself wondering if their presence on the river might not be evidence of some all-powerful, omnipresent being whose party trick was to point out the ironies of existence by using either coincidence or juxtaposition. Congreave's voice hauled him round.

"Shall we have a look at it then; the piece? Sorry to have to rush you like this. I mean, it's not ideal for me, but the bloody printers say they've got some new machinery or something coming in and they want to have a few more days, 'Just in case'. Nothing I can do about it, old boy, there it is. Ah!"

He took the document Mark had extracted from his folio during the previous speech, receiving it with almost mock reverence. Congreave smiled, then looked at the top sheet.

Mark had never been able to work out how Bruce managed it - nor adopt any form of the technique himself - but Congreave had a knack of being able to speed read at an incredible rate. He should - Mark had told himself in the past - only be skimming, certain that detailed reading at such breakneck speeds might almost be physically hazardous; yet he had been caught out more than once by Congreave quickly dispelling this illusion with some telling comment or another. Perhaps - and this was an idea that had grown over time - his speed reading was simply the other side of the same coin that allowed him to prattle on at ninety miles an hour. Perhaps he did everything at the same impossible pace.

No sooner had Mark finished his thoughts than Congreave looked up. The article spanned three pages, but a few paragraphs was usually enough to give an indication of quality; it was certainly enough for Bruce, and Mark guessed that the other's powers of editorial dissection were probably far in advance of his own. This selective pre-judging had resulted, in Mark's case, in a number of books only partially read, abandoned within the first few pages. It was (he now felt ashamed to recall) the fate that had befallen one of his Father's books; one completed only recently, and more from a sense of duty and research than anything else.

Congreave was smiling at him.

"About that last piece of yours." The change of tack rocked Mark, who had been prepared to discuss the political shenanigans of Kuwait. Indeed, the shift proved so violent, that he interrupted Congreave without any indication of a pause to offer such an option.

"The last piece? Don't you want to talk about this?"

The editor followed Mark's eyes down to the surface of his desk where the three sheets of paper lay stapled together.

"Looks fine; fine. Of course, it's only a draft - I know you're going to tell me that; something about knocking the rough edges off it, I shouldn't wonder! - but it looks fine. I mean, I accept all that about it not being ready and everything. You've still got a few days left (though I'll have to insist on next Wednesday - damn those printers!) so, basically, I'm not worried. OK? It's not like you've never finished something for me, is it?"

Congreave left his rushing there, with a deliberate question. Mark, suddenly sensitive to every nuance of phrase or tone, was instantly alarmed. Congreave rarely asked direct questions he expected to be answered; things tended to be rhetorical, or if tangible and valid questions, these would tend to get lost amongst the morass of his general verbal outpourings. There was, however, something of an intonation on this last phrase that bucked the trend; an invitation to respond, to actually answer the question.

Mark wondered what he was supposed to say. He tried to calculate as accurate a response as possible. Had he ever let Bruce down? Was there ever a time when a piece was late, or unfinished? Had his timing ever been a problem?

"No." It was all he could manage.

Bruce picked it up and ran on.

"No, of course not. And you're not going to now, are you? Even though the pissing printers have pulled the plug on us, you'll still make next Wednesday. I know that, so that's OK. OK?" Bruce paused, but it was the type of pause that scared off interruptions. "Now, about your last piece."

"The Irish thing?"

"The Irish thing. Went down a storm, by all accounts. Even had one or two letters - which is unusual, isn't it? Political mainly; people making some point or other depending on their persuasion, saying how your piece had been biased. But then as both sides said that, I guess that proves it wasn't, eh?"

Congreave whistled a short laugh which failed to entice Mark into accompaniment.

"There were a couple of letters complaining about certain - how shall I put it? - 'inaccuracies'."

It was the slowest Mark had ever heard him deliver a word. Despite the implication, he teased it out, though not from uncertainty; he teased it out wilfully. It was most definitely the word he wanted, and he laboured almost lovingly over it.

"'Inaccuracies'!" Mark, missing the subtlety, swept down on the word venomously. "When have you ever known me to be inaccurate!"

Congreave leant back, smiling, picking up Mark's rage like a striker picking up a loose back-pass in football and sweeping towards the goal.

"Exactly! Exactly! 'When' - I said to myself - 'have I ever known Mark to be inaccurate?' And do you know what my reply was? Never. 'I've never known Mark to be inaccurate.' That's what I said to myself. Stupid sods, I thought; those geezers writing the letters and complaining. Daft, bigoted sods." Mark eased back a little in his chair, at which Congreave rushed forwards from his own and leant across the desk. "But. But, because of that - because I couldn't recollect anything like this happening before - I thought I'd check it out."

Mark, facing this verbal barrage and suddenly sensing how hot it was in the office, felt himself to be swimming. The roller-coaster (which, given the circumstances, was likely to make him sick) showed no signs of stopping.

"'Check it out'?"

Congreave reclined in his chair. The smile that had been ever-present since the meeting began, faded slightly on his lips. He let the air get a feel of the silence. Outside a ship hooted.

"And they were right. I didn't believe it at first, but they were right. There were one or two things in that piece that were historically inaccurate. I got Mike to check it when I didn't believe it myself. And there it is. Afraid we managed to upset the punters a bit, old chap. Not got our facts precisely correct."

"Which facts? Where? I researched everything, thoroughly. As usual."

Congreave shook his head.

"Doesn't matter now. Water and bridges, and all that. See Mike if you want chapter and verse. I can't remember off-hand."

There was another pause. Mark, uncertain whether or not the interview had been rather abruptly concluded, shifted in his chair, preparing to depart.

"And then," Congreave's phrase pinned him to his seat, "I had a look at your previous piece too. The Health Service one. Found a small error there as well."

"Error?"

"A historical faut pas, shall we say? Look Mark," the smile was completely gone now, and Mark had reverted to being the young journalist in awe of his editor, "there's no easy way to say this, but... Well; I'm concerned. I'm worried that you might be slipping; getting careless; losing it. There are historical facts, and there's historical fiction. We are responsible for putting the facts before our readership. It's what we get paid for; the truth. There's no room for anything else. You know that. Shit, you're the best, OK? And I'm sure this piece on the Kuwaiti thing will be just fine. I just wanted to mark your card - in case you weren't aware of it. That's all."

Mark looked at the draft of his Kuwaiti article as it lay face-up on Congreave's desk. Suddenly he felt unable to remember any of it at all, and found himself wondering if any 'inaccuracies' were hiding within it. He could recollect nothing remarkable about the production of either of the pieces Congreave had referred to: the research had gone smoothly enough; he had used his standard authorities; he had spoken to knowledgeable people. From somewhere the image of Neville Chamberlain came to him.

"About the Chamberlain biography."

Congreave, who had half turned away from Mark and had allowed his attention to be taken by goings on outside, looked back at him. The professional and soothing disposition had returned, and, in consequence, Mark began to feel as if the previous few minutes had not happened at all, being the creation of a somewhat stressed imagination. Instantly he began constructing a re-run of the conversation, with Congreave thanking him for his new article, praising the previous two, and offering to buy him lunch. As if to support this fiction, the smile that greeted Mark's last comment was pretty much the same as that he had first encountered on his entry into the office; something that indeed seemed only seconds away.

"The Wallace book? Bloody great thick thing with the 'usual' picture of the old boy on the cover; 'Peace in our time' and all that, eh? What about it? Not finished the review already? Don't need it for a couple of months yet really; though if it is ready early we could try and squeeze it in before then."

"No, it's not that. It's just that the book's shit. I mean, I've started to read it, but I don't think it's very good."

"Not up to your standards, eh?"

Congreave's geniality was more in line with his default behaviour - all of which went to reassure Mark that things were, after all, fine. Happy to be returned to this normal, comfortable relationship - to the environment he was expecting to inhabit - he even laughed.

"No, it's not that. It's just that I don't like the way Wallace handles his subject."

"Chamberlain? How many ways can you handle him, eh?"

"Not Chamberlain. History. He's too off-hand, too casual. He's got this kind of 'well you can disbelieve it if you like, but here's my version' attitude to it."

"Sounds like an Aussie soap or something!" Congreave laughed. It was a quiet, unexplosive laugh. "Well, I shouldn't worry about that just at the moment. I mean, you've got enough on your plate with the article - not to mention your book - so I wouldn't even think about it. And if you're that dead set against the thing, then I'll get someone else to do it. Mike maybe."

The notion of someone else undertaking the assignment came as a surprise to Mark. There would - he instantly recognised - be merits in delegating the review; after all, he would not be able to commit himself as wholly to it as he might have liked. Yet, despite this - and despite the immediate sense of relief knowing he would not have to read the Wallace biography, and that he would, in consequence, be freed to spend even more time on his own work - he did not want to leave Congreave with the impression that he was just going to duck out.

"Oh, it's not that I don't want to do it, Bruce. I mean, don't get me wrong. I just wanted you to know that I think the book stinks; and that's probably what my review will say. That's all."

Congreave rose.

"OK. Say no more. I'll have a think and we can catch up later, can't we?" He checked the clock on the wall and extended his hand. It was Mark's cue to rise. "Got to cut you short, old son; got an editorial meeting in five minutes and I need a slash first! You'll pop the Kuwait job in next week then? Just leave it with Jackie or Mike or someone."

"You're not around?"

They had reached the door which Congreave was now holding open. Outside, Jackie replaced the hand-set of the telephone and began typing, the keystrokes sounding like Morse code, tapping out some secret message which Mark imagined he should be able to decipher.

"Just taking a few of days off. Going up to Scotland to play golf."

"It'll be good this time of year." Mark flicked through his memory to locate something relating to golfing in Scotland. All he could come up with was a fading image of his Father and the real physical presence of the jacket he was wearing.

The wind had picked up a little since he had entered the building, and walking back towards Waterloo, he felt it full in the face. He tucked his folio under his arm and buttoned up his jacket. This seemed to make little difference - certainly not as much of a difference as it once would have - and Mark wondered if time (not to mention considerable wear and tear) had a detrimental effect on cloth.

Despite the discomfort from the wind (it felt like the last throes of a dying winter) Mark chose to deviate from a direct route to the station having decided to drop in on the National Theatre to pick up a copy of the new season's programme. It had been a while since he had been to the theatre (he recalled a rather dour version of 'The Seagull' which he had wanted to leave at the interval, but had been persuaded to see it out by Julia) and, now that he was in the vicinity wondered if it might not be time to think about taking in another play.

The warmth of the building caused an involuntary shiver as he entered, and he instantly recalled the blast of the heater in the doorway of the shop in Regent's Street. Unbuttoning his jacket, he noticed how few people there were milling around. Midweek or not, Mark seemed to recall that the NT could always be relied upon to offer sanctuary to a number of people browsing, meeting, or drinking coffee in the cafe.

Five minutes later, having decided to dally a little longer, he sat down in the cafe (a dark espresso on the table in front of him) and opened the small booklet boasting 'an exciting summer at the National'.

The format for the following months seemed not to deviate a great deal from what was becoming a standard pattern: a few new and avant-garde things in the smaller auditorium, with the more lavish and traditional productions reserved for the main theatre. There was a Miller (which seemed to be the norm in recent seasons); a revival of George Bernard Shaw; and what was described as 'a modern feminist reading' of Oscar Wilde, rather un-cryptically entitled 'The Importance of being Ernestina'. And of course, there was Shakespeare.

Mark had - despite several attempts on his Aunt's part to change his view - never been much of a Shakespeare fan. Previously, he had struggled through a rather limp version of 'A Comedy of Errors' and both parts of 'Henry IV', proclaiming the later to be short on both entertainment and historical fact. Beatrice, who had accompanied him on the first of these visits, had assured him that taking the production they had seen as indicative of Shakespeare in general would be a mistake; yet the experience - as theatre - had achieved little except to confirm the prejudice that had been instilled in him as a result of the rather flat teaching of the subject from his school days.

Julia - whose attitude to Shakespeare owed more to her feelings with regard to live theatre in general, rather than the playwright in particular - seemed to like just about anything, and they had once resolved an argument over the quality of the Bard's writing by agreeing to differ. For Mark, the not inconsiderable doubts over the authentic source of the plays could only detract from the praise heaped upon the man from Stratford, unwilling as he was to accept the relatively unquestioned belief in him as to the plays' Author with only slim evidence of indisputable fact to hand. Despite all of this, however, he would admit to something of a liking for Hamlet (which he had only read) and the prospect of attending the National's new production filled him with what he might have chosen to regard as an unusual degree of interest. At school, he had been required to learn several of the major speeches off by heart, and now, as he sipped his coffee, he tried to recall the most famous of them:

> "To be, or not to be, that is the question:
>
> Whether it is nobler in the mind to suffer
>
> the slings and arrows of outrageous fortune,
>
> or to take arms against a sea of trouble,
>
> and by opposing, end them. To die, to sleep,
>
> perchance to dream: ay, there's the rub,
>
> for who would bear the whips and scorns of time
>
> that makes calamity of life."

He was aware, as he took another sip of coffee, that those internally recited phrases may not have been the exact words that he had learned; nor, for that matter, the exact words initially written by the author of 'Hamlet' - though that was a different story. Memory, over time, played tricks, and Mark was a little uncomfortable nowadays on being dependant upon it. The book had something to do with this of course, especially as it was likely to rely - more and more - on him dredging things up from his own recollections with the necessity of treating them as historical fact.

In addition to the whims and vagaries of memory, he felt a similar dilemma with reported speech too. He had been given, mainly by Beatrice, several accounts of conversations she had participated in with his Father where the assertion 'he said' was often made during the re-telling. This felt like little more than circumstantial evidence, and unless he had heard the words himself or had proof that they had indeed been spoken (such as BBC archive footage) then Mark was determined to exclude them from the account of his Father's life - except where he felt he had no alternative or option. This, as Beatrice herself had pointed out to him after he had objected to one of her tales, was likely to present him with insurmountable difficulties later on - especially during the affirmation of his own experience - and she suggested (a little harshly, Mark recalled) that something would have to give.

On the way out he noticed a poster for the production of 'Hamlet', created with a dark and menacing style of brush stroke and lettering. Hamlet (for it could only be he) faced outwards, his hair - whiter than Mark would have imagined it - long and wild in the wind. In the background and against the darkness of the castle, the Ghost of his father staring hard, his eyes burning with some unsatisfied desire. Hamlet, though discernibly younger and darker than the Ghost - the whiteness and wildness of whose hair seemed to surpass any similar image Mark could recall - bore more than a passing resemblance to his dead progenitor, and left one with the distinct impression that you might just be looking at two versions of the same person.

Chapter Nine

"I had expected to see you over at the house this week, Mark. After the weekend, I mean."

The words had come from Simon as he sat alongside his nephew in the back of a black cab. They had stopped at some lights on Lodge Road where, just beyond, the dome of Regent's Park Mosque was illuminated against the darkened sky.

Mark, staring out of the opposite window, was watching a frail Indian man step nervously off the pavement, encouraged by the dimly lit green man beckoning from the other side of the road. By the time he had reached half way the all clear had been usurped by a crimson warning, and so - to avoid being a witness to a possible tragedy, if nothing else - Mark, in that split second between green and red, turned to tackle his Uncle's question.

"The weekend?" Mark knew what Simon was referring to - or at least, he thought he did - but he wanted to be sure, to be absolutely certain that he wasn't going to answer the wrong question or make any affirmation based upon a mistaken premise.

"You seemed to be pushing on with the book; making progress, you know? Perhaps you didn't say anything specific - my memory's not what it was, of course, not like Beatty's! - but I had the impression you'd be working at home quite a bit."

Simon's words, delivered as always, evenly and without any form of innuendo, hint or threat, struck Mark as a starkly significant contrast to Bruce Congreave - in relation to whom he had just been replaying 'and if you're dead set against the thing, then I'll get someone else to do it'. This was a link now particularly apposite given the matter of his Uncle's question.

"I had intended to, but then Bruce hit me with that sudden deadline for the Kuwaiti piece, so I had to finish it."

"How is he?"

"Bruce?" - Simon gave an affirmative 'Hmm' in response - "Oh, you know Bruce!"

The ultimate outcome of the Waterloo interview had been that, once Mark had returned to Hampstead and - in some way - regained his equilibrium, he determined to re-examine not only the draft of his article thus far, but also to re-check his research. This had even extended to the extreme of telephoning the Kuwaiti embassy to ask them to verify the facts they had already disclosed. The conversation had not been particularly easy.

The cab was moving on again and Mark, re-aquatinting himself with the outside world, half-heartedly tried to catch sight of his Asian pedestrian. He was no where to be seen - not surprising since they had already travelled at least two hundred yards - and as there had been no recent squealing of breaks nor sounds of physical collision, Mark assumed that the man was still extant.

He had himself, just two days previously, 'made it' under different circumstances. Given that he had undertaken to re-do some of the work already carried out on his article, Mark had made Bruce's deadline reduction even more difficult to accommodate since he had, of his own volition, virtually doubled the workload. The consequence of this was not only his non-appearance at Simon's for a few days, but also little public showing anywhere else, much of the week being spent closeted in his study in Hampstead fighting with both his keyboard and the vagaries of history. Coming within twenty-four hours of his deadline, he had been forced to call Congreave to beg a stay of execution for another day. He had forgotten that Congreave was in Scotland (had he been *that* wrapped up?) and had been both surprised and relieved to be dealt with by Mike. Mark had explained the situation, asked for another day, and Mike had acquiesced. The ease with which the copy date had been extended struck him - on the Thursday, as he walked away once again from the Waterloo offices (this time avoiding the National Theatre) - to be a little odd, considering Bruce's rather aggressive selling of the Wednesday date. Still, he had comforted himself with the fact that the ordeal (for that was how it had become to feel) was over, that the piece was good and solid, and that he had checked and double-checked his facts.

In order to restore not only his own sanity, but also a little domestic harmony, he had booked a table that evening in a local Bistro and had treated Julia to a champagne supper. It was something they had often done in the past (especially in the early days) and although Julia might have chosen to interpret the dinner as a form of replaying those 'embryonic' evenings, Mark's motivation had been little more than the expression of relief.

"So you finished it then?"

Mark looked at Simon, shaken from his reverie. Julia had used those very same words the afternoon he had emerged victorious from his cocoon with the peace offering of dinner.

"Finished it?" Mark reiterated his Uncle's works to re-establish himself in the correct conversation and context.

"The Kuwait article."

Satisfied that Simon's question was entirely innocent - and that, from his own point of view, he was perfectly 'safe' despite the coincidence - Mark laughed lightly.

"Of course, yes! And on time too. So now I'm a free man for a while."

Mark recalled something from Julia during the meal: "And will you do the Chamberlain thing?" she had said. He looked at Simon, half-expecting the same words - but they were not forthcoming. He hadn't known the answer when Julia has asked him and didn't know now; but, driven by a sudden desire to ensure equilibrium (even if Simon wasn't - in the long run - going to maintain it), he offered, "I may not do the Chamberlain biography I was supposed to be reviewing, though."

Simon frowned slightly. Mark wondered if he might have made a mistake after all. He was sure he kept his Uncle abreast of his projects, if only as a form of courtesy.

"Well then. Especially as you've your own little history to work on, eh?" The phrase sounded strange, as if Mark were actually working on his own biography rather than someone else's.

They travelled in silence for the remainder of the journey. Mark, allowing himself to become absorbed in lights as they flashed past him - lights from cars going in the opposite direction; street lamps; shop windows. He tried to imagine how he might have felt seeing all this for the first time. Indeed, there must have been many occasions when he did see things that way - or at least an approximation to it: the same principle again and again on different streets and with different sets of lights. How had he felt then? Could he remember? He tried to recall a reaction to the freshness of such an image, knowing that somewhere, buried, he had a log of those moments, a record of the experience. The lights flew past in a blur as his gaze became fixed in mid-distance (almost as if he was incapable of doing two things at once; remembering and looking) and he found himself only able to recall similarly blurred images, none of them the original he sought.

Travelling down Baker Street, the familiar symbol of the Underground - that bright red ubiquitous circle - pulled him from his reverie, as if an alarm had been triggered somewhere in his head. He noticed Simon glance at his watch.

"What's the time?"

"Just after eight."

"Plenty of time then."

Mark knew that there would be. Simon was legendary for his punctuality. Given the choice between being late and being early, there would never be any doubt as to his preference. They were due at the hotel at eight thirty - which, if past 'events' were anything to go by, meant that the dinner would not start until nine-thirty at the earliest, and allowing for the guests to get suitably lubricated, suggested the awards ceremony itself might not commence until nearly eleven.

His attendance (by invitation through his liaison with the magazine rather than as a result of anything in his own right - "After all", Bruce had joked, "we have to give the invitations to someone!") he viewed as responding to a sense of duty rather than pursuit of pleasure. Discovering that Simon would be there loosely disguised under the brim of his 'publishing hat' - and managing to swing a seat at the same table - made the chore of appearance less odious. He wondered (they were near Oxford Street now) how different his attitude might have been had he found himself in line for one of the prizes. Bruce had hinted - in his vast, expansive manner - that one day he might find himself hot favourite in one of the categories.

"Who knows? Maybe 'Best Biography'? After all, it simply takes enough pushing from a publisher - and Simon is your Uncle, after all..."

The remark had deserved little entertainment at the time, but now, as they turned into Hanover Street and drew towards the threshold of the event, it returned to him, echoing uneasily.

A second, more tangible echo, was soon to displace the first with something of a jolt. Getting out of the cab in front of them - smiling to the Doorman; waving his hand at someone in the lobby; waiting, with that distinctively superior and predatorial air for his companion (in a glittering off-the shoulder gown split on one side to the thigh, a stunner bearing a remarkable resemblance to Claire) - was Bruce Congreave.

Mark entertained a sudden dialogue with himself, a hail of questions flying rapidly and unanswered. Wasn't he supposed to be in Scotland?

Why had he not told him he would be at the dinner? Had he forgotten? Who was the glamorous woman? Could it be Claire?

"Isn't that Congreave?" Simon said as they drew to a standstill.

"Yes; it would appear so." Mark had his hand on the door handle; for a split second he harboured some vague notion of flinging the door open, rushing over, and denouncing Congreave as he stood there, making him look small in front of his public and his concubine. Perhaps he was uncertain exactly what form the denunciation would take, but revenge seemed appropriate as it was revenge that he suddenly wanted; vague, undefined revenge. The disappearance of Congreave from the pavement and into the hotel saved Mark the scene (which he probably would never have initiated anyway) and as he descended to the pavement to await his Uncle, he recalled that first unspoken rhetorical question - "Wasn't he supposed to be in Scotland?" - and in doing so remembered his tweed jacket, and looked at the unblemished pocket of his tuxedo.

"Problem, Mark?"

"Sorry?"

"Not stained or torn or anything, is it?"

"No nothing like that." He looked through the open doors of the building and to the mass of evening dress. "Shall we?"

He tried, for a number of minutes after their entrance, to re-locate Congreave. Not that he had any wish to make contact with the man; it was the question about the woman - his own question - which demanded an answer. They had lost the scent as early as the lobby of the hotel when Simon had been hailed by one of his cronies and the subsequent pleasantries and introductions had done the damage. Had Mark harboured any notion of locating his prey through a general gaze about the dining room upon his own entrance, then this too was thwarted by the sheer number of people both seated at and milling around the tables.

"Lots here, eh?"

Simon had offered this some thirty minutes later, almost as a delayed response to Mark's expression as they paused upon the dining threshold.

"Millions." Despite the general disappointment at not being able to see anyone he knew - let alone Congreave - given numerous attempts at the 'casual glance', the wine had begun to loosen Mark's demeanour.

"Not seen anyone you know?"

"Are you telepathic Uncle?"

"Sorry?" For a moment Simon seemed thrown by the question, then chose to ignore it. "Your Father hated these affairs."

"Father?"

They were sitting next to each other at a table for eight where the majority seemed to be interested in all matters Russian: the language, the politics, the philosophy. Two of the party were women, one of whom - a smallish, bespectacled thirty-something with close-cropped red hair - had already exchanged smiles with Mark. His proximity to Simon allowed not only for their general inclusion in the table conversation, but also their exclusion from it at moments such as this.

"You knew he attended one or two of them. Similar, you know. For fiction writers, or playwrights or something."

"Yes, of course."

"Came with him once." Simon drained his glass and looked up for a wine waiter as he spoke. "Most difficult experience. It was the drink probably. Got completely drunk."

Arrival of the waiter and replenishment all-round interrupted Simon's anecdote.

"And?"

"And? Oh, yes your Father. Well, it was probably a good job he didn't win (if he was up for anything that is; I can't remember). God knows what he would have said; what he might have come up with in his 'acceptance' speech. Eh!"

There was a little laugh that finished the reminiscence, as if Simon were recalling someone with affection - or attempting to script Charles' speech posthumously.

This was not the first time Mark had been to such a function - but the first of this nature with Simon, in spite of their familiar and present professional relationship. He had attended smaller, more 'focused' events, where the sphere from which the guests were drawn was decidedly restricted, and where the awards (if indeed there were awards) carried with them some degree of prestige; the acclaim of one's peers. The present jamboree smacked of gaudy self-publicity, and Mark wondered if such events as the Booker or the Turner Prize were similar.

His Uncle, having completed his reminiscence and replenished his glass (which was rapidly emptying again, like an oasis in a drought) was now talking to the man on his right. Mark could not make out the subject; the dialogue seemed to him to be vague and unfocussed - which was probably just as well considering Simon's advancing state of inebriation. He recalled his Uncle's recent phrase - "Got completely drunk" - and wondered if he had been a little inaccurate in assuming that Simon had been referring to his Father alone. Perhaps it was being absent from Beatrice that gave Simon licence.

"So you're a journalist; is that right?"

The seat to Mark's left was now occupied by the bespectacled woman with the short flame-red hair. He glanced up to see where the former occupant had gone, and found him sitting in conversation two tables away. They were between courses and it seemed that many of the diners were taking the opportunity to stretch their legs and indulge in a little relaxed networking.

The woman extended her hand.

"Maxine Priest."

Mark smiled.

"I've heard of you. Foreign Affairs Editor at the BBC."

"Oh?" Maxine offered a slightly concerned frown.

"Good things only! I know one or two people there."

"Some of our production staff perhaps?"

"Afraid not. Researchers mostly. And no; I'm not a journalist. What made you assume that?"

"Something I heard you say earlier on, when you were talking to that gentleman," she nodded slightly towards Simon, "and because you know Bruce."

"Congreave?"

"Yes."

Again Mark looked up, expecting to see his Editor's face beaming at him from close range.

"I bumped in to him just before I sat down. 'I see you're on the same table as young Packard' he said. Apparently you write for him."

"Apparently."

"And you're not a journalist?" She smiled playfully and waited a response.

Mark, beginning to relax after the unexpected assault, wanted to make sure that his answer was entirely correct. He could see Simon engaged on a nearby table, so knew he could afford to be a little extravagant in his response without fear of contradiction. Indeed, there might be some pleasure in such an approach, especially with a partner who appeared herself to be a little untied by alcohol. The young woman was attractive in an austere kind of way and, because his relationship with Julia meant that he had no need to be predatory as far as Maxine was concerned, he decided that a little flirtation might be fun.

"Yes - and no."

"That's hardly an answer!" Maxine complained. "Bruce says you write factual pieces for him. Historical things."

"That makes them sound like A-level essays! Bastard!" They both laughed. "I do write some factual studies for him, yes; and they are researched. But that doesn't make me a journalist."

"What does it make you then?"

"First and foremost, a historian. And secondly - I suppose - a writer."

"A writer!" There was a little exclaim in her voice at this, and she furrowed her brow in a mock expression of serious regard. "That's different, isn't it? Not a journalist at all then."

Mark drained his wine glass, choosing not to respond to the little baited hook that Maxine had just teased before him. Leaning across the table, he rescued a half-bottle of Pinot Noir and replenished both their glasses.

"So, Mr Packard."

"Mark."

"So, Mr Mark Packard, when you are not being a journalist (which is not, of course, writing in any way shape or form!) what do you write."

"At the moment, a biography."

"Really? Of who?"

"My Father. Charles Packard."

"The writer?"

"The writer."

She smiled warmly. There was something inviting in her manner which Mark had not experienced for quite a while. He tried, in that split second, to remember when he had last encountered it. Who had it been? Julia, surely? And if so, then it must have been ages ago. Or was it Claire? More recently perhaps. He teetered momentarily.

"The famous Son of a famous Father then."

From the far end of the hall came the sudden rap of the Toastmaster's gavel which signalled, as if by some magic spell, a chorus of voices and rustling chairs. Maxine, in rising from the seat next to Mark, added her own contribution to the song.

"Prize time!" she said with a slight shrug.

From his right, Mark felt Simon tug on his sleeve which, almost simultaneously, was accompanied by the return of the rightful occupant of the other place next to him.

As soon as the speech-making began (he managed to hold on to the general thrust of things for only a few moments) Mark found himself relegating the microphoned words from the top table to little more than background noise. As he was sitting with his back to the stage, making the effort to turn round was too uncomfortable for all but the committed attendee, and so he resigned himself to a small period of purgatory solaced only by the remaining red wine in his glass.

Simon, who had a better view, appeared to be over-enthusiastically enwrapped in the proceedings. There was a glint about his eye which, were it not for the flush on his cheek, might well have been mistaken for something other than the advanced stages of inebriation. Occasionally, at Christmas or family celebrations, Mark had seen his Uncle sliding this way; but his present state of alcoholic avalanche was more disturbing.

Whenever Mark saw Simon, he normally saw Beatrice. They were a couple, an equilibrium - though strangely enough a balance which Beatrice was quite capable of maintaining on her own. Simon let loose almost seemed a different man. It was not the drinking that was the most unsettling; indeed, were he honest with himself, that element of the pageant was more amusing than anything else: it was Simon's commitment to the event, his whole-hearted support for the sheer fraudulence of the thing - a professional charade and its attendant lack of quality or integrity - that made Mark wince. Here was a man - not only family and a man he loved, but his professional partner in the most dangerous enterprise of his life - who was showing up, in some profoundly base way, everything he stood for. Mark felt suddenly let down, betrayed. He wanted to shake his Uncle sober, or to see Beatrice walk through the door and escort her errant knight off the premises and back to the castle where he would be chained to the battlements in punishment.

But Beatrice would never do that; neither walk through the door nor punish her husband in such a crude fashion. She had no need. She had other weapons. And Mark knew - as he had to know - that none of this slithering into babbling intellectual stupor would be news to her. She was too wise for that; she had known Simon too long. Perhaps in the past they had exchanged words - fierce, bone-crushing words no doubt - but almost certainly Beatrice had been able to engineer an occasional freedom for Simon which was granted under her terms, and for which he, in an absurd expression of gratitude, made the most off by climbing comprehensively out of his box.

Giving up his Uncle as a lost cause, Mark cast his gaze around the hall. He caught Maxine's eye by accident as he did so, and she rewarded him with a funny cross-eyed expression of boredom. It was then, after he had returned her smile and she had returned dutifully to concentrate again on the speakers, that he noticed Bruce Congreave sitting on the table immediately behind her.

Mark wondered how he had missed him. Indeed, he argued internally, surely he could not have been there before. Surely he had looked at that particular table several times already that evening. One of the chairs next to Congreave was vacant, the other occupied by a rotund man he recognised from Simon's earlier diversion in the lobby. Mark's major question - the identity of Congreave's companion - would not, it appeared, be answered as readily as the former's location. Perhaps it didn't matter as much, he wasn't sure. If it did, well he could always make enquiries later.

He felt a tug on his line of vision and, refocussing on his more immediate sphere of interaction, found Maxine looking hard at him. There was no smile on her face this time, but the gaze was somehow nonetheless warm for that. He raised one eyebrow and glanced sadly at the ever-diminishing volume of wine in his glass. At this she smiled a little, and then there was an accompanying burst of applause.

It was not a little later that Mark, supporting a decidedly tottering Simon on one arm, stood outside the hotel, his other arm raised in hopeful salute to any taxi that might be coming their way. The rounds of speeches and applause had continued almost interminably like a rather poor yet infinite roundel until, only a little before midnight, the final award was presented and the massed throng was released to burst out into the hotel lobby. Simon had stopped to pay one last visit to the Gentlemen's cloakroom before they left, only to be waylaid by another of his old publishing colleagues who - apparently equally pissed - kept him talking for a full ten minutes. As they stood on the chilly pavement, Mark felt his patience had been tested to the very limits and in consequence his responses to his Uncle's affirmations that it had been a 'bloody good evening!' were little better than monosyllabic.

Four headlights - which would have been identifiable as a pair of black cabs by any true Londoner irrespective of the location, weather, or time of day - suddenly swung into view and began to decelerate. "Just like buses!" Mark thought to himself as he prepared to propel Simon gently forwards.

As he opened the door of the first cab - which drew obligingly to a halt immediately in front of them - he felt a light pressure on his shoulder. Releasing Simon - who seemed to switch to automatic pilot now that his carriage had arrived - Mark turned to see Maxine standing just behind him. She removed her hand from his shoulder and placed it on his free arm, squeezing it gently.

Mark felt the cab door move from his other hand. Simon was attempting to close it.

"You take this one Uncle," Mark said, and repeated the Belsize Park address to the Cabby. "I'll take the one behind. Are you OK?"

The slamming door obliterated Simon's response.

"I'll see you later. Give my love to Beatrice."

Chapter Ten

"You must maintain a sense of balance."

Beatrice had taken the somewhat unusual step of bringing, unbidden, a cup of coffee to Mark in his study, with the result that she now sat - somewhat uncomfortably, it seemed - on the large green chair that dominated the middle of the room.

Mark, his coffee now steaming gently on the desk behind him, had swung round in his own chair in order to talk to his Aunt. With his own posture also now being far from ideal, it seemed that they were fated to hold their present discussion under the additional strain of some physical discomfort. As he looked at Beatrice, he could see, peering over her shoulder almost, the large brown shape that was Laura's mirror.

"Do you think that I won't?"

"There's a danger, isn't there? I mean there must be."

"I suppose so."

"You could of course go either way; and quite legitimately too."

"Either way?"

She shifted slightly.

"Being too critical - or not critical enough. 'I come to bury Caesar, not to praise him'."

Mark smiled, and pulled his coffee from the table, twisting at the waist to do so.

"I don't think I own any rose coloured glasses in relation to Father, if that's what you think."

"Perhaps not. But you can never be too sure. I mean," - and this she added hurriedly - "you can't know. Can you?"

"I don't think that it would be possible for me to be so praiseworthy - considering everything else - for the book to become unbalanced. He was, after all, 'human'."

He had paused fractionally before uttering the last word. There was a need, he was sure, to depict as faithfully as he could the events of his Father's life; perhaps there was also a need - or, more so, a duty - to give his writing all the credit that was rightly its due. If Beatrice was arguing for some kind of equilibrium then it would surely fall out naturally: the former was negative, the latter positive. Charles Packard had been no angel. Indeed, could there be anyone other than himself - apart from his poor Mother - who could better testify to this? It seemed important however (and this importance seemed to be growing almost daily within his consciousness) that he attempt to understand, that his depiction was never 'cold'. It was, he knew, a diversion from the factual; but that could not be helped. He would not be changing history, he would be merely offering a gloss upon it. After all, wasn't that why Simon had wanted he - and he alone - to write the biography?

"Oh, your Father was human all right!"

A small laugh escaped from Beatrice as she tried to relax a little more into the chair. The upholstery was comfortable enough; indeed, Mark had spent enough hours sunk into its accepting cushions to know that. His Aunt's discomfort - which seemed still to be present even after her latest shuffling - was evidently a manifestation of something else.

"Where are you - in the book I mean?"

Even though he knew immediately - intimately, in fact - the answer to the question, he glanced back to the desk at the small pile of papers spread there.

"1963. The publication of 'Dawn'."

"I see." Beatrice paused. "'It was the best of times, it was the worst of times, it was the age of wisdom, it was the age of foolishness'."

Pushing quotations about in a conversation - like moving pieces in one of those square puzzles where there is a picture to be made by rearranging the sliding segments - was one of Beatrice's occasional idiosyncrasies; especially when she wanted to avoid using her own words to express something. Mark might offer a salvo of his own that would be, in part at least, a little gambit to prove that he could do it too. They never entered into any kind of open warfare - it was not a game of that sort - and only on rare occasions (which often made a Christmas or something of that ilk quite memorable) did they exchange shots with any volume or rapidity. This occasion - from both the quote, and the manner of its delivery - Mark recognised as not being one of those opportunities.

He suddenly wondered when they we due to be taking the mirror to Laura's, and glanced back at the calendar that stood on the desk. It was unmarked; the future was empty.

"Sorry?" He had lost the thread of the conversation, thrown partly by the Dickens' quote, and partly by the sudden contemplation of the mirror's departure.

"1963," she clarified, "was not an altogether good time."

"Nor 1964 and 1965. Yes, of course I know that; but you asked me where I was, and it's there."

"Have you mentioned Stella?"

There was something troubling Beatrice after all, and perhaps this was it. Perhaps she was concerned as to how Mark was intending to portray the less laudable side of this Father's character. He replaced his empty mug on the desk and turned his chair a little, to make himself more comfortable.

"Not yet. But I will of course. I have too."

"Yes, Dear; I know you do."

"And others in that vein too."

"But Stella is different, isn't she?"

"Because she was the first woman father was unfaithful with? Or is there something else? I have the facts Aunt; I can only write the facts."

"Ah," and here Beatrice caught her breath slightly, "but that is not so. There is no such thing as 'only the facts'! How will you write these 'facts', can you tell me that?"

"I'm not sure I'm with you."

"Facts or no facts, you're telling a story Mark; and, like it or not, your story has a hero of sorts. In that respect it's no different from a million other stories. What I want to know is..."

"Yes?" Mark seized on her pause, her uncertainty. Yet he knew that she could not be uncertain; that she knew very well what she wanted to know.

"What I want to know is what sort of hero is Charles going to be? Make no mistake, in the wrong hands that affair with Stella could be turned from what it was into some kind of romantic fantasy. We could have on our hands a dashing hero, swashbuckling his way from one novel to another - and from one mistress to another."

There was something hostile in Beatrice's voice; a hostility only mildly disguised by a prevailing sense of nervousness.

"But he was your brother!"

"Oh, I know that!"

"What do you want Aunt? You sound like you want me to crucify him, or condemn him."

"I just don't want you to forget that at times he was a complete bastard."

The word hung heavy between them. She seldom swore; and when she did, even less rarely did she not mean it. 'Bastard' had been meant, and now, taking on a life of its own from all the power she had invested into it, Mark could almost see it in physical form, hovering tauntingly before him.

"I'm sorry."

She rose, offering a small smile. For a second the bold and capable front that was the Beatrice he grew up with; the woman who kept his Uncle in check, together, alive; the woman whose equilibrium had, over the years, kept the whole family stable; for a second, she was stripped, and vulnerable.

"I'll take that shall I?"

Mark turned to where she was suddenly pointing. He picked up the mug.

"You're right of course," this as he passed her the mug. "I did love him. He was a charming and very brilliant man. And I want you to tell his story. But I also want you to tell the story of the faithless man; the man who betrayed his family."

"Did he betray you?"

The question hit Beatrice like a slap, hard across the face. At once she was upright, solid; Mark could see her puffing in the corner of a ring, boxing gloves on, ready to take on all-comers.

"Yes, he betrayed me. He betrayed us all. I suspect, deep down, he knew that he had even betrayed himself." There was fire in her now. "Don't lose sight of that Mark. We all suffered at times, in between the glory and the champagne. Charles more than most, I suspect."

"And you never forgave him."

It was an idea that had come suddenly, formed from the remnants of her word 'bastard', as she stood there. The word had popped like a balloon, and the letters that had made it up had reformed and come to him as a completely different phrase, a new premise.

"No. I did not. I could not; then or now."

"Because it was him?"

She looked slightly quizzically at him.

"Because it was Father. Or not? I mean," he paused, for now he was on wholly uncertain ground. He felt as if he had climbed a fence (knowing all the while that he shouldn't) and that there was no going back. It was only a single step perhaps, but the chance of trespass that now presented itself - the chance to know something about his Aunt, rather than deduce things by guesswork or supposition - made it worth the risk. "I mean, do you forgive with difficulty? I don't know if I do; I suspect not."

"Does it matter? Is it of any relevance, my personal inclinations?"

"I think so - in this case. After all, you are my star witness in all of this - "

"Excluding yourself," Beatrice corrected.

"Indeed. So don't you think I need to understand what you think and feel too? After all, what you tell me - the way you tell it to me - that has its own gloss on the truth; it has been interpreted already. Maybe I need to be able to peel that varnish away as best I can."

"You don't think I would lie, Mark?"

He smiled.

"Never. But you asked me what kind of hero I was painting; I just want to understand what kind of hero you see."

Beatrice smiled, took a single, half-step towards him and stopped.

"Touché!"

"Take Simon for example."

"Simon! What has he to do with all this?"

"No; the other night. After the awards dinner. Did you forgive him for that?"

"Was there anything to forgive?!" Now she laughed, spurred on by either the memory or his own naiveté; Mark was uncertain which. "He slept in the spare room, and felt dreadful the next day. The day after that he was contrite - as usual - and bought me flowers."

"As usual?"

"Simon likes these dinners; it gives him a chance for him to let his hair down."

"And it gives you a chance to give him the chance too!"

She wagged the index finger of her free hand at him in mock admonishment.

"You have some of your Father in you, young man!"

"So forgiveness was never a question then?"

It was plain enough that Simon's revelry had been innocent enough; endorsed even. If there was to be forgiveness required on one side, then, he assumed, that there would be guilt on the other. If there was an equilibrium in all things, then perhaps this was the equation.

The first kiss had taken place in the back of the taxi. He had held the door open for Maxine who had given the driver her address before Mark had taken the seat next to her. They had not gone far when she leant towards him, her mouth purposeful yet uncertain, her tongue asking a question which demanded a response. It had been a brief enough moment, but it had set out the terms of the encounter: Queen's Gambit, accepted.

As he watched Beatrice disappear from the room, he knew that she left behind (as she always seemed to) some 'big' questions. Guilt and forgiveness, their opposition and interdependence, had sparked a memory. More than that, it had stimulated within him a desire for a little self-searching. The question - 'Would Julia forgive him?' - that had taken root the following day, had now been suddenly replaced by another - 'Was there anything to forgive?'. If guilt spawned forgiveness then, more than anything, it had its own prerequisite; to have caused pain or suffering - and there had to be guilt there in the first place.

"God knows what time you'll be home! Or what state you'll be in! I bet Simon drinks like a fish given half a chance!"

Julia's announcement that she was going to stay with Laura for a couple of days was delivered with the air of a pre-emptive strike; a shot of invective across Mark's bows that carried the tone of 'Oh yes, I know what boys get up to when they're let loose at one of these functions!'. She had meant getting drunk, and Simon (as she had predicted, and with a degree of insight that surprised him now that he considered it in retrospect) had obliged in quite a satisfactory manner! What she had not meant of course, was leaving the dinner with another woman.

Would she even know? And if she did not, how could there be any pain or suffering on her part? Wither guilt then? Simon's recollection of the tail-end of the evening had been non-existent (Mark had quizzed him that far) so his trail was safe there. As far as Maxine was concerned, there he was less certain; but his instinct (and one which he did not know he possessed, or which was not yet proven) was that she knew the form and had no intention of rocking anyone's boat.

The taxi had not travelled that much further before it pulled off the main thoroughfare and into a small mews. They had joined hands, loosely, after the kiss, and Mark had taken to vague abstraction as they journeyed on in silence. When they pulled to a halt (Maxine freeing her hand to pull some money from her purse for the driver) Mark had all but lost his sense of direction. Stepping from the cab was little help either.

He looked back to the entrance of the small cul-de-sac as the driver reversed out: he thought of Marylebone; it felt about right.

Maxine was standing in the open doorway of one of the small mews cottages that made up the single-sided terrace. He walked towards her as casually as he could; an action partly helped by the amount of alcohol he had drunk, but partly hindered by an uncertainty over the turn of events.

She turned her back on him as he reached the threshold.

"Drink?" She had removed her coat and was standing in the small hallway as he closed the door. "I've got brandy - but that's a little heavy perhaps. Do you like Cointreau?"

"Yes; fine, thanks."

"Through here."

He followed her into a surprisingly large sitting room which was furnished impeccably. On the walls, a small number of paintings - originals, undoubtedly - hung in modest splendour.

"Very nice."

She smiled from the drinks cabinet as she poured.

"Daddy was very generous."

"Ah."

There were two small leather sofas, each camouflaged by colourful cushions. He chose the one nearest, and sat down. Maxine walked over, holding out his glass.

"I don't usually," she began little nervously, once she had sat next to him.

"Neither do I." He smiled. The reply sounded almost text book.

The sweet orange flavour was sharp and strangely reviving after the red wine. He sipped a second time and took a slow glance about the room.

"Do you always do that?"

"What?"

"Examine other peoples' rooms so carefully?" She smiled. "Not that I mind; I've nothing to hide. The dead bodies are buried under the patio."

"Not very original."

"The patio? No, I know. But I have so little space. Where else am I to secrete the remains of the poor men I lure back here?"

He leant forward and placed his glass on the small coffee table that bridged the space between the two settees. Maxine brushed the back of his head as he did so. He straightened, took her hand, and kissed it.

"Where's the bathroom?"

"Oh dear! I thought you were being so charming, yet all you want me for is my Armitage Shanks!"

"Absolutely!"

"Top of the stairs, and straight in front of you." She watched him stand. "Why don't you take that jacket off too - that is, if you're not rushing off."

The bathroom was Laura Ashley blue sea shells. Mark hated Laura Ashley, mainly because people had a suicidal tendency to overdo it. It was as if they had invested so much in their expensive choice that they were going to squeeze every last pattern out of it. Tasteful Laura Ashley was, in its place, something else; and Maxine's bathroom was undoubtedly tasteful. It was (he decided, as he was drying his hands and indulging in another inquisitive look round) only what he would have expected, given the example set by the decor of the room downstairs.

Maxine was waiting for him outside on the landing.

"Hi."

"Hello. Nice bathroom."

She moved closer and placed her arms round his waist.

"Thanks."

She pulled him to her. They kissed.

There was no uncertainty in her now. They stood for a few moments, the kisses gentle, exploring; tongues caressing, each running along the insides of the other lips, probing softly. She pulled away. Mark opened his eyes; she was smiling.

Taking his hand, she led him into the bedroom.

"Did you want to take a good look round here too, Sir?" She adopted the air of an Estate Agent, and flashed her eyes at him. "We have a small built-in wardrobe over here - with full length mirrors of course. Radiator over there, as you can see. Wall lights are on dimmer switches, and there's a small light especially for the bed."

He had felt relaxed enough as Maxine started her little play-acting, but suddenly he lost track of what she was saying. He wanted her badly, suddenly. He stepped forwards and pulled her towards him, stopping her mouth with his own, this time less gently, more assertively. Her response was instantaneous, her hands hard over his back then running down the front of his shirt, beyond his belt, gently squeezing his stiffening penis through his trousers.

His hands found the zip of her dress which he pulled. A small gasp escaped from her as his hands touched her flesh. She tugged at his shirt buttons. He slipped the dress straps from her shoulders. Her breasts were small, their nipples small too; small and pink and hard. He rolled his tongue around one of them as she began to remove his shirt. In seconds they were naked.

She took off her glasses, throwing them down softly onto the discarded pile of clothes. She smiled.

"I take it that Sir is quite interested in the property. Is there anything else I can show you?"

They had reached the edge of the bed. Mark, his mind racing now, driven on by something so basic that it denied any rational thought, eased Maxine down onto the duvet. He knelt on the floor and kissed her navel, allowing his tongue to roll around it. He kissed her stomach, then her hips, nibbling little kisses that made her squirm. He could smell her now, and nuzzled his nose into the rough of her pubic hair, breathing warmingly, deliberately.

Maxine, her hands on his head, pulled him up onto her. Her tongue found his ear, then round under his chin to the other ear. She slipped her hands along his back, one of them moving under him, feeling him, encouraging his erection. Their mouths met. She shifted under him, holding him, then - suddenly - she guided and swallowed him.

There was a mutual groan. She was smiling, rocking beneath him. Mark arched his back and began pumping slowly. He bent his head and kissed her breasts roughly. She let out another small moan.

"As you can see, Sir," she started talking again. Mark tried to stop her mouth with kisses, but his rhythm wouldn't let him. "It's a small establishment, but perfectly furnished," she paused. He was driving hard now. He could feel the surge building at the base of his penis. "but open to all sorts of opportu..."

Maxine's last word was interrupted by an aching grown from Mark as he drove himself, exploding within her. She grabbed the flesh of his back and held him, encouraging, pulling him on, again and again and again.

Chapter Eleven

There was a way in which the early morning sunlight, shining in a slice through the bedroom curtains, made Mark think of foreign climes. It was - for some reason - Bangkok, or Thailand, or somewhere of that ilk, where he could imagine himself waking beneath a pure white mosquito net, and seeing slats of light making their slow progress down the wall as the sun rose outside. There were no such blinds in his bedroom of course (it would have been a fantasy too strange for Julia to entertain, even if he had divulged it) but the window - a modern incarnation of lead-framed square glass panes - leant itself to such an interpretation; and when the curtains weren't quite drawn (as was now the case, with Julia having already peered out to check the weather) the overall impression, to his mind at least, allowed for an Eastern fantasy.

Julia reappeared in the room with a small tray upon which two cups of tea steamed invitingly.

"I forget to tell you," she began, as she set the tray down on her large bedside table, inviting Mark to look up from his book, "you had a phone call."

"When?"

"Yesterday. When you were in town."

"Oh?"

"Someone from the BBC."

"A woman?" he wanted to say, but said nothing.

"He said something about getting in touch. Some piece or other they wanted you to consider." She paused, passing him his tea as she did so. "I didn't know you knew anyone at the BBC."

As he placed the mug on his own table, he considered his response. The fact that it had been a man who had called gave him some possibilities - and an insight into Maxine's modus operandi.

"Someone I met at that awards do the other night. Max. Maybe they've got a job they'd like me to think about." This suggestion was not an impossibility, of course. Indeed, having invented it, he was momentarily uncertain which motive for the call he wanted to believe in. Either way, he was certain that Maxine was the instigator.

Julia snuggled down next to him, laying her left leg across his thigh.

"That would be good, wouldn't it? I mean, a little more public recognition? Something to look forward too?" There was an element of uncertainty in her voice; an uncertainty not related to her own philosophies or desires, but a doubt as to Mark's present ambitions.

He smiled dutifully, missing the inference in her voice, his mind occupied by things to look forward to other than 'public recognition'.

"It's a little unexpected, perhaps;" he offered, "but maybe there's an opportunity there."

Although Mark was using his Aunt's house as the base for the work on his Father's biography, he still maintained a significant workspace in the Hampstead house. This study, larger and somehow 'cleaner' than his room in Belsize Park (it still carried the feeling of being newly decorated, and the matching study furniture - desk, shelves, and filing cabinet - leant it an air of an office above all else) was where Mark carved out the freelance journalism that he had, thus far in his career, chosen as the means by which he should make his name; an undertaking made especially important given that, being his Father's Son, he had already been born into a 'name'.

Consequently, the bookcases were dominated by volumes of history: first-hand accounts, second-hand perspectives, third-hand theories. They bore an order about them, arranged by period (though there was little that could not be considered 'modern') and then sub-classified by topic. The research for each article Mark produced saw another small batch added to the catalogue, and - in advance - a small space prepared for the next. He had already decided where the Chamberlain reference material would reside.

In the study later he looked up from the small pile of Kuwait-related books that had been temporarily removed from their home, and cast a general gaze about the room. It was not a gaze to identify anything in particular, but rather a plea to the god of domestic inspiration.

"Julia!" His call was to the room in general, and beyond that, the whole house. He waited.

"Yes?"

From the sound of the reply, the way it came to him bouncing off walls, doors, ceilings, he located its source as the kitchen. Automatically he moderated his response, targeting it almost through the fabric of the house.

"Have you seem my old photo albums?"

"What?"

Julia was on the move. He waited. She appeared through the door a few moments later.

"What did you say?"

"Have you seen my old photo albums?"

"No. Should I have?"

"The black volumes," he ignored her reply, "there were three of them."

She followed his eyes as he scanned the room again. It was not a real search; there was nothing penetrating about his looking, as if he were scratching the surface knowing that he was going to be disappointed.

"You had a clear-out a while ago." She remembered a whirlwind Sunday morning devoted to making the study spick-and-span, where Mark had endeavoured to clear the 'detritus' - his word - from his professional life. "You put some things in that big box, up in the attic."

"But not my photos!"

Despite this assertion, within ten minutes Mark was lifting the loft hatch and gazing from floor level into a large and relatively well-kept boarded attic room. He had toyed (at various intervals in the past) with going the whole hog; going beyond merely having the void boarded, and putting in stairs, a window, proper lighting. There was a part of him that liked the idea of having the roof space as his study, a space entirely of his own - and of his own making, too - away from the remainder of the house. A space which could, in his eyes at least, never be construed as anything other than that which it had been designed to be.

There were several boxes almost within his reach from the top of the stairs. After a brief attempt to reach them from his initial vantage point, he clambered the remainder of the way until he stood in the loft proper, head slightly bent. Moving the contents of each box in turn, he soon came upon the albums; dark, leather binders, each differing slightly from the other in terms of shade, weight, and size.

From somewhere, he had a recollection of his Father; an image that he was certain he held - in the true physical sense - within his possession. It was this he had been determined to seek out.

One of the albums (he had returned with all three of them to the lounge, and they now sat sharing the settee with him) was evidently older than the others: its leather was more cracked; its colouring had faded further. This had been the volume started by his Mother. He had vague, child-like recollections of her talking to him about 'her photographs'; recollections that had, years later, been supported by his Father during one of their rare quiet moments when they spoke openly of her. She had insisted, amongst all the photographs they held (a growing number, Mark remembered; at least until her death) there should be some that were endowed with a certain 'status', ones that were 'special'. Her desire was that should anyone wish to see, encompassed in a single place, a composite of the Family Packard, then one should be available. Because the size of the album was finite - and she had insisted on maintaining only one - there were numerous occasions when old needed to make way for new, and she would sort the entire collection into those that represented the history she wanted to keep, and those that did not.

Mark could remember - again in one of those childhood images blurred by the flames of the living room fire as much as time - Mary sitting on the floor surrounded by small squares of black-and-white and sepia-stained paper, ordering and re-ordering, talking quietly to herself as she did so.

It was a ritual that all but died with her. 'That volume' - the one Mark now held in his hands - remained as she had left it. It was nearly full: indeed, it had always been nearly full; the only thing that changed being the balance of the old against the new, an inexorable decline which saw the more modern all but triumphant.

He had tried for a while to maintain her tradition. It was not an immediate undertaking - at twelve years old he would not have been ready - but later, once he had learned from his Father the secrets behind those fireside memories, he began his own collection, the evidence of which resided in the relatively ramshackle accumulation in the two other albums next to him.

Whilst photographs held a fascination for him, this was for reasons apart from his Mother's. She had seen them as a means of record for others; they were dispassionate things and nothing of sentiment - something in her that ran counter to the Pre-Raphaelite romantic image of her which he had attempted to treasure. More than anything else, they were to her receipts for a life. There was nothing of memory in them: he had no recollection of sitting on her lap and being shown images of himself when small, or of his Father when he had been a dashing young man. Mark had never seen any evidence of the Accountant in his Mother, except in her photograph album.

Carefully - though trying to avoid within himself any sense of religious devotion - Mark opened the album. The photograph he sought was taken in the late fifties, an image of his Father sitting writing; something that the modern world would have endowed with the title 'portrait'. Such elevated ambition had been far from Mary's mind that Sunday morning when she crept into the room where Charles was bent over a book. She had never truly understood what drove him to write, and the sudden whim - to surprise him with a photograph - perhaps was motivated by an unspoken (or unrecognised) desire to capture something of that drive.

Whatever the reason - and whatever the motivation - Mary had, in all innocence, succeeded perfectly. The Charles Packard that now stared out of the page at his son, was a man rapt; in the eyes that peered upwards (the face half-bent, turned on the sound of intrusion) was a depth of feeling and understanding beyond comprehension. Mark had never seen an image of genius to compare with this. In the bottom corner of the page, slightly beyond focus, Charles' right hand held a pencil, suspended momentarily above the page. It was, for Mark at least, a pencil charged with imagination; he could almost feel the words, transferred to its tip from behind those eyes, waiting to burst out.

Of course the photograph was famous now. Mark had - during those early days with Julia - taken her to the National Portrait Gallery where, for a short while, a print been taken and hung. And it had appeared on the cover of the most recent reprint of 'Sixteen Sonnets (and other poems)'.

-*-

After the publication of "Sonnet Seven", Charles became more open to accepting George Walker's assertion that his work was of some merit. Although he had no "grand plan", Charles continued to write poetry. It was never easy. Work at the factory was in undertaken in shifts, and the hours were long. Often the tedium of the day, or the length of the night, would return a tired and drained Charles home to Mary. Bringing up a new baby failed to make matters any easier, too. Finding time to write was difficult.

> "I used to try and find time between waking and sleeping, but it was never easy. I even tried to get something done when I was on night shift, but the Foreman became suspicious when I began to spend too long in the toilet! If you took a newspaper and a packet of Woodbines in with you, that was OK; but I didn't. I wasn't streetwise yet!"

(Interview with Melvyn Bragg, 1986)

Gradually, as the months passed, Charles' cannon grew. He wrote - always in pencil - in cheap notebooks he bought in packs of four from the corner shop. The paper was rough and of poor quality, but this was of little matter for a man with large, expansive writing, and a tendency to cross things out aggressively and start again.

Mary, content that her husband was happy enough and fulfilling the role she would expect of him, turned her attentions to their young son. The first six months were difficult. Mark suffered badly from colic, and attempting to keep the household running on an even keel - especially with Charles on night shift half the time - was difficult. The goal for which she strove was to achieve a balance such that the whole family was functioning and as happy as they could be. Charles was always her barometer in this. If he seemed content, then all was well. If he suddenly appeared from the sitting room holding one of his notebooks and smiling, then things were especially well. The things she feared most of all was a deeply unsatisfied Charles and any consequent return to drink.

> "Did she understand? No, I don't think she did. That was difficult for me to come to terms with, you know? After all, I'd met her at an art class and she could draw! I assumed, again naively, that because of that she was an "artist", that she would understand about my writing. But she never did. In the end perhaps I realised that she was more a draughtsman than artist. But she did make it all possible. Oh yes."

> (Interview with Melvyn Bragg, 1986)

By the end of 1960, Charles had a collection of some thirty-four poems. He had been badgered by Walker to submit more to Orbit but had refused. Walker was determined that Packard's work should see the light of day and so, one week when Charles was on day shift, he went to the family home and, with Mary's blessing, copied them all by hand.

"I knew I was taking something of a chance. Charles was a fiery character - look at his long-standing hatred of Harriman - and I knew what I was doing was risky. Charles was not a man to deceive lightly, but I knew it was an important thing to do, to get his work published."

As the Sixties began, the working environment at the factory began to change. There was a change of Ownership, and a change of leadership within the Trade Union. Confrontation became more regular than it had ever been in the past, and Charles, who had no desire for a political life or to become involved, found himself gradually embroiled.

> "I guess I was more on the side of the Workers than the Bosses, though that had never been the intention. Shit, life was hard enough without making it worse. Or more complicated. I tried to steer a middle ground; I didn't want hassle, I couldn't afford the time. It wasn't easy. Sometimes the Bosses saw me as an ideal middleman; sometimes I was a Commie agitator. And whatever

they thought, the Union guys - hard-arsed, thick skinned ignoramuses mostly - thought the opposite. It was a real shit sandwich!"

(Interview in The Sunday Times, 1973)

Packard's creative output suffered under the barrage the factory put upon him during early 1961. There were two strikes, one going the Union's way, the other not. In the latter case he obtained a promotion that he did not want and which he tried to refuse. It was only the strength of his opposition to the job that saved face with his shop floor colleagues.

At home, Mary was as devoted as ever, and the young baby - just turned three years old - seemed to have sprung up before Charles was aware. He once described Mark as 'suddenly a toddler', as if the young boy had somehow taken him by surprise.

Trips to the corner shop to buy notebooks had been replaced by purchases of beer, and quiet evenings around the times of Union wranglings saw Charles return home and put his feet up, wanting nothing more than a bottle of beer and a smoke.

On July 19th, a little after seven thirty in the evening, George Walker made an impromptu visit to the house. With him he brought a large brown envelope and a bottle of wine.

> "I was immediately suspicious. I'd had a heavy day at work and the last thing I wanted to do was to be sociable. It was only because Mary was upstairs putting Mark to bed that I opened the door myself. George was a funny bugger; never could keep much to himself. Played poker with him once and he lost a packet. Anyway, we never had wine. Never. And there he was, trying to look serious but with this fucking great grin on his face and holding a bottle of wine. I thought he'd just got married or something; I mean I knew he was seeing some lassie from the local, and thought that maybe she'd just said 'yes'."

(Interview with Melvyn Bragg, 1986)

What Walker had brought with him was not only his original copy of Charles' poems, but also a contract from a publisher for a one-off collection.

Charles invited George into the sitting room and they sat for a few moments, mainly in silence. Walker asked about the factory.

"I don't think I'd ever been so nervous in my life. It was an excited kind of nervous; but I was scared too. If he didn't take it right, I knew that Charles was quite capable of killing me stone dead there and then."

Walker waited until Mary returned downstairs before speaking.

> "He was holding that bottle of wine so tight I thought he'd crush it in his hands. It was actually quite funny. I asked him if he'd finally managed to knock off the girl from the "White Hart" and he seemed to ignore me completely! Then Mary came in and George was off, talking all at a gallop and stumbling over his words like a nag in the National! I told him to calm down and start again."

> (Interview with Melvyn Bragg, 1986)

Walker had sent the drafts of Charles' poems to the editor of Orbit and asked for an opinion - and for the name of a Publisher who might be interested. Both were forthcoming. George travelled the short distance to Birmingham that rainy Wednesday to meet the owner of a local publishing house, later to become part of the Faber group. They had done a little research into Charles Packard once they had read the poems, and Walker found himself talking to a man - Samuel Dawson - who was already familiar with <u>Pieces of Eight</u>. After two hours he was on his way back to Warwick, wine in hand.

Beginning again, Walker related the story and his news. Mary sat on the arm of Charles' chair, resting her hand on his shoulder. The whole thing lasted no more than a minute, and then there was silence.

> "I couldn't believe it. I mean, I just couldn't believe it! Maybe if I'd been less tired, or it had been a different day, or Mary hadn't been there - I don't know, maybe I'd have been angry with him. Perhaps I'd have felt betrayed. But I was too tired - and in front of me was the spectacle of the most inept, bumbling, and nervous specimen I'd ever seen! Maybe that helped. But George was a wonderful man too. A selfless man. All the while I'd been dragged down by work - just like I'd been dragged down in the past - and he'd been there, constant. Fuck it, he was more true to me than I was myself! He offered me the envelope; his hand was shaking. I felt a lump in my throat bigger than I could stand. I leant forwards and took his hand. He dropped the envelope. 'George, you dozy bastard', I said, 'I love you.'"

> (Interview with Melvyn Bragg, 1986)

-*-

"Maxine Priest, please."

"Who shall I say is calling?" The voice at the other end was female, professional, and BBC through-and-through. The fact that Mark had a legitimate reason for making the call - more than that, a 'professional' reason - made him feel sufficiently more at home and relaxed than, had he given himself enough time to think about it, he probably had cause to be. Indeed, having decided the instant Julia had given him his message from 'Max' at the BBC, that he would return the call, the only matter that begged resolution was when the call would be made.

"It's personal. Thanks."

He had come downstairs from his Belsize Park study after a concerted effort on the book. It had gone particularly well and, despite telling Beatrice earlier in the day that he expected to only be there until midday, lunch had come and gone. The clock in the hall chimed three, forcing him to glance up. His Aunt would be back around three thirty, she had said, with the promise of some fresh carrot cake and tea if he happened to still be around.

He had phoned Julia too.

"There wasn't anything we were supposed to be doing was there?"

There had been a pause.

"Like what?"

"I don't know. Anything."

"Not that I'm aware of. Why?"

"It's the book. Things are going really well and I don't want to break off just yet."

"That's OK. When will you be home?"

"Not late. I'll call before I leave if you like."

"No need. Don't forget Peter and Claire said they might pop over later for a drink."

"Of course. See you in a while."

He had forgotten, of course, though being reminded forced an image of Claire into his head just as the telephone came to life again.

"Hello?" The voice was distant and uncertain. He realised that he had not given his name.

"It's me; Mark. Mark Packard."

"Ah!" There was a slight pause. In the background he thought he could hear a door closing. "Mr Packard, my Real Estate friend! How are you?"

"I'm fine." Mark was struggling. He had kept a note of Maxine's number in his wallet and, as he was suddenly alone in his Aunt's empty house and standing at the telephone, impulse had demanded that he satisfy his earlier resolution and make the call. He suddenly wished that, given he knew they would be speaking again - and on his own invitation - his strategy had been a little better planned.

Maxine rescued him.

"Me too. Did you get my message?"

"Your message?"

"Well not mine, exactly," there was a laugh at the other end of the line, and Mark saw instantly Maxine's short red hair, and her small round glasses behind which bright devilish eyes hid, "I mean, I didn't phone. It was one of my crew."

"I guessed as much." He paused, wanting to be certain that there was no possibility of misconception; that he had - as he suspected - gained something of an insight into the way Maxine worked. "Which means, of course, that there is no work?"

She laughed again.

"Not unless you're really desperate! I mean, I might be able to dig something up for you if I had to; but it's not your work I'm interested in - if your professional ego doesn't mind me saying so."

"Not at all," he was more relaxed now, "and I'm too busy to fit anything else in right now anyway."

"Oh dear, does that include me?"

Mark found himself smiling. At that moment, he couldn't give a damn about his 'professional ego', as she called it: there was something special about being wanted, sexually; about being found stimulating, attractive, desirable. That was a better drug than anything else he could imagine. The fact that it was clandestine: that too was something else!

"What did you have in mind?"

Chapter Twelve

"I may be playing a bit more squash at the club."

Julia looked up from her crouched position by the open door of the dishwasher. Mark handed her one of the dinner plates they had recently used, the remnants of Dijon mustard near his fingers.

"Why's that?"

It was not a real question. Mark watched as Julia tried to slot the plate into the rack; more difficult than it should have been as a result of the rather random way in which Julia had tackled the job from the outset. The inner trays were segmented with various guides to indicate where each piece should go, but Julia - as was her character it seemed - chose in the main to ignore them.

They were making conversation, that was all. Mark had reason enough to make his statement - indeed, he had reason enough for most things - but it seemed of late that all they did was to 'make conversation'. He wanted, suddenly, to ask Julia when was the last time she had asked him a 'real' question. It was fitting he did not; and more fitting that he lied.

"Oh, I just feel a bit out of shape, that's all. So I've signed up for one of those informal ladders they run down there."

She looked up again.

"I thought you said you hated those things. How you ended up playing against the same people all the time and never progressed."

He pulled a saucepan from the table and held it in his hand, looking uncertainly into the dishwasher.

"I know, but that was when I took it seriously. I'm not planning to take it seriously this time."

"You, not take something seriously?" She gave a small laugh and held out her hand.

"I just want to feel in better shape, that's all. For the summer. I've done nothing of late, spending most of my time between here and Belsize working. And Peter's not been around much either. I need some physical stimulation."

There was a short pause. From near the cooker, the agitated bubble of the espresso machine. Mark could suddenly hear the ticking of the clock on the wall.

"Are you going to give that to me or not?"

A ring from the front doorbell saved Mark the trouble of responding. Julia stood up.

"I expect that's Peter. He'll tell you you're daft to go back into those squash ladders."

Mark watched Julia leave the kitchen, then bent down to address the dishwasher. As he removed the last plate Julia had inserted he listened for a greeting from the hall.

"Claire!" came Julia's voice on cue.

He tried to catch the rest. Something Julia said sounded like 'Where's Peter?', but as the volume and tone dropped from the heights of greeting he lost contact with what was actually being said.

When Julia and Claire eventually entered the kitchen, he was in the process of replacing the last of the items in the washer.

"Guess what?" Julia paused, looking down at Mark as he rose from the now perfectly organised dishwasher, closing the door on his handiwork as he did so. A small frown passed momentarily across her brow and was then gone.

"No Peter?"

"No Peter," she confirmed.

"He sends his apologies," said Claire as she came across to kiss him on the cheek, "but something's come up at work. He's got to get some report or other ready for the States. Has to be emailed this evening."

Mark heard the espresso machine again, nudging him through the conversation.

"Coffee? Or something stronger?"

"Coffee will be fine. Thanks."

"You two go on; I'll bring it through in a minute."

He watched the two women walk out of the kitchen, then addressed himself to preparing the coffee tray. He was suspicious of Peter. He knew that work was going incredibly well, and that things were very busy; but there were times when he wondered just how far he went in pursuit of the good-time, wide-boy image he sometimes tried to portray. Perhaps he didn't have a fax to send. Perhaps it was just an excuse - as much as the squash ladder had been an excuse.

Mark placed three small cups on the tray and filled them with the hot, dark coffee. From one of the cupboards, he pulled a small sugar bowl filled with brown, shiny crystals, and a box of dark chocolate mints.

He wondered if it were possible for Peter to be having an affair. He remembered Claire on the squash court: her magnificent physique; how it had felt in that moment to brush himself against her. The cups clinked together on the tray as he walked through the hall. As Julia looked up at him from the sofa, he tried to remember the last time he had seen her in sports clothes. How would she appear to someone else if there were to be an accidental collision on a games court?

"Julia says you're going to be playing more squash." Claire looked up at him from the armchair by the fire. As he handed her a coffee, he noticed that she was wearing the blouse from the wine bar.

"Just a touch; to keep in trim."

Claire laughed.

"You're a fit as a fiddle Mark; why do you need to keep in trim?!"

Mark smiled and offered the box of mints from the table.

-*-

<u>Sixteen Sonnets (and other poems)</u> was published early the following year. Dawson was a strict editor and made it plain to the young Packard that there some work to be done on the poems before they would be ready for publication. The notion that they were not complete as they were came as something of a shock to the poet who had seldom in his short career faced professional criticism.

The argument with Arnold Harriman over <u>Pieces of Eight</u> some four years earlier centred on financial rather than artistic matters. Harriman had agreed to take on the publication of Packard's small collection of short stories with the promise of producing a book. Charles - who at that time, was still just a man in his mid-twenties - duly signed the contract placed before him.

> "It was getting into print that was the most important thing. When I let Harriman read my stories - and then when he offered to publish them - well, I thought I'd arrived! I thought that suddenly someone had waved a magic wand and my life was to be changed forever. That was all I saw; all I was looking for."

(Interview in Time Magazine, 1986)

The contract Charles signed had a number of clauses within it which, although written plainly enough, were hidden within a mass of jargon. The key points were that a) Charles was to pay half of the publication costs; b) that all proceeds from the book would go to Harriman in the first instance until all his personal costs had been covered, after which they would be divided equally between them; and c) Harriman would own all future copyright over the work. If this were not enough, there was no explicit mention of the nature of the "book" Harriman was contracted to produce nor the publicity he would put behind it.

On 17th October 1957, Anthony Harriman arrived at the Packard's home with a small box containing one hundred and fifty copies of <u>Pieces of Eight</u>. He had printed two hundred. Two local stores had agreed to take twenty-five copies each on a sale-or-return basis, along with a small A4 black-and-white poster announcing the arrival of 'a New Work from a Local Author'. Also within the box was the demand for half the publication costs, and a schedule - explaining in plain words this time - the agreement Packard had signed.

According to Harriman later, it took all Mary's guile - not to mention her physical strength - to prevent Packard from killing him there and then. As he walked away from the house, he could hear Packard's abuse following him down the street.

> "It was betrayal. Not just of me, but of my dream. And I'd had the dream such a short time. I had expected a book, and all that Twister had produced was a shoddy little pamphlet. It was hardly fit to light the fire with."

> (Interview in Time Magazine, 1986)

Harriman followed his visit with a solicitor's letter a few days later. Packard was forced to comply, and virtually emptied the family savings account in doing so. Only six copies of the book were sold; he never saw a penny from it. It was only on Harriman's death in the mid-sixties, that the rights over the work transferred back to their Author - but by that time Packard had sworn never to have the stories re-published.

With an experience such as this behind him, Packard was understandably wary of Dawson. Not only that, but he was immediately suspicious. This time however there were three things that were in his favour: he was some four years older and certainly wiser; Dawson was not a crook; and he had George Walker at his side.

> "The first meetings were difficult. I think I stormed out of one of them! But George brought me back. In fact, considering the hand he had in it, it was more George's project than my own. Dawson was a sound man though. After a while I began to realise that he wasn't trying to take me for a ride, and that all he wanted was for the poems to be as good as they possibly could be. It was difficult for me though. "I don't like that" he used to say, or "you can't use

that word". He was right - mostly. And when I stuck to my guns, well, give him his due, he respected me for it."

(Interview with Melvyn Bragg, 1986)

This time the publication was more like the sort of book Packard had in mind. It was half-way between soft and hard cover; there was a design on the front; and the forty pages inside were not made of tissue paper. Dawson had been in publishing too long not to have done his work properly. Thus the fanfare that greeted <u>Sixteen Sonnets (and other poems)</u>, although not loud, was certainly a little more tuneful than the 1957 launch. The publisher had managed to get copies into most of the bookstores in Warwick, in twos or threes mainly, and even some as far afield as Coventry and Birmingham.

Coincidentally Dawson printed two hundred copies in the first run, placing over half of them straight into shops. Eventually, by the end of 1961, nearly all had sold. There would be no second printing just yet, however.

The most significant event to occur as a result of the book was an invitation for Charles to read at a local poetry workshop. As ever, Walker was on hand that evening - March 12th, 1961 - when Packard made his first public appearance.

> "I was shitting myself. I made George take me into a pub just round the corner from the library where this group held their meetings; I felt I needed a stiffener. There were two things that scared me: the first was that I'd never actually spoken aloud to a group of people; the second was that I'd never talked with anyone about my writing. Not even Mary. What I didn't realise of course was that my Union business stood me in good stead as far as the first fear was concerned. And the second? Sounds corny; but the people were actually very nice. They liked what I'd written, and they were interested. Once I'd relaxed, well, then it was easy!"

(Interview with Melvyn Bragg, 1986)

Charles Packard gave two more readings from <u>Sixteen Sonnets (and other poems)</u>. One meeting was attended by a journalist from a local newspaper who managed to fill a couple of column inches in one edition, saying how much he had enjoyed the evening. Despite the disappointment that not all the books were sold and that after a few weeks things seemed to go back to the way they had always been, for the Poet the spark had been well and truly lit.

-*-

Mark smiled and offered the box of mints from the table.

Maxine moved across to the side of the bed where he was now sitting, her white towelling robe draped about his shoulders.

"We should rename these," she said, taking one from the centre of the box.

"To what - 'After Lunch'?"

"No, 'After Sex'!"

She pulled his hand towards her face and gave it a brief kiss.

"Thanks."

"My pleasure, Sir!"

Mark moved his hand away, brushing it through her hair as he did so, and then stood up. He felt tired; a strange, mid-day kind of weariness that beckoned him back to bed, only this time to sleep.

"I'd better have a shower."

"Isn't that a bit of a giveaway?" She asked the question without looking up, studying the box of mints to choose the next dark envelope she was going to take.

"It's essential. Julia thinks I'm playing squash, so if I don't go home all refreshed..."

"And just a little tired?" Maxine suggested playfully.

He left her lying on the bed. A few minutes later, she joined him in the bathroom. As he showered he could see her robed figure via the mirror as she sat on the lowered toilet seat. She was looking at his shape through the curtain as he washed his hair.

"Mark?"

Even with the noise of the shower, he could hear that the smile had gone out of her voice. He stopped lathering and allowed the hot water to run down the back of his head.

"Yes?"

"I don't want us to get off on the wrong foot."

"I thought we'd 'got off' rather well!" He laughed, but his humour was not reciprocated.

"I'm being serious. I don't want any misunderstandings; that's all."

He dowsed his hair once more, turned the water off, and pulled back the curtain. He could see her properly now.

"Pass me the towel, can you?"

She leant forwards and handed him a white and blue patterned towel. Not Laura Ashley, but it went well. He caught a glimpse of her breast as she leant back, and he suddenly wanted to have her all over again.

"I mean, I don't want to upset anything. I'm not trying to steal you away from Julia."

"I know you're not."

She smiled.

"No you don't, lovely, and that's why I'm telling you. I'm not looking for anything like that."

"'Like that'?"

"Commitment." She watched him rubbing himself dry, her eyes following his hands as they went about his body now knowing every inch of it. "I like my life the way it is. And I like the occasional..." She struggled briefly for the word.

"'Excitement'?" he suggested, hopefully.

"Diversion. Fun. You know. I don't want to jeopardise the way things are, because I've got them the way I like them."

Mark stepped out of the shower, pulled the towel round his waist and walked over to where she sat. She seemed so terrier-like most of the time, but just now she was a little unsure of herself. He kissed her forehead.

"I quite like the way things are too." He paused, turning to look at himself in the mirror. He seemed a little younger, his hair damp and disarranged, the odd bead of water still on his shoulders. A frown began to form and he caught it before it had a chance to develop. Still looking at himself, he went on, "I don't want things to change either. And I'm not going to threaten your space. OK?"

She had risen as he had been speaking, and the last phrase had been delivered face-to-face. She smiled, stood on her toes, and kissed him closed-mouth.

"Good. Now we'd better go back to work. My turn."

As he left the bathroom to regain his clothes, he heard the whoosh of the shower resume.

-*-

Things soon returned to normal at Morgan Street. With the excitement of
<u>Sixteen Sonnets (and other poems)</u> and attendant readings out of the way,
Charles' life became once again dominated by his work and his family.
For the first time in quite a while, he began to take an active interest in his
young son. School was a little over a year away, and Charles was
concerned that Mark should get the right sort of start in life. All the while
he had been preoccupied with the factory and his writing, Mary had been
getting on with things as far as her son was concerned, and Mark was
already making good progress in learning English.

Charles set himself the task of helping teach Mark to read and write, and
for a few days would return from work and immediately sit down with the
boy in an attempt to make the most of the limited time they had together.
The enthusiasm was short-lived. Charles, expecting too much from the
young child, rapidly lost patience, and after a while Mary gradually
resumed her former role, carefully deflecting her husband away from any
domestic situations which might lead to an unhappy outcome.

With his interest in Mark almost instantly on the wane, Charles became
restless.

> "The challenge was, of course, that I'd had a taste of it. There was
> a life out there - a different life from the routine of the factory and
> hum-drum things - that I wanted more of. How to get it was the
> problem. Or rather, not the problem. I mean, I knew instinctively
> what I had to do. If I wanted more of the same then I had to write.
> So I sat down and tried to get back into the old routine."

> (Interview in Time Magazine, 1986)

On sitting down to start work on the sequel to <u>Sixteen Sonnets (and other
poems)</u>, Packard was immediately faced with something that he had not
realised: with all the effort that had gone in to preparing the book, he had
not actually written an original word for many months. Sessions with
Dawson at his office - followed by long sessions at home alone, or in
discussion with Walker - were focused on re-work after re-work; his mind
was concerned only with honing that which he had already produced,
there was no room for original thought. After such an effort over a
considerable period, Charles had simply forgotten where to begin.

> "It was as if I'd never written a word in my life. I felt as helpless
> as young Mark trying to come to terms with simply how to hold a
> pencil! Oh I tried various things; read books about "How to
> Write", and followed their little tips on subjects, spontaneous
> writing, free verse - the works. All I could produce was garbage."

(Interview in The Sunday Times, 1973)

What Packard had also forgotten was his assertion from a few years earlier that he never considered poetry to be where his talent lay. Two things - the difficulties with <u>Pieces of Eight</u> and the recent success of the volume of verse - had successfully masked the fact that it was indeed prose where he would be most at home.

George Walker was a regular at the Packards' house at this time. Ever since the breakdown of his marriage in 1957, he had been trying to get his life back in order. His wife, Eunice, had taken their young daughter away to Scotland where she had a sister who had offered to put them up. After a few months, George had lost touch, and had been in a desperate state on more than one occasion. His friendship with Packard had succeeded to their mutual advantage: it had given Charles a crutch at the times he had needed one the most, and it offered George a diversion from his own problems.

Buoyed by the general euphoria surrounding Charles' limited but successful publication, George had begun to feel that all was well in the world again. He changed jobs for the better in mid-1961, going to work as an Administrator in the local bus and coach company. The friendship with Packard blossomed too.

"It was a good time. Charles was a marvellous man when he was on form! A man's man; good to be around. Of course he didn't drink as much then - hardly at all in fact - and was as good a father and husband as he possibly could have been. But I always felt sorry for Mary and the boy. She was an absolute jewel, and he took her for granted."

In August of 1961 Walker, on a sudden impulse, asked Irene Wilson (the barmaid from the "White Hart") to marry him. She refused. The rejection hit him hard; all the forward strides that he had made in recent months seemed suddenly for nothing. Now it was Packard's turn to be supportive.

> "I took him for a drink - though not to the "White Hart"! He was really low. Looked ill. I hadn't realised that he had invested so much in his relationship with the girl. I'd heard a few things, of course - jokes at work mostly; if I'd have known I would have been able to warn him. Anyway, we sat in this pub - the "Lion", I think it was - George drinking and talking, me listening. Quite a turn about! After a while he became quite relaxed, quiet, resigned. He looked as if he'd aged ten years overnight, but was suddenly calmer. He even wanted to talk about my writing."

(Interview with Melvyn Bragg, 1986)

And talk they did. Walker, in his inebriated state, reminded Charles that he had never in the past considered himself a poet - so why should he be acting like one? He wanted to know why he had not considered writing a book and 'getting it over and done with'.

That thought stayed with Packard as they left the pub. Indeed, it remained with him for the rest of that night and the following day. And for many days after that too. Walker visited the house again the following weekend, and though not as vibrant as he had been of late, was less distressed than the last time Packard had seen him.

> "After he left - he came for a cup of tea and stayed for supper, I remember; he sat playing with Mark on the floor for ages, and then went and helped Mary in the kitchen. Anyway, after he left, Mary came down from putting the boy to bed and sat opposite me, quietly staring into the fire. The she said, "I wish we could do something for George". Just that. No ideas, no suggestions. "I wish we could do something for George"."

> (Interview with Melvyn Bragg, 1986)

Mary's wish, echoed deeply by Charles, sat as an idea alongside the one he had been carrying since the evening in the "Lion". Packard would identify that evening, as he sat mediating about his friend and staring into the dying fire, as the moment when the impulse to write <u>Dawn</u> arrived.

> "It was all I could do to help him; the only way to express my gratitude. If I'd had money I would have given it to him; but I didn't, and George was worth something more than money anyway. So I decided to take his advice. After all, listening to him in the past hadn't done me any harm had it? "Why don't you just write a book?" he'd said. So that's what I decided to do. A book for George. That was all I could do, really."

> (Interview with Melvyn Bragg, 1986)

The next day Charles asked Mary to get him some notebooks from the shop while he was at work. He was earnest and thoughtful when he arrived home in the evening; Mary knew that something significant had happened. For that evening, and the evening after that, Charles spent the time after supper sitting in his chair writing, crossing out, and writing again. Mary sat opposite, knitting and tending the fire. It was a picture to be repeated most evenings for the next year.

Chapter Thirteen

DAWN - by Charles Packard

First things first. *Dawn* is a flawed book. It has many imperfections, some so evident that one could - to use an old cliché (and *Dawn* itself has many of them) - drive the proverbial coach and horses through it. It is also a first book; which means, of course, that in many places there is just a little too much of Mr. Charles Packard peeking at us from beneath the thin veneer of the story he is telling. But more of the story later.

Given such reservations, how can I recommend that you should go to the trouble to even consider reading it - because read it you should. As a first novel - even a flawed first novel - there is something in *Dawn* that is magnetic, enthralling, promising. It reads like the work of a man who is stretching his literary wings for the first time, having just awoken from the slumber of his creative cocoon. If nothing else, it may prove to be the interesting initial salvo from a career worth following.

Dawn is essentially a "Domestic' novel. It charts the progress of its hero, George Maxwell, through a difficult and traumatic period in his life as he struggles along the road to self-knowledge. There is nothing particularly original in that, one might argue; or in the rather gritty and earthy nature of the plot's backdrop. After all, it is not that long since *Room at the Top*; and *Look Back in Anger* is recent enough to still reside in our collective literary consciousness. Packard's book does, however, manage to avoid any hint of pretentiousness; and his hero (for in many senses, George Maxwell is indeed a true hero) is devoid of anything which over-complicates his character. If Packard's aim is to represent a 'simple' man struggling with his lot, then Maxwell - his 'Everyman' - is never far short of the mark.

The novel opens just after Maxwell's wife has left him and taken their young child with her. Packard never attaches blame to this circumstance, neither does he attempt an over-long psychological essay into how it has come about. It is, quite simply, 'one of those things'; and while we get much in the way of background, we are never far from the conclusion that neither Maxwell nor his wife are absolutely to blame. This deliberate lack of definition is manifest in the character of Maxwell who starts the story as a confused and lost individual; and as much as we might try to locate the reason for the separation and failure, so we tread the same path that he has trodden.

Given that Maxwell has been cast adrift from his moorings, much in his daily life - and especially those things which (to continue the nautical metaphor) he has used to navigate by - have also let him down. The departure of his wife opens up his world - or, more exactly, opens him up to the World. Thus we see a man sliding, through no apparent fault of his own, into emotional decay. And Packard is deliberate here; there is no blame to be attached to Maxwell, who is beset by a collection of 'one of those things'. When he reaches his lowest ebb, Packard gives us - through the clever motif of Maxwell re-reading his poorly written and clumsy diary - the chance to re-examine the case for ourselves. The only conclusion we can reach is that Maxwell has been desperately unfortunate, and there - but for the grace of God - go us all.

Sombre though it is, the book succeeds in never being totally depressing. And, when - standing on a river bank, in tears and contemplating suicide - something jolts Maxwell into believing that there is something worth fighting for (namely himself), Packard succeeds in bringing a lump to our throats. From that moment we are out of our seats and rooting our Champion on.

The vehicle for Maxwell's self-discovery is his role in a dispute at the factory where he works. Having never been a militant or political animal, local conflicts of this kind had always passed him by. This time however, the dispute centres around the owners of the Factory wishing to sack a key machinist for taking three days unauthorised leave - during a critical drive to meet a significant export order - to tend his wife who has suddenly fallen dangerously ill.

Maxwell, who does not know the machinist particularly well, sees all too clearly through his own experience the importance of his wife; and although not well educated, he has enough common sense to appreciate his employer's point of view as well. There are messages here about principles and values, and what we should regard as important in life; there are elements of the David and Goliath struggle too, and - at times - Packard struggles to keep his head above trite sentimentality and hogwash.

Although Packard leaves us with a positive message, he is prudent enough never to suggest that there is a pot of gold at the end of

George Maxwell's rainbow - something, he makes clear, none of us should expect.

Frank Wilson

-*-

He stared at the door. He was close to it now, his nose no more than six inches from it. He could see the grain of the wood beneath the green gloss paint. In the past he had seen this door only from the end of the corridor. It was a dark shape, beyond Miss Trowbridge's desk, like a castle beyond a moat.

And now he was there, close enough to touch it. He looked down and watched his hand, clenched as a fist, rise from his waist and pause before the raised drawbridge. Looking up again, through the mottled glass, he could see shapes, dark and disfigured. In front of an oblong of light, one shape, non-rectangular, moved awkwardly, its grace distorted by the opaque pane.

Silverman. He had seen him from a distance, when he occasionally walked the floor. Or in the car park as he made his way to that large black car, later to sweep past on his way through the gates. And he had heard him too, addressing meetings; a far-off figure in a dark suit, raised on a platform, face half-hidden by a megaphone, or by shadow, or by sheaves of waving paper.

And now. And now.

While he was not watching it, his hand moved of its own volition. The shape - Silverman - froze at the sound. Knock. Knock. It was too late. He could not go back. And what was there to go back to; the river bank?

'Come.'

He was unable to move. He had come this far - past Miss Trowbridge's desk; past the solitary plant on its solitary stand; past the bright red fire extinguisher; beneath the bright fluorescent light - to be greeted by a distorted shape and a disembodied voice.

'Come!'

There was no retreat. He turned the handle of the dark green door and pushed, his feet leaden. The glass swung away to reveal the oblongs beyond in all their straight-edged glory. And Silverman at the window.

'Maxwell, is it? Come in then man, come in!'

He had imagined a small man. Small and squat and old. He had imagined a man it would be easy to despise on sight. But Silverman did not fill the image of the

133

man he had seen on the platform, or at distance in the car park. Silverman was a man much like himself; a medium, average kind of a man.

He walked towards the desk; towards the chair that waited for him, four feet from the mahogany altar, angled towards the sun. He walked slowly. Silverman sat down on the other side of the desk, facing him, waiting for him to take the seat.

'Sit down then; there's a good chap!'

He had not known what to expect: a warm smile? a handshake? a cigar and brandy - for he had heard of such men. He looked at the chair, at its green, fading leather, then wiped his hands on the legs of his overalls and sat down. In front of him the oblong of the window, and in front of that Silverman.

And he saw that Silverman had a glass eye.

'Miss Trowbridge said you wanted to see me. I've got a meeting at eleven, so you've not got long. What is you wanted to see me about?'

He looked at Silverman's impassive and inexpressive half-smile, at the face of a man committed to nothing. At that blemished, thwarted face. How old was he? The war perhaps? An accident? No-one had said anything. Perhaps no-one knew. Perhaps no-one had ever been this close. Except Miss Trowbridge. Miss Trowbridge, who had been astonished at his approach; at his request; as if no-one ever asked to see Mr Silverman; as if he had asked to play in goal for England, or to marry the Queen.

'Partridge, Sir.'

The words came together, but the second slowly. He was not an arrogant man, but seldom had cause for deference.

Silverman's half-smile slipped slowly from his face, like cooling fat from a plate.

'I've seen the Union. Matthews has seen the Union men; Taylor and the like. If I'd have known...'

'I'm not from the Union, Sir.'

He had not intended to interrupt, but he had noticed Silverman's hands begin to press the desk; had sensed Silverman's body beginning to rise with his voice; and he did not want to be thrown out. He had not come this far to be thrown out.

'Are you one of his Pals? Is that it? Partridge is not, I gather, a popular man, but I suppose he must have Pals, eh?'

'No, Sir; I wouldn't say as I'm one of his Pals.'

He watched Silverman's hands relax against the desk. He felt the voice falling. He could see in his eye - his one good eye - a spark of interest. He wiped his hands on his legs again and waited. There would be another question.

'So. Maxwell.'

Silverman leant forwards on the desk and pulled a cigarette from a packet, then lit it with a Vesta. He glanced at the desk; he had heard of silver cigarette boxes too, but could see none.

'You're not a Union man. And you're not one of his Pals. But you want to see me about Partridge?'

'Yes.'

'All right then, I'm listening. But make it snappy.'

A puff of blue smoke floated between them, hovering above the desk. It removed the clarity, obscured his vision. Somehow it made things easier, but he still had no idea where to start.

He searched his memory for images of men he could imitate; men who would have revelled in his situation, who would have known what to say, who would have had Silverman eating out of their hands. He could think only of heroes from the cinema, and he knew he could never be Humphrey Bogart or John Wayne. He looked again at Silverman, for the first time just long enough to make eye contact.

'I don't think you can sack him, Sir.'

Silverman smiled again, and eased himself back in his chair. Glancing at the clock on the wall - it was ten fifty - he pulled on his cigarette.

'You don't think I can sack him, eh?'

'No, Sir.'

'Where do you work, Maxwell?'

'Me, Sir?'

He suddenly wondered if he might be told to leave himself, there and then. Out, just like that; just like Partridge.

'Loading bay.'

'Been extra busy recently, haven't you Maxwell?'

'Yes, Sir.'

'All those lorries from Antwerp. The red and gold ones with the funny number plates.'

'They're Belgian, Sir.'

'I know.'

Silverman smiled more broadly, staring at him, waiting for a little more eye contact.

He looked up at the silence, and caught the glass eye. The safe eye. It blinked lifelessly at him.

'And you know about the Belgian order?'

'It's a big one, Sir. I know it's a big one.'

He nodded.

'Now,' Silverman rose, and turned to the window, 'you know where Partridge works, don't you? On one of the presses. And Partridge is an important man for this Belgian order. That press is an important machine. If it doesn't run - if I can't rely on having someone there to run it - then we might not make the order, Maxwell. We might upset the Belgians.' He turned back. 'Do you understand?'

He did. He knew the story of the order; or at least part of it. No-one had told him how important Partridge was; and he knew he didn't want to lose his job too.

'There is another man on that press now, Maxwell. We had to hire another man for that press. And now the machine is running. And we will fill our order. And we will all keep our jobs.'

He watched Silverman bend forward to stub out his cigarette in the small crystal ashtray that sat on the desk.

'Except Partridge.'

There seemed little to do now. Silverman had told him what was happening. Maybe he knew more than anyone else in the factory. Perhaps Silverman had told no-one else about this.

He stood up. Silverman, standing, but still slightly bent at his desk was suddenly looking up at him. He thought of Alan Ladd; how, because he was so small, they made other actors walk in trenches to make him look bigger. Because if you look bigger, if you are taller, then you are 'the man'.

'Do you have a wife, Sir?'

Silverman blinked up at him.

'What?'

'A wife, Sir?'

'Is that any of your business?'

'I have. Or I had. She left me. Not long ago. Ran away up north to stay with her sister. Took our young boy.'

'I'm sorry for you.'

Silverman sat down, but *he* remained standing; ready to walk to the door at a moment's notice; ready to run if he had too. But he wanted his moment, to be the man, just once. Alan Ladd, dark and brooding in 'Shane' waited for him.

'I don't know why, but she went. I came to work the day she left me, and the day after that; and every day since then. I might not have done. I might have been like Partridge. And you might have sacked me.'

He looked at the man with the desk, and the crystal ashtray, and the glass eye. Silverman said nothing.

'I went to the river on Sunday. The meadow just below the weir. There's a small bridge there, and I stood on it, looking down into the water rushing by. I can't swim, you see, Sir. And I thought I might just... But I didn't, Sir. Because something stopped me. And do you know what that was, Sir?'

It was his question. The one real question he was allowed. He was Perry Mason defending his greatest case. He was Shane waiting to draw, his finger poised over the trigger.

Silverman drew.

'No, Maxwell, I don't.'

'Partridge, Sir.'

'Partridge?! In Heaven's name, why?'

'Because I thought if he got the sack, then he might just do the same thing as me. He might go down to the meadow. He might stand on that bridge. And he might not have anything to stop him. Or anyone to try and save.'

He turned and began to walk to the door, waiting for Silverman to say something, to call him back, to tell him to leave the factory, to jump off the bridge.

Hearing nothing. he stopped and looked back. Silverman was watching him, intently.

'You see, Sir; if I'd had to skive off work for three days to stop my wife from leaving me, I'd have done it. And if she'd still been with me, and had been taken ill, I'd have skived off then too, Sir, just like Partridge. I know the job's important, and I know the Belgium thing is important too; but I love my wife, Sir, and that's more important. Which is why I wondered if you had a wife, Sir. That's all.'

He had his hand on the door handle before Silverman spoke.

'Maxwell.'

There was the half-smile on Silverman's face, but it was sadder than before.

'To answer your question; yes, I do have a wife.'

'Good, Sir; I'm pleased for you.'

His left foot had crossed the threshold when he heard Silverman's last words.

'Thank you for coming to see me, Maxwell. Would you ask Miss Trowbridge to pop in on your way past.'

But Miss Trowbridge was already in motion between her desk and the office, and must have heard in disbelief Silverman's words. She looked at him askance as he walked away: he was Perry Mason leaving the empty courtroom; he was Alan Ladd riding into the sunset.

Chapter Fourteen

For him, Foyle's had once been a daunting place; a place where the size, the variety, the sheer volume of books - even, if he were honest with himself, the ornate old trellis-work lift - had actually taken his breath away. This was a reaction - very much a young person's reaction, bereft of experience - which Mark had shared with many of his then contemporaries: green students who spoke of the place in hushed tones and with a reverence that almost brought tears to their eyes.

They had all ignored - as he himself had ignored - the difficulty of finding things amid the plethora of shelves and the apparently indiscriminate (or at least mystic!) way in which subjects were sectioned and books sorted. The consequential and almost religious wandering through the wisdom-laden shelves - like lost souls in an oasis of books! - was part of the experience of the place: what did it matter if it took hours to find what you were looking for, or if you emerged on to Charing Cross Road shell-shocked or traumatised by the experience? Perhaps if you didn't, then you had probably failed in some profound sense.

Mark had, since those novice days, discovered that the passing of time not only bought wisdom but also abstinence. The need to visit the bookshop was removed; he had ceased to be a student; he had ceased to need the buzz that Foyle's - like some addictive drug - had often induced. That particular Holy Grail - the quest for knowledge, experience, 'life!' - had, within a very few weeks, been replaced by something other. Or, as it seemed in his own case, had been taken away altogether and replaced by nothing of much merit. It was something perhaps he might have been warned about. So many had trodden that selfsame path that it might have been reasonable to expect danger signs posted at significant places - about the bookshop seemed as valid as anywhere! - to indicate that there was a fall of some indeterminate nature soon to be experienced.

It was, he might have argued, a Father's responsibility to take his juvenile son aside and explain one or two things about 'the Ways of the World'. He could not recall such occasions; indeed, thinking of moments when they simply sat and talked was difficult enough. There were mitigating circumstances; things which, if taken in his father's defence, exonerated much of the blame when facing a charge of wilful mis-information. In the first instance, his Father had never experienced the traumas and delights of sophisticated degree-level education, so the disappointments borne from the transition out of such a rarefied and unique environment were not available to share. In the second, Charles Packard was too busy making his own way in the world - unearthing his own discoveries - to have time to divest his ever-growing vault of wisdom on his son. This, of course, warranted the bringing of a charge other than that of mis-information.

In Mark's case, the specific instance that made manifest the general 'let down' (for that was exactly how it felt, much like being told that Father Christmas did not actually exist, or that Rock Hudson was gay) came two years after he had left University and was partially immersed in his new 'professional' career. He had needed to find some reference material on the abolition of Slavery and, by a choice more automatic than conscious, had decided Foyle's could be the only possible place to satisfy that need. The disappointment of the experience - despite his eventual success in locating suitable books - had been sudden and profound, and the emotion had been one more of relief than triumph.

Pausing once again on the threshold of the History section - the very place which had once represented the verge of Nirvana! - Mark felt his presence there to be more an admission of defeat than celebration of victory, something that should not be revelled in but rather endured and undertaken as speedily as possible. Three floors below, he had left Julia to wander through Fiction - 'rummage' had been her word, as if she were pawing through a sale box in Harrod's - whist he, eschewing the lift for the stairs, made his way heavenward, his quest specifically directed at reference material on Neville Chamberlain.

It was mid-week and quiet. The lower floors were always the busier, mainly with Tourists who, as if on ancient pilgrimages, had Foyle's on their list of 'Things to Do' in London. Few made it beyond the popular paperbacks, except perhaps to transgress into Classical literature or Global travel.

"I went there once," Beatrice had said, when quizzed about her love of 'great' literature, "but couldn't stand the place. Too many books!" She had mis-remembered, she confessed later, owning up to an equally unsatisfactory visit to lend his father moral support during an early book-signing adventure.

With the History department came something of an oasis in the expanse of both furtive and furious bustling and browsing. Perhaps, as a direct consequence of this, there also came a restriction on floor space, with shelves towering ever closer together. Mark wondered if each department secretly tried to out do the other by having the maximum number of books on display, and that reducing aisle space - along with other tactics like stacking books so high that half of them were out of reach - was specifically designed to achieve this.

The upper floors also added an extra subliminal dimension to the place; here, the shop's labyrinthine nature actually took physical form, laying traps for the unsuspecting. Mark wondered, as he crossed the threshold only to pause again before a small, bi-directional sign - '<= Modern - Pre-Twentieth Century =>' - if, in those formative years, he might have regarded chasing his own shadow as part of the 'mystical'. Experience - both recent and past - had given him some level of expertise in terms of navigation, yet not enough to prevent him, on following the direction for the 'Modern', walking straight into a dead end at his first deviation from the main path.

It was ironic that he should find himself face to face with volumes covering recent Middle Eastern history, the word 'Kuwait' - with all its present connotations - leaping into his line of vision. Resisting a very limited inclination to dally here, he retraced his steps, acquainting himself once again with the hand-written signs.

"Can I help you?"

A young male assistant - still hard at work on both his spots and his personality - peered at him bookishly from behind glasses that looked old, unfashionable and cheap; which, Mark knew, meant that they were probably the opposite of all three. Knowing that, he smiled to himself; it was, he found, a strange comfort that his extra years had given him something invaluable - that particular bequest of time, like part of a bargain struck on one's behalf and beyond one's control. There was even something malicious in Mark's smile, as if he held a secret that the young man - probably still only a student - would be forced to learn quite painfully in the immediate future, and on his own too. He might have taken the role of signpost himself here of course, and cried out 'Look around you! Look to the future! What do you see!', but the enlightenment of his fellow man on such an intimate level was not something he was particularly keen on. In addition to which, he was not a little put out by such a youth asking him if he needed direction in the History section!

"I'm OK. Thanks."

Of course locating Chamberlain - in the historical sense - was not a problem. His studies had given him such a breadth of exposure to the past (a breadth made even more impressive by his passion for the subject) that Mark already had a skeleton of knowledge which prevented him from coming to his subject cold. Chamberlain, christened Arthur

Neville, was the famous Son of a famous Father; a man who completed the family's transition from Liberal to Conservative, and who, as Prime Minister of the National Government (1937-40), chased appeasement until it led to war.

Mark knew (as he stood before an eight foot high row of shelves, allowing his eyes to methodically scan spines of various heights and thicknesses) that it was a little more than the bare facts he needed. If he was to make a meaningful impact with his review, then he needed to ensure he knew all the historical facts that were being represented in the book under his particular microscope; for him, the accuracy of the interpretation would always be more important than the quality of the writing. Mark caught a glimpse of the bookish assistant as he passed the end of his cul-de-sac, a young lady in tow.

"The blind leading the blind", he thought.

He lighted upon his prey two shelves from the bottom; an inconvenient height where bending down from the waist was out of the question. His memory suggested that, during his own far off student days, he would almost certainly had either knelt or squatted on the floor, but such positions were no longer viable options for him. It was, Mark reasoned, not only a question of logic - he was wearing pale trousers that were prone to staining at the slightest provocation - but also one of dignity, and so he resorted to a kind of uncomfortable crouch with his knees severely bent and the bulk of his weight transferred through tense quadrupeds.

Not only had Mark been unprepared for this unnatural physical position, he was also discomforted by the small selection on which he was forced to focus. The Wallace he was reviewing immediately caught his eye, sitting boldly in its dark blue jacket among its peers; indeed, so proudly did it rest there that in an Amateur's search for the most authoritative volume it might well have been the first choice on the basis of some strange qualitative transference based upon nothing more than image and size. This was not the impression he had been seeking; quite the reverse in fact: he had been expecting to find others that would instantly appear to be the favourites for that particular prize.

But it was worse than that too. Even if he were to disregard that important first impression, he was faced with a collection where each appeared to boast - in various ways - that they should be considered as his prime source of knowledge and the repository of 'the truth'. The titles of the books - 'Neville Chamberlain', 'The Life of Neville Chamberlain' - seemed basic and fundamental (indeed, how could a title be less minimalist than simply the person's name?) yet each potentially belied the deduction that they could therefore be nothing other than the truth.

He had become wary of 'authorised' biographies, finding that many presented an approved and sanitised version of events; books that were destined to promote a particular slant, or to be dominated by some form of vested interest. He was even more cautious of auto-biographies, because nowhere could the vested interest be more to the fore! His Aunt's words - and her caution in respect of 'balance' - echoed suddenly back to him. He shivered at a spasm in his legs - the pain coinciding with a realisation that he too was engaged in the production of such a work: that the book about his Father was - quite profoundly - an 'authorised' undertaking, and that, in the absence of his Father - and because of his own presence in the history - he was, in may respects, very close to the parallel writing of his own autobiography.

He pulled at one of the volumes in front of him and turned it over in his hand. On the back cover there was a picture of the biographer, a few notices of critical acclaim - '...the definitive biography...' - and a summary of the Historian's pedigree. Mark flicked to the contents page and saw listed there a series of chapters, each titled and with the respective years covered noted in brackets: 'Berchtesgaden (1938)'. It was similar with the other books too: '...an unsurpassed account...'; '...a seminal work...'; 'Compromise and Capitulation (1936-1938)'. He had not expected to find himself confused in such a manner. Despite his experience, the years of reading and research, he found himself wanting to find something other than this. Perhaps it was his newness to biographical reviewing that inclined him to be seeking the impossible - a jacket that offered 'The True Story' and chapters that simply promised '1937', '1938'. Fiction - for it seemed that he was in danger of uncovering little more than that - was something else indeed!

There was, of course, a question Mark - as author - would be facing soon enough himself: how would he choose to title the sub-divisions of his Father's life? He had given little thought to the structure of the book, deciding on no more than a basic framework which offered itself as self-evident logic. He was, to a certain extent, obliged to follow the signposts and milestones already laid down by his subject: he had the works of Charles Packard by which to navigate, and his subject's affairs and relationships with which to chart them. But even so, would '1963' be sufficient for the title of a chapter - assuming there would be chapters - or would he need to be more elaborate or expansive? It seemed (there was the pain in his thighs again and he found the shelves blurring slightly in a semi-focused vision) that such a simple choice - indeed, that fact that there was a choice to be made at all - was something other than history, a creative activity for which he had not been trained and for which he was unquestionably not prepared.

"Didn't they have anything?"

Julia had seen Mark almost immediately on his reappearance on the Ground Floor. She had caught sight of him - glancing up from her search - over the banks of low shelving, as he paused at the exit from the stairwell, his brow furrowed slightly, scanning the store for her. She had watched him steadily from the moment he acknowledged her wave to his arrival at her side. He was empty-handed.

The wave had annoyed him. Despite the fact that there seemed even more people milling about compared when he left her a few minutes previously, he had been confident that he would quickly find her on his own. After all, he had significant experience of hunting Julia out in shops, and simply because they were now in Foyle's was no excuse for her to indulge in a theatrical - not to say, public - demonstration of her whereabouts. That she had watched him - as perhaps others had also watched him, their attention caught by her gesture - was galling too. There was little chance that, having settled on her location, he would fail to make it across twenty or thirty yards of shop floor; yet she insisted on using her gaze as if it were some kind of homing beacon, drawing him magnetically to her. For a moment, as he walked towards her, he considered a deviation, breaking from the obvious route to indulge in a little off-piste browsing, but finding nothing that would present a credible excuse, completed the pre-destined manoeuvre.

He glanced down at his hands on hearing her words. She had delivered them in innocence, a slight, off-the-cuff remark with the aim of nothing more than welcoming him back. He could still feel the tension in his thighs, and the sense of disappointment he harboured in relation to his visit upstairs - if, indeed, disappointment were the correct word - was not something that allowed him to easily absorb light remarks of this nature.

"Apparently not."

Julia offered him a slight smile of condolence, but he was not prepared to be bought off quite so easily.

"Though it would be more accurate to say that they didn't have what I was looking for, rather than them not having anything at all."

She said nothing, turning to re-address her own search.

"Will you be long? This place gives me a headache."

"No, not long," she offered him the small pile of books she held in the crook of her left arm. "Hold these for me will you?"

He glanced down at the collection of which he suddenly had custody, rotating them in his hands to view the spines. The cover of the uppermost suggested itself as little more than a pot-boiler of some kind, and its title - 'Sicilian Summer' - forced him to adjust his gaze away from the spine to confirm that impression. A raven-haired lovely, so obviously designated to suggest a stunningly attractive yet vulnerable heroine, stared sadly back at him; an image, he guessed, to promise that somewhere within its pages, the book might offer a Universal dream for its female readers to buy-in to. It was not Mills and Boon - it was far too thick for that - yet Mark was comfortable that he was justified in condemning it instantly.

The other two books seemed to him strangely akin to 'Sicilian Summer'. He knew of Jeffrey Archer, of course, and found himself objecting to him on principle rather than because of the content of his books. It was not his politics that was the problem - after all, Mark was a fair shade of blue himself - but rather that he had allowed 'Cain and Abel' to be produced as a Hollywood mini-series on television. Mark sided with Archer in terms of philosophy well enough (in spite of his Father's background) but he was unable to forget - or forgive - television's turgid interpretation of that fictional history.

He looked up and across the shop. On a wall not that far from him, a poster advertising the National Theatre's production of 'Hamlet' stared back, the image of the ghost intermittently blotted out by passing shoppers like an irregular strobe.

The name Atwood rang some kind of bell within him, though he was uncertain why. Perhaps it was an alliterative association with Attlee that confused him - and Attlee because of Chamberlain. He lifted 'The Robber Bride' to the top of the pile to offer it his consideration. On the front cover, dark and mysterious, was a mask with the eye-slits cut out to reveal intense pupils beyond, as if the publishers were trying to convey more than just the picture. Beyond the cover - appropriately stiff, though strangely so for a paperback - the equally dark and mysterious face of a woman stared back at him. She was, of course, too dark, and too mysterious; her eyes too wide to bear any resemblance to a real person.

Mark looked up. Julia had moved on a little. Her collection annoyed him. He glanced back at it, deciding which of the three he should display at the head of the pile in order to convey as strongly as he was able that the books did not actually belong to him. He chose 'Twelve Red Herrings' then caught Julia up.

"Isn't this enough?"

She looked up at him. He saw how totally unlike either of the women on the cover of the novels she was, and how, if there were something within those books to which she aspired, she would undoubtedly be disappointed.

"I want to get something for Laura. Won't be a minute."

They were nearer the front of the shop now. Outside Mark saw a black cab waiting in the traffic, its passenger - a woman - looking towards the shop. Even though the fare looked nothing like Maxine, Mark found himself recalling an image - the small frame, her glasses, that shock of short red hair - and wondered what it might be like shopping for books with her.

He looked down again, suddenly contemptuous of Julia's choice; of the rancid, second-rate things he held in his hand; things that bore no relation to the real world. The house in Marylebone had bookcases - he had seen but not studied them - and he was certain that the editions he would find there would reflect the real world, the world he existed in, and not representations of some fictional fantasy land where all men looked stunning in tight swimming trunks and women had breasts from which one could ski jump.

"Finished!"

Julia's voice carried a note of triumph that belied her wary expression.

Mark looked away from the window and at the final book - by someone called 'Colette' - now in Julia's hand. She pulled the others away from him.

"Now I'll pay for these and we can go."

"I don't know what you see in this crap."

She stopped and looked at him.

"Is your headache really bad?"

"Sorry?"

"Your headache? You said you had one. Is it really bad? Why don't you wait outside?"

"No, I'm fine. Really."

He followed her to a small booth nearby, within which - secured by parallel bars inset in a glass frame - an Assistant waited. It was the bookish Young Man from the History section. He smiled as Julia handed over her books, calculating the total price by considering each in turn.

There was an equanimity - or abstraction, Mark could not tell which - in the way the youth handled the books. Mark had assumed that the other had held some affinity with History, that his place in the History section was ordained by preference, or inkling; but here he was - the person who had actually offered to help him out! - now standing in a small Ground Floor cubicle, seemingly at home dealing with books from a completely different sphere.

"Did you find what you were looking for?"

Mark looked up. The Young Man was staring at him.

"Sorry?"

"Upstairs. Did you find what you were looking for?"

"Yes; thanks." Mark offered an uncertain smile, and the man completed processing Julia's transaction.

"You said they didn't have what you wanted."

They were walking towards the exit, Mark leading, Julia talking to him from behind his back.

"I know," he said, half turning his head to make sure she heard, but not wishing to compromise his escape.

"So why did you tell that young chap you had?"

It was a question for which Mark had no logical answer, only a pragmatic one.

"Sometimes you have to lie."

He reached the door and pulled it open, pausing to allow Julia to leave before him. But she was not instantly there. He looked back into the shop. She stood, completely still, about ten feet away from him. There was a pained expression on her face, and the newly acquired white and brown carrier bag she held in her hand, hung limply at her side.

"Do you want a coffee?"

"Sorry?" She was with him almost on the instant, the pause so brief that he had quite missed any significance it may have carried. As he stood holding the door, he noticed - somewhat blurred and indistinct - the reflection of his jacket in the window.

"Coffee? Perhaps down Old Compton Street or something."

"No, I'm not in the mood. And it's getting on. Shall we go home?"

Mark waited until she was outside, released his grasp on the door then checked his watch. He wondered what sort of 'mood' Julia might be in that dictated at eleven thirty in the morning the need to be 'getting on'. Checking his reflection one more time, he turned and walked after her.

Chapter Fifteen

The publication of <u>Dawn</u> failed to bring any immediate change in the Packards' domestic circumstances. Charles, who had harboured naive hopes of being shot to stardom on the back of his novel, was to be sorely disappointed. There was little fuss made and, apart from the review by Frank Wilson, the only tangible sign that something had happened was the evidence offered by a few copies in local bookstores.

At work, Charles' colleagues greeted the news with nothing short of distrust. Those who worked with him at arms' length, could only regard the publication as something to distance Charles even further from them. Owing to his interest in things other than football and horse racing, he was already beginning to be seen as 'not quite one of us', and now there was additional evidence to support that prejudice.

> "The Management were, of course, deeply mistrusting. I don't think they could make out exactly what I was "up to". They seemed uncertain where to be most upset: was I likely to hand in my notice instantly and walk out, or was I setting myself up as some management-bashing Commie agitator? There was a strange scene in the Personnel Director's office where he seemed to be trying both to persuade me to stay as well as force me to leave!"

> (Interview with David Frost, 1984)

George Walker had warned Charles that his return to work - 'once word had got out' - would not be easy. Packard, immediately buoyed by his publishing success and yet to feel the disappointment of anti-climax, had been ready to march in to his Manager's office and hand in his notice, but Walker had successfully cautioned against this.

"It wasn't in the bag yet. And if the book failed, if it didn't sell, what would they have done then?"

Consequently Charles persuaded his employers that the book had been something he had been working on for a long time and that it bore no relation to his experience with them. He even cited an anonymous friend and a fictitious company in Birmingham - 'Harriman's Ltd.' - as the source for his story. He also made them believe that, having written <u>Dawn</u>, he had exhausted his literary ambitions.

> "That had been really difficult; standing in that office and attempting to deny the very thing I wanted more than anything else in the whole world. Had there been anyone there who had

read the Sonnets I might have been scuppered. "To have written one book..." etcetera, to paraphrase Oscar Wilde. But I guessed that none of them had, and I guessed right."

(Interview with David Frost, 1984)

-*-

Mark looked across from his desk at the brown oblong now partially hidden behind the easy chair. It had been a warm day and sunlight poured through the window, illuminating the dark green pattern of the chair and throwing a black shadow across part of the papered parcel.

They were seeing Laura and Tim for lunch the next day, and Mark had - only a couple of hours previously - tried once again to persuade Julia to let them take the mirror with them. It would be - he had argued - the ideal opportunity to hand it over; they could even check to see if Laura liked it. Perhaps they might offer her the receipt, and allow her the freedom to change it if she wanted.

Julia had listened good-heartedly enough, but he could tell - perhaps because of her smile - that any argument he might choose to put forward would flounder on some unshakeable and sacrosanct feminine logic. At the appropriate time they would take the mirror to Laura's new house and put it up ready for their return from honeymoon - and that was that.

There was a breeze coming through the window, and despite the warmth of the day, Mark shivered. He wanted to smoke. It had been an urge that he had felt on and off for a few days now, but sitting at his desk, working, it had suddenly become particularly strong. He had smoked once, but as an Amateur, never reaching the dizzy heights where nicotine intake could be measured on the scale of 'packets per day'. It had been a brief enough flirtation towards the end of his University days, and - apart from the odd cigar when he was drunk - he had abstained for years. Mark imagined that, like most things one did not truly believe in, identification of cause and effect - the reason he began or the event that stopped him - would always prove impossible, either to divine or to care about. He had discussed smoking once with Julia (she had been a smoker when she met him, but found it easy to give up once she realised that he was not to be converted) but, as with most of their conversations, he could remember little of the detail. When they talked, they seemed often to have a theme - but that was as far as it went.

He picked up one of the transcripts of his Father's few interviews and began leafing through the pages, not attempting to read it, but rather feeling the weight of the words in his hands, content to recognise the

150

odd phrase or sentence that he had already used. He had read many of them in the past or seen them on television (the Bragg interview in 1986 had been his favourite) but it was only now, now he was actually working with what had been said, getting his hands on the raw material as it were, that he had begun to appreciate their real worth. Perhaps his Father's life had been ordinary (something he had argued himself a long time ago but which now he would vigorously deny) yet even if it had, even if someone managed to persuade him of this, then his work - his words - proved that there was something else that most certainly was not ordinary.

Outside, two birds darted in turn between the trees in the front garden. With the window open he could hear the continuous drone of traffic from the nearby arteries of the city; a sound punctuated by the chirping of the birds.

On his desk was a small photograph frame, ornate and silver. It had been given to him - 'on loan' - by Beatrice who, possessive of things that were important to her (even the smallest and the most abstract) had offered him the use of it for the study. Smiling up out of the frame - and leaning against one of the very trees which now hosted the darting wildlife outside - Julia in a bright orange summer dress. He leant forwards slightly, trying to examine the detail in the face that stared back at him. It was an action and an investigation not motivated by fondness or recognition, but undertaken as if he were looking for something, engaged in a search for what had been lost like an archaeologist hunting forgotten treasures.

-*-

During the first two or three weeks after the publication of <u>Dawn</u>, Charles made numerous telephone calls to his publisher in an attempt to discover how well the book was selling. Dawson, the publisher of <u>Sixteen Sonnets (and other poems)</u>, had been persuaded to take Packard as a client once again. However, after fielding the first few of these calls himself and trying to explain that they would have no idea as to the sales volumes until much later, Dawson then used his Secretary to intercept the enquiries. After a while, Charles stopped ringing, preferring to use the evidence of his own eyes as a guide. The day one of the copies of <u>Dawn</u> disappeared from a local book shop provided a brief moment of high excitement.

> "It meant that someone was reading it. That they had actually gone into the shop and paid money! I was still fairly green then, and it took all George's powers of persuasion to lead me away

from the idea that all four shillings and sixpence (or whatever it was) would be coming directly my way!"

(Interview with David Frost, 1984)

Two months after publication, Charles received a letter from Dawson informing him that of the thousand copies distributed thus far, two hundred and seventy-four had been sold. A cheque for thirteen pounds and fourteen shillings was enclosed. Although it was not as much as Packard had hoped in terms of his first royalty cheque, he reconciled himself to the fact that, for the first time in his life, he had been paid for something other than labouring. Returning the complement of many months previously, he invited Walker to dinner, this time providing the wine himself.

The three of them - Charles, Mary and George - had become very much a triumvirate. As had been his experience after the publication of <u>Sixteen Sonnets (and other poems)</u>, Charles was experiencing great difficulty in getting started again, primarily because of his lack of subject. George, who had recognised himself in the Maxwell character, spent more and more time with the Packards. He believed that some kind of precedent had been established and that, through their recent experiences, he and Charles had developed some kind of unshakeable bond.

"Charles was like the brother I'd never had. We had both been low at times, and the other had been the one to rescue the situation. I had never been as desperate as George Maxwell, standing on the bridge over the river, but Charles was perceptive enough to know that such a thing might not be too far away."

At work, things were beginning to improve. The air of disquiet had begun to subside and business was booming. The Management made generous awards during that year's pay round, and, evidently impressed by the apparent diligence with which Charles had resumed his duties, had given him a new job with both more responsibility and more money.

> "Strangely enough, it was the very thing I didn't want. I knew that I could only be happy if I managed to get out, and here they were making it all the more difficult for me. Had I been a weaker character, had I been less convinced of where my destiny lay, then it would have been all too easy to just pack the writing in and settle down into a comfortable and mindless routine."

(Interview with David Frost, 1984)

The extra income from his job - supplemented by the odd cheque from Dawson - saw Packard reaching a state of financial security that was new to him. He had never been the kind of man who was careless with money, and with George on hand to offer advice, began the task of rebuilding the meagre savings which had been decimated in the fiasco with Harriman.

All this while, through the spring and summer of 1963, Mary continued to fill the role of dutiful wife. Mark was growing up a quiet and thoughtful child under his Mother's influence. Moments of intimacy between Mark and his Father were rare however, and it was more often than not the ever-present George who would help with paternal duties if Charles was working late or trying to write.

-*-

Mark pulled a small bundle of photographs from the desk drawer, flicking through them until alighting on the one he was searching for. He leant it against the small silver frame, obliterating the image of Julia.

"I have a problem."

He had been sitting opposite Maxine in a small coffee bar at the northern end of Regent Street. She had slipped out for lunch and had joined him in the lower-level of the cafe. They had exchanged a polite kiss - discrete enough to be passable as platonic friends meeting for lunch - and allowed their hands to touch briefly as she sat down. Mark found such meetings difficult. He appreciated that there was some need for caution, after all - as the presentation dinner where they had first met had proven - the journalistic community in London was not as large as one might have imagined, and it took very little to spark the jungle telegraph. But caution was beginning to feel more and more unnatural, especially considering his ever-present and growing desire for her.

The first coffees and the small club sandwiches that were their accompaniment, saw them play out the preliminaries of the conversation; what had each been doing, where had they been, how was work. It was the latter topic - and a direct question from Maxine - that had led Mark to his statement.

"Oh?" She leant forward slightly across the table, smiling apologetically as she withdrew her hand in response to Mark's advancement of his own.

"The book. I've come to the point where I can remember things, where I think I need to add my version of events."

"So, what's the problem with that? You knew it would happen."
"Of course."

Her eyes sparkled behind her large spectacle frames and he wanted to grab her and kiss her hard until it hurt them both.

"What would Beatrice say? I mean, you usually ask her about these things don't you?"

"Yes, but this is a question of style, of reportage if you like. I need to add my words to the thing, what I think - and what I remember - without mixing it up with fact."

"How do you do that now?"

"The reportage thing?"

She nodded, picking up her espresso.

"I use quotations for my Father; articles, interviews - things that can be authenticated."

"And for others?"

"Reported speech I suppose," he thought of George Walker's words. "Not guaranteed to be accurate in many cases. 'Handed down' if you like. What I say will be accurate of course; I mean how can it be otherwise? But I don't want to vie with my father's words as being the most important in the book."

She smiled again and drained her cup.

"I think you have your answer then. You have to treat yourself as any other witness. QED."

Mark watched her as she checked her watch then rose.

"Sorry, Lovely, got to go."

She leant forward and kissed him on the cheek, close enough to his mouth to allow her tongue to brush his lips.

"Wednesday. Call me."

He found himself staring out of the window. The branches on the trees swung in the breeze and he allowed himself to search for the birds that had been flying there earlier. He could not see them, not could he hear their chirping; the only sound was the London hum punctuated by individual vehicles passing in the road outside.

He allowed his eyes to drop to the small image resting before him: in the foreground a small boy seated in a bright pedal car, and although the picture was in black-and-white, the gleaming newness of the car's paint work was unmistakable. Crouching alongside the car - dressed plainly enough, though not to the detriment of the air of brilliance that hung about her too - a woman with a pretty smile and long flowing hair. Behind them, almost as if he were attempting to retire from the picture somehow, a tall, fairly slight man, dressed in a tweed jacket, collar and tie, his hair already beginning to show signs that it was on the retreat.

-*-

"It's one of the first things I can remember. It had been a bright Summer's day and we had gone for a day trip to Margate, which was a real treat. Father didn't have a car - couldn't drive at that point - so we were reliant on Uncle George (as I called him then) for such expeditions. I was walking with Mother along the promenade when Uncle George suddenly appeared in front of us. It was as if he'd appeared by magic. And there, in front of him, was a bright red pedal car!"

George Walker's present for the 5-year-old Mark was the most expressive gesture he ever made towards the boy. The trip to Margate had been Walker's idea, and, although he had been invited, Charles had declined, preferring instead to remain at home working on a new idea he'd professed to having. So the party for three - armed with the new camera that Charles had bought Mary for her birthday - spent the day at the seaside. Walker's present came as a surprise for Mary too who, almost as overwhelmed as her son, at least had the presence of mind to request a passer-by capture the moment for them on film.

"In a way, that day marked the high point in the general state of affairs. It also signalled the beginning of the decline. When we returned home, we found Charles sitting in the chair by the fire. All around him on the floor were shreds of paper. Flames were licking at some embers in the grate, and it was evident that he had been feeding it with some of his discarded efforts. And there was the smell of drink too. I don't know which hit me first; seeing the paper, or smelling the booze."

Packard's efforts had, throughout the day, become less and less fruitful. He had been struggling with making something of a fledgeling new idea, but to no avail.

> "The harder I tried to chase it, the further it ran from me. It got to the point where I didn't even know what I was trying to do. About mid-day I went to the pub, had a couple of pints and brought some bottles back to the house. I suppose I'd been drinking on-and-off all afternoon."

> (Interview with Melvyn Bragg, 1986)

Not only did Charles tear up his efforts from that day, he also condemned to the fire his first drafts for <u>Sixteen Sonnets (and other poems)</u>; it was only good fortune that prevented him from laying his hands on the originals of <u>Pieces of Eight</u> and burning them too.

Having had such a disastrous day and being the worst for drink, seeing his family and his best friend returning in buoyant mood was enough to send Packard over the edge. His frustration at his inability to write, which had been growing over the previous few weeks, suddenly had vent.

> "It was the little red car that did it; don't ask me why. I flipped. It was all Mary could do to get Mark safely out of the room and away to bed. Poor George bore the brunt of it. I asked him what the fucking hell he was doing buying my son presents; didn't he think that I was father enough to do those things for the boy? Things like that. I'd a poker handy to stir the flames, and I remember picking it up and crashing it down on that bright red car."

(Interview with Melvyn Bragg, 1986)

That one act of violence broke the spell and Packard collapsed back into his chair. Walker, who had momentarily feared for his own safety, managed to calm his friend down, persuading him to drink some tea and eat some bread, eventually getting him to go up to Mary who - on hearing the crash of the poker - had remained in Mark's bedroom. The next day Charles tried his best to repair the damage done to the pedal car, but it was impossible to remove all traces of the dent, the top coat of paint having been damaged irreparably.

It was not only the car that suffered from that day's events. Gradually, as he struggled with what seemed a fading ambition, Charles became ever more wrapped up in his internal problems. He became less warm towards George whose visits to the house began to lose their frequency. Nothing changed in respect of Packard's attitude to Mary. He had taken to sitting on the floor at her feet during the latter part of the evening, and resting his head against her knees as they listened to the radio. If the house was quiet and Mary was knitting, Charles would stare at the fire, hypnotised by the rhythmic clicking of her needles and the flames and sparks disappearing up the chimney.

For his part, Walker did not welcome the change.

"It was plain enough that Charles was going through some kind of crisis. After the affair with the car, well, I kind of backed off. But I didn't want to lose touch. They were all special to me; had become my own family in a way, and I couldn't afford to lose them."

George would occasionally meet Mary in the park where he would play with Mark, and ask her about Charles. They would return to the house together sometimes, but Packard, though still polite to his oldest friend, was cooler towards him.

Towards the end of October, Charles received a letter from a woman, Stella Thomas. She explained that she was a member of a local writing group, unofficially known as 'The Sunday Scribblers' though advertising themselves in the local press as 'The Meade Road Writers'. She had read Sixteen Sonnets (and other poems) two years earlier, and had been in the audience at one of Charles' first readings. She had also recently read Dawn and was so impressed by both that she wondered if Charles might consider attending a meeting of their group as a guest speaker.

The news so buoyed Packard that he immediately invited George to go out for a drink with him to celebrate.

> "It had been so completely unexpected, you see. Just as I thought that, well, maybe I'd got it all wrong; that perhaps I was destined for a life in a factory or something, here was a little glimpse - a little proof, if you like - that there was still something to shoot for. Drinking with George had been an automatic reaction. I'd been completely shitty towards him over the previous couple of months - ever since that thing with Mark's car - but I didn't really see it. Mind you, George could. We sat in the pub for ages, me talking mostly, him curled up tight like a spring. It wasn't until we'd had four or five pints that we'd both relaxed enough to bury the hatchet."

> (Interview with Melvyn Bragg, 1986)

The meeting at Meade Road - Stella's home - was scheduled for the 5th of November. Packard invited Walker along, for moral support, but George was already committed to helping out at his firms' firework party so could not attend. Charles worked hard in preparation. Having read some of his poems aloud, he had assumed that reading prose would be as easy; however, his first dry run proved this would not be the case, and for three successive nights prior to the fifth, Packard spent at least some portion of the evening reading to Mary in their front room, using her opinion as his sounding board.

Guy Fawkes' night proved to be cold and blustery. Packard made his way along Meade Road with his collar high against his neck, his cold hand clutching a copy of Dawn and a small card file containing scraps of other things he had managed to put together. Approaching the street from the wrong end, he saw several people apparently disappearing into the same house further up the road. Consequently, when he eventually knocked at number seven, he expected to find himself confronted with dozens of people. There were, in fact, five; the majority of the pedestrians he had seen were attending a fireworks party in the house next door.

> "I was immediately struck by Stella. Perhaps it was the comparison with the other members of the group - either sad or elderly individuals - that helped. She was not an especially attractive woman, I would say. But the important thing for me was that here was a woman - a passable, fair woman - with whom I had an assumed and shared interest. The other members of the group were all pleasant enough; indeed, they said some nice things about my work - but the important person there was Stella. During the reading - which was horribly difficult - I had to focus on something, and that something could only be her."

(Interview with Melvyn Bragg, 1986)

The first tangible result of the reading was that the other members of the 'Meade Writing Group' promised to buy Packard's book. They had, they told him, enjoyed his reading and had been impressed by his style. Later in the week, as if to test them out, Charles asked Mary to visit the two local book shops to see if they still had copies of <u>Dawn</u>. She reported that only one remained.

Three days later, Packard received another letter from Stella. It thanked him for his reading which, she said, 'they had all found stimulating', and asked if he would like to attend their next session. She outlined the format of the meetings and suggested that, as a published novelist and poet, his experience would be of great value to them all. It was flattery plain and simple, but it worked. Indeed, both Mary and George (who was back in favour again) added their weight to Stella's request. He had, they said, been a different man since the reading, and if the group could help to stimulate his writing and overcome his present block, then he should make all efforts to attend.

The next day, Packard wrote his reply to Stella, promising to see her in three weeks at the next meeting. The die was cast.

Chapter Sixteen

Even though he had only met him a few times, Mark had taken an early dislike to Tim that was proving difficult to shake. Having graduated from Oxford and now making his way in the world as a relatively junior barrister, Tim had cultivated all the necessary attitudes and opinions essential for his job. Mark wondered - as he sat across the table from him in the restaurant - whether or not there had been a time when Tim's accent had been a little less pompous and his mannerisms a little less studied. He didn't know enough of his background before Oxford to make any sound judgement on this, although his understanding from Julia was that there had been a period at one of the 'top' public schools.

Having been forced to attend such a school himself after his Mother's death (though one considerably down the public school league table in comparison to Tim's, no doubt) he was well aware of the nature of the beast; looking at Tim, it was easy to recall how such an institution might mould and shape young men to deliver tailored and neatly pressed Under-Graduates - and later Graduates - ready to take their rightful place in the world. He was grateful that his own school had been more pragmatic in this regard than most: in the vast majority of cases such moulding was carried out more or less unconsciously, almost as a by-product of historical tradition rather than the pre-disposition of the more modern Masters. As such, Mark found unintentional influence easy to both understand and forgive, especially since it had been relatively simple for him to resist such conformity. Whilst vulnerable to some of the influences to which he had been exposed - though in his own mind of course, these were only those to which he chose to be open - he discovered, with some surprise, that his Father had already managed to instil in him a limited range of values which, in certain instances, were wholly incompatible with particular aspects of the more class-focused doctrines he had been taught. Consequently, by the time Mark went up to University, he did so confident that he was without the more obvious trappings of a public school education - such as the accent of which Tim seemed so proud - whilst still retaining in his personal locker a kind of 'mix-and-match' set of values that seemed, to him at least, totally appropriate and far superior to any packaged dogma as boasted by many of his contemporaries.

Mark's personal - though often, not private - assertion that his own set of values were probably the most balanced to be had, brought its own problems, however. During his first few months at College, his dominant characteristic - which he saw as self-confidence - was viewed by others as blatant arrogance; in consequence of this, he was prepared to admit that he found it initially difficult to make friends at anything other than the most superficial level, and his relationships - with both sexes - had, to his chagrin, been less than satisfying. He gave himself credit for being able to recognise this minor short-fall in his character however, and once recognised, undertook an almost ruthless plan to re-address the situation; a plan which required him to take an interest in different social activities where possible, to join different clubs, and to cultivate a new set of people from scratch. Only his devotion to his subject remained constant.

Mark looked up at Tim. He had been intent on his salad and had missed much of what the other had been saying. The words 'wedding' and 'honeymoon' floated into his consciousness from the conversation to his left where Julia and Laura had locked horns over details of the Maid of Honour's dress.

Tim finished speaking and burst into laughter. Mark smiled politely, then flagged down a waiter.

"Another Perrier please. Anyone else?"

His question, and the glance round the table that accompanied it, broke into the other conversation and pulled them all back together.

"Please," said Julia.

"Make that two. Thanks." He watched the waiter walk away, wine cloth draped expertly across his arm. It was details like that one paid for in expensive restaurants.

"How's the salad?"

He turned to Julia, offering almost as evidence, the piece of tomato currently speared to the end of his fork.

"Splendid; very nice. But so it should be, shouldn't it - at these prices?"

She offered him a slightly quizzical look.

"Not used to dining in decent eateries, eh?"

As seemed almost inevitable, Tim punctuated his comment with a short nasal laugh approximating - in Mark's mind, at least - to little more than a snort. He wondered if Tim believed everything he said was funny.

"I wouldn't go that far."

There was the briefest silence, sufficient to allow a change of direction.

"How's work, Mark?"

Laura bore a strong physical resemblance to her sister. She was a little younger and still witness to the very last remnants of youthfulness upon her slightly more rounded face; her eyes offered something of the sparkle about them that he had once seen in Julia - perhaps it was age that took the lustre away. He smiled at her. Despite their similarity, he had never found Laura particularly attractive; there was something in her manner that promised the very opposite of stimulation, as if her purpose in life was to deaden and dull. Tim, waiting for his response, seemed in many respects, the ideal partner.

"Work? You know, compared to Tim here, what I do isn't fit to be called work!"

"Mark!", Julia remonstrated, offering to come to his defence. "How can you say that?"

He was supremely confident in the knowledge that he *could* say such a thing because that was exactly what Laura and Tim felt about his so-called 'work', and that rather than debating the point with them - which, even if the argument could be won, he was convinced they would choose to ignore their defeat - he preferred to pander to what he regarded as their small-minded assumption. He could almost sense Tim swelling in self-admiration.

"Well, things have been rather hectic of late, you know. Big case coming up at the Bailey in a couple of weeks. Helping out our Silk in a murder thing."

"Of course you can't give us any of the details can you?"

"Sorry Old Man; absolutely not. But you'll know the one I mean when you read the papers."

Tim, Mark knew, had a desire for public acclaim.

"Never mind."

The waiter returned, set down the two glasses of Perrier then cleared the empty plates. They were silent until he had finished doing so and departed.

"Won't be long now!" Julia squeezed her sister's arm across the table. "Only another five weeks."

"Five weeks?"

All three looked at Mark, who had been in the process of lifting his glass.

"Sixth of June," Laura smiled back at him.

"It seems like it should be tomorrow or something; after all, we've been talking about it and making preparations for so long."

The image of the mirror, silent, waiting for him in his study came suddenly to him.

"Preparations?" Laura seemed puzzled.

"Mark means arrangements. Hotels, cars; that kind of thing." Julia looked at him quickly. "We were actually thinking of taking some time off ourselves; you know, see you off then take our own holiday."

"How romantic!"

Tim cut Laura's approval short.

"Oh, where to? Hope it's not Venezuela. Wouldn't want to see my in-laws on my honeymoon!" He snorted again, this time with Laura adding a little falsetto backing.

Mark had picked up the thread of the conversation again.

"Maybe Tuscany; it's great in early summer, before it gets too hot. Or the Rockies. Or maybe Iceland. Who knows?"

Laura, missing his sarcasm, winked at him openly.

"Maybe you'll be planning your own honeymoon one of these days, eh?"

He had begun to look away as she spoke, catching an image of her in one of the restaurant's mirrored pillars as she did so. Behind her, now in mid-guffaw, Tim's face appeared almost in profile. Thrown by the fact that from this strangely distorted angle Laura looked identical to her sister, for a second it seemed as if, in Tim, he might almost be looking at himself. He could see Julia there, leaning slightly forwards, holding her glass with that idiosyncratic arrangement of her fingers about its stem, laughing, talking, chiding, cajoling; behind her, changed beyond all recognition, Mark Packard reduced to a buffoon who laughed at his own jokes even when they weren't funny.

"Mark; that last review of yours was a complete flop!"

"Yes, shit wasn't it!"

"Mark; wife's looking awfully frumpy. Shagged that secretary of yours yet?"

"Won't even let me get her a coffee, let alone shag her!"

"Mark; when was the last time you were free to do your own thing?"

"When they cut the cord, Pal; when they cut the cord!"

"Mark. Mark!"

A real voice, Julia's, intruded on his vision. He looked away from the mirror, focusing first on the waiter (servicing another table) as he tried to regain his bearings. There were other voices too; Tim and Laura, engaged in their own discussion. He looked at Julia and smiled.

"You OK?"

"Me?"

"You seemed miles away."

"No," he laughed unconvincingly, "thought I saw someone I knew, that's all."

"Wasn't a ghost?"

"A ghost?"

The idea amused him. There he had been, looking ostensibly into the future, and Julia had assumed an image of the past. He wondered if his vision might not, after all, have something of the spectral about it; people claimed to have déjà vu all the time, though he could not - hand on heart - admit to such himself.

"I don't think so."

Across the table Laura and Tim had reached a lull in their conversation, each looking away from the other and off into the mid-distance of the restaurant. It was a peculiar image. At that instant, they seemed like strangers who had not yet been introduced, having been placed at the same table for the convenience of the restaurant staff rather than by choice. He wondered, considering their dispassionate and solitary gazes, how they had met. Julia had probably unloaded the story on him at some point, and he - with all good sense - had allowed it to float within his consciousness for a very limited period before expelling it with the status of the most basic of trivia.

Julia spoke and, simultaneously, they faced her. Mark watched the transformation with the air of a detached observer, divorcing himself from any emotional tie to the situation playing out before him. Both Laura and Tim had, within a split second, turned, taken each other back into their personal space, and resumed their former postures. It was as if they had let slip - for the briefest of moments - their attachment to each other, and in doing so, had reasserted their independence. Was that a good thing in their case? He suspected not; he suspected that they would be lost without each other.

Mark listened to a few words of the conversation, establishing whether or not he would be needed - or required - to take part in it. Knowing - by his non-participation - that he had gained for himself some kind of detachment from Julia too, he searched for a mirror that might allow him to examine how they - he and Julia - might appear in such a divorced circumstance. He did not expect to find himself with the kind of lost expression he had seen on Tim's face. Indeed, he was confident that he would maintain an air of independence under any circumstance; that, when re-joined with Julia in such a fashion, there would be no change in his demeanour and that people would be unable to ascribe any form of 'need' to him whatsoever. After all, had he not so very recently proved his independence, and would he not be doing so the very next day?

Finding no suitable looking glass (despite subtle attempts to shift in his seat for the purpose) Mark chose to scan the other tables. It was possible that there would be other people in the restaurant having similar thoughts to his own, or - at the very least - who might have been looking his way and who, from their reaction to what they saw - Mark and Julia together, but apart somehow - might give him a clue as to the external view he sought. As with the mirror, his search was fruitless.

He wondered - and this was the horrible thought! - if his vision of the future, his future with Julia, might not be so far off beam. He allowed himself to toy with the idea that Tim had, once upon a time, actually been a regular kind of bloke who, under relentless grinding from Laura, had been transformed into the man before him now. This was a difficult premise to entertain, but one - he was sure - not beyond the realms of possibility. Even now, perhaps, Tim still maintained, secretly hidden within some cavern of his personality, that little gem treasured from his past; a jewel which, once in a while on 'men only' occasions, he would retrieve from the protection of its cellar and allow to shine in natural light. If this were the case - and if Julia and Laura were of the same stock (as they appeared to be of the same mould) - then was it not possible that such a fate might await him?

There would, Mark assumed, cautiously raising his glass, be signs of such a transformation; after all, he had seen little in Julia's personality thus far to suggest that she could be that manipulative - unless that were her precise skill, and she was a truly consummate artist! And in any event, he would certainly be aware - all too painfully! - of changes in himself to allow his metamorphosis to pass unnoticed. Julia glanced towards him as he lowered his glass to the table, moving her hand towards the wine bottle a she did so. He shook his head slightly to decline the unspoken offer and smiled. She smiled back. He watched her hand retreat back across the table and wondered how it was that he had no desire to grab at it and hold it tight. Perhaps he had changed of late, but only by the slightest degree; and if Maxine were anything to go by then he could surely argue that his change (even though this was a theory that he was reluctant to endorse) had, from the point of view of his individuality, been a positive one: insurance, if insurance were needed, against his capitulation.

Chapter Seventeen

"Have you ever been unfaithful?"

Peter had been leaning back in a chair in the sports club bar, looking down through the balcony windows to the court below where two of the club's more experienced squash players were in the middle of a close match. Mark's question made him look round.

"Sorry?"

"You know; played away."

"I thought that's what you said." Peter sacrificed the ongoing game to give his full attention to Mark. "Why do you ask?"

Mark paused, trying to gauge the depth of his friend's interest which seemed - in that he had swung round so readily - to be quite considerable. He wondered what significance this might have, if any.

"Just wondered really. Partly because of the book, my Father. Set me thinking. And there's a guy I know - at the magazine - who was boasting the other day about some conquest or another. Maybe that's what made me think of it." Mark had conjured an image of Congreave in his mind along with the conceit of a vague history to help him deliver the question.

Peter smiled.

"No, then. I can't say I have 'played away' - or that I really want to."

Mark recognised that Peter's position was enviable: he recalled instantly the image of Claire in her too-short squash skirt; the feeling of her body pressed lightly against his own; the glimpse of her breast.

"You've no need, anyway."

"Need?"

"Claire. I mean, she's perfect really, isn't she?"

A slightly quizzical look came to Peter's face.

"Perfect?"

Mark wondered why Peter was now repeating everything he was saying, as if he failed to understand the language he was using.

"You know: attractive, intelligent, vivacious - that kind of stuff."

"Yes."

"So you're a lucky chap, that's all I'm saying. Why should you want to mess around?"

Peter's features eased. He raised his orange juice to his lips, pausing before he drank.

"And so are you."

"Me?"

He watched as Peter finished his drink, placing the empty glass on the table with his usual authoritative and self-confident flourish of which Mark had, in the past, been occasionally jealous. There was no such jealousy now however, and - despite the recent on-court thrashing Peter had dished out to him - Mark felt, if anything, Peter's superior.

"With Julia. Smart, refined, pretty; all those good things. And she's crazy about you, which can't be bad."

It had been a long time - perhaps not since Julia's first visit to Beatrice and Simon - that Mark had received any form of independent critique on her. It sounded odd, as if the words (ordinary in themselves) were taking on an alternative connotation in this present context. He contemplated Julia as 'smart', in both senses of elegance and intelligence. Perhaps Peter had some justification for his analysis, but he was doubtful whether, given more intimate contact, he would have been so ready with his praise.

"So have you?"

The question pulled Mark from his thoughts - thoughts which were taking him further into an examination of Julia in terms of both character and form.

"Have I what?"

"Been unfaithful."

His laughter was instant and unplanned. As he became conscious of it - and of a sudden image of Maxine, naked on her bed - he hoped it had been devoid of any trace of falsehood.

"No, of course not. It was this guy at work."

Mark paused on the verge of quoting Bruce Congreave's name, feeling that he needed, by means of authentication, something concrete to justify his enquiry; after all, he was aware that citing anonymous friends carried a certain danger of guilt by implication. Pausing over Congreave's name however, brought back the evening at the awards ceremony.

"Would Claire, do you think?"

"Have an affair?"

This time it was Peter's turn to laugh, though he did so - Mark judged - with a little less confidence than he might have.

"No! No, I don't think she would. She's not that type to be honest. Oh, I know she seems a bit flighty at times, but that's just show; that's not what she's really like."

Mark wondered exactly how Peter would define 'a bit flighty'. He was convinced that Claire was well aware of the image she portrayed and that, if he were to be blunt, there was little that might be regarded as 'innocent' in the picture she conveyed. He had long since ceased to believe that most things people did were generated from some kind of naiveté, that they simply went with the flow; life was too complex for such abdication, and Claire - in the overt display of her femininity (if he could describe it as such) - was simply another witness proving his view of the world.

Although he had not seen her for a couple of weeks now, he had become all the more convinced that it had indeed been Claire hanging off Congreave's arm at the awards' dinner. He debated whether or not it was more important to prove his theory than refrain from disturbing his friend, especially as his only true means of corroborating his theory - apart from direct confrontation of Claire - was to adopt the 'professional detective' approach and demand of Peter if he knew the whereabouts of his girlfriend on the night in question.

"I thought you said you'd signed up for another one of the ladders."

Mark's deliberations had him coming down on the side of Peter's protection when the latter interrupted him.

"Did I?"

"Well, not to me. But Claire mentioned it; something Julia said I think."

"Right."

"So have you?"

"Signed up?"

Peter nodded.

"Yes. After today's thrashing I need all the practice I can get, don't I!"

They laughed together.

"I didn't see your name on the board; that's all."

"Really? Maybe they've taken it down to sort it out, or something. I've never quite worked out how they look after those things anyway."

"So how's it going?"

Avoiding an immediate answer, Mark waited while Peter checked his watch. They were killing time before one of them made the first move to leave. The game was over, and they had followed it with the ritualistic shower, sandwich, and pint of orange juice. Mark could imagine Peter trying to decide - at a little after three thirty - whether to go back to the office or to treat himself to a short day. Taking the initiative, he rose.

"Shall we?"

-*-

After his first evening with 'The Meade Road Writers', Charles became a regular attendee. On the 3rd of December, the date of the next meeting, the group seemed to have swelled, Stella's house appearing very cramped under the circumstances. All those to whom Charles had read the previous month were there again, along with a number of new faces. These, Stella was to confess later, were the more 'casual' members of the group who had been encouraged to come along and meet their new star.

> "I knew, of course, that the first reading had gone well. The practice with Mary had been invaluable and everyone seemed convinced that I really was some kind of pro. When I arrived at Stella's the second time, well! The house seemed to be packed, people occupying every possible place for sitting down, with one or two even standing. I guess there were probably no more than nine or ten there in reality, but it felt a bit like the Albert Hall!"

> (from 'Writers' Lives', Granada TV, 1986)

Some of the group had attended that December evening on the mistaken assumption that Charles was going to read for them again or hold some form of workshop. During the break, when Stella served (as usual) Custard Cream biscuits as well as tea and coffee, a number attempted to solicit Packard's attention with the explicit aim of getting him to help them with their writing on a one-to-one basis. Without exception, all those who had attended the Fireworks' night meeting had bought and read <u>Dawn</u>.

> "It was surreal, suddenly being a minor celebrity like this. I guess I hadn't really thought about the group; what to expect, I mean. After all, I didn't yet regard myself as anything particularly out of the ordinary. I'd set my sights so high so early, that my expectation of glory, the fame and fortune that would come from being "a Writer" had already been dashed. It was because of this I guess the whole thing took me by surprise."

(from 'Writers' Lives', Granada TV, 1986)

With the exception of the occasionally volunteered comment, Charles kept fairly silent at the December gathering. "There were some people", Stella recalled, "who were particularly disappointed. I think they expected Charlie to be some kind of performing animal. One or two never came back."

Packard had his own agenda as far as 'The Sunday Scribblers' were concerned. Having previously encountered the difficulty of finding a way to start writing again, he saw the group as a means by which he might be stimulated into creativity. With the promise of regular 'literary exercises', the chance to hear other people's work, and the opportunity to talk about the act of writing itself, Charles had no initial ambitions beyond being a member of the circle.

> "It was difficult for me to maintain any kind of anonymity. Indeed, there were some people there who were ten times brighter than me; people who, if I'd have met them on the street, I'd never have had the courage to speak to. There was even one guy who looked for all the world like one of the managers from the factory! But the strange thing was that it didn't matter. What mattered was that I'd had something published, and this seemed to endow me with almost super-human qualities as far as everyone else was concerned. For the first couple of months I tried to block it out, tried to pretend that it wasn't real, but eventually I just gave in. Of course there was actually quite a large part of me that wanted to play the star anyway…"

(from 'Writers' Lives', Granada TV, 1986)

-*-

"Did you ever meet her?"

Mark looked across from where he stood, picking his trousers from the back of the easy chair Maxine kept in the corner of her bedroom. Propping herself up on one elbow, she stared at his recently-showered figure from the bed, the quilt half draped across her body. There was an aura of satisfaction about her; a quiet contentment that seemed strangely at odds with the still up-tempo beating of his own heart.

"Stella?"

"Yes."

He sat on the chair, retrieved his socks from the floor and pulled one on his right foot. There was something satisfying about the routine of dressing, of knowing the order of things. He had once tried - quite deliberately - to put on left sock before right, shirt before trousers, only to find himself thrown by the experience and generally disquieted.

"Only once or twice."

"Recently?"

"For the book, you mean?"

Maxine nodded, still in the same position and showing no inclination to move. Mark stood up and pulled on his trousers. The clock by the side of the bed showed that it was a little before two.

"Don't you have a meeting or something?"

She smiled.

"Later. About three." There was a pause. "So what about Stella? Was she some kind of femme fatale?"

The memory of her, of their last meeting - a remarkably plain woman who, to look at, gave no indication there would have been any excitement in her past at all - came back to him; the juxtaposition of the reality with the image he sensed Maxine held made him laugh.

"She came to the funeral, though by then it was safe of course. After all, there was no-one left who had cause to remember her. She was just a face in the crowd."

"But you recognised her."

"I'd seen her photo once, that's all. At the funeral she kept to the back and left before I had chance to speak to her."

"Did you want to?"

"Speak to her?"

He had assumed that he had, that it would have been the natural thing for him to do; but now that Maxine had asked the question - well, things seemed to exist in a different light.

"Not really I suppose. Though I would have done - if she'd come up to me."

Fishing his shirt from the floor where it had fallen, he stood and faced Maxine. He watched her watching him, a slight smile on her lips. From within he could feel his recently satisfied hunger beginning to stir again. He forced himself to return to her original question, and turned back to face the mirror, watching his body disappear beneath the gradually buttoned garment.

"But I saw her later. Because of the book. Yes."

A rustle from behind, forced him to turn. Maxine was standing now, duvet wrapped about her.

"You knew where she was?"

"I just wrote to the address in Meade Road. She hadn't moved. I didn't know, of course; I was just guessing." Maxine moved up and put her hands about his waist. "I told her about the book. She was cautious at first, so I offered to go round and see her. I think that spooked her. She said she'd think about it and would ring me back."

"She did, obviously."

"About a week later. She said that she'd see me, but that she wouldn't make any promises. And I wasn't to go to the house. It had to be somewhere public. Maybe she thought I was going to rape her or something."

Maxine laughed and gave him a squeeze.

"You haven't got it in you!"

He spun her around and aimed a kiss at her mouth, missing and catching her high on the cheekbone.

"See!" She moved her head and found his mouth briefly, pulling herself away and reaching for the dressing gown hanging on the back of the door. "So where did you meet?"

She seemed to slip seamlessly between duvet and gown, allowing but the briefest glimpses of flesh to meet his gaze. He readjusted himself mentally, tucked in his shirt, then ran his hands through his still wet hair.

"Warwick Castle, of all places!"

-*-

Early in 1964, after two more meetings of the writing group, Stella proposed an outdoor event. As one of their recent exercises, they had been considering ways in which they might achieve a sense of the historical in their writing, and how, through the use of various linguistic devices, they might instil a sense of periodicity in their work.

> "The whole exercise thing had been something of a shambles! All we managed to come up with were a few twee paragraphs which, instead of truly invoking a sense of the Medieval or whatever, simply ended up as primitive paraphrases of Shakespeare. Of course, no-one would admit it. We spent an entire evening saying nice things about each others' work, all the while knowing that it

was complete bollocks! Well, I'd assumed that we all knew it was bollocks…"

(from 'Writers' Lives', Granada TV, 1986)

Stella's idea was to hold a meeting away from Meade Road in favour of a location where the influence of the historical might subliminally come to bear. One or two of the group were dubious about the idea and doubted its validity, but she carried sufficient weight in her argument for Charles and two others - Elizabeth Morrison and Bernard Styles - to agree to the expedition. The location she chose was Warwick Castle: it was sufficiently convenient not to require excessive travelling, and endowed with sufficient historical gravitas to promise some degree of inspiration.

One of Stella's fundamental reasons for promoting such a radical alternative to the normal programme was her desire to extract Charles from the 'safe' environment of Meade Road and out onto neutral territory. She had, over their previous four encounters, become besotted with him. His success as a published writer, accompanied by instant pre-eminence at the group, endowed him an immediate and powerful allure. Following on from this was a strong and ever-growing physical desire.

"I knew he was married of course; but somehow that didn't seem to matter. After all, he was a Writer, and Writers lived extraordinary lives not bound like ordinary people by sterile and outmoded conventions."

Her somewhat romantic ideal of Packard was fuelled to a certain extent by the man himself. Lacking anything relating to a kindred spirit in the group, Charles would focus on Stella as being the only individual there capable of communicating on his wavelength.

"It was easy to be pleasant with Stella. Out of all of them, she was the only one who seemed to come anywhere near to understanding what was actually going on. Most of the others made certain unrealistic assumptions about what I was or what I believed in, but Stella never appeared to let herself be totally preoccupied with any idealistic interpretation of who I was or what I did. I actually thought that she understood some of the struggle too. Of course I'd also had an early inkling that she'd taken a shine to me. It was kind of flattering. Maybe I thought it was all a part of my success - if you could call it success, that is."

(from 'Writers' Lives', Granada TV, 1986)

In the week before the Warwick Castle expedition, Charles and George experienced another falling out with the former accusing his friend of having designs on his wife. Walker had been following his reinstated routine of visits to the Packard's house, often walking with Mary and Mark in the local park. Once or twice, he would load the red pedal car in the back of his Austin and take the young boy alone. Despite their recently recovered relationship, the friendship Packard witnessed between his wife and George began to rankle with him once again.

"Things were going well enough at work, and attendance at the Writing Group had given Charles a fresh impetus of sorts; but despite this, there was something amiss. He began to grow a little colder towards me; I was forced to back-off a little. Mary said she hated these mood swings, even to the extent of questioning whether or not she had actually done the right thing all those years ago. I was caught in the middle and I hated it."

There was no specific incident that sparked Charles' accusations this time. His simmering, possibly born of an essentially restless nature, had turned more to boiling and, as was usual, Walker was the first to suffer. Packard's charge, delivered in the same front room where he had so recently re-embraced George, was vague, unsubstantiated, and spoken in the presence of the entire family.

It was this preoccupation with his unsatisfactory domestic background - and the suspicion that Mary and George were having an affair - that proved to be a major diversion for Packard at this time. Consequently, when Stella made her own declaration, Charles was in the appropriate frame of mind for it to make sense to him.

> "We had become separated from the other two; I can't remember how, but Stella confessed later that it had all been part of her grand design. Funny; I would never have credited her with the imagination for such subterfuge. Anyway, I had been looking at some picture or other, struggling - or pretending to struggle! - with how I might turn my vision into some kind of acceptable 'historical' image, when Stella simply came up alongside me and took my hand. Although we had lost the other two from the group, there were still other people about, so I could hardly wrench my hand away and create a scene. And in any event, maybe I didn't want to."

> (from 'Writers' Lives', Granada TV, 1986)

When Charles and Stella finished their tour some fifteen minutes later they were still holding hands. During that quarter of an hour, Stella had chosen to accompany their slow meandering with a commentary of her own.

-*-

"I told him that I loved him."

She sat with Mark on one of the benches that fringed a large and immaculately dressed lawn at the back of the castle. He had waited, as arranged, at the exit from the castle to the grounds and had almost given her up when she appeared, walking nervously towards him. They had shaken hands and moved in silence to the seat.

"And did you?"

It had taken him a little while to persuade her that he was genuine and that the book was not 'some sordid little fable'. Mark had been taken slightly aback at her words, surprised not only by the vocabulary but also with the realisation that the woman who sat but a couple of feet from him - a small, timid kind of woman, now well beyond middle-age - had been the vessel of so much passion.

"I did. And I still do." She added the second phrase without both hesitation and doubt. "Those were wonderful minutes, those fifteen minutes, just walking quietly around here with Charlie."

She looked over Mark's shoulder to the large building behind him. He felt almost as if he were a visitor to a shrine, so great seemed her reverence for the place.

"What did he say?"

Stella looked at him briefly, then away again, across the lawns.

"Very little. When we were outside we went for a walk. He spoke the most then, giving me a potted account of his life. He told me about Mary," she paused, checking to see if he were still paying attention, "and you. And about George Walker."

"Did you ever meet George?"

"No."

A small silence fell on the conversation. Mark struggled slightly with perspective; he was involved on two levels: keeping to the role of detached biographer was difficult, knowing that he was talking to the woman who had nearly split the family asunder and who had a major part to play in breaking his Mother's heart.

"And then? After you came out into the garden?"

She searched the trees beyond the lawn as if reconstructing her memory.

"He kissed me. Over there, by the trees." She allowed her voice to direct his gaze, keeping her hands folded on her lap. "It was a hard, desperate kind of a kiss. For me it was heaven."

Mark had run out of questions. As he sat there, next to Stella, he felt strangely out of place, as if he were intruding on someone's secret and most sacred past. Yet it seemed to be Stella's past alone. Though his Father had spoken of her seldom, he knew their relationship bore slim resemblance to the one imagined by this sixty year old woman.

"We left the other two; didn't even bother to wait for them. We went back to Meade Road. The first time Charlie let go of my hand was to take my clothes off."

The sun began to appear from behind the far trees, catching Mark unawares as he looked in their direction. The sudden light caused him to blink and look down. When he turned to face Stella, he found that she had risen and was walking away from him and towards the trees.

-*-

With the certainty of Stella's faith now as security for him, Packard's accusations of Mary's infidelity grew in both regularity and vociferousness. Walker, rarely on-hand, always fought such verbal onslaughts on Mary's side; a defence which, in Packard's eyes, simply compounded proof of guilt. He began to invent reasons for being away from the house: there was more overtime at the factory; they had changed the shift patterns; even extra sessions of the writing group.

> "I was wild, I guess. Convinced that Mary and George were being unfaithful to me, in Stella I had the ideal safety valve. It didn't strike me until much later that I was actually indulging in the very thing I was accusing them of. Of course, it was all very easy. Stella constantly pandered to my ego - especially my writing ego - and she had her own house, which made liaisons simple to arrange. You might ask me why I became involved, or what I saw in her. I never loved her. Sounds terrible, but it was too easy; I mean, I think I was some kind of god in her eyes."

> (from 'Writers' Lives', Granada TV, 1986)

Three weeks after the trip to Warwick castle, Charles packed a single suitcase and moved to Meade Road. Mark's memory is understandably sketchy:

"I was too young to know what was really going on, I guess. I knew that things weren't right; no-one seemed happy, or wanted to play. George seemed not to be around for a while, then, when it dawned on me that Father was not there, suddenly he came back."

Packard stayed with Stella in Meade Road under a month.

Although his doubts had been gathering, the final act that caused Packard to leave Stella occurred when he returned from work one day to find her dressed as an imitation of Proserpine from Rosetti's painting, complete with a rich red wig. The Pre-Raphaelite connotation instantly brought back memories of Mary and along with that an overwhelming sense of guilt.

Uncertain of his ground, Packard filled his suitcase for a second time and made his way home.

-*-

Mark returned to the study to find Beatrice at his desk. Despite his quiet footfall she looked up instantly. In her hand she held a few of the photographs he had been considering for inclusion in the book.

"She wasn't a beauty was she?"

"No; that's certainly not how I'd choose to describe her."

Beatrice laid the photographs back down.

"Well that's something."

It seemed an odd remark for her to make, as if behind it lay acres of disappointment or sensitive scars where she had somehow been wounded.

"Have you made it romantic?"

Mark was suddenly angry with her and offered to allow her the privilege of interrogating his computer and seeing for herself what he had written. She laughed gently, dispelling his anger.

"No thank you, Dear. I'll wait." She paused. He sensed some hesitance in her; a hesitance that was unusual for Beatrice. "Because it wasn't you know."

"Romantic?"

"Charles called it a 'sordid little fable'."

"A what?" The echo hit him hard.

"A 'sordid little fable'. That's what he called it. Can't remember when exactly, but it was a phrase he used to trot out occasionally. You seem surprised."

He looked down at the image of the plain woman smiling weakly at him from a poor quality snapshot. In the background, on the very edge of the picture, the suggestion of a large building. Perhaps Warwick Castle.

"She said she wanted to be sure that I wasn't writing it as 'some sordid little fable'."

"Why?"

"Because that wasn't what it was. Not to her."

"And to you?"

"Me?"

"What kind of a fable to you think it was Mark? Sordid? Little? Romantic? Large?"

There was something in Beatrice's cross-examination - that was a shade disturbing.

"I'm not trying to think, just to relate. I just want to be as accurate as I can be; that's all."

"Well, you met her. That must tell you something."

"Yes, I suppose so."

Beatrice, having risen by now, turned, then stopped.

"I don't suppose she mentioned her other 'little fable', did she?"

"Which was?"

"That a year after your Father threw her over to go back to Mary, she was committed to a mental institution. Spent three years there." From somewhere else another echo; Mark shivered. "You won't find any reference to it in your Father's papers. She wrote to him and he threw her letters away. She pleaded with him to visit. Said she would kill herself."

"She didn't."

He spoke slowly, his mind fixed elsewhere. Beatrice stopped her diatribe, surprised by the tone of his voice.

"No, Mark," she said slowly, "she didn't."

Composed again, he looked up at her.

"So that's that; the end of another chapter."

Without responding, Beatrice left the room.

Chapter Eighteen

'The white of the bow sliced through the blue water, magically turning the blue waves into white cascades that fell in an arc back to the sea. And as the boat slowly turned into the entrance to the tiny harbour, the brilliant white buildings shone in the strong sunlight, fringing the harbour and spotting the hillside. The sky was a precious and untarnished blue. White and blue. It was as if all impurities had been removed from the world and only the pure essence of things remained.'

(from the Hydra notebooks, 1964)

With reconciliation to Mary came also a restoration of Packard's friendship with George. The first few days after Charles' return from Meade Road were tense affairs with the Prodigal Husband attempting to make some form of atonement for his absence. Mary did not ask for any details as to where he had been.

> "I guess she knew. I mean, she must have had some idea; people don't just walk out and stay nowhere for three weeks, do they? But she said nothing; not a single question came from her. I suppose I must have been mortified. I don't know if it was guilt - somehow I don't think it was - but there was something that demanded I show some kind of remorse. I tried to help around the house; I took Mark to the park once or twice - on my own, to give her a little space, you know? But it didn't matter. There was something different. Something irrevocable. When we made love again, for the first time, she cried in my arms."

(Interview with David Frost, 1984)

With Walker things were initially strained too. Packard was certain that George had known why he had left Mary and where he had gone, but once again the two men did not speak of it.

"Mary was out shopping when she bumped into me. She asked me to go back for tea; said there was something she wanted to show me. I remember that young Mark seemed pretty excited. I carried her shopping back; perhaps the weight of it should have given me a clue. It didn't; so I was stunned when I walked in and saw Charles sitting in his old chair by the fire."

Mary took Mark into the kitchen to make some tea, leaving the two men alone.

> "I really didn't know what to do. Maybe I was as surprised to see George as he was to see me! It was odd. Despite our various

adventures together, it was still difficult for the two of us to be completely open with each other. I think I offered George my hand. It was all I could think of."

(Interview with David Frost, 1984)

Things would never be completely the same for Packard in either of these relationships. Attempting once again to show due diligence at home - getting in from work early; trying to give his son the attention he believed was expected of him; helping Mary with the shopping whenever he remembered - Packard tried to restore the status quo by pretending the episode with Stella had never actually happened. Mary seemed to him to want things that way. The fact that she failed to question him about his absence, or to chide him over his return to drink - even though it was only in moderation at this time - gave Charles the impression that such an approach was the only one to adopt. His wife's distance, slight but unquestionable, made him all the more determined to put the past behind him.

Two weeks after his return, Walker was a dinner guest.

"It was a little after seven on the Sunday. Charles was sitting by the fire, staring into the flames, his notepad in his lap. I asked him why he was not going to the writing group. I remember Mary getting up and leaving the room. Charles watched her go, then turned to me. I'll never forget the look he gave me. "It was boring", he said. "Doubt if I'll go again." I knew then; I knew then."

With spring now established, Packard began to look forward to summer. He felt he worked better in the summer, the lighter days making it psychologically easier for him to write when he came home from work. There was also time enough for him to take Mark to the park before bedtime if he chose. The young boy, who was now six, was mobile enough to indulge in more skilful games of football without simply falling over. For Packard - who had never been a football fan - the physical undertaking of such brief evening kick-abouts was more a trial than a pleasure.

Mark had begun to take a schoolboy's interest in football, and would listen to the radio on Saturdays to see how the local clubs had fared.

"Most of the boys at school were Aston Villa fans, but I always preferred West Brom. On weekends when West Brom won and Villa lost, I used to dread Monday mornings as I'd often get beaten up in the playground because of it. Eventually I publicly swapped my allegiance to Villa - even though I still preferred the Throstles. Later, I simply gave up football; I think mainly because Dad showed no interest in it whatsoever."

On April 17th, 1964, Packard received a letter from the publishers of <u>Dawn</u> containing his royalties for the previous three months. Sales of the book had been better than expected, buoyed, they assumed, by one or two positive reviews in the wake of that from Frank Wilson. Whilst there was insufficient justification to contemplate a second printing, they were suitably satisfied to be able to make a preliminary offer to consider of any future work. As it turned out, Packard was destined to place nothing further with them.

The letter had an uplifting effect on Packard who had once again begun to struggle with his writing.

> "Form was no longer the issue. The relative success of <u>Dawn</u> proved to me what I had known all along really; namely that prose was to be my forte. I guess I'd always thought that - except for the time I allowed myself to be distracted into thinking that I was a poet! The problem was content, subject. I'd already written about the thing I thought I knew best - Man in his workplace. Since then I'd been tinkering; trying things out. But thus far I'd found nothing. Because of this failure, I began to wonder just how shallow and uneventful my life had been."

> (Interview with Melvyn Bragg, 1986)

The royalties windfall once again brought wine into the Packards' home, and once again George Walker was there to share in Charles' good fortune. After dinner, the evening turned into something of a debate as to what should be done with the money. Mary was in favour saving it, a position countered by Packard who openly admitted that he could quite easily have spent it several times over if he were given the chance. Once again, it was Walker who was to offer the most sound advice.

"I simply suggested they did both: save some and spend some. And rather than spend half on any old thing, I suggested that Charles should put it to good use; to do something with it that might just open up new avenues for him."

George's suggestion won favour with both Packards. Having decided on an even split, Mary was content that some if the money would be secure for the future. The debate then centred on what Charles should do with the other half of the money. Luckily he was not a frivolous man, and having lived his life thus far without many modern materialistic trappings, the option of choosing to "do" rather than to "acquire" fell on fertile ground.

Eventually, Mary proposed that Charles should consider a holiday. Her argument had been that by going somewhere different - possibly abroad for the first time - he might find the subject matter he sought for his writing. Packard, although enthusiastic, tempered this with counter arguments about the cost of taking both her and Mark, the disruption to Mark's schooling, and the general upheaval.

"I remember Charles' face when he heard Mary's words. "I don't want to go," she said, "we'd just be in the way." He looked like a man who'd been let out of prison. Then, quick as a flash, he turned to me and said "George, where shall we go?"."

That Saturday, Packard and Walker made a tour of the Travel Agents in the High Street. Given their somewhat restricted budget, their options were limited. Over a pint in the 'Green Man', they discussed the potential of each destination. Eventually they settled for a week in Greece. Packard paid for half of Walker's ticket.

-*-

As he walked in to the lobby of the hotel - the Doorman deferentially holding the open door for him - Mark checked his watch. It was a little after ten past one. Maxine had been most insistent that he be on time.

"We'll have finished the morning's shoot by one. The crew normally go off for lunch then, with a view to starting again at two - but as we're interviewing a 'star', we'll probably start the afternoon a little later. So be there at one fifteen. A minute later and I'll assume you won't be coming."

He had tried to joke with he over the demand for punctuality, but it had not, apparently, been a joking matter.

"I'll looking for Miss Priest; she's filming here with the BBC."

The Receptionist smiled professionally back at him. He thought of the Assistant who had sold Julia the mirror.

"Just a minute, Sir."

The reference to time made him check his watch once again as the uniformed Receptionist scanned her computer terminal. Twelve minutes past. Surely three minutes would be enough time for him to find her?

"They're in the Aberdeen suite; tenth floor, rooms 1002 and 1003. The lifts are just there, Sir."

Mark followed her gaze to the shining sets of doors just across the lobby. As his finger pressed the silver 'Call' button, the sleeve of his tweed jacket rode up to reveal his watch. Two and a half minutes.

He had expected the lift to be there instantly, but it was not. As he waited - seconds now beginning to race by in such as fashion as to lead him to the edge of a mild panic - he cast his eyes about the lobby. He had been to the Regent's Park Hilton only once before, though being too busy at present trying to fathom why Maxine had chosen such a place to see him, the reason for that earlier visit has slipped his memory.

The "ping" of the lift, its doors now opening behind him, caused him to turn. A large, corpulent man emerged, sweating heavily. There was something familiar about him, though Mark was unable to place who he was. He nodded to Mark. Inside, the lift bore the faint traces of the man's smell; a dusky combination of cologne and perspiration.

He checked his appearance in the mirror, adjusting the open collar of his polo shirt at the neck of the jacket. His raised his arm to check his watch again. A little over a minute now. Tugging gently at the bottom of the jacket beneath each pocket, he caught a glimpse of the errant tweed pattern; it was always there now, and however he might try, he could never fail to see it.

Another "ping", this time to herald his arrival on the tenth floor. Mark stepped from the lift and paused, catching a breath of fresh air - of hotel air-conditioned air - and looked for the sign that would direct him to the Aberdeen suite. There was a board that indicated the direction of 'Rooms 1001-1029'.

The doors of 1002 and 1003 were side by side a little way along the corridor. Mark, checking his watch again (there were still thirty seconds to go, so he knew he could indulge a little) tried to imagine the rooms beyond. They would, he guessed, be more or less identical - perhaps with furniture and fittings arranged diametrically opposite to each other - though today it was likely that one had been turned into something of a mini-studio. The question of course (and this as he held up his hand ready to knock, his watch counting down the last few seconds to one fifteen) was which door should he knock; which room would Maxine be in?

He rapped on 1003 and waited.

"It's open."

Although it was slightly muffled (had she been in 1002 after all?) Mark recognised Maxine's voice immediately. He pushed the door open.

Inside it was dark. The curtains were drawn and there were no lights on. The communicating door to 1002 was also closed, though a chink of light escaped from beneath it. He moved his hand towards the light switch.

"Leave it off." Her voice was close, but although his eyes were beginning to adjust to the dim light, he could not yet make her out. "Lock the door."

There was something urgent, insistent in her voice that he had never heard before. It was excited too, impatient almost, and not to be denied. He turned and fumbled for the catch. As it "clicked" into place, he felt her emerge from the bathroom and stand behind him.

"Don't move," she whispered.

As her hands found his shoulders, he felt himself smile. He recognised the source of the excitement in Maxine's voice now; she had invented some kind of game, an attempt at the mysterious, the secretive. From his shoulders he felt her hands move upwards to the back of his head, then forwards. Suddenly, darkness. He started slightly.

"I'm afraid you're now my captive, Lovely; there's no point in trying to struggle."

Mark wondered if he was supposed to speak or not; indeed, half-expecting the blindfold to be followed by something else - some other part of Maxine's fantasy - he said nothing. She returned her hands to his shoulders and eased his jacket off.

"Turn round."

As he did so - blind as he was - he wanted to see her, wanted to see what she looked like. He moved his hands forwards and upwards; they were met by hers.

"Not yet," she said, gently forcing them to his side.

Her hands undid the buttons of his shirt then tugged it from where it was tucked inside his trousers. He could feel himself hardening in anticipation. If Maxine's little game had been designed to encourage him, to stimulate his desire, then it most certainly had not failed.

He waited. It seemed an age before she touched him again. He had been expecting to feel her hands on his chest or on his arms, but instead he felt her fingers tugging at the laces of his shoes. He made to lever them off himself.

"When I say," the voice said firmly.

The words - the orders almost - seemed momentarily to be coming for someone else. Without sight of her, without evidence that it was indeed

Maxine who was saying these things, he suddenly imagined that it might be anyone there, impersonating her, taking advantage of him.

"Shoes!"

He lifted his feet in turn; two hands removed his shoes and socks simultaneously. He felt his bare feet on the carpet and waited. There was a pause, and no sound.

"Maxine?"

As her fingers touched the fly of his trousers, he jumped. Suddenly he felt vulnerable, out of control. Although he knew that it was Maxine slowly unzipping him - after all had he not recognised the voice behind the words? - what if it was not her? What if they were not alone in the room? He felt a warm hand rub gently against his penis through his boxer shorts.

"Maxine?"

He suddenly needed more acknowledgement. As much as he wanted her, he need to know that it was indeed her he was wanting. His trousers fell to the floor and her hand slipped inside his shorts. He felt her fingers moving gently through his pubic hair. At his side, he felt his fists clench; he rocked his head back. At that precise moment, he felt himself to be completely at her mercy.

"Maxine!"

Violently he rushed his hands to the blindfold, and pulled it from his head, her hands leaving his body as he did so. The blackness had given way to a strange kind of instant twilight; he blinked, quickly, then looked down. Maxine was on her knees at his feet. With the exception of a camisole, she appeared to be naked. In the faction of a second as they both paused, he took her in: the shape of her breasts beneath the soft material; her wide eyes, their whiteness exaggerated in the darkness; her hands, close to his body.

He bent slightly, suddenly unshackled from his imaginary prison; suddenly convinced that it was Maxine - and Maxine alone - in the room with him. Now he was free from her command; free to assume to control; free to lift her roughly from the floor and, as she gasped, press her pliant body hard against him.

-*-

The small villa they had arranged to rent from fifteen hundred miles away was a short walk out of town, across in the next valley. It stood in a small cluster of white dwellings, so basic that to the two Englishmen it appeared more a shell than a complete house. The rooms were sparsely furnished, and there was an absence of electricity. Running water was available from a rusty standpipe just outside the back door.

Packard, whose mood had gradually shifted from anxiety through to euphoria on their journey, had accepted their accommodation with an enthusiasm that surprised Walker completely.

"I had expected him to be distraught when he saw the place; I was. But there seemed no denting his passion. I don't think I had ever known him so enthusiastic for anything."

Despite their arduous journey, Packard was keen that they instantly explore, haranguing Walker who was intent on taking a rest. They reached an agreement to return to the town together a couple of hours later; a deal which allowed George a short sleep and left Charles free to wander locally.

Not being able to speak Greek had been a major concern of Packard's prior to departure, but now that he had arrived on the island it seemed the smallest inconvenience.

> "It was quite exciting, trying to find a way of communicating without a common language. Gestures - like pointing, smiling, nodding and all that - became very important. I suppose it was something of a lesson for me - in respect of my own writing and my attitude to language, I mean - especially as it didn't stop me from returning to the hut with some fresh fruit and a small bottle of ouzo!"

> (Interview with Sue Lawley, BBC Radio, 1987)

The discovery of ouzo was not the last Packard was to make during the holiday, although it did end up being the one which was to re-emerge most evidently at various stages throughout the remainder of his life. Sometimes during moments of crisis or uncertainty, he would shut himself away with a bottle of the pernod-like liquid and attempt to recreate Hydra.

That first evening, they ate in a small bar along the waterfront.

> "Watching the light fade from the sky - seeing the blue replaced by indigo, the white by soft grey - seemed such a natural transition. Perhaps it happened like that back in England, but until then I'd never seen it. Come to think of it, I don't think I've seen it since."

> (Interview with Sue Lawley, BBC Radio, 1987)

Enlivened by this new adventure, he was in buoyant and expansive mood.

"I don't think I'd ever seen Charles as relaxed as he was that first evening. Boyish, almost. I could almost have forgiven him those more beastly elements of his past, he was so winning."

The evening was more remarkable for Packard than simply the picturesque sunset. At the table next to them was another English couple who introduced themselves on hearing the two men talking. Thomas and Kitty Brakespeare were artists who had come to Hydra to paint, and had already been on the island for three weeks. Kitty was beginning to get homesick and had virtually stopped painting, failing to find any inspiration in the landscape. Her husband, on the other hand, had immediately fallen into a reverie similar to that engulfing Charles and, as a result, had begun to paint wild and colourful semi-abstract paintings at a prolific rate; a success which did not endear him to his wife.

Packard immediately latched on to Brakespeare as something of a kindred spirit, and they exchanged their emotional responses to first contact with the island. Thomas was interested to see if Packard's art would respond in the same positive manner as his own had, and suggested that they undertake a joint exploration the next day. The result of that undertaking - 'Chasing the Muse' - now hangs in the Tate Gallery, London.

> "Tommy was a marvellous man, and such a tremendous find for me. It was as if I was suddenly on a roll, like a gambler who couldn't lose. Poor George was cast adrift in my wake a little I suppose; in the end he spent more of that week with Kitty just reading and talking than he did with me! And it wasn't only Tommy, of course; there was Constantina too."

(Interview with Sue Lawley, BBC Radio, 1987)

The harbour bar was owned by an Athenian who had come to the island as a youth and never returned home. He had married a local girl and their daughter, Constantina, helped him to run the bar during her vacations away from her college on the mainland. In 1964 Constantina was nearly twenty and looking forward to a peaceful spring vacation in preparation for that Summer's examinations.

Packard's exuberance had so enlivened him that in consequence he appeared closer to twenty-two than thirty-two, and the attraction between he and Constantina was immediate. The fact that she spoke a little English made her the only person who could sensibly wait on any British tourist who happened to visit the bar, so she and Packard were forced into immediate contact.

"She was quite simply the most amazing woman I'd seen for years. I know that it was probably the heat, or the excitement, something like that - but I was completely in awe of the kind of statuesque quality she had. Maybe I was being over-romantic about the whole thing, but she seemed to possess something of the goddess about her."

(Interview with Melvyn Bragg, 1986)

It was not only the newness of Hydra and Packard's present vitality that influenced him at this point. He was still attempting to come to terms with Mary's change towards him, and the somewhat unsatisfactory nature their relationship had taken on. More than this, he was also a man whose ego had been boosted by his affair with Stella: his manhood had been re-established, and this, along with the success of <u>Dawn</u>, made him feel particularly good about himself.

After the first day's excursion with Brakespeare, Packard returned to the bar alone. It was early evening and the place was quiet.

"I asked Constantina what she was studying at college. Literature, she told me. Mainly ancient classics, but some more modern stuff too. Then she asked me what I did. It was the first time I'd tried it, more for effect I guess, but partly to see how it felt too: "I'm a writer", I told her. Both the effect and the sensation of saying it were tremendous!"

(Interview with Melvyn Bragg, 1986)

Packard asked Constantina if she would like to go for a walk with him the next day. Partly as an excuse, he told her that he had been recommended some ruins by Brakespeare and wanted to find them but was wary of getting lost. She did not respond at first. Later, when Walker had joined him and they were eating supper, she agreed to go.

By the end of the next day, Packard and Constantina were lovers. They had left the town early in the morning and had walked in relative silence for a little over an hour when Constantina slipped as they scrambled up a rough path. Catching her about the waist, Packard managed to break her fall, but in doing so sent them both to the ground.

"She had fallen slightly on top of me and I was unable - or unwilling - to move. I remember those black eyes of hers - pure, like the sky and the sea were pure. They swallowed me up. She leant forwards and kissed me. We made love there and then. It was wild, carefree and abandoned; but it seemed right. It was

189

what the place demanded of us; anything less would have been treasonable."

(Interview with Melvyn Bragg, 1986)

During the following five days of the holiday, Packard spent some time each day with Constantina. Every day she would show him a different part of the island - sometimes borrowing her Father's old van - and every day, with one exception, they made love.

"Only once did Charles insist I went along. Maybe he was feeling guilty about neglecting me. I can't remember too much about where we went, but it was obvious I was just in the way. He never chose to hide what was going on, or to justify it. Perhaps I should have been outraged - for Mary's sake at least - but I wasn't. Somehow I couldn't be. It was as if I was witnessing a new man being born."

On the last day, Packard persuaded Constantina to sit for Tommy. He wanted something to remember her by and Tommy had volunteered to paint her, promising to bring the finished work home with him for Packard to collect at some stage in the future. It had taken him a considerable amount of effort to get her to agree, but agree she did, and so the three of them set off after breakfast for a secluded spot along the coast where they would not be disturbed.

> "When it came to leaving... I remember George waiting for me at the top of the gang plank; the ship's crew ready to man the ropes; there had been a toot on the ship's whistle. Standing there and holding Constantina in my arms, I could imagine how it must have been for her father; how it had been impossible for him to go home. For a brief moment, as I kissed her for the last time, I think I actually contemplated staying."

(Interview with Melvyn Bragg, 1986)

Now part of the Brakespeare family's private collection, Packard never did collect the portrait of Constantina.

As the journey to Hydra had seen a gradual rise in Charles' spirits, so the return to England brought something of a decline. The new man that Walker had witnessed being born on the island apparently began to regress, and the closer they got to home, the more Packard relapsed. There was, however, sufficient of a change - and sufficient inspiration remaining - for him to begin writing again.

"I don't know if Mary saw any difference in him. To be honest, if I hadn't been away with him, I would probably have assumed that it was the same old Charles returning myself. I don't know how much she was able to glean from him. She asked a few questions; the answers she received were limp in comparison with the reality of the thing. Charles mentioned the Brakespeares I think, but that was about it. I think one of the reasons he seemed so low was that a part of him hadn't wanted to come home at all."

Walker's theory was to be proven. The next nine months saw Packard working solidly on his second novel. He approached the project with a dedication that suggested a passionate belief in what he was doing, as if only in the execution of his writing was he able to express the passion he felt.

In <u>Under the Olive Tree</u>, Packard was to draw heavily not only from his experience on Hydra, but also from the failure of his relationship with Stella. The novel tells the story of an artist, Anthony Shipley, who travels to a Greek island with his partner, Sandra, for a painting holiday. Shipley is inspired by the place - much as both Packard and Brakespeare had been - and finds tremendous creative drive there. Sandra does not however, and begins to be a drain on him. He meets a local girl and they begin an affair. Eventually Sandra leaves, her relationship with Shipley broken, and the artist remains.

> "I guess it was a kind of exorcism. I mean I knew I had wanted to stay on Hydra, but I also knew that I couldn't. Or I thought that I couldn't. So I wanted to try and explore that possibility; to live out what life might have been like; to see what might have happened. And I was scared that I might lose some of the feeling for the place, so I had to write it as quickly as I could."

> (Interview with Melvyn Bragg, 1986)

By mid-Autumn of 1965, Packard had completed his first draft of <u>Under the Olive Tree</u>, and began turning his thoughts towards publication. His experiences with publishers thus far in his career had been variable, and although reasonably satisfied with the way Dawson had handled <u>Dawn</u>, he was uncertain of placing his new book with the relatively small publisher again. As a result of this disquiet, Packard wrote to Frank Wilson - the critic who had been so praiseworthy of <u>Dawn</u> - and asked for advice.

Walker, who was consulted less by Packard this time, was convinced that Charles should remain with Dawson. However, something of the old distance had returned to their relationship since Greece, and Packard was set on establishing some new links on his own. Wilson's reply, when it finally came, was gratifying for two reasons: firstly, it showed a degree of enthusiasm for Packard's work that was morale boosting; and secondly, it offered the name of Peter Healey at Macmillan as a contact.

On October 17th, Packard travelled down to London, carrying with him the first few chapters of <u>Under the Olive Tree</u>. At a little after twelve thirty, he met Healey in Lyons Corner House, near marble Arch.

> "I liked Healey immediately. I guess what impressed me most about him was the sense of professionalism you got from him. Sure there was a nice suit, good shoes, that kind of stuff; but you also got the satisfying sense that he actually knew what he was doing. Wilson had obviously primed him, and he had read <u>Dawn</u>. Whilst he never committed himself - show me a publisher who does! - he was reasonably enthusiastic about the prospects for the new book."

(Interview in The Observer, 1976)

Healey took Packard's draft chapters away with him, promising to get back to him before the end of the month. On 24th, Packard received a letter from Macmillan offering to take on publication of the work. Included in the latter was a draft contract, an outline schedule for completion of the work, and another invitation to visit London in order to agree the financial arrangements.

-*-

Mark looked up. He suddenly realised with something of a shock that he had never actually discussed payment for his Father's biography with Simon. Perhaps because it was a family affair there was a sense in which it would have been 'bad form' to broach such a delicate matter. As there had been no advance, nor any mention of reward for his labours, Mark wondered if his Uncle might not be attempting to get the book written for nothing. He wondered if Simon suddenly appeared and said 'Mark, I'm not paying you a penny!' how he would react. There would be anger and bluster of course, but the critical question was whether or not he would actually stop.

A case could be made for him writing the book out of a sense of love or duty, he knew; but that would be a case made by other people, not himself. He was uncertain just how far his 'love' for his Father would take him, possibly little further than the preface. Yet despite this, he suspected that he would have to continue, that he had come too far to stop, and that the book would grow. Was it the historian in him that would force him to carry on, or the social archaeologist that was bent on uncovering the truth behind his Father's life? On the screen in front of him, the words stared back at him accompanied by the whirr of the computer's fan, blurring as they did so. They became a maze, an abstract pattern through which he sensed he might be searching for more than just his Father's chronology.

Chapter Nineteen

He stood on the hillside above the harbour entrance and watched the long white ship glide silently away. Up here, close to the sky and with the gentle breeze masking the heat of the sun, no sound carried. And so the ship's leaving was devoid of all nuisances of noise, a departure coming to him more as image than reality. It seemed fitting that way.

Somewhere on board, Sandra would be thinking of him. Perhaps already couched away from the sun; or leaning against a deck rail and waving towards him. Perhaps she would be crying once again. He was occasionally surprised by a woman's capacity for tears. Even though there had been many during the previous two days, he would not have been surprised to know that someone might at that moment be witness to a few more.

Overhead, a cry from a gull also observing the departure. Anthony looked up, shielding his eyes. All he could see was the blue canopy, a stunning natural umbrella that had provided him with his light, his backcloth, and his inspiration.

He shifted on his feet, re-establishing his sense of balance. The path was uneven here and the drop from the edge of the cliff severe. Beneath him, cutting through the blue water, the silent vessel edged out into the channel, her wake a churning froth of white, muted gulls whirling off the stern. He thought of waving. Just in case. But if Sandra were looking on, he perceived it as a cruel thing to do; far better to appear as a simple silhouette, framed against the untarnished sky.

It would take them two hours or so to get back to Piraeus. They would be in shallow water only a short while and then the waves would build and the swell would take over. Sandra would hate that. He had been amazed that she had managed to refrain from sickness during their passage to the island. And he was certain that, with her spirits already low, she would succumb on the return. Perhaps she would find a friendly Samaritan to take care of her. Perhaps that was why she had not responded to the place as he had done, always holding a grudge against it because it had made her feel ill just getting there. And because of him, and the fact that he loved it. In her own mind, surely it would always be because of him.

He had yet to decide how long he would wait and watch. Already the ship was considerably smaller, but it would take a while before it had gone completely. Waiting until he could no longer see it seemed strangely wasteful. He put his hands in his pockets, turned, and began to walk away. It was not as if there was anything he had to *do* now. There was no longer any pressure of that kind upon him. Indeed, picking his way along the rocky path, it felt peculiar to realise that he could have simply stayed there for two days until the ship returned and no-one would have known or cared. No-one except Soulla.

A few yards down the hillside the path twisted to the left. For a moment the view of the sea was gone. He could hear the tinkle of goat bells in the sudden stillness. It was hot, like an oasis of heat. The path forked. To the left, it wound its way back up across the hills, away to the next village. Soulla's village. He bore right, and the view opened out again and he could see the town. His easel remained where he had left it, near the olive tree. His satchel lay at the tree's base, resting in what little shade there was.

Not wishing for a difficult farewell, he had been up early. In the cool of the morning, the light played softly upon the white structures of the port. It was an image that returned to him through the half-finished painting he paused before now. Lifting his hat, he dragged the back of his hand across his forehead. It was a good picture, he knew that; another good picture. He looked down at the town, searching for some green; he had one day decided to banish green from his palette and his work had come to life. There seemed little need for it; he found he was able to use other colours in its place, as if the island demanded it of him. As if he were compelled to reduce the spectrum he used in order to get at the essence of things.

Sandra had not understood that.

There was green to be seen of course, and green that could not be painted away. He thought of Soulla's eyes; pale and undeniable. If he was to paint her, then he would need to restore the banished hue to his brush. There could be no substitute there. It was a prospect that made him vaguely nervous. And then there was the tree. He had yet to paint the tree. "I have plenty of time", he told himself; "neither the tree nor I are going anywhere just yet." As the green of Soulla's eyes was undeniable, so the green of the olive tree was compulsive, demanding. Its darkness made him nervous. He had banished green - yet the tree was a reminder that he could never banish it; not always; not forever.

He picked up his brush and allowed it to swirl in pale ochre. As he touched the canvas, the memory of Sandra's departure left him.

~

The package arrived for him on the tourist ferry from Piraeus. He had been walking in the hills when Petros had left it at the bar. "Hela! Soulla!" - he could imagine him shouting - "a box here for your Englishman". The sneer never left Petros' lips, not even when he was happy. Petros bothered Anthony. There was something disturbing about him.

"Has he ever been happy?" he had asked Soulla.

"Happy?" She had laughed, flashing her perfect teeth at him. "Who knows?"

When he arrived for a beer after his walk, the box was lying on the bar. By accident he noticed it was for him. It was open. He pulled back the cardboard lid and checked the contents. Brushes, linseed oil, tubes of paint. He searched for green and found none. Beneath a layer of packing, some small canvas panels. She had been as good as her word.

A sound roused him. Soulla came towards him, her brow furrowed. He had seen her this dark before, but never in his direction. She pulled a piece of roughly folder paper from her pocket and tossed it onto the box.

"You still want her? Your English woman? Then Soulla not for you."

He watched her turn on her heel. He knew she was angry. Her language gave it away. Despite her fluency, at moments of significant passion grammar was the first casualty. Waiting until she was out of sight, he picked up the letter. It was from Sandra. His "English woman". Soulla's tongue - which had a Mediterranean venom all its own - had chosen its poison for Sandra.

The letter began brightly enough, asking after his health; itemising the contents of the box. It had been a reference to the non-selection of green that had seemed to trigger Sandra's degeneration, as if the unnatural practice had brought back not only her painful memories, but also a notion that somehow Anthony had been led astray. Having picked up this tack, the language soon became hysterical. Sandra professed her love for him; said how she would have him back; begged him to come home.

There was nothing in the letter to fuel Soulla's reaction. She had been let down by her misunderstanding of the text - that and a violent prejudice. Anthony smiled sadly to himself. He would need to read the letter to her word for word. That would be the only way to prove to her that she was wrong.

He corrected himself. It would only be the first thing he would need to do to prove that she was wrong.

He folded up the letter and walked after her through the bar.

~

If only he hadn't insisted. If only he had been patient; waited. Perhaps she might have made the suggestion herself.

It was an exceptionally hot night; he tossed uncomfortably in the large empty bed, stretching his limbs to all four corners. The thin cover had fallen to the floor some time ago, and his naked body lay exposed to the burgeoning dawn. Anthony opened his eyes and checked his watch. It was not yet four. He had not slept. The dream had not let him sleep.

As he turned again he saw the outline of his rough suitcase leaning against the wall. It was ready to go. There was no uncertainty there, no lack of sleep. The presence of the case offered him proof, confirmation that it was time. The fact that he had packed the bag just a few hours before had been evidence enough of his new resolve. Hoping he would be able to stay - hoping that, in some perverse way, he might be able to pretend that nothing had happened - he had tried to go about his normal business. But there had been no routine for him to fall into, nothing artificial to fall back on. He found himself devising plans for walking, sketching, painting. The walking was easy. Occasionally he would even manage to unpack his satchel and arrange his oils.

But he could go no further. The magic had left the island. He had painted his last picture there.

But if only he hadn't. Turning in the bed again, the stack of canvasses - covered in cloth and bound by rough twine - stood ready to make the long journey with him. They too were prepared. Even the one with the olive tree was there. Something in him had wanted to hurl it from the cliff, to have it follow the path of Soulla's fall. It would have been poetic for the instrument of this tragedy to meet the same fate. But something else in him was stronger. It wanted a record. It wanted the history.

He screwed his eyes shut and forced himself to count. Trying to imagine sheep leaping an English fence, the soft sound of a bell outside turned the sheep to goats. And instead of jumping fences, they were leaping from the cliffs.

It had taken him days to persuade Soulla to pose for him. She had been suspicious, taunted him. He promised her that there was nothing obscene in his desire. She would be fully clothed. She had seen his paintings; the image would not be an exact copy. Where would he paint her, she wanted to know. He suggested the tree; he wanted to paint the tree too. The conversation reverberated inside his head over and over, as it had every night. When she agreed, he remembered how elated he had been; how relieved; how impatient.

Now all he wanted was to return, retrace; to undo the words. He wanted to tell her that he did have obscene desires; that she would be naked; that the whole world would know that it was her. She would slap his face, but she would still be lying next to him.

The boat would not dock in the town until around midday. It would not be properly light for another couple of hours. He felt trapped, now in a world he could not see, and then soon in a world he could see only too well. He remembered watching Sandra's boat leave and wondered how long it would be before he could no longer see the island.

From somewhere he recalled an image of his arrival; the initial impression of the island seen from the sea. And he remembered it being green, Between the blue of the sea and the blue of the sky, a shape of olive green punctuated by the white of the buildings.

Green. Once he had completed the background, he remembered how he had started with the tree. Soulla was already there in vague outline, but he needed to paint the tree first. His hand had shook slightly as he mixed the colours: cobalt blue, cadmium yellow and ochre. The green he made - dark, powerful, fit for the tree - had taken him aback. It seemed foreign to his palette; foreign, but perfect.

God knows he had tried to maintain his style: the bold, almost abstract rash brushwork; striking rather than smoothing the strokes across the canvass. But the brush would not work this way. The tree would not allow such treatment. It demanded honesty.

Standing back, thrown by the concoction of styles that had been forced upon him, he had actually considered stopping there and then. Or he thought he had. Surely he had! And if so, why had he not? What was it that drove him on to his final subject? He remembered the feeling of the brush in his hand; his hand shaking; the deliberate strokes which began to shape Soulla's form.

And there was no stopping. As she began to appear within his composition, she did so under some control other than his own. His brushwork was painstaking; the detail fine. There was another artist at work here. An earlier version of himself. Or a later one.

He turned again, conscious that he was now sweating profusely. He checked his watch again. And from somewhere came an echo of her laugh, and of the question swept towards him from beneath the tree wanting to know how long he was going to be. How long? He had stepped back and something told her he was finished.

She reached his side within seconds. His stare remained fixed; a stare now conjoined with her own. Soulla stared at Soulla. An almost perfect duplicate; a canvass replica. Except. Except.

He rose from the bed and pulled on his trousers and shirt. This was not him either. This was some other force; a force ripping at the twine and pulling the picture from the stack. A force that drove him out of the hut and off towards the hill, towards the tree. His sweat became profuse, instigated by his exertion, his effort, his pace as he drove himself on. Passing the tree, he followed the path. Followed her steps as she had run away from him, her scream of betrayal trailing behind her. He stumbled up the path as she must have stumbled. He dodged the rocks as she must have dodged them. Or tried to dodge. Except. Except.

As he reached the cliff edge the sun was rising. Only then could it rise, just as he paused where he had paused a few days before. Paused where Soulla had failed to pause. Paused where Soulla had suddenly lost her footing; where a rock had caught her; stolen her balance. There and now he held up the picture for one last time. The olive tree. And Soulla. A perfect portrait. But it was a Soulla, naked. It was a Soulla whose eyes were not green but fiery red.

His courage did not fail him now; not as it had then. Twisting the canvass behind him, he uncoiled from the waist and sent it skimming out through the air. Hovering momentarily, then sliding, face towards him in a last glimpse of the green tree, it dived out of sight.

~

He felt the deck vibrate beneath his feet, his canvass shoes offered him inadequate insulation. Beyond the white wake of the ship, the island began to recede. The passenger at his side, a middle-aged American, glanced his way.

"Sure is pretty."

Anthony returned his look but said nothing.

"And so green."

"Green?"

The American smiled uncertainly.

"Have you been on holiday?"

Anthony looked back to the shrinking green shape beyond the wake. It seemed as if there was more than just the island he was leaving behind. In many ways he had much of the island with him, wrapped up and tied in twine. But there were other things less easy to carry.

He was going back, but not home. Perhaps he would see Sandra again, but he doubted it. Perhaps he would be able to rediscover the style the island had given him; the abandon; the confidence. Perhaps he would be able to resurrect something of the man he had been there. It seemed a not unreasonable goal. Except. Except.

Anthony turned back to the American.

"No, not a holiday. I came to watch someone die."

Chapter Twenty

"I'm thinking of taking a trip to Hydra. For the book."

Working the text from 'Under the Olive Tree' into the biography had sparked something in Mark's mind that was now trying to persuade him that the next logical step was for him to physically travel in his Father's footsteps in preference to the rather abstract manner of reliving this part of his life through his writing. If he ignored his interaction with Beatrice - as far as tracing out the history were concerned - then his meeting with Stella had been his first tangible collision with his Father's romantic past. Indeed, part of him was still struggling to come to terms with the fact that, when they shook hands, he was actually completing some kind of fated circle; touching the hand that his Father had once held far more tenderly. It seemed bizarre - in fact, almost obscene - that such a trick should be available to him. Ignoring conversations with Walker and Healey, reading the books and transcripts of the interviews was a sanitised way to get to the truth - but it had been the only way he'd been able to access such events thus far. It was also the way he had been taught. That he had never considered the possibility of crossing the channel to shake hands with Napoleon or General de Gaulle owed as much to prescriptive learning as the restrictions of reality.

Had he taken time of weigh his argument more fully, he might have conceded that in talking with Beatrice he was also making the same kind of physical connection as he had with Stella; but Beatrice being family - and being no more than a 'witness' as opposed to a 'participant' - disqualified her from any such consideration. Following this line of reasoning also marked him out as a non-combatant.

The allure of Hydra - or one of its temptations, at any rate - was for Mark to be able to *actually* tread in his Father's footsteps. He would be able to sit in the bar where the conversations with Brakespeare took place; perhaps visit the hut where his Father and George Walker stayed. Also - and his meeting with Stella provided some fuel here - he might also re-discover Constantina and be able to judge for himself whether she was the 'amazing' woman of his Father's description.

"Hydra?" Julia was retrieving clothes from the washing machine and had paused when Mark arrived on the kitchen threshold to make his statement.

Mark looked down at her, his mind in mid-thought, attempting to manifest Constantina from a few of his father's phrases. Would there be more women such as Constantina still there? If there were, then what if he should meet one? What if his visit were to begin - in some remarkable fashion - to do more than allow him mere academic research?

"It's where Father went with George. Where he met," he paused fractionally, taking a breath mid-sentence, "Brakespeare."

"Oh yes, you did say." Julia busied herself again, her words bouncing back to him from the frame of the Hotpoint. "When would we go?"

How would he react in such a situation? Mark tried to project himself onto the quay with a white boat beckoning him back to England. His Father had returned home: wanting to stay, he had not. So badly wanting to stay, he had later created Anthony Shipley who had been endowed with the opportunity to do so. As a result, there had been tragedy, but that had only been fiction. Who was to say which of the lives, real or fictional, he might choose to live? And was there an olive tree there as well, naked on the hillside overlooking the town?

"Mark?" Julia was standing now, her arms filled with clean clothes. "Did you hear me? And pass me that basket will you, please?"

He picked the wicker basket from the floor and took three steps towards her, replaying their stilted conversation as he did so. Filtering out irrelevant words from his most recent memory he reconstructed her sentence, realising - just as he held out the basket to receive the weight of the laundry - that Julia had asked when *they* would be going. Not only did it dash the notion of him going alone, the question suddenly implied a set of practicalities that he had not even considered: there would be flights to be booked; hotels to arrange; a car to be hired - or more probably a jeep. And would they be able to stay in Hydra anyway? Were there hotels there of the sort they were used to using? And how hot would it be? Julia's skin did not respond terribly well to heat and humidity. Attempting to decipher such a list, brought his musing of Hydra to an abrupt end, and he found his suite of available replies strictly limited.

"Soon, probably."

Julia took the basket from him.

"But not until after the wedding, obviously. After all, that's not far away now, is it?"

Mark didn't know for sure. It was not a key date he carried around with him. Indeed, the coming together of Laura and Tim could only be for the worse as far as he was concerned, because ahead of the nuptials it demanded the man-handling of the mirror once again.

Out of the kitchen, Mark made his way up to the bedroom where he fished his dark tan brogues from the bottom of the wardrobe. As he tied the laces, sitting on the bed and facing the now empty laundry bin, he caught a glimpse of his watch. It was nearly ten and he had promised to meet Congreave at eleven for coffee.

"Nothing critical," Bruce had said, "just want to catch up, that's all."

Mark's hand paused as it reached out for his tweed jacket, hesitating over what would have normally been his natural choice. He looked down at his trousers - a pair of fawn Chinos - and wondered if he might try an alternative accompaniment.

"How long will you be?"

Standing in front of the hall mirror, checking his hair - and the fractured tweed once again - Julia's voice reached him from the kitchen. He turned to see her approaching.

"Not too long. Bruce said he wants an update, that's all. Coffee. And we're not meeting in his office anyway."

"Oh? Where are you seeing him?"

"Apparently he's off to Hampshire for some reason and suggested we meet in the National. It's on his way from the office to Waterloo. His train's before twelve, so we can't be very long can we?"

"I see." Julia paused, smiling uncomfortably. Mark wondered for an instant if she might not be well; she had seemed a little below par of late, not her buoyant self. "You're not playing squash after?"

"Squash?" It was a word that now had a dual meaning for him, and Mark was forced to chase through his mental diary checking on plans for squash with Peter and meetings with Maxine. "Not today, no."

He turned and walked to the front door; as he opened it, Julia - who had followed him along the hallway - spoke again.

"Are you driving?"

"I thought I might. Even though it's Waterloo. I might get back a little quicker." Mark stopped and turned, then - as if caught off-guard by his concern for her well-being - bent to kiss Julia's forehead. "Why don't you arrange for us to see Peter and Claire for dinner or something over the next couple of days? Might be a nice thing to do. Perhaps we could go out to Kew or something, if they've time."

Thanks to the kiss - and the suggestion - Julia's smile seemed to him a little more reassured now.

"You haven't forgotten that we're going over to Beatrice and Simon tomorrow for dinner, have you?"

"Tomorrow? Are we?"

She laughed.

"You *had* forgotten!"

Mark ignored the joke and pulled his car keys from his trouser pocket.

Unaccustomed to the lighter than usual mid-morning traffic, Mark found himself walking into the foyer of the National Theatre earlier than expected. It was a little before ten forty-five. He paused as the heavy glass doors swung closed behind him, taking in the scene. Although it felt an age since he had last been there (a visit not entirely unconnected with Congreave, he recalled) the place seemed not to have changed. There were a fair number of children about, but rather than being there in uniformed presence, they seemed more relaxed, as if visiting the theatre on their own terms - or at least, on their parents' terms rather than those of their educational establishments. Mark paired children with parents for a second, realising as he did so that the general population might be explained by it probably being some kind of school holiday; a fact which would, in part, help explain the slightly quieter roads.

From the far side of the Foyer, the image of Hamlet - with the wild haired Ghost at his shoulder - stared back at him. He remembered with a slight shiver Julia's words about their dinner date at his Aunt's, and simultaneously recognised the need to spend more than just the evening in Belsize Park.

"Coffee, please."

"Filter, decaf, cappuccino or espresso?"

As he asked for an espresso, Mark tried to remember when ordering coffee had been a more simple affair: half-and-half boiling water and hot frothy milk served in plain white china. He picked up his clear glass cup - which, despite its metallic ring-like handle, was almost impossible to hold - and walked towards the small bookshop.

Sitting on a vacant seat just outside its door, he watched prospective customers wandering in and satisfied customers wandering out, most bearing brown paper bags of various sizes, with each bag carrying the emblem of the 'NT'. He noticed how those visitors cradling bags seemed to leave the shop in a more purposeful manner than those who did not, as if they were about to take their purchase off to a secret hide somewhere and devour it immediately. Such a reaction to book buying had never been something Mark had experienced himself. Even when leaving Foyle's after successful student days' expeditions, he failed to recall any keen anticipation associated with the prospect of reading his new purchases. Perhaps it was the forced nature of study that removed some of the pleasure of reading - for he was certain (or as certain as he allowed himself to be) that he did actually enjoy researching into history. In any event, at the time it appeared that the only way one could find out about the past - let alone research into it - was through reading. His very recent thoughts - those which leant towards Greece and suggested that there was a possibility of tracking down the past through some other kind of shared experience - offered a little further evidence to counter the kind of focused zeal he was witness to now.

It might be different with fiction, of course; and Mark's assumption was that the NT book buyers were indulging in the purchase of such work. To explore a new and unreal world might - and here he was guessing slightly - *need* some kind of anticipation; indeed, it might just offer such a freedom. If it were impossible to really 'share' historical events, he found himself wondering how likely it might be to share any fictional experience. There was, he reasoned, imitation; but Mark felt certain that imitation - taking the fictional and making it real - was somehow a less pure translation than his own undertaking, namely taking the real, the historical truth, and writing that down. Taking truth and making it fiction - that was another matter, of course! There had been one student at University who specialised in the lineage of English royalty. More than that, however, the young man had been something of a Shakespeare scholar too. Mark wondered, even now, if it had been possible to keep the two apart: if he had written, for example, an essay on Richard the Third, then whose Richard would he write about; the real historical King or the Bard's fictional one?

From somewhere a clock began to chime eleven. Mark looked away from the shop and scanned briefly for a sighting of Congreave. Undoubtedly the other man would be late and would rush through their conversation, his coffee, the foyer, in the same way as he seemed to rush through everything else. In expectation of a slightly longer wait, Mark drained his coffee, stood up, and walked into the shop.

There were a few names familiar to him: Keats and Wordsworth in the small poetry section; Shaw and Shakespeare with the plays. There were a whole variety of texts, especially in the expansive section reserved for the man from Stratford where each play was offered by a variety of publishers. Mark selected a couple of editions of 'Hamlet' and opened them at the beginning of the first act. The words to be spoken by the actors were, of course, the same, but the variety in the books came from the layout of the text, the way footnotes were inserted, and - most especially - the gloss applied by the editors. It seemed to him almost as if they were unsatisfied with the original, and in consequence had decided to supplement and improve it. Mark smiled. The thought of trying to do that with history - providing spice, puffing out conversations or meetings, even adding events that never happened - was a parallel he found instantly amusing.

"Mark! Espresso, isn't it?"

A voice called him from the books. He turned. It was Mike.

"Bruce is getting the coffees. You usually drink espresso, don't you?"

"Mike," Mark was a little surprised to see him in the doorway. "Yes, espresso's fine."

Mark watched Bruce's assistant leave, then returned the copies of 'Hamlet'. As he was leaving, he noticed the shelves also offered a considerable number of biographies alongside original texts and scholarly critiques. This threw him a little; perhaps he had not expected to discover such a large element of history - was he not writing a biography? - amidst the fantasy. And what if some of those little brown bags so keenly carried off the premises contained such works; what then?

He found Bruce and Mike seated at a small round table near the coffee bar. Mike's short wave reminded him of Julia in Foyle's; a parallel that ended with the gesture. Both men were wearing suits which, though not unusual for Congreave, suggested to Mark that their Southern visit was an important one.

"Out to make an impression?"

It was odd that he had been able to get the first word in, considering Congreave's tendency to rush ahead full pelt, and this - along with the other's failure to put down his coffee and offer Mark his hand - immediately put him on the defensive.

"Impression?" Congreave smiled, "Just a business meeting, old chap; that's all."

Mark nodded and took the seat designated as his by the presence of another small espresso cup.

"Difficult to pick up these things, aren't they?"

"Sorry?" Mike queried.

"The coffee cups? Too small. Difficult to get a hold of."

"Ah."

"So, Mark," Bruce suddenly launched himself into the conversation, "how's it going? Keeping busy? Working on the book, I expect. Tough, I'll be bound; research and all, eh?"

Mark was jolted by the sudden injection of pace.

"So-so, Bruce; you know how it is."

"Yes, indeed. Only saying to Mike the other day how you were probably slaving away over your Dad's story; you know, little time for anything else, that kind of thing." Congreave turned to his colleague. "Said that, didn't I Mike? 'Bet old Mark's working his balls off on this one!'"

"Something like that," Mike affirmed, joining his boss in looking at Mark.

Mike's approach - being that much slower and more methodical than Congreave's - always threw Mark when they were together. He saw them as peculiar opposites, a strange kind of incarnation of the 'good Cop, bad Cop' scenario popular in the mythology produced for the masses. Mark tired to gauge his own pace to fit between them, uncertain as to the response they were looking for.

"As you say," he said noncommittally.

"Look Mark," the Editor raced away again, "you're probably wondering why we suggested seeing you. God knows we're got our train to catch in a while, and this isn't necessarily the easiest place, but such is life."

"Easiest place?"

Congreave shook his head slightly, still smiling as he did so, suggesting that there was a rogue thought in his head he might be trying to shake off, or that what was about to be said failed to merit the importance the words might imply.

"It's the Chamberlain biography," Mike offered, causing Mark to shift his attention to him.

"The Wallace? What about it?"

"Bruce has asked me to do it."

Congreave, sipping his coffee, was ready to receive Mark's gaze as he shifted his eyes towards him.

"Why? I mean, I know I said that I didn't think much of it - but I didn't say that I wasn't willing to do it. I mean I can fit it in, if that's what you're worried about." Mark felt uncomfortable, pressured. In trying to pick up his drink, the small cup tilted in his hand and he spilt a little of the coffee on the table.

"I see what you mean," Mike offered in sympathy.

"It's not about your willingness," Congreave sprung on him while he wasn't looking. "Your willingness isn't in question, dear boy."

Mark expected to hear more; he wanted to hear more. The way Congreave had left his sentence, the way both men were now looking at him, demanded a response; and there was only one response he could give. He felt - even as the words slipped automatically from his mouth - as if he had been set up; they had laid a trap in this pre-planned conversation and he had fallen into it. Perhaps there was a way out, a way not to play their game: if he stood up, threw the table back; if he simply walked out - they wouldn't have planned on that. But then the words were already out, spoken as if by a character in someone else's play.

"So what is?"

Congreave put down his coffee and offered Mark his steady, professional gaze.

"We've pulled the Kuwaiti piece, old son," Mark was mesmerised by the sudden lack of pace on the delivery, as if Bruce were talking in slow motion. "After our last little chat I had a couple of the team check it out."

"Check it out?"

"I hoped I'd been wrong. I said to Mike, 'Bet that Irish thing was just a minor lapse' - didn't I Mike? 'Bet old Mark's been thrown by that book of his. Lapse of concentration; that sort of thing.'" Mike nodded as if to confirm this. "But there you are. There were things in the new piece we simply couldn't let go out. We're gong to change them. Mike will do the rewrite and we'll put it out next month, Of course, you'll still get the credit."

"Credit?" Mark, still holding the espresso two or three inches above the table, was trying to assimilate Congreave's message. What could have been wrong with the article? After all, hadn't he checked and re-checked his facts? Hadn't he been thorough? As usual?

"With Mike. Joint effort. Your name first, of course."

Congreave's smile helped rouse Mark a little from his punch drunk stupor. He replaced the cup on the table then attempted to fix the other man with as serious stare as he could muster. He knew that Mike was there somewhere, but he needed to focus, he needed to try and cut down his peripheral vision to almost nothing. There was something important going on here, and he wanted to understand it.

"What are you saying, Bruce? That my Kuwaiti piece isn't good enough?"

"Accuracy..."

"That you're going to get someone else to re-word it?" Mark carried on, for once ignoring Congreave's attempt to interject as much as he was ignoring Mike, "That you're pulling me off the Wallace biography, yes? And why, Bruce? Why?"

"Mark," Mike cut in, "its just that we think that you're a little..."

"Distracted," Congreave suggested.

"Distracted by your book, that's all. Maybe a little tired too. We think it might be best if we just left you alone for a while; that's all."

"That's all?"

"Mark," Congreave was checking his watch as he spoke, "don't get this out of proportion. Come on, we all know that you didn't really want to do the Chamberlain book, don't we? So don't make a big thing out of it. Shit, we've probably done you a favour!" Congreave was up-beat now, rushing towards his conclusion as if his checking the time had given him cause to do so. "And anyway, we've got something we might want you to pick up in a couple of weeks or so."

"What something?"

"A small project. Just an idea at the moment - but once I've worked on it a little bit, we can talk about it then." Congreave motioned to Mike who, following Congreave's lead, rose. "Take a break from the magazine for a few weeks. Forget about history. Why not forget everything and take the gorgeous Julia off to the country or something? When you get back, give me a call."

Congreave spoke as if it had already been decided that - without any power to make up his own mind - he would be going away. Mark made to get up.

"Don't worry about us," Congreave placed his hand on Mark's shoulder, "we've got to dash. Finish your coffee in peace, eh? And call me in a couple of weeks. Or whenever. OK?"

The two men were already retreating as the last words reached Mark's ears. He picked up the coffee cup and sipped the dark liquid which had cooled considerably by now. Somewhere Mark could feel wrath inside him, but it was a strange, buried kind of feeling that had not yet surfaced. Perhaps - and he was still clear minded enough to see this - Bruce had expected some kind of explosion; perhaps that was why Mike had been with him. He was right of course; he hadn't wanted to do the Wallace review. And yes, it might be useful to forget about the magazine for a while. Perhaps the project Bruce mentioned would be a little more up his street, something he could get excited about; something that would suit his style and approach, his method of research. It was, he conceded to himself as the pulled open the heavy door, more likely to be a blessing in disguise; a chance for him to really focus on the biography.

As he walked away from the theatre, the wild eyes of Hamlet and the Ghost followed his departure.

Chapter Twenty One

Beatrice and Simon's bedroom was, to all intents and purposes, 'foreign territory' for Mark. His well-trodden route from the top of the stairs to his 'den of inequity' (as Simon rather abstractly called it once) was so direct - even allowing for the one hundred and eighty degree turn around the banister - that their nephew had little need to venture any further. It was, therefore, a circumstance out of the ordinary which found Mark pausing at its threshold.

In fact the catalyst for his minor trespass - the sound of something dropping to the floor and a half-stifled curse from Beatrice - proved to be far from calamitous, and when Mark arrived (having been, coincidentally, at the top of the stairs when the crash came) Beatrice was already bending to recover the broken object from the floor. Having her back to him, Mark's view of his Aunt was also something a little outside the run of the mill. There was, of course, little in her actual appearance that took him by surprise; he knew well enough her taste in clothes, and so the sight of her in cord trousers - her 'weekend baggies' she liked to call them - failed to surprise him, even if from this angle the view presented to him was a trifle undignified. There was also little in the way in which she went about her physical activity which he might legitimately have noted as odd. Indeed, there was nothing about the situation at all which he could have pointed to with any authority and said 'There it is! That was what gave it to me.' However despite this, there was - as he paused trying to decide on whether or not to make a silent and unobserved retreat - an aura about Beatrice that alarmed him. Not that it should have of course, given that the message he received - unheralded and triggered silently across twenty feet of bedroom carpet - was that she was getting old.

This thought, having come suddenly to him, did just enough to hold him there, postponing his decision to move sufficiently to allow Beatrice - as she rose from the floor, broken china in her cupped hand - to catch sight of him in the mirror of her dresser.

"Just one of my silly trinkets," she said, straightening and turning towards him, her hand half-outstretched as if in explanation. "Actually they're not really my trinkets at all, but little things your Uncle has persistently bought me over the years on the mistaken assumption that I like them."

She was upright now, with a slight flush to her cheek. There was no sign that she was suffering any lack of breath or discomfort through her exertion, and Mark wondered if that momentary image - Beatrice as an ageing woman - might have been illusory.

"Why didn't you tell him?" he said, managing to tag on to the thread of her statement.

"That I didn't like them?" She shrugged her shoulders as she let the pieces of porcelain tumble into a waste bin. "Maybe I didn't want to hurt his feelings."

"Really?"

She smiled.

"Well, once I would have cared about that sort of thing - though you might choose not believe it, Mark! - and as soon as one misses the chance to nip something like that in the bud, then the lie just goes on living with you."

"Until it becomes a truth perhaps?"

Beatrice brushed her hands together.

"Not in this case."

Mark turned, assuming that the brief cameo was over, but Beatrice, gathering herself together before she went back downstairs, wanted him to see the time out with her.

"Do you do the same thing?"

"What same thing?" He stopped and waited for her at the head of the stairs, his left hand resting on the banister rail as he responded to the disembodied voice.

"Buy things for Julia that she doesn't want?"

"Like trinkets?"

"Like anything." Beatrice allowed a short pause, time enough for Mark to respond in the affirmative if such a response was going to be the natural one. Sensing nothing coming, she carried on, meeting him again physically as she spoke. "But then you're just a man after all, aren't you Dear? Shouldn't really expect meaningless tokens, should we?"

Mark wondered if this combative attitude had been triggered as a direct result of his seeming to question the more sensitive side of her own nature.

"Not meaningless, surely? And what about Simon?"

"Perhaps not meaningless, no; but you can't assume your Uncle to be some kind of norm for the male of the species. And certainly not in your case."

This was a little too close for comfort. Mark straightened himself.

"My case?"

"You are, are you not, your Father's son? And there's no way in the world he would have succumbed to such feeble gestures."

"Are you sure he didn't?"

"You think he did? Have you any evidence - either physical or in remembrance - to suggest otherwise? You know, it might have helped him to have been a little softer."

Mark was uncertain as to his Aunt's exact meaning, especially in terms of 'helping' his Father. He tried to take Simon as the embodiment of her notion of 'softness', just to see what he might be able to conjure up; however, the exercise proved fruitless as the only connection he was able to make between Simon and any tendency towards 'softness' was not (he was sure!) of the kind presently being lauded by Beatrice. Despite this - and his inability to refute her direct accusation - there was the need to respond, to offer something in his Father's defence.

"But he was romantic."

Beatrice laughed quietly. Having reached the top of the stairs, she had stood poised to make her descent, but his last comment drew her hand away from the supporting rail to pat his own.

"Oh yes; but he was too romantic!"

"Too romantic?"

"He was full of the stuff - and much of it of the wrong kind too. If he had one dream, he had a hundred. Maybe that was why he drank so much - and why he wrote."

"To act out his dreams, you mean?"

She smiled again, and began to walk down the stairs.

"Good Lord, no! To fulfil them."

-*-

The decision to give up work was one Packard did not take lightly. By early the following year, <u>Under the Olive Tree</u> was promising to be successful enough for him to be able to sustain his family without needing to resort to the factory. Having now had two novels published, Charles also found himself being asked to write small pieces in magazines and newspapers which, along with his limited royalties, gave him an income totalling around two-thirds of that which he had been used to. More than that, this income also gave him his freedom.

As was his usual practice, George Walker was involved in some of the early discussions with respect to leaving full-time employment, though in the end it was Healey at Macmillan who proved to be the major influence.

> "George's advice was sound enough, but it seemed a little biased. He was quite obviously concerned about Mary and Mark above all else; how I fared or fitted in was of secondary importance. Perhaps that was just as well; after all, I guess I was feeling pretty gung-ho about things, and George held me in check just long enough for me to take further soundings."

> (Interview on Radio 4, 1983)

Peter Healey at Macmillan was the man to whom Packard turned. They met at Healey's office towards the end of 1965 to discuss sales of <u>Under the Olive Tree</u> and possible future projects. At that stage, Charles had nothing in mind, and was in any event being kept busy enough with his minor articles to think very far into the future. During their conversation, Packard asked for Healey's opinion on the subject of his giving up work. Healey took him through the projected sales of his book which, though modest, were sufficient to secure a limited income. Taking into account other additional fees, Healey suggested that if Packard were careful - and if he was able to follow up with a third novel in a reasonable timeframe - then there was no reason why he should not consider writing to be his sole occupation.

> "I remember the words that did it for me. He said, "If you're serious about this Charles, then you've got to do it; you have no choice". I knew I was serious. I knew I wanted nothing else. OK, perhaps there was a part of me that was being driven by the desire to quit work, but I don't believe - even to this day - that it was a very large part."

> (Interview on Radio 4, 1983)

So the decision to leave the factory was taken. As it turned out, the follow-up novel was longer in the making than either Charles or Healey had anticipated, events in 1966 overtaking them rapidly.

-*-

From the end of what was probably - Mark surmised - a logically interminable communications cable, the electronic 'burr, burr' of the unanswered phone came back to him. As he waited, he turned slightly on the small chair that sat alongside the telephone stand in the hallway, attempting to look through the kitchen door and out of the window beyond. He had been standing there around an hour earlier when Beatrice had delivered what he could only interpret as a definitive answer to the question which he had presented (he had been certain of that!) in the most sensitive way he could. Not that there was any need to be especially sensitive in his Aunt's case, of that he was sure; but the event with the trinket - and its consequent verbal cuffing - had left him sufficiently wary.

"Photographs?" she had said, looking up from her preparation of the meringues they would be having for dessert that evening, "Oh, I don't think so. Not of her."

Although Beatrice's words had implied uncertainty, their delivery had come in such a manner as to dispel all possible doubt as to their veracity.

"Why do you ask?"

"I've just finished writing about Hydra and, well, I thought that a picture of Constantina might be suitable."

Beatrice returned to her whisking, flicking the thin steel implement about the mixing bowl with a practised hand.

"'Suitable'", she echoed, as if taking the word and folding it in with the egg whites and sugar. Without breaking from her rhythm, she batted a question back to him.

"When you say you've finished, what do you mean exactly?"

"The first draft of that part of the book."

"Yes, Dear; but where are you in time?"

Mark was relieved by her returning to gentle familiarity, and dismissed their conversation at the head of the stairs to the back of his mind.

"I'm in early 1966. Hydra was nearly a year ago; the 'Olive Tree' has been published; and he's just given up work."

There had been the slightest of hesitations - as usual - when he needed to refer to his Father when talking to Beatrice. Neither 'Father' nor 'Charles' seemed accurate somehow, each lacking something from one perspective or the other - if not both. Except when absolutely essential,

Mark always chose the nondescript 'he' as the most appropriate term of reference; it was one which Beatrice never challenged, after all, they both knew who they were talking about.

A 'click' interrupting the monotone purring of the telephone brought him back from the kitchen.

"Hello." The voice was female, but sounded younger than Mark had expected.

"Mrs Brakespeare?"

"Who is it please?"

"Mark Packard; Charles' son." Sensing caution in the other speaker, Mark offered the qualification almost as if it were a password that might gain him access like Ali Baba to some secret cavern.

There was a moment of silence.

"Please wait."

Mark looked up at the hall clock; it was a little after three. He watched the slim second hand slip round its face and wondered if he should see how long he was kept there: five, six, seven. In the unseen distance, there came the muffled sounds of voices and then nothing. He looked back at the clock. The second hand had moved beyond the twelve and was now making its descent once again. As it came to the four, he tried to recall if that was thirty or thirty-five seconds he had been waiting.

"Yes?"

This time the voice was considerably older, crackling softly down the hi-tech line to him.

"Hello. Mrs Brakespeare?"

"Yes."

"My name's Mark Packard. You don't know me very well, though we did meet at the memorial service for your husband a few years ago."

There was no response.

"I was a little younger then. I don't suppose you remember me."

Again nothing.

"You knew my Father; Charles Packard."

"Charles?"

"Packard, yes. The writer. You met him in Greece, when you were on Hydra with your husband." Mark felt his words trailing off, beginning to feel that his call - a long-shot, the possibility of which had come suddenly to him - was ill-conceived. He had not expected her to sound so old. When he had met her she had still seemed a sprightly lady.

"Charles Packard." Mrs Brakespeare's voice suggested a degree of hope. "The writer. Yes."

"You were together in Greece," Mark prompted again.

"It was very hot. How is your Father?"

The inappropriateness of the question took him aback slightly, though not enough to prevent him pressing on with something rapidly turning into a fruitless exercise.

"I wondered if you had any photographs."

"Photographs?"

"Of Greece. Of my Father when he was on holiday with you."

"Photographs?" The voice began to sound a little disembodied, and its response directed not to Mark at all. "Photographs? What photographs?"

"Mrs Brakespeare." There was no response. "Mrs Brakespeare."

"I'm sorry," - it was the younger woman - "I'm afraid Mrs Brakespeare can't talk to you any more. You'll have to excuse her. I shouldn't have let you speak to her in the first place; I'm sorry."

There was another 'click', this time leaving Mark holding the unresponsive receiver in his hand.

The importance of photographs had crept up on him suddenly - this as he sat back at his desk fingering the only shot he had of his Father and the younger, male Brakespeare. He remembered similar prints in the books he had seen on the artist over the years of course, but had only recently - through his own immediate experience - realised their intrinsic part in the re-telling of history. In the same way that Mark had lent some thought to the naming of the chapters in his book, he had also gently wrestled with the best way to include the images (mainly black and white) that would accompany them. The two basic choices open to him - or at least those with which he was most familiar - were to include the pictures within the body of text at the appropriate point, or to house them all together in a kind of supplement which would be located somewhere near the middle of the biography. Neither of these seemed quite right somehow, and his ambition to make such inclusions as true to history as possible would have been to have been able to inter-weave them between the lines of text themselves and thus arrive at an amalgam of both word and image.

It would have been impossible for him to say what had triggered this realisation in respect of the photographs. Perhaps searching for those ancient prints of his Mother had been the catalyst, stirring, as they did, something within him that was even more personal than the function for which they were intended. Indeed, his pursuit of such collaborative material had been ever more serious since Beatrice had been able to provide him with a selection from her own private hoard. At such times Mark had almost felt himself to be on more of a journey of personal discovery (much of it was his own history in one way or another, after all) than the definably more simple task of historical translator.

Because of his growing need to satisfy this impetus and the now recognised belief that such tangible back-up was essential to establishing the most able and accurate representation he could muster - because of this, Mark had reached the inescapable conclusion that a picture of Constantina was a vital ingredient in his Father's biographical recipe. It had not registered with him (and why should it have, indeed?) that part of his desire to catch sight of Constantina was to allow him to verify for himself the magnificence of the woman who had captured his Father's imagination.

_*_

Two weeks after the meeting with Healey to discuss the practicality of living off his writing, Packard was back at Macmillan's. He had received a letter from the Executors of Arnold Harriman in respect of <u>Pieces of Eight</u>. After a long struggle against cancer - a struggle not assisted by Harriman's persistent smoking of twenty roll-ups a day - Packard's first publisher had died in St. Mary's Hospital, Portsmouth, on 4th April.

His publishing house - which had also been ailing - was taken over a few months previously by American publishing giants Bell & Withers, who, on the divestment of Harriman's estate, had uncovered the papers relating to Packard's dealings with the dead man.

> "As far as I was concerned, Harriman had been dead for years. The sordid little fable of <u>Pieces of Eight</u> was long since over, and the last thing I expected was for the old man to "rave from the grave", as it were!"

(Interview in "The Sunday Times', 1981)

Since the publication of both <u>Dawn</u> and <u>Under the Olive Tree</u>, all remaining copies of <u>Pieces of Eight</u> had been sold, many of these privately by the Author himself. Bell & Withers' contention was that, not only did Packard owe them the appropriate share of the moneys received for those final copies, but maintained that the original agreement with Harriman provided for a tie between the writer and publisher in the event of success unless the publisher chose to waiver that tie. Bell & Withers could find no such waiver, and were therefore now demanding substantial recompense for Packard moving his affairs first to Dawson and then to Macmillan.

Given the amount of support he had so recently received from Peter Healey, Charles had no hesitation in making him his first port of call on this occasion too.

-*-

He was interrupted by the remarkable occurrence of a knock at his open door. Beatrice waited for him.

"You don't have to knock, Aunt," Mark said cautiously. Her appearance - and the fact that she had announced her arrival in such a fashion before crossing the threshold - immediately put him on his guard.

"I could see you were busy", she said almost timidly.

Mark looked back at his keyboard and the last character - a full stop - he had typed there. He spun the computer's mouse to the toolbar and saved his work before facing Beatrice square on. She had walked a little further into the room, not so far as to be away from the wall but close enough to Laura's mirror, upon which she decided to rest her hand.

"Don't you want to sit down?" Mark, torn between the brown oblong and his Aunt's presence, found he could only cope with one distraction at a time. Beatrice moved to the chair and sat down. Her hesitancy was new to him, alien almost. "Is there something wrong?"

She shook her head, but it was only a half-denial, the manner of her action - rather than the action itself - being more telling.

"How do you feel about unsubstantiated truth?"

"'Unsubstantiated truth'?"

"Rumour; instinct; gut feel."

"Depends whose gut it is," - she smiled at this - "and the context."

Beatrice's silence allowed his mind to race ahead, and Mark found himself wondering what he might possibly have to do with 'rumour' or 'gut feel' - especially in his Aunt's house. It had been an idle and unfocussed kind of thought - until he remembered Simon. And remembering Simon, he recalled the dinner they had attended together. And remembering the dinner, he remembered Maxine. He felt a shiver emerge from between his shoulder blades and slip, out of control, towards the small of his back.

"You ask for context." Beatrice paused, threatening to reward Mark with a second tremor. "How about in the context of your book?"

"My book?" The words had tripped out too quickly and Mark found himself hoping that they had not carried with them undue signs of relief. Indeed, if Beatrice were approaching him on the subject of the biography then she would surely expect him to appear very concerned indeed. He tried again. "What do you mean, exactly, by 'my book'?"

"You said that you had finished with that Greek girl."

"Constantina? Yes, I have"

"Presumably you mean that you have exhausted your supply of factual material?"

"Indeed."

"I see."

"Why?"

His Aunt paused before repeating her original question.

"How do you feel about unsubstantiated truth?" She repeated the original question.

"About Constantina?"

"Yes."

"I'll have to hear it first, of course."

There was a slight pause before Beatrice spoke again. Once more she denied him immediate access to her thoughts, preferring - as he saw it - to lay as much foundation for what was to follow as she possibly could.

"You have tried to contact her, I suppose - directly, and through all the usual channels?""

"I have."

"Without success?"

"Indeed."

"So if there were," - again she paused, though seemingly more relaxed now, and almost into the flow of what she was doing - "something else, you wouldn't be able to do much about it?"

"Aunt! What are you on about?" Mark felt as if he had suddenly been cast in the denouement of an Agatha Christie thriller and the sleuth was holding on to the identity of the killer until the last possible moment.

"Presumably the last you have of the girl is your Father waving goodbye to her at Hydra."

"If you don't include his portrayal of her in the 'Olive Tree', yes. Why?"

"Well; I suspect that there were letters."

"Letters!" He had sifted painstakingly through all his Father's correspondence - not to mention his bills, accounts, and tax returns; the last thing he would have expected to hear of was the presence of further letters. For this reason, as much as any other, Mark was immediately struck by a sensation that, even though he might be on the verge of an important discovery, he might somehow perversely - ironically even! - need to face up to the possibility that he had not actually done his research properly. Proof was easily gained. "You have letters?!"

"I didn't say that, Dear. I said that I 'suspected' that there were letters."

"Did Father show them to you?"

"He did not."

"Then how do you know there were any?"

Beatrice laughed.

"I feel as if I've walked into an episode of 'Perry Mason'" - Mark was struck by the parallel with his own feelings - "and I'm being grilled by the Prosecution or something! I don't know, Dear - but I suspect. From things your Father said at the time, little hints in conversations; you know the kind of thing."

"Conversations with him?"

"Mostly. But with your Mother too. She suspected."

"That something had happened? But that's not news for me; not as far as the book is concerned. I mean, what relevance do a few non-existent letters have to the story of Constantina?"

"Perhaps none, unless they revealed that she was pregnant."

He had once toyed with the question as to why his Father's various adventures - both during and after his marriage - had failed to result in further issue. It had been a thought process triggered one day by something of a dismissive comment from Julia which he had immediately ridiculed. Under the circumstances however - and given the factual evidence of these liaisons which Mark could certainly not contradict - did this mean that his Father had been particularly careful? There was, he believed, no prominent 'safe sex' culture during his Father's sexual heyday. Indeed, he was certain that the sorts of precautions now liberally taken - and here he immediately recalled Maxine as being a confessed practitioner of modern methods - were less popular then. Perhaps his Father had just been lucky. If so - and Mark took this next step instantaneously without any possibility of checking his stride - did this mean that in his own presence might be evidence of bad luck?

"Pregnant?"

"I know Dear, but there it is. It's something I've been sitting on, oh for too long now. Not even your Uncle suspects."

"But you almost speak as if it were fact." Mark had regained a little of his equilibrium, trying to hold on to the conversation as distorted images of a Grecian half-brother threatened to overwhelm him. "You said you had no letters. Where is the evidence?"

Beatrice smiled, as if trying to soothe his excitement.

"As I said, there is none. All I have is instinct."

"Gut feel!"

He was angry now; angry that his Aunt should have raised such a spectre before him, stirring such wild and virtually uncontrollable thoughts. It was, he reasoned, all very well for her to casually slip in the odd accusation, but to do so without any regard for the integrity of what he was trying to do, let alone his own equilibrium! From all people, he would have expected her to display some regard for equilibrium.

"And."

The word hit him like a bullet from a gun whose silencer had softened the sound of its coming.

"And?"

"Instinct and something else."

She waited, but Mark said nothing. In his hand, he rotated a pencil he had picked up from the desk. Looking beyond her, he noticed that on one corner, the wrapping of the mirror appeared to have come a little undone. He would need to fix that.

Aware of the silence, he looked back at her.

"I asked Charles."

"You asked him?"

"If there were letters. If the Greek girl had written to him."

"And if she was pregnant."

Beatrice nodded.

"He refused to talk about it; but he denied nothing."

Chapter Twenty Two

By the time Bell & Withers' case had progressed through the various stages of dispute to finally arrive in Court, Charles Packard had become something of a minor celebrity. Healey, having decided to support Packard, had carefully orchestrated the Macmillan publicity machine behind the writer. Consequently, the popular press had been guided in such a way as to portray the clash as one between the plucky British Underdog fighting the mighty American corporation.

> "It was vaguely surreal. I found that, not only did the reports of the affair hardly resemble reality, the person about whom some of these rags were writing - namely me! - was someone I didn't even recognise. Of course as Peter continually reminded me, there was no such thing as bad press, and the consequence of this sudden attention - and especially the TV interview - was to see sales of both my novels rise. I was fully aware that Peter's motives weren't wholly altruistic, of course, but he knew the game and how to play it so well... Well, we couldn't go wrong."

> (Interview in "The Sunday Times', 1981)

The matter was never as clear cut as Healey made out in his morale boosting meetings with Packard. Indeed, only three days before the court appearance that was to settle the matter once and for all, he received independent advice that they should stop fighting and agree to settle out of court.

"It would have been tempting at one stage, but we had come so far. And okay there wasn't a huge bandwagon following our progress, but there was some. The key thing for me was what the whole thing was doing for Charles, and for his career. He handled it so well, so naturally. I guess my gut told me that if we made it out the other side, then we were likely to make it out big time."

The hearing lasted a little over four hours with the Judge retiring to make his ruling a little after three p.m. on Wednesday 7th July. The case had progressed pretty much in accordance with the Packard-Healey game plan - with the one notable exception of Charles' sudden outburst after a period of intense cross-examination, when his vehement rhetoric in defence of the rights of the individual earned cheers from the small but well attended public gallery.

> "I felt like Lincoln must have felt at Gettysbury. Or maybe Hitler at a Berlin rally, I don't know! The speech hadn't been planned,

and I guessed that the Judge hadn't appreciated the slight disruption to the proceedings that followed it. Later, as we waited in the corridors outside, some of the public - and even one or two of the Press - came and asked my for autograph. Some of them even had copies of <u>Under the Olive</u> tree. It was bizarre!"

(Interview in "The Sunday Times', 1981)

When four o'clock passed, suspicion grew that the case would be adjourned to the following day, Judge Michaels being particularly well known for his long deliberations. So, when the court was suddenly recalled at eight minutes past four, the level of expectation and excitement was particularly keen. The summing up and delivery of judgement was over within five minutes. Michaels began by recognising the legitimacy of Bell & Withers' case, and confessed that in other countries their petition may well have been upheld. He stated, however, that he felt in this instance their case had not been sufficiently proven, and that - taking into account all the mitigating factors in terms of the passage of time as well as the rather dubious origins of the contract in question - Packard had enough moral right on his side to gain the day.

For the second time that day there were cheers in the Court, and outside Packard and Healey found themselves pursued by a small posse of Journalists searching for soundbites.

"We made the evening news. Just a small piece, but it was enough. And Charles was asked to appear on a lunchtime programme the next day. It took him a little while to settle down after all the excitement. To be honest, I think he went AWOL for a time. But later we were able to rein him back in and talk about his next book."

What Healey was soon to find out, was that Packard had been rewarded by more than just a moral victory from his day in Court.

-*-

The sound of a car door slamming outside caused Mark to look up. Through the slightly open window, he heard the familiar sound of Julia's voice bounce towards him from beyond the hedge as she paid the taxi driver. Dusk was imminent, and, in its accompanying chill, he shivered, and stood up to close the window. The sound of its closing (a tight, comfortable sound, he thought) made Julia look up as she walked towards the house; seeing him, she offered a brief wave.

He thought of the wave in Foyle's and wondered how a single action - or an apparently single action, if one was to believe the solitary word given to it - might have so many different interpretations. Someone once told him (or had he read it?) that the Eskimos had dozens of different words for snow; presumably because snow was important to them, and its variety was both critical and meaningful. All he had to describe Julia's action was 'wave', and in his mind he was forced to play with various adjectives as he tried to qualify the difference between this most recent example and that from the bookshop. They were different, of course (this as he resumed his seat, preparing to listen to Julia's progress through the house) although his attempting to pin those differences down in a strictly linguistic sense was proving difficult.

In front of him the last words he had written stood out - black against white - on his computer screen. Occasionally - usually when he was stuck, or had lost his train of thought - he would play with the display colours on the PC, seeing how the text appeared in different formats: red on yellow; or white on grey. Thinking about Julia's gesture, made him wonder how well-qualified some of the things he had written might be; after all, it was surely possible that he had written something simple - even a single word - where what he was trying to say was perfectly plain as far as he was concerned, and yet someone reading it cold, as it were, might construe things very differently. Mark wondered (hearing greetings from downstairs parenthesised by the front door opening and closing) if he would ever write that his Father had 'waved' to him, and, if so, would it be possible for someone to interpret exactly what that meant - after all, as he had just reasoned, a wave was never simply just that. Perhaps he would need to review what he had written thus far in order to root out such examples, now concerned that there may be opportunity for misunderstanding in such cases - and misunderstanding would mean that the historical truth might fail to come across. But in such circumstances what was he to do? If he resorted to deliberate and complex qualification in order to try and ensure that there was no possibility of such a disaster, how much more would he need to write? And worst still, would he not be swerving dramatically away from his task - his Father's history - and turning it into something quite different?

Mark sensed a presence behind him. He had missed the footfall on the stairs (not difficult of course, given the excellent quality of the house's carpets). He turned. It was Beatrice.

"Julia's here", she said.

"Oh," Mark had not expected to see his Aunt. "I saw her, just a minute ago."

"And Simon's downstairs too."

"Has he been out?"

"Only in the back garden tidying up the vegetables."

Mark nodded. There was a pause.

"We'll be having dinner soon. I think your Uncle's doing sherries, if you want one."

He never drank sherry; Beatrice knew that.

"I'll come down for a 'G and T' in a minute, once I've finished up here."

"Mark." Beatrice's voice prevented him turning back to the screen.

"Yes."

"What I said earlier. About your Father."

"And Constantina?"

"Yes."

"What about it?"

"Well, it didn't upset you did it?"

He laughed. Beatrice was evidently concerned that she had caused him offence, or that her theory had thrown him into some kind of deep angst. He knew, of course, that beneath her Commando-like exterior she was a caring woman, though it was not this - his amusement at the juxtaposition - that caused his response. Indeed, it had happened even before he had chance to request it; a kind of autonomic reaction that sprung from his natural defences.

"Upset? Me? Of course not!"

"I mean, I only wanted you to have the complete picture. That's all."

'The complete picture': what was that? As he looked at his Aunt - the woman who he had so recently realised was ageing - he wondered just how many more pieces of 'the complete picture' she might be keeping to herself. Were there other things? She had said that his Mother had suspected that there had been contact after Hydra: this meant that the two woman must have had some reasonably intimate contact, yet Beatrice had consistently denied such events. How much more about his Mother was she privy to? And how many more instances of 'gut feel' were awaiting the right moment which would allow her to reveal them to him?

He maintained a polite smile throughout all of this; a smile that endeavoured to convey: "Don't worry Aunt, of course everything's fine'.

"And that's all I'm after too," he said.

Mark watched her as she turned and left the room, calling behind her that she would get Simon to ready his gin for him.

Proving to be as good as Beatrice's word, Simon had prepared a large gin and tonic which - resting on the small table alongside Julia's sherry - was awaiting Mark on his entrance to the lounge. Both Julia and Simon rose when he entered; Julia to offer him a welcoming kiss, Simon to indicate the whereabouts of his drink.

"Your Aunt said that we should go through as soon as you came down, if that's all right. We can talk as we eat, can't we?'

"Hmmm," said Julia enthusiastically, having now slipped her hand through Mark's left arm, "I'm starving!"

"Busy day?" Mark enquired dutifully - though without any real interest - as they followed Simon to the dining room.

"Not really. Didn't get much to eat at lunchtime that's all; and as I went to the gym with Claire in the afternoon, I'm now really hungry."

"And tired?"

She looked up at him and squeezed his arm.

"A little. You?"

Mark took a large sip from his drink.

"Me? I'm fine."

-*-

"Does it do you any good?"

Beatrice had been relatively quite during the meal, but now that the main course had been eaten - and the prerequisite degree of praise and thanks come her way - she began to relax a little more. As she honed in on a conversation between Julia and Simon about keeping fit - all triggered by recent revelations with respect to the Princess of Wales - Mark noted how she seemed restored to her normal, combative self.

"Going to the gym?" Julia picked up the question.

"Yes. I mean, I've never been near one of those places in my life, and it doesn't seem to have done me much harm!"

"But you're a bit different, Dear," Simon offered loyally.

"Different? Nonsense!"

"I think it does. I mean, I always feel a lot better for it afterwards."

"'Better'? Do you mean slimmer?"

Julia smiled, recognising Beatrice's thrust.

"Partly. But fitter too. More generally healthy, and that's important."

"Healthy body, healthy mind", Simon suggested.

Mark watched his Uncle with a little disquiet. Simon had been attacking the wine steadily, and his most recent comments had signalled the beginning of a descent into mild inebriation. Mark recognised the symptoms from the awards dinner, and in doing so, found his fears about the possibility of Simon both recalling and retelling the events of the evening uncomfortably resurrected.

"You might as well ask Mark why he goes to the club to play squash; it's the same thing." Julia attempted to gain an ally against Beatrice.

"Squash?" Beatrice was having none of it. "That's different. Competitive. And as a man, Mark needs a competitive outlet, don't you?"

The three of them looked at him, and he adopted a mock defensive attitude. It was, he knew, part of the role he was supposed to play on occasions such as this. Indeed, during their earliest meetings as a foursome, he would often leave Julia on her own in a battle against his Aunt, the nature - and outcome - of the contest a measure for both he and Beatrice to judge Julia by. He had refrained from such tactics of late - after all, the need had long since gone - but at moments such as this when the topic of conversation held no interest for him, he was quite happy to draw on those old skills and remove himself from the firing line.

"Leave me out of this! Don't start psychoanalysing me, please!"

"But do you play it for the competition, Mark?" Beatrice was on the trail and, even though she must have recognised his tactic, was unwilling to let him off the hook quite so easily. "Would you play the silly game if it weren't about beating someone?"

Mark paused, resigned to having to contribute.

"Probably not."

"See!" Beatrice signalled her triumph, "It *is* different. Not like this aerobics nonsense at all."

"How are you getting on in the ladder by the way?"

Julia's question took Mark aback; dragged him further into the fray - and on terms that were suddenly very unfavourable to him. Mark emptied his glass before responding.

"Competing, as Beatrice would want me to say."

"But doing well?"

"So-so; you know."

"Claire says that your name's not in the ladder at the moment."

It was a continuation Mark had not expected, like a sudden sacrifice in a game of chess. Such manoeuvres almost always proved too complex for him to process, and he usually found himself accepting the poisoned pawn either to get the game over and done with or hoping that his opponent would make a mistake along the way which would let him back in. He laughed falsely.

"She must have missed it."

"No, I don't think so. Peter told her."

While they had been talking, Simon had pulled the cork on another bottle of wine and was topping up their glasses. Mark watched his actions for a moment, allowing the thread of the conversation to fray a little, hoping that, on its resumption, Julia would have lost the head of steam she had been building up. When Simon had finished, Mark - having found a refutation to Julia's sacrifice (intended or not) - spoke again.

"My ladder wasn't up the last time Peter was there."

He had offered it to close the conversation. Julia, whose eyes had not left him for the last few moments, was suddenly re-appropriated by Beatrice who had decided to return to her theme of physical activity as a fashion accessory promoted by the activities of certain 'noble personages'. Seeing Julia dragged away - their little game of chess abandoned as a draw, perhaps - Mark watched her in semi-profile as she once again crossed swords with his aunt. It was impossible for him to say how deliberate Julia's question had been, but it had unsettled him somewhat.

As he allowed the two women's conversation to slip away from him slightly, Mark turned his attention to his right where Simon picked up his now refreshed wine glass with a hand that was beginning to look a little unsteady. Watching Simon's glass take the less-than-direct route from table to mouth, he tried to recall how - during those early years - his father had behaved under the influence of drink. It was a pertinent enough thought as all the while in some philosophical sense there existed - but only in their unwritten form - further chapters of the biography that were destined to unfold. By the time Mark had been old enough to truly recognise what was going on, his father's drinking had progressed from the social to the habitual, and he could only rely on second-hand reports for the early detail. There were times where, on reflection, he might well have chosen to interpret certain of his father's actions as being drink-induced; yet this seemed particularly dangerous ground to him, and whilst accuracy demanded that he would be unable not to make reference to the drinking problem - for problem it undoubtedly was - the last thing he wanted to do was to either embellish or underplay the phenomenon.

Simon rose from the table.

"Just popping upstairs; you know."

Mark watched him leave - his words just failing to carrying the 'nudge, nudge' innuendo of a man about to indulge in some kind of elicit 'fix' - then turned back to the women. They seemed oblivious to Simon's departure. From somewhere an old craving suddenly hit him hard.

"Aunt."

Beatrice broke off mid-sentence to Julia.

"Yes, Dear?"

"Does Simon still have any of those half-coronas left?"

"Cigars!" Julia feigned horror.

"I know. But it's been ages, and - well - I just fancy one."

"Before dessert, too!"

"Try the end cupboard in the drinks cabinet," Beatrice ignored Julia's protestation, seemingly still keen to make up for her earlier intervention. "And don't smoke it in here; go and smoke in the conservatory - then you're close at hand if we need you."

At the end of the dining room, two large French doors opened out onto the conservatory, and from thence to the garden. After a brief search, Mark returned with a cigar and some matches, and - with both the garden and French doors open - prepared to strike.

"That's not too cold is it?" A cool mid-evening breeze edged through the now open garden door. It had been a surprisingly warm day, and the house had been feeling a little too hot. Mark assumed that the central heating needed further post-Winter adjustment.

"Fine, Dear," came his Aunt's voice. "You can hear us, can't you?"

"Of course. I'll keep one ear open!"

He could hear very well; certainly well enough to then pick up Julia's voice even though she had lowered it slightly.

"That's unusual."

"What is?"

"Mark smoking. I mean, he hasn't had a cigar for ages. Not that I can remember anyway."

Beatrice gave a little laugh. Mark, who was now seated and with his back to the house, could imagine her placing her hand on Julia's arm.

"It won't hurt him. I think he's under a bit of pressure with the book."

The mention of the book recalled the subject of his Father's drinking, and as he half-listened to their conversation, he tried to outline the next section in his head.

-*-

During the wranglings with Bell & Withers, Packard had begun to drink again, though at first more regularly than heavily. This trend became most noticeable during preparation for the trial, when he and Peter Healey spent a great deal of time in each other's company.

-*-

"Pressure? From who?"

"Oh, not from anyone really - apart from himself."

"Well, I don't suppose it can be easy. Writing about your Father and all that."

"It isn't easy", Mark confirmed to himself as he tried to remember the interviews with Healey.

-*-

Healey, for all his professional virtues, was a man who liked to drink. Years of working in the capital's publishing industry had defined the format for the post-work social life that needed to be followed if one was to be successful.

-*-

"And it must be getting to be a little more difficult too," Beatrice suggested.

"Why do you say that?"

"Oh, because he's writing about things he's beginning to remember. And he's reached a time where - well, where things are becoming a little more complicated."

"Complicated!" Mark smiled to himself. "They don't know the half of it!"

"I'm not sure I'm with you."

"1966 - or thereabouts. Charles was beginning to find himself, you know? Make his way in the world. Things were beginning to change quite dramatically, and Mark must have been a little bemused by it all."

-*-

"Oh Charles liked his sauce; that was evident very early on - especially when we'd had long days preparing our defence against B&W. We'd wander over to the "Toad and Gown" from the office and spend most of the evening there. We paid for Charles to stay in town whenever necessary, so there wasn't very much else for him to do."

-*-

Except to indulge himself in the odd one night stand with Healey's secretary, perhaps. This was an accusation Mark knew - drawing on his cigar as he ruminated - that had sprung from an unnamed source just after the trial. Healey suspected that it had been invented by a rival publisher as an attempt to discredit Macmillan's rising new star.

"Because he was so young?"

"And because he was watching his Father changing - growing up too, in a strange kind of way. Now he's got to write about it, that strange time."

"Strange? Why was it strange, Beatrice?"

"Oh, the drinking, the women. I'm sure Mark must have told you all about it."

Women; drinking. Mark listened to the words as they floated out to him, an exchange for the cigar smoke that hung for a moment in the air before the breeze diluted it onwards. There would be a great deal of his book about such topics, because there was a great deal of his Father's life that seemed devoted to them.

"No. He's kept most of it locked away really. For the book, I suppose."

"Yes, I expect so."

"But was his Father so bad?"

"Bad?"

"The stories about his infidelities; the way he treated Mark's Mother?"

Mark, watching the smoke, waited for Beatrice's reply.

"I have no reason to believe that Charles abused Mary; not in the physical sense."

It was true that he could never remember any violence. There had been anger of course; but this was usually either taken out on inanimate things

233

(Mark remembered his damaged pedal car), on George Walker, or on himself - and then via resorting to the bottle.

"But mentally perhaps?"

"It can't have been easy for her, Julia - after Greece, and the things that followed on from there. Of course they weren't to know that she was ill; not right then."

And he would need to write again about his Mother too. That might not be so easy, and there would be some pressure on him then for sure. He recalled being old enough to know about things, to see things. He recognised the changes in his Father for himself - the way only you can recognise changes in someone that you know and have lived with.

"You think Charles might not have been unfaithful if he had known?"

"I don't know, Dear. What makes - or does not make - a man faithful? Do you know? I don't think the wisest woman in the world knows the answer to that one. I mean, is Mark faithful?"

"Mark?!"

Mark's hand froze with the cigar an inch from his lips.

"There you are, Old Boy! Left the women in there gassing have you? Well, can't say I blame you, eh?"

Simon, returning to the dining room, had immediately made for the conservatory on seeing Mark there, and his greeting - loud and close, coupled with a hand on Mark's shoulder - had made his Nephew start so much that the cigar slipped from his hand to the floor.

"Oops, my fault! Shouldn't have made you jump, eh?"

Mark retrieved the cigar from the floor.

"That's OK; no damage done."

From inside, Beatrice's voice called to them.

"Do you two want any dessert then? Meringue, strawberries and cream. Or ice cream, if you prefer."

"Ah, pudding!" Simon slapped Mark gently on the back and walked back into the house.

Mark rose, tossing his cigar butt into a nearby planter as he did so. Reaching the French doors he halted. Julia was not there.

"She's just popped upstairs," Beatrice said, reading his gaze, "powdering her nose! Won't be a tick. Now you two, come in and sit back down."

Chapter Twenty Three

"Not getting nervous are you, Lovely?"

Once again they had met for a snatched lunch in the Regent Street coffee house, and Mark - partly to see how Maxine would react, and partly to hear how the story sounded himself - had chosen to divulge the basic content of Julia's conversation with Beatrice. Thanks to Simon's ironically well-timed intervention, he had failed to hear the remainder of Julia's reply to the question put so bluntly by his Aunt. Indeed, her absence from the dining room had fuelled such thoughts in his head that when Julia quickly reappeared - and in a humour that was entirely consistent with an absence driven by nothing more sinister than having to satisfy a call of nature - he was relieved to be able to banish the notions he had found the most alarming. Having raised the spectre however, and indulged - for even the briefest moment - in the possibility that Julia might actually suspect his infidelity, the thought remained with him still, resolutely refusing to return to the oblivion from whence it had come.

Mark's story had made Maxine laugh, a reaction that immediately riled him. However, as he then watched her sipping her coffee and gazing out onto the passing traffic, he became convinced that her response had been little more than a show of bravado, and that, were his worst fears to be realised, then there was indeed something that would need to be dealt with.

"What are you going to do?"

The question, delivered flatly and without the emphasis that it perhaps merited, roused Mark from his thoughts. He had not rationalised the situation in such concrete terms as identifying the need to 'do' anything. Indeed, to take a such speculative course would, of necessity, demand that he answer a few fundamental questions of his own. Thus far his relationship with Maxine had progressed along very simple lines: they met - frequently, if not regularly - and usually taking advantage of either Julia's house in Marylebone or some other discrete location, would indulge in what was euphemistically and popularly referred to as 'uncomplicated sex'. Operating a relationship on such a level required little mental input from him; physical presence was normally sufficient. There was, of course, no question that he was enjoying their liaison; indeed, he was having a better sex life outside his permanent relationship that he was within it. The question he had avoided facing thus far - and which he wished to continue to duck - was why this should necessarily be the case. Mark had no desire to analyse his relationship with Maxine; its spontaneity and abandon - the whole absence of questioning - was proving to be something of a revelation for him and a remarkable indulgence to boot. At times, he even began to wonder if he might not be experiencing a similar encounter to those enjoyed by his Father.

He looked up. Maxine was sipping her coffee again and waiting for his response. He wondered if she had yet asked herself those difficult, internal questions about what they were doing - even as she sat there waiting for him. In her own mind, how far had she progressed beyond a liaison borne from casual inebriation to something that had begun to represent more than that? From his point of view, Mark could not conceive how she would have done anything other than regard him as just a casual affair. Perhaps she had begun to wonder if she loved him; perhaps she was about to go back on her initial statement that the last thing she wanted was a relationship that implied 'complications'. If so, then this might warrant having something 'done' on a completely different plane.

"Do?" he echoed, watching her as he spoke, the bright spring sunshine outside adding a certain sparkle to her green eyes. "Nothing. I mean, there's nothing to be done is there?"

"In what sense?"

"Changing things. I don't think Julia does suspect; I can't see why she should - or what grounds she would have, come to that."

"You don't want to," and here Maxine paused, her face serious for once, "you don't want to call it a day?"

It was a notion he had never entertained, and he responded - as she had earlier - with a laugh, though his own was low, confident and calculated.

"Why should we? I haven't had so much fun in years! The last thing I want to do is..." He allowed the sentence to trail off, uncertain of exactly what the last thing he might want to do would be. To stop seeing Maxine - to forsake their haphazard meetings - certainly did not figure on any list of potentials he might choose to draw up.

She nodded and finished her coffee.

"Just wondered," she said, noncommittally.

Her eyes averted from him again, Mark watched he as she became distracted by a conversation between a French couple on a nearby table. They were holding hands, but the tone of their words suggested something other than perfect harmony. Mark reached across and stroked the back of Maxine's hand with his index finger. She looked up and smiled. It was a sad, preoccupied kind of smile.

"You're not worried are you?"

"Worried?" she said.

"By that little story about Julia?"

Maxine withdrew her hand and began to fumble in her bag.

"Why should I be? Ah," she withdrew her purse, "my turn."

He watched her as she pulled the bill from the table and walked over to the counter to pay. She was wearing a dark green suit that carried a feint tartan pattern. The skirt was short - a little too short, some might say - and made the most of her legs. He imagined other men gazing at her and cursing him for being so lucky. As he rose, he smiled to himself: they didn't know how lucky he was.

Outside, she joined him on the pavement.

"Why do you always wear that old jacket?" she asked, tugging at the tweed material.

"This?" He looked down at the right hand pocket. "Because I like it; it's comfortable."

There was a pause.

"Boring production meeting this afternoon, I'm afraid," she said, looking in the direction of Bush House. He wondered if she was just making conversation, or trying to excuse the fact that they had not met in Marylebone.

"That's OK. There's Friday afternoon to look forward to."

Turning, she looked up at him, the sparkle having returned to her eyes. He felt himself stirring, wanting her; she seemed to be able to fire him up so easily.

"What time did we say again?"

She was to be on a shoot early in the morning at Victoria but was due to have the afternoon free. Mark had suggested that they meet in the Tate Gallery: 'lunch, art, sex' he had said, as if making choices from a menu. Maxine had laughed.

"Time? Oh, around twelve. You'll be free then won't you?"

"We're scheduled to finish about eleven, so it shouldn't be a problem."

He saw a flash of recognition fall across her face as she looked beyond him, then, suddenly, raised herself on her toes and pulled his face towards hers. The kiss was long and deep; his head span for a second as their tongues met.

"Thank you," he said, slightly breathless as she released him, taken aback by such a public show of affection.

She laughed.

"My pleasure, Sir! See you Friday!" And with a sudden twirl, she was away into a stream of pedestrians.

Mark tried to watch her as she left him, losing sight of her distinctive hair, the green outfit - and her enviable legs! - within a few yards as she was subsumed into a bevy of Japanese tourists.

-*-

The pattern Packard established - once the fuss over the Bell & Withers affair died down - in many ways resembled the time when he was writing <u>Under the Olive Tree</u>. The court case had provided him with the inspiration for his next work which began, at least according to Healey, as a vague notion.

"Charles said he had an idea, but wouldn't let on until he'd had a chance to get something down on paper. As I heard only reports of progress from him over the next few weeks, and - without seeing anything - I began to get a little concerned. Finally, when a sample of <u>No Easy Fight</u> turned up, along with a synopsis for the whole thing, I knew we were going to be all right."

Packard, the idea for his next book firmly in his mind, worked hard on developing the material. As was the norm, he spent much of his time at home slaving over various long-hand drafts, forcing himself through the peaks and troughs of the creative cycle. However in 1966, and the two years that followed it, things were subtly different from previous times. Packard was developing as a writer not only in the sense of his technical ability, but also in terms of his professional persona.

The time spent with Healey had taught him much about the world in which he was destined to move. He learned a great deal about how the press worked - and how they might be manipulated; Healey opened his eyes to the machinations of the publishing world too, and he became aware of exactly what he needed to do to keep Macmillan happy.

> "It was a time of tremendous learning, really. Maybe I matured over the period of those few months. Maybe they did a lot of

damage, I don't know. Consciously or not (and I suspect the former) Peter proved to be a sound and efficient mentor - just as the trial itself was to prove a tremendous inspiration. Perhaps I thought I was fated. Just when I needed something to get me started again, along came the trial. The same way Hydra had given me <u>Under the Olive Tree</u>, so I was gifted <u>No Easy Fight</u>."

(Interview with Frank Wilson in "Stand", 1975)

The other thing Packard had been 'gifted' was the reintroduction to alcohol. Although he had never been dependant on drink at any time in his life up to that point (and, he would always argue, he continued to remain independent of it) the early evening drinking sessions with Healey had re-awoken a desire in him that seemed only to be satisfied through the bottom of a bottle or a glass. Charles' indulgence was compounded by the need for him to develop an identifiable 'writer's persona', and, as he would later admit, there was a degree of naiveté in his somewhat self-conscious development of this.

In terms of his domestic life, he saw much more of Mary and Mark. Although reconciled with his wife, their relationship had never recovered from his infidelity with Stella. They maintained a public face that seemed entirely plausible as a loving couple, although Mary shunned anything that attempted to force her to be seen as a part of Charles' career. The escapade on Hydra remained, as far as Packard was concerned, a secret, and George Walker was to keep the promise made to his friend as they journeyed home.

"She knew, I think. I never said a word, but I think she knew. Oh, she still loved him, that was plain enough; and she was proud of what he was doing, and what he was making of himself. But, even though it might have been her greatest dream coming true, she never allowed herself to be drawn in to it. I think he had ruined it for her, and something vital had died."

Mary's devotion to Mark remained undiminished. As Packard began <u>No Easy Fight</u>, Mark was a seven year old enjoying his long summer holiday. An intelligent child, he showed little of the technical artistic ability of his Mother, nor the burgeoning artistic temperament of his Father. Like most boys of his age, he was interested in football and science; at home, his new model railway - one of the few presents from his Father that turned out to be exactly what he wanted - took up a great deal of his time.

From the summer of 1966, Packard's working pattern saw reasonable periods when the family would be together. He would break off from his writing and help Mark construct a new station building; or, seeing Mary quietly developing their home, even turn his hand to a little decorating. At least once a month however, Charles would declare that he needed to travel to London to meet with Healey.

"He would suddenly be gone. I'd come downstairs and find he wasn't there any more. Mother told me that he'd gone to London on business and that he would be back soon. Sometimes it was a day or two; sometimes longer."

Packard would usually come back to the house either buoyant or depressed, and would throw himself back into his writing with renewed vigour. After a couple of days, the normal cycle would be renewed and so the pattern would go on.

> "Those were wild days. Sometimes I did actually go to see Peter; often I stayed with him for a few days. We'd talk about the book - and possible future books - mapping things out like a grand stratagem over a bottle of Port or something. Sometimes I'd stay elsewhere. Often I didn't see him at all. What did I do? There were so many nights over the next couple of years - right up until the publication of No Easy Fight in 1969 - that I can't recall them all. Very few in fact. To be honest, they were quite dark days, and those I can remember I now don't like very much."

> (Interview in "The Washington Post", 1981)

For nearly two years - until Packard submitted the final draft of No Easy Fight in October of 1968 - the life of the family, revolving around Charles, maintained its uneasy stability. Financially, Healey's predictions were unerringly accurate, although a short contract with the 'Sunday Telegraph' for monthly book reviews helped boost Packard's modest income. Along with sales of his previous novels (which had, in early 1967, been brought under the Macmillan wing) and a small advance on No Easy Fight - which Healey was cautiously drip-feeding through - the Packard budget proved adequate rather than healthy.

Mary, however, began to be far from healthy. Occasional pains in her lower abdomen saw her make an increasing number of visits to their local General Practitioner, Doctor Keene, during the latter half of 1967. Keene's diagnosis had been initially woolly, and had suggested a variety of common complaints as the possible cause, treating each one in turn as time passed. Eventually, in the spring of 1968, Packard accompanied his wife to the Surgery for the first time.

"It was obvious that she wasn't well. Oh, for weeks at a time she'd be as right as rain, and then, suddenly... I hadn't been too concerned at first. She said that it was probably "just women's' trouble", but as time went on even I could see that it was something else. Keene had been surprised to see me, I remember. I think he was even more surprised when I refused to leave the building until he had taken Mary's plight seriously!"

(Interview with Melvyn Bragg, 1986)

On 3rd August 1968, Mary took a bed in Ward 'D' of St. Katherine's hospital in Warwick. For two days she found herself subjected to a number of tests before being released with a revised prescription. Under the new mix of medicines, the frequency with which Mary suffered her spasms died away, and when, three weeks later, a letter from the hospital reported that the tests 'had found nothing conclusive', both Charles and Mary assumed that there was nothing to worry about, and that the new medication was working well. It was a theory Dr. Keene did not disabuse them of when Mary visited him in early September for a repeat prescription.

-*-

One of the few photographs Mark still had of his Mother was taken in late September of that year. He had withdrawn it early on from his collection and had managed to rest it (despite being a little bent and with one bottom corner torn) at the back of his desk leaning against the window ledge. His Father had been out and returned with a new kite; something unheard of in the family. Mark remembered it as a bright yellow affair, with a large red and black dragon emblazoned across it, the dragon's tail culminating in two long streamers that flew away at the bottom of the trapezoid. His Father had insisted that they go to the park and fly it, and he could recall running up and down the park, launching and chasing this fiery dragon. In the photograph his Mother is smiling at them as the two male members of the family attempted to unravel the beast from a tree. It had not, as far as he could recall, flown particularly well.

-*-

Not long after the publication of <u>No Easy Fight</u>, Packard met Frank Wilson for the first time. Wilson, who had written the first serious review of <u>Dawn</u>, had pestered Healey to arrange a meeting. The two men had known each other since the days when they were both young aspirants at Faber & Faber. Diverging fairly early on in their respective careers, they had met up again one year at a Booker Prize ceremony and from then on kept in touch. Each was useful to the other: Wilson as a potentially tame critic for Macmillan's authors; Healey as an inside source for the well-respected journalist.

> "The meeting wasn't much to write home about. In fact, Frank was a bit of a disappointment. Peter had given him something of a build-up, and as he was the first person to publicly recognise <u>Dawn</u>, I guess I had my own expectations too."

(Interview in "The Washington Post", 1981)

Wilson had declared to Healey that it was his intention to write a piece on <u>No Easy Fight</u>, and that before he did so, he felt he needed to meet Packard for himself. Wilson's other motivation was his rivalry with Derek Shutts, regular columnist for the 'Observer'. Shutts had a habit of latching on to new talent like a leech, praising and promoting in such a way as to ensure that his own name and reputation rose with any new star. Having heard through a mutual acquaintance that Shutts was reputed to have shown an interest in Packard, Wilson was determined to stay ahead. Healy recalls:

"He was very bullish about it. Said that Charles was a great find; that I'd earned my place in the great scrapbook of publishing, and so forth. And what the hell - I knew it wouldn't do any harm. Of course, as far as I was concerned, news of these two apparently wanting to slug it out in order to promote Charles could only be good for us."

-*-

RESURRECTION OF THE HERO

'No Easy Fight' - Charles Packard

by Frank Wilson

It is not insignificant that the hero of Charles Packard's latest novel, 'No Easy Fight', should be called Smith. Indeed, Packard's choice of an unremarkable name for his central character - Arnold Smith - would appear to be deliberate; a critical requirement in order for the hero to sit comfortably as a modern Everyman.

Given where Packard has most recently come from - 'Under the Olive Tree', where the story centres around an artistic and charismatic individual whose lifestyle is Romantic with a capital "R" - the juxtaposition is particularly striking. Second to the primary question of "Is 'No Easy Fight' a good book?", we might conceivably ask ourselves "Why is it so different to its predecessor?".

The answer to the first question is, thankfully, yes. Once again, Packard refuses to allow himself to be seduced by the wiles of complex plot construction and intricate sub-themes. Smith's story - of a man wronged by Society, who then fights to have that particular wrong righted - is simple and linear. Packard's strength lies in the effortless way he develops his main characters, gradually allowing them to expose themselves as the story progresses.

This light touch is an improvement on the handling of George Maxwell in 'Dawn', with whom Arnold Smith has much in common. Both men are loners in one sense or another; and both are preoccupied with a fight for justice. In 'No Easy Fight', the Smith character is fighting for himself however, and this immediacy - and the growing talent and experience of the man who created him - gives us a more rounded and polished performance.

If 'Dawn' and 'No Easy Fight' are from the same stable (as they certainly appear to be) one of the key questions for us to address should be "Where does 'Under the Olive Tree' fit in all of this?". Of course, the three novels are not intended as a trilogy in any sense of the word, and the Grecian piece is - one might argue - something of an "occasional" work. Yet to dismiss it as such would be a mistake, for there is a progression here too, and the link is provided through Packard's heroes.

From George Maxwell, through Anthony Shipley, to Arnold Smith, Packard takes us on a tour of descent and resurrection. Maxwell is very much a picture of a "man's man"; a solid, working class chap who knows what's right. Shipley - who at heart also knows what is right - chooses an alternative, hedonistic and self-centred path which, through the metaphor of Soulla's plunging death, sees him fall from grace. Smith, who at the beginning of the book has already 'fallen' (he is a convicted criminal, after all), pursues the course that will see him exonerated, vindicated, and restored to his rightful place.

Packard's contention that this is "no easy fight", is a moralistic one; and with Smith as his Everyman figure, he maps out for us the kind of dilemmas and struggles that each and every one of us faces in our daily lives. Smith is victorious, and crowned by the very symbol of his Society - the God-like legal system - which cast him down. Such a struggle proves to be a substantially good read, and shows Packard at his righteous best. Unanswered questions there are -

for example, where do we end up in relation to our feelings for the court? - but one suspects with Packard there will always be such loose ends. The trick is that they fail to detract from a quality product.

-*-

Mark had always been a little suspicious of Wilson's analysis, mainly because the man seemed to fail in his primary aim - that of reviewing the book - by being deflected into an attempt to be intellectually clever. The piece on 'No Easy Fight' was typical of what was to become Wilson's journalistic style. Opinion on this tended to be divided between those who felt that the intellectual slant added a certain weight which implied quality, and those who rubbished the whole enterprise as being obviously amateur. Mark knew that his Father's own reaction had been a little ambivalent; whilst being able to see the flawed nature of the end result from a professional viewpoint, he remained constantly flattered by the notion that someone was prepared to take him that seriously.

It was a situation which, although failing to elicit a great deal of his own sympathy, was nevertheless one which Mark was able to understand. From his time at University, he could still recall a somewhat painful discussion with his first year History Tutor concerning an essay he had written on Ruskin. The Master had been scathing: "This is all very well as an introduction to a book on the man - perhaps a 'Life', or something of that sort - but as a rigorous piece of historical research I'm afraid it won't do at all!" As Mark sat at his desk, there still seemed a strange kind of irony in his Professor's condemnation; almost as if he had been privy to the future undertakings of his young charge.

Mark had met Wilson at his Father's funeral. He had seemed a small, prematurely old man whose life had gradually been overtaken by the kind of obsessive religious belief so common among born-again Christians. At the time of 'No Easy Fight', Wilson had just begun to embark on his personal crusade.

He had extracted his hand from a raincoat sleeve that looked as if it belonged to someone else, and offered it to Mark.

"A great loss. A great and tragic loss, God rest his soul."

-*-

In the 'Observer' on 14th August, 1969, a brief review of <u>No Easy Fight</u> appeared under Derek Shutts' banner. It was a short, concise four column inches which meted out some not unqualified praise. Having already read Wilson's piece, Shutts was positioning himself.

"Peter told me that having the second review - and one by Shutts too - was really significant. OK, I hadn't made it yet, but it was a step in the right direction; and the right kind of step too."

(Interview with Melvyn Bragg, 1986)

245

Chapter Twenty Four

Although it was not a walk he had undertaken particularly often - away from Pimlico Underground station, across Vauxhall Bridge Road, and then along John Islip Street and past the Barracks - it was one Mark allowed himself the luxury of feeling he knew well enough to be comfortable with. Despite this, it was not what he would consider to be a pleasant walk - especially as it was one where, considering the final destination, seeing an over-large group of tourists or students heading in the same direction was a bad omen. With this in mind, Mark's emergence into daylight saw him immediately on the alert for such talismen. The weather, although dry, was cold, and this - allied with the fact that it was a mid-week morning out of season - saw the pavements pretty much deserted and contributed to his feeling mentally un-harassed. Once away from the continuous roar of the traffic (in as much as he could ever be away from it) Mark began to relax, feeling a little more at home in relative rarity of tree-lined streets bordered by imposing Victorian houses.

Having declared a need to visit Congreave and the consequent intention of taking the tube into town, Mark had left Julia at Hampstead station where she had dropped him en-route to her sister's.

"Laura thinks she's found new caterers for the reception, the first lot having let her down, and she wants me to go and see them with her," she had announced as they turned away from the Heath.

"To make sure they look OK?" he had asked, somewhat sarcastically; a reaction that any mention of the forthcoming nuptials seemed to elicit from him only too easily.

"To see what sorts of food they do," Julia had refused to rise to the bait, "and to discuss the menu."

By the time he had changed trains at Warren Street, he had managed to eradicate any residual thoughts relating to Laura, the wedding or her potential caterers, and allowed anticipation to sharpen up his appetite for the journey.

Having already checked his watch once between Green Park and Victoria, Mark checked it again. Although he had effectively been a Londoner all his adult life, the capacity for the Underground system to surprise him remained undiminished. Having experienced negligible waits for each of his two trains, he found himself turning the corner into Atterbury Street - with the large blank edifice of the Tate Gallery to his left

- over half an hour ahead of schedule. Maxine would certainly not be there until twelve at the very earliest, and if he made allowance for her tendency to be late, Mark knew that he should not expect to see her for an hour or so. It was a prospect that would normally have stimulated nothing but frustration in him, although on this occasion he felt remarkably unperturbed. It had been a while since he had visited the gallery, and though he would admit to knowing little about Art (it wasn't his subject, after all) when in the right frame of mind he did enjoy looking at the pictures - or, more precisely, at those he felt he could understand. The presence of hoards of other visitors - and hence, the reason for his surveillance all the way from the station - was usually sufficient to topple his rather limited concentration, and, as he appeared to be in the mood for some light artistic contemplation, any indication of relative peace and quiet was to be welcomed.

When they had still been living in Warwick, his Mother had attempted to stimulate any artistic leanings he might have been harbouring by taking him to the Museum and Art Gallery in the centre of Birmingham. She had even gone to the not inconsiderable trouble of relating his Father's somewhat exceptional experience of the place in the fundamentally vain attempt to invest some degree of mystery and magic in the affair: but all he could remember were the replica rubber dinosaurs available for sale in the small gallery shop, and the chocolate cake she had bought him when he had begun to flag.

As he turned the corner, Mark saw a large coach divesting itself of its load; a group of thirty or so teenage students, each casually uniformed with personal rucksack and Walkman. In attempting to take them all in such a way as to weigh up their threat to the success of his visit (though not the ultimate outcome of it, of course!), the simultaneous recognition of the Coach's origin and the prevailing accent of its passengers, allowed him to place the newcomers as being French. Having had no particularly bad experience of relatively mature French students previously, Mark allowed the sighting to pass without further thought, and began to mount the steps to the entrance in a calm frame of mind.

The Security Guard nodded to him as if in recognition as he crossed the threshold. Beyond, the large central exhibition area - lightly dusted with sculptures - awaited. He had promised Maxine he would be early, and that he would wait for her somewhere in the vicinity of Rodin's 'Kiss'.

"It's a big space, but you shouldn't have any trouble spotting me."

"Will you wear a red carnation," she had pouted, "just for me?!"

To either side of him - beyond the entrance to the shop on the right and the stairs down to the cafe opposite - arches led to rooms which, from what Mark could recollect, represented (more or less) the chronological beginning and end of a circular tour. Whether or not it was out of habit - after all, a clockwise rotation did seem to be the automatic choice in almost everything circular - or because he had a preference as yet unrecognised, Mark moved to his left and walked into the first room.

The theory that he would immediately find himself at the beginning of something - and of something that would lead him quickly and comfortably around the entire building without really having to think too much about it - was immediately unsettled upon the discovery that he had walked into a temporary exhibition of modern portraits painted by women. At the far of the room, another arch promised - once again - to offer him another beginning for the brief historical tour he sought; but rather than walk immediately towards it, he decided to scan the works now on offer before him.

Rather than address each painting in turn, Mark chose to occupy a central position in the room and turn slowly there, allowing the various paintings to pass before him as he rotated. In doing so, he vaguely recalled a toy had he owned as a child where you looked through a spy hole on the outside of a drum and then turned a small handle, allowing the pictures on the inside of the cylinder to spin before you. This circus-like effect did little to enhance his opinion of the figures he saw now; their mainly abstract and non-representational shapes were alien to him, and only one or two painted in a style with which he was comfortable. Given that all the painters were women, he would have expected to see many more portraits of men, but there were only one or two; the bulk appeared to be celebrating the naked female form (in all its distorted offerings!) and, as he left the room, Mark found himself reflecting that, had the exhibition been populated by male artists, he might have expected pretty much the same sort of display.

He followed an elderly American couple through to the next room, excusing himself as he was forced to squeeze past them when they instantly stopped on its threshold and looked up at the ceiling. Their action forced him to do likewise, though for little reward, and he attempted to establish an appropriate focus for his attention. The portrait exhibition had thrown Mark a little off balance, and as he allowed himself to stroll slowly along the left hand wall of the gallery - vast images of Heaven and Hell, and painstaking depictions of the English countryside sliding in and out of his vision - he tried to recall the calm he seemed to have lost.

His watch told him that it was a little before a quarter to twelve. Aiming to be back at the main sculptural hall by twelve, he allowed his pace to quicken, attempting to judge the appropriate stride which would allow him both to complete some kind of tour and, at the same time, not let it appear to everyone else that he was just racing round. Occasionally Mark would pause before a painting - usually one that he recognised - and stare at it. He was unsure whether, at such moments, something was supposed to happen. He had, in the past, noted various people who would appear transfixed before certain pictures, remaining stationary in some trance-like state, as if they had been welded to the spot by an alien power. Part of him wondered - and it was the cynical part of him that disliked both pretentiousness and forms of intellectualism to which he could not relate - whether some of these people might not be adopting such a pose for effect alone, as if to demonstrate to their fellow gallery-goers that they could really appreciate what they were seeing. He had tried such an approach himself once, but had become almost instantly bored and consequently concerned that there might be others considering him with the same disdain that he might well have taken as a prerogative he reserved for them.

The result of these experiences - and this general philosophy - was to allow him the freedom to wander through the various rooms untouched by what he was seeing. In some cases - not unsurprisingly - he was well aware of the historic event depicted by an image before him, or - and this was more rare - possessed knowledge of the artist, though in a strictly historical context. In the main, however, Mark's progress through the gallery was generally consistent with simply picking up eclectic scraps of images or detail - even to the extent of the construction of the frames - with such fragments remaining with him for a split second before being cast aside and replaced by another.

Mark had moved on a little further when he suddenly found himself thrown once again from his intended itinerary. He knew, of course, that the Pre-Raphaelites had been an influence in his Father's life - or at least during those early days with his Mother. Stories he had from her - that he could now scarcely remember - had been reinforced on rare occasions by his Father, who would usually be suffering from alcohol indulgence at such moments of weakness. The notion, heavily promoted by his Father, that he had in fact first seen Mary in a painting before he actually met her in the flesh, had failed to gain any credence with Mark, suspicious that the fabrication had arisen as romantic manifestation, rather than from hard reality. Despite this, Mark had, once in a while, actually looked for his Mother in the images painted by these mid-nineteenth century men; a search that - whilst he would admit to it being somehow peripheral - had failed to offer any reward at all.

On this occasion, however, Mark had not been looking. He had turned into the Pre-Raphaelite room and instantly noted that the walls seemed to be a different colour from his previous visit. Whilst he would never dare to suggest that he was the vessel of a photographic memory, there was something about the arrangement of the shapes on the wall ahead of him (and at first blush, they were just shapes) that suggested some form of reorganisation or rehanging. Glancing to his left, he stopped, his feet frozen, his arms motionless. He was staring at his Mother.

For a second Mark felt cold, and then sensed the blood rushing to his face. He was conscious that, if someone were observing him at that precise moment - rather than looking at the paintings - they might have been a little amazed to see a man turned suddenly crimson. Perhaps they had been admiring that same painting before which he had now come to rest, and been taken aback by his sudden - and presumably, dramatic - change of appearance. Pulling his handkerchief from his pocket, he feigned a sneeze and looked around. There were about a dozen other people in the room, none of whom appeared to be looking his way. A little reassured (though no less disturbed) he turned back to the painting. According to the card to the right of the frame it was Rossetti's version of the Annunciation: 'Ecce Ancilla Domini!' 1849-50. His Mother, in a long white robe of some kind, was kneeling on a bed, head bent slightly as she stared at the Angel who stood before her. In the Angel's hand was a triple-headed lily, and in his Mother's eyes was a kind of fear. She looked young and pale: young as he was unable to remember her; pale as she had been during those last few weeks of her life. It seemed as if she were about to take the flower, the poisoned chalice, knowing what taking it would mean for her - and that ultimately she had no choice but to do so. Mark stared hard at the Angel; was there not something of his Father in that profile? The hair was different, of course, but perhaps in the nose - that slightly pronounced bridge - or in the lips? They had both been younger then, of course. And what of the lily? Was it really a lily, or was it something more than that? What could his Father be offering her that would cause such fear, that she would be compelled to take even though she had an inkling of the future? The Annunciation; the immaculate conception?

A pressure, hard against his right side, roused Mark from his study. The smiling face of a middle-aged Oriental lady begged his forgiveness. Finding himself standing full square in front of the painting with his nose no more than a foot from the canvass, he moved slightly to the side to allow her a better view. From the corner of his eye he caught a glimpse of one of the Museum staff looking his way. Feeling surrounded somehow, he moved away, his back to the painting, and out of the room. Once in the next space he stopped, and closed his eyes.

Realising almost immediately that he was, once again, in danger of drawing attention to himself - what, after all, was a tweed-jacketed, normal, adult male doing standing in the middle of the Tate gallery with his eyes closed? - Mark opened his eyes and moved slowly forwards. Once again he caught a glimpse of the uniformed attendant looking his way, so he bent to examine the card alongside a picture of Venetian canals, then stepped back to give the appearance of further contemplation. The image of his Mother - more waif than woman, it seemed - had yet to leave him. He wondered (feeling comfortable enough to move on) how it must have been for his Father to have undergone the experience in reverse, the image before the flesh. It would, he assumed - now a little more in control - have been a different painting that had started that particular chain reaction. There were many Rossetti in Birmingham too, and - for Mark, at least - all of the Pre-Raphaelite women had the dubious distinction of looking pretty much the same. As he considered the notion, he realised that the woman in the Annunciation was not one that would traditionally set men's blood racing, and, even though he was talking about his Mother, he could only assume that this was further evidence for another Rossetti being the catalyst.

The whole experience had set something off inside him that Mark, now resumed on his tour, tried to decipher as he walked on. He was fairly certain it was nothing especially tangible; the perfectly concrete image of his Mother had, he assumed, been the spark for the somewhat nagging sensation he now felt. There was nothing physical in the experience; rather it was, he could only say, a kind of 'knowing' that, for the present moment, was refusing to make itself public.

One thing he did need to consider - and this in relation to his Father's book - was what pictures were capable of doing. He knew, of course, that in this particular case his consideration was solely for photographs, but as he had just witnessed, the potential link - in all its forms - between image and reality was something not to under-estimate. Mark knew that, in the main, there was nothing for him to worry about; the photographs he was planning to include in the book were little more than illustrations, examples of what people actually looked like. The purpose they served - for him, at any rate - was to add a little reality to the history he was depicting; a little reinforcement to the veracity of his own words. In one or two cases, they offered proof of fact, and that - for Mark - was the ultimate gift they could give him.

Paintings were, of course, different, although Mark found himself struggling in the attempt to define an appropriate boundary or rule for them. Thinking of the Rossetti, he might have chosen to argue that such works offered - in as much as any photograph could - simply images of individuals. After all, did the Brakespeare portrait of his Father not bare a remarkable resemblance to the sitter? Indeed, had it not, for many people, become the authentic image of what Charles Packard actually looked like? And this was no special case either: there were many other such examples, from James Joyce through to Oscar Wilde. It would have been convenient for Mark to have been able to accept such a notion - even as ill-defined as he might make it - but his experience of the portrait exhibition had, within the last few minutes, done enough to disprove it. Perhaps (this as he stood before another representation of Venice) it would be easier for him to comprehend the relationship between art and a reality he might understand - that which he could touch or feel - if he considered only inanimate things. He tried to force himself to answer the simple question 'did Venice look the same as the picture now before him?' - but could only find himself asking other questions. How exactly the same did he want it to look? Did water really ripple and wave quite like that? And, if he was to accept the truthfulness of the painting, then did that mean all Venetians were misshapen and deformed?

Mark could find no simple conclusion here either. Something undeniable was the thing he would have liked to have found, but it remained elusive. He recalled a painting of Nelson's death from somewhere: was that how it was, an exact and truthful copy of the event? There was probably little denying the historical accuracy of it. He suspected that, any artist worth his salt, would have made sure that he had correctly identified - and then painted - all those present at the scene; but the unanswered question here seemed to be where did historical accuracy cease? Where did the factual take a back seat to make-believe, interpretation, and fiction?

By this time Mark had wandered through another couple of rooms and now found himself in the midst of the early twentieth century where the most common question he historically asked himself was what he was supposed to be looking at. Wild abstraction had taken over from representation, and the cul de sac exposed by Impressionists and Cubists had, as far as he was concerned, now been completely walled-off at one end. He knew there were probably many forms of abstraction, but for Mark there were only two that mattered: those paintings that truly looked like nothing but what they were; and those that chose to disguise the subject they were conveying almost to the point of obliteration, but not quite - which sounded to Mark similar to cryptic crosswords, and he never been any good at those.

He had just walked through the Rothko room; walls hung with large canvasses solidly painted in just one or two colours. As far as he was concerned that was all they were - and that being the case, quite comfortably met his first definition. Standing before something by de Kooning, he now found himself face-to-face with his second model of abstraction. According to the small blue card, the picture was supposed to represent a girl welcoming home her sailor boyfriend. Through the rough and violent brush strokes, the girl in question appeared to be naked, and facing the viewer with her legs spread in anticipation. Mark paused. He could just about see what the artist was painting, but there was something else in the image that he found familiar. It was true that in the flashes of red and yellow the woman was hardly visible as being such, but he could see - even in the wild inaccuracy of the piece - a reflection of something. When it hit him, he took a sudden step backwards. The girl reminded him of Claire.

Moving towards the canvass again, he tried to see what it was that had caused him to make the link, after all there was nothing in the representation that looked remotely like her. The hair - if it was hair - was the wrong colour, and the smear that appeared to be her mouth was also completely wrong. Try as he might to discover the link, he failed, and yet Mark knew that Claire was there somewhere. Of course, he had never seen her in such a position, and found himself - without premeditation - wondering exactly what she would look like if *he* was her sailor boy come home. He had been teased with the glimpse of a breast in the wine bar, but now they would both be exposed; she would be completely naked, legs apart, those amazing thighs of hers flexed, ready for him.

He found himself beginning to race away with the notion and, with something of an effort, forced himself out of it by checking his watch. It was just after twelve. Mark looked up to gain his bearings, and attempted to locate the most immediate route back to the sculptures. He had promised Maxine he would be early and did not want to break that promise - especially as he suddenly found himself once again fired with anticipation.

A quick scan a few seconds later, failed to reveal Maxine's presence. Mark walked to the Rodin and paused there, looking out towards the front entrance and the daylight beyond. It seemed a little brighter outside, and there was a steady stream of people coming in to the gallery. He decided to move from piece to piece, staying towards the entrance end of the hall so that she might find him more easily. For a second he thought of waiting outside, but that was not what they had agreed, and, for all he knew, Maxine could have already been inside the building.

After five minutes, he was checking his watch again. He had ventured as far up the gallery as to find himself standing before the infamous bricks, laid out in their standard pattern on the floor. Mark smiled to himself; art he could touch and feel perhaps. Sounds of French voices to his side made him glance round. A small group from the coach were making notes in the pads each of them seemed to be carrying. He tried to judge their age; something he found easier with boys because clues such as the presence - or absence - of facial hair was such a reliable guide. Perhaps the boy next to him had been shaving for a couple of years; he decided they were nineteen.

Turning to walk back towards the entrance once more, he noticed a slim girl, slightly taller than average, with long fair hair. Judging from her manner and her clothes - the way she wore her jumper loosely about her shoulders, the way she stood - he guessed that she too was from the French coach party. There was something un-English about her; an indefinable air that announced a cosmopolitan attitude and promised so much more. She was attractive too; even from this distance - a little over thirty yards - he could see that she was out of the ordinary.

Glancing briefly towards the entrance, he began to walk towards her. Years previously - when he had been much younger - Mark would have imagined how he might engineer an encounter, or find an excuse to talk to her. Even now, he could conjure up fantasies that would draw them inexorably together in a collision that would explode all his preconceptions with respect to romance and passion. Feeling discomfort, he caught himself up. That would be like reliving the real past.

He was within a few feet, when she moved away from the sculpture she had been examining and went past him, dragging Mark's attention with her. He caught the scent of her perfume - a light and delicate smell - and for the briefest of moments her eyes met his. There was a kind of preoccupation about her that added to the attraction. Mark, having stopped and turned to watch her walk away, suddenly found himself a little mesmerised and began confusing images of this girl with the de Kooning picture. He found himself beginning to wonder, to imagine.

Suddenly, there was the sound of a voice behind him. It was a call; low enough to be spoken and not shouted, but loud enough to be noticed. And there was something in the tone of it which was immediately familiar to him. Mark watched the French girl stop and look his way. For a moment, it appeared as if she were looking directly at him - or if not at him, then just beyond.

Chapter Twenty Five

In turning away from the painting in such a sudden fashion, Mark bumped hard into the person standing behind him. He felt his foot press down on something uneven and, simultaneously, an unexpected impact against his shoulder, a combination immediately followed by a cry and the sound of something hitting the floor. There was sufficient time in that moment for him to register - through a combination of both sense, sound and sight - the toppling form behind him, but insufficient for him to do anything about preventing the young woman in question from hitting the ground. His automatic reaction was to bend to pick up the pen he now found at his feet, a physical movement swiftly followed by the sensation that there were now a number of heads turned his way.

He felt himself blush. Still bending, he looked at the person he had so comprehensively felled. Mark's instant assessment took in a girl of about his own age, whose own reaction to her sudden tumble had also been to redden. There was a pained look on her face.

"I'm sorry. Really," Mark began, trying not to speak too loudly in an attempt to dissuade inquisitive eyes from staring in his direction, "I didn't see you there."

"That's OK," the girl said, though evidently in some discomfort, "I was standing a little too close."

"No, no," Mark offered her the pen, "I just didn't see you. It was my fault."

They rose together, the girl's first attempt to put weight on her left foot leading to the further expansion of the pained expression she could not fail to hide.

"Are you all right? Was that your foot?"

She tried to smile, but the combination of pain and embarrassment prevented anything other than a brief grimace from reaching him.

"I'll be fine. Thanks." Having regained a little composure, she took the pen.

"Are you sure?"

"Yes."

Mark was unprepared in as far as knowing what he would have done had she said 'no', but decorum - and an upbringing which had ensured his possession of a modicum of decency - made his question unavoidable. There was a short pause as he watched her drop the pen into her bag. She looked up at him.

"Well," he said, uncertain how to close the scene. "Sorry, again."

Having offered a short smile, Mark made his way to the centre of the room - steering well clear of any other possible contact (either physical or by eye) - and then out into the next hall, leaving the girl stationary behind him. Once away from the scene, he took a moment to replay the incident. He had been trying to decipher something in the Klee landscape and failed; it had refused to yield anything to him, keeping its message - if indeed it had one - a tightly guarded secret. He had become frustrated with it and moved accordingly.

He looked round. It was still fairly quiet - which somehow made the collision even more absurd. Had the gallery been packed he would have understood the accident a little better; indeed, he might well have been in a frame of mind which might have ensured - however unconsciously - a degree of care when moving about the place. As it was, the fact that the girl had been exactly there, and at precisely that moment, seemed a little short of bizarre.

Mark had, at various times recently, wrestled with the notion of coincidence. Given his field of study, it was a potential that remained comprehensively ignored. Perhaps - and here he was on the verge of drafting some sort of theory of his own - history could not possibly include coincidence. It was, at the most basic level, the retelling of factual events: things happened to particular people and in a particular sequence, and these things inevitably led to their own historical outcome: it seemed almost chemical in the its nature of cause and effect. He was unable to recall any particular instance where he had been told - or encouraged to believe, even - that one of the parties in any interaction had been there by accident. Archduke Ferdinand had been shot; that, for example, was the historical fact. It might have been that just before the fatal moment he had paused to stroke a cat or shake someone's hand, and in doing so had allowed his Assassin just enough time to get a clear shot at him. If so (and as far as Mark knew, this was not so) should that be set down as an unfortunate coincidence? Somehow he doubted it. If it were, then surely the vast majority of historical fact - indeed, the whole of recorded history - could turn out to be founded on a bizarre series of happenstance, and not be causal at all.

It was a notion he allowed himself to carry round the gallery, pondering how individual pieces might have looked if the sun had been shining in a different direction, or if the artist had been suffering from a hangover when he or she began their work. Attempting to divine what might have been was, of course, so ludicrous - and opened up such an infinite number of possibilities - that he took on the proposition almost as if it were a game he were playing. Proving to be such amusing speculation, Mark found his light-hearted attitude was still with him when, having finished his tour, he decided to go down to the restaurant for some coffee.

The cafe was surprisingly busy considering the relatively empty nature of the galleries upstairs. He examined the price list on the wall to decide what he might have - or rather, considering that he was only a student without a bottomless bank account (despite his Father's assistance), focused on what he could afford. Picking up a tray, he walked on to join the tail of the queue. As he waited to move forwards - and having completed a general sweep of the notices on the nearby wall - Mark realised that immediately in front of him was the young woman he had so recently knocked over. At precisely that moment of realisation, she turned towards him.

"Oh." It was as if she had been taken by surprise again, only this time without the physical discomfort that accompanied their last coming together. A hint of uncertainty in her eyes was immediately evident.

He stopped, still around five feet from her.

"Don't worry; I'll stand well back, I promise."

The comment, intended more to allay her fears of repeated assault rather than anything else, evidently carried sufficient charm - even humour - for the girl to respond with a slight smile. Mark had not intended such a reaction, but when it came - and whatever actually triggered it (for he could not be certain) - he found it not unpleasant. There had been no time to examine the young woman upstairs; indeed, the sudden nature of their meeting, its discomfort - both physical from her perspective, and in terms of his own embarrassment - precluded any such undertaking: but now, in this more organised and safe environment, Mark allowed himself the kind of superficial examination upon which first impressions are invariably made. The result of this was that he judged himself to be face-to-face with a person who would, were they a character in one of his Father's books, in the very least be described as handsome.

"Are you all right?" Her smile - and the picture she presented to him on a more general level - encouraged the attempt to prolong the discussion.

"All right?" she quizzed, a little hesitantly.

"Your foot."

"Oh, that." This time the smile was a little brighter. "Yes, fine. It did hurt for a little while, but it seems OK now. Thank you."

"Bruised, I expect."

"Probably."

"My big feet; sorry."

Ahead of them the queue had moved on, and there was a gap in front of the girl. Mark was conscious of several people now behind him. He took a step forwards.

"We should move up," he said, looking beyond her as he tentatively offered the pronoun.

She half-turned, then began to slide her tray along the counter, both in manner which did not quite relinquishing contact with him. By the time she arrived at the station where a young man was dispensing hot drinks, Mark had closed the gap between them to such an extent that their trays were nearly touching.

"Coffee, please," she said.

"Make that two."

As the young man rattled two cups and saucers from their respective piles, she shot Mark an inquisitive look.

"It's the least I can do. Buy you coffee, I mean. That is, if you don't mind."

He allowed the offer to hang between them, her expression giving no clue as to how she would respond. The smile had gone again, to be replaced by a look Mark found he could only interpret as tentative neutrality. Two cups of coffee, each with a small pot of cream in their respective saucers, had slid towards them before she spoke.

"Thank you. I'll find a table."

Mark allowed his eyes to follow her as she made her way along the line and out into the body of the cafe, depositing her still-empty tray on a nearby pile. She was plainly dressed: jeans and ribbed sweater, with her footwear - by not being training shoes or pumps of any kind - suggesting, in a generally uninformative ensemble, the most about her personality. She seemed a little above average to Mark; a little taller, a bit better educated, a little more attractive. Watching her move away from him, he allowed the sight of her bottom - undoubtedly appealing in her well-fitting jeans - to rouse him a little.

A sound from behind encouraged him to move on, and the reached the till.

"Seventy pence, please," the woman demanded.

From his trouser pocket Mark fished the fifty pence piece he had, in earlier preparation, withdrawn from his wallet, then - handing this over - went into his back pocket for some more money.

Having completed the transaction, Mark found himself at a small table which hosted cutlery and sugar. He selected two spoons, then, uncertain as to his ground, a single sachet of white sugar and another of brown. Once these were placed on the tray, he moved on again, head up, trying to search her out.

She had found a small table in a far alcove - a destination Mark finally managed to reach only after she had risen from her seat to wave at him. There had been a moment when - as he stood scanning the busy tables for her, and beginning to panic as he realised that he was not familiar enough with her to know, instinctively, what she looked like - he found himself on the verge of deciding that she had run out on him.

"There you are," he said, somewhat automatically as he set the tray down. It was a pedestrian phrase he regretted almost instantly. Trying to cover up, Mark place a coffee in front of her and indicated the sugar. "I wasn't sure..."

"Thanks, I don't."

He watched her as she emptied the small carton of UHT cream into the coffee and stirred, before doing the same. He had been almost certain that she would not want the sugar, and being right gave him a strange degree of confidence.

"Mark", he said, having taken the first sip of his coffee and breaking the awkward silence. There was, he felt, some onus on him as the instigator of the conversation to take the lead, and even though it was not a role he was particularly comfortable with, in this instance it was something at which he was determined not to fail. Even if the girl were to walk away, the fact that they had taken coffee together and - he hoped - enjoyed a pleasant discussion, would be triumph enough. "My name's Mark."

She offered her hand across the table.

"Lydia."

It was a subversive kind of offering, almost undercover and secretive Mark felt, and the handshake he exchanged was limp, weak and without conviction. The touch was over in an instant.

"Are you a student, Lydia?" He tried out the name for the first time, tagging it on to one of the few opening questions he felt he had available to him (especially in such a foreign environment!) and delivering it much in the manner of his Father. He had witnessed him at readings or visiting places of learning where - through years of experience, rather than natural charm - he could, if he desired, disarm an admirer by appearing to take a personal interest in them. Of course, in Lydia's case, Mark *was* taking a personal interest. Indeed, he had sufficiently qualified his original categorisation of 'above average' to such a degree as to want to offer more than just courteous compensation for the personal discomfort suffered at his hands. He had not, however, refined his thoughts far enough as to be able to endow himself with any clear goal.

His question restored a demure smile.

"Is it so obvious?"

He thought of the shoes.

"To be honest, no, not really. Just a guess. I mean, you might have been a tourist..."

"'Might have'?" she echoed back at him.

"But you don't have a foreign accent."

"I still could be - from Newcastle say, or Nottingham, down to see the Big City for a few days."

"But you're not, though."

"No." She paused to pick up her cup. "So what gives the game away? And why was it a guess?"

Mark smiled. The fact that she was beginning to relax took much of the pressure from the situation, and he felt the need to manufacture their conversation begin to leave him.

"I don't know. There's a sense isn't there? Among students, I mean? You get to be able to spot them a mile off?"

"Especially Engineers!"

He laughed at her joke, but a sudden thought brought her own laugher to an abrupt halt.

"You're not one are you?"

"An Engineer?"

She nodded.

"You said they were easy to spot, didn't you? So; do I look like one?"

"No, but...you might be."

"And you think I'm a student too, right?"

"Well, yes."

"See!" he said triumphantly, "I said that it was easy to tell, didn't I?"

"OK. And can you tell what people study, then?" The smile had returned to her lips - and Mark found something comforting in the shape of her face, the line of her cheeks, and the angle of her eyes when she did so.

"Apart from Engineers?"

"Apart from Engineers, yes. What, for example, would you say about me?"

He thought of a number of things instantly, some of which he recognised - and not without a little guilt - concerned his response to her attractive walk. He feigned deep thought as he allowed himself to supplant these with other, more relevant ideas. Mark knew that he was not - compared with many of his peers - that experienced with the opposite sex. Indeed, his catalogue of conquests thus far read more like a catalogue of disasters, with no relationship managing to last any significant duration, let alone allow him to fulfil himself sexually. Given such a track record - and one about which his Father occasionally ribbed him - a find like Lydia was, in many respects, potential manna from heaven.

"You're not an Engineer, that's for sure!"

"Thanks!"

"And being here is a bit of a clue," he sensed her preparing to respond immediately to this, so quickly added, "though not, by any means conclusive."

"So?"

"Arty, I'd say - but in the broadest sense. Not literature, and probably not languages. And I'd say definitely not history either. Psychology? Too scientific. Economics? Too dry. How about Geography?"

To be honest, he had no idea, and Lydia's sudden peal of laughter - with which he was obliged with join in - proved as much.

"Sorry Mr Holmes," she said after a short pause, "but I'm afraid you're completely wrong."

"The Butler didn't do it?"

"No," she said. "Classics is the answer you're looking for."

"Latin and stuff?"

She smiled.

"That's what most people think. No; mythology, literature, art. A broad spectrum really. It's fun. I expect you think it sounds boring - most people do - but it isn't; I like it."

"So why are you here?"

"I like Art, I guess. And I can pick up a few things - like how more modern societies have used and developed the ideas and myths of the Ancients."

"Paul Klee?" he said, recalling the location of their collision.

"Ah. That I like for me."

He allowed the conversation to tail off for a moment, taking the time provided by a further sip of his coffee to allow his eyes to sweep round the room once again.

"And what about you?"

"Me?" He looked back to her.

"Shall I guess what you do?"

"Can you?"

She smiled.

"It's easy. History."

Mark was surprised. He wondered if it could possibly be that obvious - like having it tattooed on his forehead or emblazoned across the front of his shirt.

"Why? How?"

"You told me."

"I did?"

"The way you said 'definitely not history' - like you knew *all* the sorts of people who'd study history; and because of that, you knew I didn't. You could only be that confident if it was your own subject. Am I right?"

There was a degree of playful expectation in her eyes now, and Mark, determined to keep sight of it for as long as possible, declined to respond immediately. He glanced up to the ceiling, tilting his head back slightly, as if thinking about his response. The pressure of Lydia's hand on his arm brought him back.

"Tell me!" she said, withdrawing her hand.

"Tell you what?"

"Ha!", she said, mimicking his earlier triumph, "I knew I was right. History; absolutely!"

"I give in."

"So why are you here? Not studying the history of Art?"

"No, nothing like that. I just had some free time, and thought I'd take another go at trying to come to terms with Art and stuff. I mean living in London makes this sort of thing really accessible."

She clouded, ignoring his invitation to probe into his domestic situation.

"'Come to terms with Art'; what do you mean?"

He found himself faced with something of a dilemma. Having avoided the first trap into which he might have fallen - that of pretending he knew a great deal about Art (especially as she would have probably exposed him instantly) - he now had to decide how far to go in telling the truth. Mark knew that there was, in this instance, nothing wrong with the truth; the key would be to tell it in such a way as to make him interesting enough from Lydia's point of view. It would be all too easy to blow it right here.

"I don't know. I guess I've always had a bit of a problem with it. You know, the capital 'A' kind of stuff. It's like I've never quite managed to get on the wavelength. I'm no philistine - or at least I don't think I am! - but I can't seem to get any further than knowing what I like."

"What's wrong with that?" Lydia's tone was positive. "There are plenty of people who go through life without even looking; without even trying. You're already ahead of the game if you know what you like. Jesus! Some days I'm not sure if I still like the things I did the day before!"

Mark decided to push on

"Mum was arty, you see. And she tried to help me; to see if I'd inherited her genes I guess."

"'Was'?" Lydia had taken the bait.

"Yes. She died about nine years ago."

"I'm sorry."

"Thanks." He paused for a second. "Anyway, she dragged me around galleries and the like when I was younger, but to no avail. I used to like traditional museums more. Guess that's why I did history."

"But you could see this as a museum rather than a gallery, couldn't you?" She indicated the entire building and its collection with the inflection in her voice.

"Yes, I guess so. Technically. But it wouldn't help me." He paused again. "Anyway, at least I haven't given up trying."

"Your Father. Doesn't he like Art?"

Mark laughed briefly.

"No, afraid not. He tried it when he was younger too. About my age. Pottery, woodwork, painting; everything I think. But it wasn't for him."

"Maybe you've inherited his genes?"

This notion was spontaneously amusing, and Mark's laughter - though somewhat softer - was at least more genuine. Lydia appeared surprised.

"Is that such a bad thing?"

"No, no. Sorry, I didn't mean to laugh really; it's just a funny idea, that's all."

"Why, what does he do?"

This was a big question for Mark. He had, in the past, played it a number of ways: the big build up, the understatement, the straight bat. Having enjoyed a positive run of luck thus far with Lydia by being fairly honest, he decided on the latter tack.

"He's a writer."

"Really?" She was instantly interested. "What sorts of things does he write."

"Books - novels, I mean. And the odd play. For the telly." The last phrase had been deliberate. Having reeled Lydia in this far, he could not help but prepare the keep net. She stopped struggling.

"Wow! What's his name? I mean, have I heard of him?"

"Maybe. His name's Charles Packard."

"Not the 'Suburban Bandit' Charles Packard?"

"The very same."

"But that's brilliant! If I were you I'd be praying I had some of his genes!"

Mark smiled.

"Well, his talent at any rate."

Fifteen minutes later, Lydia was excusing herself outside the gallery, begging an appointment with a college friend that she was unable to break. Mark had toyed with the notion of offering to accompany her part of the way, but declined; the clean break - he heading for the tube, she waiting for the bus - seemed the most appropriate. In any event, he was keen not to overplay his hand. Lydia had already taken down his phone number and had promised to ring him within the next couple of days. She had suggested that they might try another 'museum of Art', and Mark, privately denying the likelihood of his experiencing any kind of revelation, was only too willing to use such a forlorn hope as a way of extending their acquaintance.

Having escorted her to the bus stop, he waited for a few minutes - long enough to check that she had his number correctly recorded - before saying goodbye and walking away with a wave of his hand.

"Mark! Mark!"

An insistent voice caught him. Disoriented, he was suddenly conscious of someone having just walked past him, and although this was not the direction from which the sound had originated, that was the way he turned. In front of him, the slim blonde student was greeting her friend, another girl of about the same age. As he looked on, the second girl turned slightly towards him. There was a little difference, but she looked exactly as Lydia had looked when he had first met her.

"Mark!"

Closer now, the low voice bore a degree of impatience which forced him to turn around. Maxine was suddenly upon him, planting a firm kiss on his closed lips.

"Where have you been? You were miles away!"

"Sorry?"

"Didn't you hear me calling? Looked like you'd seen a ghost or something!" She slipped her hand through his arm.

His mind was reeling. Perhaps he had seen a ghost, he could not really say, but he knew that there had been images of his past suddenly with him. Mark looked at Maxine as he tried to readjust to reality. He felt her hand on his arm - a firm and public gesture that was unusual for her - and tried to disentangle it from the way Lydia had touched his arm. Suddenly there were memories of Claire and Julia crowding inside his head, each of them touching him in their own individual ways, each touch becoming indistinct and muddled, as if they were suddenly all one and the same.

"I'm not in the mood for Art," Maxine said breezily, "Shall we eat?"

Mark looked down at his arm and tried to resolve the confused references it was giving him. He looked back at Maxine, and then up the gallery to where two female figures were standing discussing a sculpture. He felt another pressure dragging at him and he turned again. Maxine's face looked up smilingly at him, waiting for his response. He knew that she had said something: what had it been? The word 'food' lingered just long enough.

"Fine. Whatever you want," he said, and allowed her to lead him away.

Chapter Twenty Six

He had begun a renewed search through his collection of photographs with the plausible excuse (which was its beauty, of course) of uncovering more significant material for the book. Such was the reason Mark had given when Julia had discovered him - or half of him, as his upper torso had already disappeared from view - once again ascending into the loft.

"But you must have been through them dozens of times," she had remonstrated.

"Not all of them."

"So what are you looking for that you haven't found already?"

"Constantina."

He had prepared this reply, knowing it to contain enough truth for him to sound convincing. Indeed, having had the importance of the image (as opposed to the written word) so recently impressed upon him, Mark had reflected again on the rather poor short list of photographs he had curated thus far. The selection process had been reasonably thorough he knew, even to the extent of including Beatrice's hand-picked offerings as potential candidates; indeed, it had been so thorough that, upon its completion, Mark had confidently banished the unwanted material back into their dark attic-bound boxes.

"But you said that there weren't any of her." Julia's voice climbed the ladder and echoed inside the loft.

"I know," he called back, wondering how distant he might have sounded, "but I'm not really sure. And anyway, I might find something else."

He left the proposition there and dragged the first box to the top of the ladder. Julia was looking up at him.

"Can you take these for me?"

"These aren't your Father's," she said, once they had managed the transfer and the box rested at her feet. "Surely *you* don't have any photographs of Constantina!"

Preparing the pass down the second box, an idea came to him.

"No, of course not. But it occurred to me the other day that, not only might I have overlooked something of my own that would be useful, I ought to consider including more photographs of other people."

"Like who?"

"I don't know. Me maybe."

Julia's short laugh told him she found the notion amusing - and the fact that she chose not to follow it up with any verbal witticism, also confirmed its validity.

There was no question of Mark undertaking his photographic exhumation in Hampstead. Julia's proximity seemed to present some kind of danger to him; after all, she only knew limited portions of his own history, and her taking an interest in his old photographs would have certainly led to the kind of deflection that he was not prepared to contemplate. It was, he knew, not only deflection that was the issue. Mark was happy enough to explain away his Father's life to her - to anyone, come to that - but his own was a different matter. This resolve, and the desire for privacy that went with it, saw him an hour or so later, unloading three boxes onto the drive of his Aunt's house.

Having prepared himself for a similar dialogue to that he had faced with Julia, Mark was relieved to find the house deserted on his arrival.

_*_

Healey, ever the consummate publishing Spin Doctor, made certain that the release of <u>No Easy Fight</u> was accompanied with heavy references to the Bell & Withers court case.

"It was obvious. After all, here was someone who had already been in the public eye: his name was known, and he had, to all intents and purposes, established himself as something of a hero with the David and Goliath brigade. All we needed to do was remind people of him; to say "Here's another book by that guy you've already heard of; go check it out"."

That Healey's strategy proved a successful one was established almost immediately. The first print run of <u>No Easy Fight</u>, though not enormous, was distributed within a week, and two-thirds sold at the end of the first fortnight. The decision to go for a second hardback run - followed, a month or so later, by a paperback edition - was taken very early.

For Packard, the success of the book came as something of a surprise.

> "Peter had warned me that things might suddenly take off. After the Bell & Withers thing, he tried to keep me a little in the public eye: a reading or two here, a review there. We even managed to squeeze in a couple of radio interviews. At times I felt more like a salesman than anything else. Which is, of course, exactly what I was."
>
> (Interview with Michael Parkinson, 1984)

It was the production of the paperback - complete with stark black and white line drawing on the cover, and excerpts from both Wilson's and Shutts' reviews on the back - which was the signal to Packard that he had finally arrived.

> "It had been something I had dreamed of, of course. I mean, you had too. Strange how a less substantial version of the same thing could somehow give you more credibility. Don't ask me what it was. Perhaps I might have flattered myself with some grandiose notion that it made my work accessible to the ordinary man in the street - although I don't think I had any pretentious notions of "my work" at that stage. Perhaps it was the fact that I could stroll into Smiths' and see my name right there between Orwell and Poe. Perhaps it was the sudden financial reward that Macmillan pushed my way. (Pause) OK; no question: it was the money."

> (Interview with Michael Parkinson, 1984)

Having been hovering close to the breadline over the previous few months, Packard's windfall, though not colossal, came to him in the same way a win on the football pools might have. His celebrations in London - except those which were shared with Healey - are not on record.

"The day the paperback came out I took Charles out for lunch; this was after a short, but well attending signing session in Foyle's. By about five o'clock I was completely done in. Charles seemed the worse for wear too, but he shoved me in a taxi and waved me away. I watched him through the taxi window as he disappeared back into Soho."

Three days after that lunch, Packard was enjoying a more restrained family celebration. George Walker was the only invited guest, and the solitary break with tradition was the buoyant Author's provision of champagne rather than wine.

-*-

For a time there had been a question in Mark's mind as to the importance of Peter Healey. Mark had met him a few times when Healey had visited his Father in Hampstead, and he remembered being struck by the strange solidity of their relationship; there was a bond between the two men which seemed more than just professional, almost brotherly. It was a sensation - that closeness with his Father - Mark found difficult to reconcile, more especially later, when he was adult enough to be able to reflect upon it sensibly. He remembered it being as if the two of them belonged to some secret society which, when they were together, rendered all others superfluous.

Despite this undoubted closeness, Mark had been struck by Healey's reticence about making any kind of contribution to the book.

"Don't get me wrong," he had said to Mark over coffee one day (they had met just off Piccadilly, in Healey's old stomping ground), "it's not that I've got anything to hide. And it's not that I don't want to contribute either. I just feel that Charles' work should do the talking. And in any event, I'm sure you've got plenty of other more important people to talk to."

Mark - immediately certain that there *was* indeed something to hide - had pushed back, reiterating the importance of the singular position Healey had occupied for the latter part of his Father's life, and probably for all of his 'career'. He had felt some confusion as he both tried to imagine what Healey might have been trying to cover up - presumably those dark and lost London days - as well as fighting the sensation that he was being sold to, and had found himself needing to try particularly hard to resist the wiles of the affable publisher. An image of Congreave broke in to his conscious, and Mark wondered if publishers were indeed a breed apart.

In the end, Healey had agreed to a single interview, with the proviso that the questions he would be asked were notified to him in advance.

"You sound more like a politician than a publisher!" Mark recalled himself saying. Healey had laughed.

There was not, Mark was to discover later - both during the initial search, and again as he trawled once more - any photographic record of the two men together. Although he found this somewhat surprising, he allowed himself to explain it away by the fact that they spent very little time together socially. They didn't go on holiday together, for example - there were many photographs of George Walker with the family - and he was certain that neither of the men went to their impromptu meetings toting a camera. Despite this, Mark had come to the conclusion that the absence of Healey's physical image within the book would create something of a gap; so much so, that he interrupted his work to write a short letter to Macmillan. They were aware of his undertaking, so a request for a photograph of a former member of their staff who was something of a key witness in his Father's life would not, he was sure, be too surprising. It was, he knew, something of a long shot, but it was not inconceivable that they might have something from around 1970. Mark, having pursued Mrs Brakespeare, was not averse to the odd professional stab in the dark, and he consoled himself with the knowledge that, even if Macmillan were unable to oblige, at least he could look forward to a coherent and supportive reply.

Walking back from the post box, Mark found himself once again wondering about his Aunt's collection of photographs. He had seen nothing to confirm the existence of anything extensive, but the impression she had given him - the way she had hesitantly handed over her own selection as if they were semi-precious gems - suggested that she might treasure such things more than she would ever let on. Of course, if that were so (and, stepping back into the house, he had convinced himself that it was) then there would almost certainly be more to be found.

The dining room was seldom used by Beatrice and Simon. They would usually eat at the large kitchen table, or with trays on their laps in the Conservatory when the weather was good; the only exception to this being when they were entertaining, and even then - as Mark had discovered - the final location for the meal would more often than not depend on who the guests were. It was a strangely dark and sombre room, out of kilter with the rest of the house, and the resting place of a small number of chests of drawers in addition to the impressive dining table.

He did not consider himself to be a devious or dishonest person, and in advance of his standing before one of the small chests, had attempted to rationalise his action as being the only course open to him. Despite such preparation, Mark expected to feel some rush of guilt or angst when his hand pulled open the first drawer, and was, in consequence, a little surprised to find he experienced nothing of the kind.

Having discovered tablecloths and sets of cutlery, Mark eventually uncovered (within the third drawer he tried) a number of slim volumes that looked like old magazine binders but which, he knew instantly, were photograph albums. He pulled out the first and began to leaf through its pages. Mainly the pictures were of Beatrice or Simon, both many years younger. A whole series captured their holiday in Kenya about which he had heard much when he was a boy. There were photographs of people he did not recognise but who, he was convinced, he might know as part of the family folklore.

Nearing the back of the album he turned to discover a page containing a single photo. It was located in one corner, and, as he could see the vague outlines left by other images, Mark knew that its partners had been recently removed. The single image remaining was a photograph of him standing alongside his Father. They were in a public garden somewhere. It was a bright day, yet despite both of them smiling, they looked worn. Mark bent a little closer to the picture. He was struck by the similarity of the two smiles; how the lips curved in the same fashion; how there was just the hint of a dimple in the cheek. More than that, the two people he was staring at shared the same look of tiredness, the identical shape about the eyes; even the same slight shrug of the shoulders. Mark concentrated on one figure then the other. There; that was him. And there, alongside; that was his Father. Mark felt himself staring at two images of the same person; he had never recognised that he and his Father had been so alike.

Underneath the image, in Beatrice's neat hand, was the date: August 1970.

-*-

After a Christmas that was, by Packard standards, verging on the sumptuous, the family prepared to settle down to a new decade.

"Although I was only partially aware of what was going on, I knew it was a very exciting time. Father was very busy, spending a great deal of time out of the house; but when he came home he tended to be buoyant. I think it rubbed off on Mother too. That Christmas Eve I had a dream that all the things I had wanted would be under the tree in the morning - and sure enough, they were!"

It was a relatively lavish time. Following on from his initial earnings from the hardback, Packard received more for the paperback which Healey managed to get into the shops just in time for Christmas. Macmillan had even decided to take on a run of both <u>Dawn</u> and <u>Under the Olive Tree</u> if <u>No Easy Fight</u> sold well.

January 1970 was a time of both old and new sensations. Packard, now with three novels under his belt, found himself on the hunt once again for a subject. Where such a quest had previously seen him rock unsteadily towards depression and over-indulgence, demands on his time - once more orchestrated by Healey - prevented him becoming too preoccupied with the future. In addition, the fact that there was more money in the family coffers made life easier too.

> "It was a wonderful Christmas; perhaps the best we'd had. Mary seemed to be over her illness from earlier that year and was beginning to look radiant again. And there was Mark. Eleven years old and at the Big Boys' school; it was like I'd missed half his life already."

(Interview with Michael Parkinson, 1984)

In addition to feeling 'radiant', Mary was also beginning to hanker after another child. She and Charles had talked about trying for a second during both the previous two years, but they agreed their domestic situation was too uncertain to take on any additional responsibility. 1970 was, Mary felt, her last chance to have a second child before time caught up with her.

"I know they talked about it, but I got the distinct impression that Charles wasn't keen. I know he used the size of their house as an excuse at one point. Perhaps it was his past that was the key, rather than anything else. And that he had fallen into this new lifestyle of his and didn't want to compromise it."

Walker's theory was, as usual, not too far wide of the mark - although it was reported later that Packard had not been in favour of the idea because 'he couldn't trust himself'. Whether or not he had in fact said that, the veracity of the statement was soon to become apparent.

Mary pressed Charles for them to move. She had taken to visiting estate agents in areas nearby and had secretly selected a number of properties which met her ideal requirement. Knowing their cost, she had made enquiries as to the cost of a mortgage and had concluded that, given her husband's recently improved level of income, such a purchase would not be beyond them.

Within just a few weeks, they would have been able to purchase more than one from her list.

> "I had a call from Peter. It was one Sunday evening. The phone was still so new in the house that it made us jump when it rang! He was pumped up. Said he'd had a call from some guy - I missed the name - and wanted me to travel down to London the next morning. I couldn't not go."

> (Interview with David Frost, 1984)

That Sunday afternoon, Healey had received a telephone call at home from Owen Colquhoun. Colquhoun was one of the major financial players behind London Weekend Television. Having trained as an Actor, Colquhoun had unsuccessfully trod the boards in Repertory for a few years without making any kind of name for himself. In mid-1964 he had been on tour when the theatre in which his company was playing - the Old Vic, a fading cause in Bristol - was suddenly hit by a financial crisis. Colquhoun had been swept up in the ensuing melee and, more by luck than judgement, found himself at the centre of a campaign to save the theatre. Within two weeks, Colquhoun had, almost single-handedly, found sufficient sponsorship to secure a year's lifeline for the theatre. Not only that, he had found a vocation.

Having quit acting, Colquhoun remained in Bristol for two years before taking up a post at LWT as a producer. Given his background, he was a natural for the drama department, and rose rapidly to the upper echelons of power.

"I had paid close attention to the Bell & Withers case of course. Even read a couple of Charles' books. The court case seemed a natural drama, and I had wanted to do it immediately. However, there were other commitments, and before I knew it Charles had written his book. That only left me one option."

The option Colquhoun was speaking of was to buy all production rights for <u>No Easy Fight</u>.

> "The next day Peter told me that his conversation with Colquhoun had been brief and to the point. Colquhoun had wanted to produce a play for LWT using <u>No Easy Fight</u> as the basis, and he wanted to buy the story. He was, he said, a no bullshit kind of guy, and made Peter an offer immediately. "Take it or leave it", Peter said he'd told him, "and don't think you can haggle!""

(Interview with David Frost, 1984)

Healey gave a preliminary acceptance to the offer which, he told Colquhoun, he would confirm the next day. When Packard arrived in the publisher's office at lunchtime, Healey simply sat him down and said 'How would you like a cheque for a fifty-thousand pounds?'.

> "I couldn't, of course, comprehend what Peter was saying. After all, this was nothing like the money Macmillan had been paying me thus far. At first I thought it was a joke. It took all Peter's powers of communication to bring me round. And Colquhoun wasn't joking. He wasn't a man you joked with - even Peter knew that. LWT was big time. Jackpot!"

(Interview with David Frost, 1984)

Contracts were signed before the end of the week. Colquhoun's conditions on the deal were simple and straightforward, and an example typical of the man. Neither Healey nor Packard were to interfere in his production; they were to have no say in how he chose to put it together; and, most particularly, Packard himself would have no influence, say, or input into the writing of the television script.

"Charles had been a little nervous of the "no say" things, and was concerned to know who would be writing the play. I told him not to worry. Actually, I told him to take the money and run!"

275

Colquhoun chose Roddy Armitage, one of the regulars from his creative stable, to produce the teleplay. Armitage had shown early promise before being brought to LWT where his output was driven by a need to fulfil contractual obligations rather than personal desire. After a slightly disappointing adaptation of Thomas Hardy's <u>Jude, the Obscure</u>, Armitage had found himself relegated to the second division, putting together scripts for sit-com pilots and the odd episode of 'Crossroads'. Healey tried to persuade Packard that Colquhoun's choice could have been a lot worse - and that, if Armitage were to return to form, it was possible he might make <u>No Easy Fight</u> 'sizzle'.

Healey's positive message proved to be delivered more in hope than anything else. On June 6th, 1970, LWT's version of <u>No Easy Fight</u> - which they had chosen to call 'The Final Chapter' - was broadcast to an unsuspecting public. Colquhoun had assembled a solid cast of reputable, journeymen actors who were well-known and, in the main, well-loved by British audiences. Some of them, however, brought baggage from other TV lives with them and this proved something of a major interference, especially in the case of the actor playing the Packard figure - Matthew Wilson had, for six years, played the dithering librarian in Granada's limp comedy 'Quiet, Please!'; an association manifestly unsuitable to a supposedly bulldog hero. That Wilson struggled was, however, more to do with the poor quality of Armitage's script than his own personal difficulties.

The critics slammed the production, and, whilst liberally slinging mud, some deliberately tossed the odd cowpat in Packard's direction. Shutts - who asked his editor if he might write a small piece on the play - defended the original book, and offered some personal thoughts on the difficulties of turning the small page into the small screen.

Packard himself was livid.

> "I couldn't believe what I was seeing! I was watching people who bore no resemblance to anyone I'd ever seen, let alone the characters in my book. In the main they used my dialogue - supplemented with garbage, of course! - but the whole thing was dreadful. It was only some desperate hope the final few minutes might redeem it that kept me watching to the end."

> (Interview with David Frost, 1984)

Healey managed to prevent Packard from what would have been a futile attempt to sue not only Colquhoun personally, but the whole of London Weekend Television.

"He had, after all, signed away his rights. There was nothing he could do. I told him I'd try and have a word with Colquhoun, but it was spilt milk by this stage."

A week after the play was broadcast, Packard received a letter from Colquhoun apologising if the play had caused him any distress. The translation had been 'a little shaky in places', but, he maintained, 'it had remained true to the spirit of the original'. Packard burned the letter and added Colquhoun's name to the place vacated by Arnold Harriman on his small, personal - and invisible - black list.

Practical demands made it impossible for Packard to give anything more than temporary vent to his rage. Between the signing of the LWT contract and the transmission, Charles and Mary had decided to move. Despite Mary's local research, the couple were destined to move south to London. In this, as in many other things, Packard had been influenced by Healey, who had told him that if he was really serious about making a success of his new profession then he needed to be in London. Too many talents had dissolved away to nothing, Healey told him, because they had been geographically divorced from where they really needed to be.

> "I was, after all, spending a lot of time in London; and, if recent events were anything to go by, I might well be spending more there. Mary had not been keen. She wasn't a big city kind of person, and pushed back on the idea. I promised that if it didn't work out, we could move away again. She said it would be bad for Mark; I told her to think of all the things he would have access to: museums, galleries, and the rest. She said that it would be more expensive. There I couldn't argue, but I suggested that just by being there we might earn even more. Peter had looked out a few places for us, and I had taken a shine to the house in Hampstead. It was the most expensive one on his list, and it took half of my LWT money as a deposit to secure it - but I had decided. Mary wasn't over the moon, but eventually she agreed to go along with it."

> (Interview with David Frost, 1984)

Three weeks after 'The Final Chapter', a dark blue Pickford's removal van carried the Packards and all their belongings away from their rented Warwick home to their house in Hampstead. When they arrived, Peter Healey was waiting for them on the threshold, bottle of champagne in hand.

Chapter Twenty Seven

Not long after the publication of <u>No Easy Fight</u>, one or two people began to espouse a theory that the book was, in fact, a premeditated political statement; an idea which gained weight when considered alongside <u>Dawn</u>. It was a notion Packard had not given any thought to, though the proposition was certainly more appealing than the religious interpretation put forward by Wilson.

> "I was interested to know where this "political" idea originated. I didn't wholeheartedly subscribe to it, of course, and when asked about it - as I was a couple of times in interviews, then and since - I tended to offer a coy response. I had to really, as I felt strangely unable to give any categoric statement. Peter told me not to worry about the source of the idea, and that such things such tended to grow of their own volition, needing nothing to germinate them. The most important thing was - and how like him to say this! - that it gave us another handle; another angle; another reason for Joe Public to go out and buy the books."

> (Interview with David Frost, 1983)

From Packard's point of view, Joe Public was doing a little more than just reading. Before the family left Warwick, Charles had received a number of letters from middle class political groups of various shades of red located in and around the Midlands. They were, without exception, interested in hearing Packard's message: what had it been like (they wanted to know) working in the oppressive regime of the factory? how had he, a member of the Proletariat, been treated by the Judiciary? did he feel he had received a fair trial, or had he just been lucky?

It all cases, Charles had written polite replies, partly deflating over-political interpretations of the two books in question, and always declining invitations to speak or attend meetings.

> "I wasn't interested. Not then. But I guess a seed of some kind was sown. Maybe there was a part of me that wondered if I might be staring at the subject for the next book and not realising it. Maybe I was more interested in politics than I knew. Whatever, the move to Hampstead seemed to crystallise a few things for me. I don't think it was as radical as me feeling guilty that I was leaving my working class roots behind, but moving - physically moving - into a different strata of society, well, that shook a few things about I guess."

(Interview with David Frost, 1983)

Before the end of July, Macmillan forwarded Packard's first batch of mail to the house in Hampstead. Before LWT's version of <u>No Easy Fight</u> he had received a few pieces of mail each month, but now Macmillan found that they were needing to make a delivery each week.

"We dealt with as many as we could "in-house", filtering out all the time-wasting crap. Letters relating to publication details we had to answer anyway. The TV play had boosted the in-coming. The only stuff we passed on to Charles was the more personal - and acceptable - stuff."

Dated June 27th, one of the letters from that first London batch was written by Prunella Amelia Hudson. In many respects her invitation to attend the next meeting of the 'Hampstead and Highgate Socialists' was no different from those Packard had turned down in the past - except in this instance he decided to accept.

"Maybe it was that "crystallisation" stuff at work; or the idea that I could ill afford to turn down anything that might give me inspiration. The letter seemed a little different to the others I had received; the tone of it. There was a kind of warmth about it, as if someone were interested in me as an individual rather than as a sabre rattler for some Bolshevik war cry. The thing that really swung it, though, was her drawing a parallel to my growing-up days - including a quote from "Sheffield Song", one of those old <u>Sixteen Sonnets</u> poems. Quoting me to me! Christ knows where she'd got hold of that!"

(Interview with David Frost, 1983)

Packard's journey to the pub in Highgate - the 'Hope and Anchor', where the group rented a room above the bar on a bi-weekly basis - brought back memories of his first visit to Stella's writing circle. On a practical level, many things were different: he arrived in a taxi; he had no intention of reading anything he had written; and he felt certain that, politically, he would be the least qualified to be there. Despite recognising all these factors, Charles would often later relate how he could not but sense an echo from his past.

As he waited for his bitter to be poured, he had asked the Barman to guide him to the appropriate room. He was directed through the back of the bar and up a narrow flight of stairs.

"The sign at the bottom said 'Toilets', and I couldn't help wondering as I ascended - pint in one hand - if this might be a very poor omen indeed! Anyway, I was a little early and when I found the room, there were only three people in it. I had no idea how many people actually attended something like the 'Hampstead and Highgate Socialists'; for all I knew, this might have been a record breaking attendance!"

(Interview with David Frost, 1983)

Of the three individuals there, one - a striking woman of slightly above average height - walked immediately towards him. Prunella Hudson, at that time in her early thirties and so eight years Packard's junior, was the type of woman who immediately gave the impression that she was a little 'different'.

> "There was something fierce about her. She wore her hair in a tightly managed way, cut short and controlled. Her clothes - though not expensive or showy - had a certain style about them. And her voice was immediately precise and definite. There was a strange kind of lilt about it too, though without any trace of accent. When she said "Hello", I found myself trying to hear her reading "Sheffield Song" out loud."

(Interview with David Frost, 1983)

Prunella Hudson had tried a number of professions since leaving University with a rather poor Law degree in 1960. She had been pushed into the course by her Father, who had been adamant that she would do well in the world, despite having the disadvantage of being a woman. When he died late in 1958, she began to lose her drive for academic study, and coasted through the remainder of her degree, finally scraping through on the strength of her work in the first eighteen months. Knowing that she was not cut out for the legal profession, she had subsequently spent her time trying to alight on another, more suitable career.

For a couple of years she had modelled, her striking figure giving her an angle which allowed her to find a small slot in a niche market. There was a little glamour work, but the bulk of her income was earned through fashion shoots. Having enjoyed some success early on, she began to tire of the life and eventually quit in 1963. From then on there were periods which saw her as a Counsellor, part-time Parliamentary Researcher, and magazine sub-editor. At the time of their meeting, she was working for the Campaign for Nuclear Disarmament as a publicist.

Packard's attraction to her was instantaneous. It had been several years since his affair with Constantina, and he had - at least publicly - remained faithful to Mary. In mid-1970, with his relationship with Mary still not having returned to its pre-Hydra norm and his public personality under

280

vigorous development, Charles was, by his own admission, 'feeling the itch'.

The room gradually filled, until around twenty-five people were present.

> "I guess they fitted some kind of stereotype: middle everything, really; class, age, the lot. There were a few old hippies - and a few young ones too. I don't know what I'd expected, but the thing that seemed consistent through all of them was a degree of intelligence, and some kind of passion in what they believed. The former was, as you'd expect, entirely daunting."

(Interview with David Frost, 1983)

The 'Hampstead and Highgate Socialists' ran their meetings along very precise lines. There were minutes from the previous meeting and a professionally constructed agenda for the one taking place.

> "I was number three - after "Minutes of the Previous Meeting" and an item to discuss recent cuts in the local services' budget by the predominately Tory council. I had no idea what to expect. The first thing seemed to take seconds, the second hours. There was a vigorous debate on the motivation behind the cuts and the effects they would have. I say 'debate', but as everyone seemed to be saying the same thing, I guess that's not quite the right word! Item three simply said "Charles Packard"; I wondered if they wanted me to do a turn - half-time cabaret, perhaps!"

(Interview with David Frost, 1983)

It was evident from the beginning that Prunella's role in the group was a significant one. The session was chaired by Maxwell Coldfield, a member of the opposition Labour Party on the local Council. Several other members of the group also had explicit political associations. Prunella sat on Coldfield's left, occasionally whispering to him as the debate was going on, or pointing to things she had written on the pad she kept on her lap. Packard, who found the style of the conversation interesting, could not help but pay particular attention to his hostess throughout the process.

After around three quarters of an hour, Coldfield proposed a motion that the group should register a formal complaint in respect of the cuts under discussion, and that he and other members of the Labour Party should make representation to the Leader of the Conservative Council.

> "Suddenly, the debate was over. They had gone from heated discussion to a calm, democratic vote, and before I knew what was happening, Pru was announcing my presence and inviting me

to sit up the front with her and Coldfield. As I walked forwards, there was a little polite applause. Quite frankly, I felt a bit at sea."

(Interview with David Frost, 1983)

It became immediately evident that Prunella was the architect behind Packard's presence, and had done a fair degree of preparation. She began by giving a brief history of his work to date, offering minor factual detail - such as his living in Sheffield, and the job at the factory - as background. There were one or two direct questions during her introduction which allowed Packard to clarify a little detail and also - more importantly - allowed him to relax.

> "By the time Pru had finished, I'd managed to get myself sorted. I'd had a scan of the people there, spotting the most radical and vigorous speakers from the previous debate, and looking for friendly faces I could focus on if I needed to. The session turned in to a kind of Questions and Answers thing. I was surprised how many of them had read <u>No Easy Fight</u>. They asked about the characters a little, but wanted to get behind them into my experience of the trial. Soon, the whole thing became theoretical and subjective: what did I think about this, and how could I reconcile one thing with another. Occasionally I felt a little out of my depth, but luckily Pru sensed these moments and managed to haul me round."

(Interview with David Frost, 1983)

In the end, Packard's session ran for a little under an hour. There were one or two dry items with which the meeting concluded, and Charles' earlier sensation that he might be there to 'do a turn' ended up being not that far wide of the mark. Prunella took possession of Packard at the close of the meeting, making sure that he spent a little time with Coldfield and several other key members of the group in the bar downstairs.

When the Landlord eventually rang the bell to call "time", Prunella asked Packard if he would like a lift home.

> "I declined. I guess I didn't want to, but I did. The Barman called me a cab. I had, of course, been knocked over by her. It wasn't just her stunning looks - I had decided by the end of the evening that she was indeed a belter - but her intelligence and commitment too. She believed in things, and she was articulate about them. And she wasn't playing at it as if it were just a hobby; or at least, it didn't seem to me that she was. Maybe if it hadn't been for that - her intelligence, her principles - then I probably

would have taken her up on her offer of a lift; but on the basis of that evening, I somehow didn't feel sufficiently equal (or sufficiently superior) to be able to get beyond general awe."

(Interview with David Frost, 1983)

Packard's appearance at the meeting warranted two column inches in the local weekly paper; a contribution written by Prunella. As far as Charles was concerned - and Prunella aside - the evening had been an interesting rather than stimulating experience. He found himself drawn towards the political aspects of the debate not for their philosophical or theoretical content, but for the way the debate itself was carried out. This exposure to a group of intellectual people discussing important and relevant issues was entirely new to him; his only previous experience of group discussions had been gained in the canteen at the factory, where the subjects for debate were invariably of a more 'basic' nature.

"I asked Charles how it had gone the next time I saw him. He seemed pretty non-committal, though he did express an interest in the format of the meeting rather than its content. Pru's name never passed his lips."

It was the excuse to Healey that he considered himself to be doing 'research' that he also offered Mary as he prepared to return to the 'Hope and Anchor' two weeks later.

> "When I arrived, Pru was at the bar buying a drink. As soon as she saw me, I knew that something was about to happen. It seemed inevitable, really. Perhaps in that instant all the reservations I had manufactured the previous week just disappeared."

(Interview with David Frost, 1983)

This time when Packard was offered a lift home, his acceptance was immediate. Driving away from the pub, Prunella asked him if he would like to stop for coffee at her flat on the way. Although he knew that he could not afford to be too late home, the invitation was not to be turned down.

As little before twelve thirty, Packard turned the key in the lock of the Hampstead house and went upstairs to bed. It was the second bed he had been in that evening.

-*-

There was, Mark began to realise, an echo. As he wrote about his Father - still maintaining his own distance, as far as the book was concerned - he found himself being drawn in, ensnared almost by the life he was recreating. It seemed to him as if here and now, the second time around, his Father was exerting a greater influence over him than he had when he was alive. It was an obscure and faintly ridiculous notion that Mark immediately tried to dispel by looking up from his computer screen and out of the window to the reality of the trees beyond. Downstairs there were sounds emanating from the kitchen (Beatrice and Simon had evidently returned, though he had been oblivious to the event) and Mark knew that if they ran true to form, he could expect an interruption for coffee fairly soon.

He looked back at his desk. A photograph of Prunella Hudson - taken in that summer of 1970 - stared back at him. Mark could see for himself the evidence of his Father's words: she had indeed been a striking woman, and wore her clothes as a model would wear them - ostensibly to show off the clothes, but ultimately to show off herself. The resemblance was not self-evident, but he could see something of Maxine in her. There was no physical parallel - after all, Maxine was a more petite individual, and her defining features, such as the colour of her hair, were entirely different - but in the manner, in the aura, there was something. Perhaps she too was 'striking'. Mark recalled the image he held of her as she walked away from him along Regent Street; yes, and there was something in the way she wore her clothes too. He wondered if his Father had felt the same desire for Prunella that Maxine stirred in him; the desire to possess, consume, absorb - and, perhaps, to be absorbed too. If so, Mark knew he was closer to being able to understand how and why his Father had embarked on the affair with Prunella.

But this was not easy. Understanding must - at least in this particular case - lead to some kind of empathy, especially if he were to maintain his parallel with Maxine. Yet such a sensation, such an echo, manoeuvred Mark into a difficult situation; he was, through all of this, trying also to remain objective, to remain faithful to his Mother - perhaps in a way that his Father had been unable. He heard again Beatrice's warning about how he must take care over the depiction of his Father; 'equilibrium' she had demanded - and now, hovering between loyalties and the reverberations of the past on his own immediate and very real present, he was beginning to gain an inkling of what she had meant.

-*-

"Pru was very different - especially different to Stella. It wasn't just her looks, you understand, it was her passion, her intelligence. I hadn't known what I was doing with Stella. I was naive. It was the situation, rather than the person that moved me there. But Pru scored on her own account. Don't get me wrong; I hadn't ceased to love Mary. I told myself I never could. But Pru had something about her that was challengingly different."

(Interview with Michael Parkinson, 1984)

Packard managed his affair with the striking Socialist in a deliberate and calculated way. He had, as he recognised, 'grown up', and there was to be no melodramatic running off to live with his new lover - and no equally melodramatic return. He and Pru met regularly. Charles attended the fortnightly meetings of the 'Hampstead and Highgate Socialists' where he became an averagely vocal participant. Though still lacking in any commitment to the political principles espoused by the group, he took part in the debates where he held a strong enough opinion. This lack of a political standpoint was something Packard would retain for his entire life. Sometimes he would find himself arguing a view counter to the general trend, and on such occasions his playing Devil's Advocate would lead to some interesting post-meeting encounters with Prunella.

> "She would get very angry with me sometimes, and in the privacy of her car or flat, harangue me for being a Tory, or ignorant, or downright stupid! But such conflict always put a little extra spark into the love-making that inevitably followed…"

(Interview with Michael Parkinson, 1984)

Between political meetings, the two would make arrangements to see each other at least twice a week, usually at Prunella's flat. Very occasionally they would rendezvous at some pre-arranged point, and Prunella would drive them out into the country for the day. Testament to Packard's management of the affair was that Peter Healey was completely unaware of it until Charles confessed it a few months later.

> "I don't think Mary knew. Or at least I like to think that she didn't. After all, the last thing I would have wanted was to hurt her again. The story about research for another book and the need to get inside such an organisation was holding up well; at times I even believed it myself! I knew, however - from very early on - that I didn't believe in it enough to write about it; and I realised too that I needed to believe in something to be able to work on it."

(Interview with Michael Parkinson, 1984)

As Packard's involvement with the 'Hampstead and Highgate Socialists' was in its infancy, Mary, who had been enjoying her role of house-maker and Mother in their new London home, began to suffer a recurrence of the ill health that had troubled her the previous year. For a considerable period she managed to hide her discomfort from her husband, getting through difficult days on a combination of pain killers and rest. She and Mark spent a great deal of that summer on Hampstead Heath when the boy, now twelve, would indulge in make-believe games with the model aircraft and motorised gun boat his Father had brought him. Often, the two of them would sit and discuss the new school Mark would be attending in the September of that year.

"I had no real idea that she was ill. There were off days, I suppose, but nothing that suggested what was to follow."

Occasionally, Packard's Sister, Beatrice and her husband Simon, would spend an afternoon with them. Beatrice and Simon had recently returned to England after a period in the Far East, and had purchased a house in Belsize Park, not too far from the Packard's new London address. If Beatrice noticed any decline in Mary's general well-being, she kept her opinion to herself.

Mary's first visit to the Doctor - Ralph Miles - was undertaken without Packard's knowledge. She told Dr Miles of the problems she had had the previous year, and Miles had resumed her on the same course of drugs that had been effective then. This time however, despite a temporary improvement in her condition, Mary's health continued to deteriorate.

> "As she managed to hide it from me, I had no idea what was going on. On one occasion I came across a bottle of tablets in the bathroom and asked what they were, but she only admitted to having a "clear out" and immediately dumped the pills in the bin. When her first really serious attack came, well, she simply couldn't hide that."

> (Interview with Michael Parkinson, 1984)

On August 24th, Mary collapsed in the kitchen. Packard, who had been working in his study, heard the crash and ran downstairs. He found Mary sprawled on the floor; she had passed out. Packard immediately phoned from an ambulance, and then called Beatrice. Mark was spending the day with them, having been taken to the zoo in the morning by his Aunt and Uncle. Packard told his Sister what had happened and asked her to look after Mark until he could get over there to pick him up.

By the time the ambulance arrived, Mary had regained consciousness and was trying to tell Charles that she was basically fine and not to worry. Packard would have none of it. Within a few minutes the ambulance had taken both of them to the Royal Free Hospital where Mary was immediately admitted. Despite her protestations, Packard knew that there was something seriously wrong.

> "She smiled at me, squeezing my arm in reassurance. She said she wanted to finish getting dinner ready for when Mark came home. She even tried to send me out to the shops to get her some salt on the pretext that she was running low, but I wouldn't have it. She looked pale. I'd never seen her looking that way, and I knew something was up."
>
> (Interview with Michael Parkinson, 1984)

At the hospital, the doctors began their tests as soon as she was on the ward. Packard was told that it would be a few hours before they would have any results and suggested that he return home. He refused. Waiting until Mary had drifted off to sleep, he made two phone calls: the first to Beatrice, to ask her to look after Mark over-night; the second to Prunella, to postpone the meeting they had arranged for that evening. Packard went back to Mary's bedside and stayed there until the Doctors made their rounds at eight o'clock. They told him that they were still waiting for the test results and suggested that he take the opportunity to get some fresh air. Packard walked into a nearby pub and ordered a bar meal and a pint of beer. He finished neither.

A little before ten that evening, Mary was awake and talking. Packard had spent only fifteen minutes in the pub, unable to remain away from his wife's bedside.

> "I hadn't been gone long, but somehow she already looked worse. So pale. She smiled at me when she woke up, but it was a hollow kind of a smile; and there was something in her eyes…"
>
> (Interview with Michael Parkinson, 1984)

The doctors returned just after ten. The tests had shown up one or two 'irregularities' and they wanted to carry our further investigations first thing in the morning. Begging peace and quiet for his wife, they sent Packard home and told him to some back the following morning. When he did so, he found that Mary had been taken to theatre for a biopsy. Once again Beatrice and Simon were pressed to extend their familial duties.

"I knew something was wrong when no-one came to pick me up. Aunt Beatrice told me that Father had phoned to say that Mother was unwell and had gone to the Doctor's. The next morning they told me she was in the hospital."

When Mary came round from the general anaesthetic, she found Packard sitting at her bedside.

"She looked a little better. It was as if the worst was over, and that the drugs they had given her had done the trick. Or at least that's what I told myself. I knew it wasn't the case; not really. She seemed to doze on and off for most of the morning. When she was awake we talked, about Mark mostly. She asked me when I would be starting the serious work on my next book.... A little before twelve, the Consultant - a chap named Hines - came to tell us the results of the tests. I guess it was difficult for him. Maybe he'd done this kind of thing dozens of times in the past, but it still didn't sit easy. You could tell."

(Interview with Michael Parkinson, 1984)

Hines told Mary that she had Uterine Cancer. The cancer had been present and growing for a number of years and had reached an advanced stage. They would, he said, normally undertake a hysterectomy, but owing to the fact that the disease had already spread beyond the uterus, they had decided that such an action would be futile.

"People usually take such news in complete silence; shock, I suppose. Or disbelief. The Packards were no exception. All I could do was state the facts and offer to answer any questions."

The Consultant told them that Mary would be best in hospital where they would at least be able to make her comfortable. In his opinion, she had only a few weeks to live. As it turned out, the end came even more quickly than he had expected.

"I didn't understand what had happened. I couldn't see how this thing had been growing without our knowing; without Mary knowing. All of a sudden she was here, in a hospital bed, and dying. Mr Hines said that she must have endured a considerable amount of pain over the previous few weeks - if not months - and that she was a very brave woman. Maybe he was right; I don't know. Mary said nothing. I held her hand as she cried herself back to sleep."

(Interview with Michael Parkinson, 1984)

Later that day, August 25th, Beatrice and Simon brought Mark to the hospital, beginning a ritual of visiting that was to last for the next eight days. Packard spent most of each day at Mary's bedside, excusing himself only to eat and sleep. When she was awake they talked, mainly about her hopes for Mark and Charles' writing.

"Mark was due to start school on the 8th of September, and she seemed more concerned that her illness would interrupt his schooling than anything else. I told her not to worry. Beatrice and Simon had stepped in and were doing a marvellous job. Mark was old enough to know what was going on, and at least he was brave enough not to crack when he was in the hospital. Beatrice told me later that he cried most nights. As for me, I just went through those days in something of a daze. It was like a nightmare I was living through. Sometimes Mary would be so lucid and bright, as if she was actually OK. And when she talked about my work, and how proud she was of what I had achieved…"

(Interview with Michael Parkinson, 1984)

On the 2nd September, a little after eleven in the morning, Mary fell into the sleep from which she was never to wake. Over the previous two or three days, the hospital had increased the dosage of the drugs she had been given in order to help her through the pain. That last morning both Charles and Mark had sat beside her bed and she had failed to recognise them.

"When I left the hospital that morning - Father still sitting at her bedside - I knew that I would never see her again. It was calming in a way, knowing that soon the pain would be gone. I knew too, that we would be left, and that we would have to get on with living, my Father and I. There had been a change in him too; I had seen it. When I used to visit the hospital those last days, it was like visiting two patients, each of whom was dying in their own way. I didn't know how Father would respond, or what our life would be like afterwards; I couldn't know. And I could see that he didn't either."

Chapter Twenty Eight

"I can't say I remember very much about the few days that followed Mary's death. It had been so sudden. It seemed as if everything had been all right, then there had been that crash in the kitchen and moments later she was gone. I guess I must have coped, though how well I don't know. Beatrice was a tower of strength; I probably leant on her more than I should have. The arrangements for Mary's funeral got made, and we managed to get along. I didn't see that much of Mark for those few days. Again, Beatrice and Simon stepped in as I tried to get myself together. I found myself thinking stupid things - like if we'd not moved to London things would have all been OK. I even thought that it was some kind of divine retribution, as if I was being punished for my sins.

"There were moments too when I found myself blaming my writing for what had happened. If I hadn't chosen to follow such a course; if I hadn't changed the kind of person I was; if I'd stayed a "normal" guy just doing my nine-to-five in the factory... There were lots of 'ifs' floating about.

"I remember wanting the day of the funeral to be bleak, fitting all those clichéd images of windswept graveyards. Maybe I was trying to cling to some romantic notion of how such things were supposed to be in order to make it seem better somehow. But it wasn't like that. It was one of those blazing late summer days: the sky was too blue; the sun too hot. It was a struggle wearing a suit and tie, and the service seemed surreal because of it. The Vicar at the Church was a young chap, and his message seemed strangely upbeat and modern; there was none of the ancient ritualistic language I had expected, and no-one wailed. As I stood at the grave-side after they had lowered her down, I suddenly realised that Mark was holding my hand. It was a new sensation. I looked at him and it was as if I was seeing a stranger, this boy I didn't actually know."

(Interview with Michael Parkinson, 1984)

Mary was buried on Friday, 6th September, at St. Matthew's Church, Hampstead; having been in London such a short time, there were few mourners. Peter Healey attended, and George Walker made the journey down from Warwick.

Whatever Packard's intentions following on from the tragedy, the practical demands of everyday life - and specifically Mark's schooling - required immediate attention. So, on the following Tuesday, it was Charles, and not Mary who accompanied their son to his new school; and it was Charles who met him later that day.

"On reflection I guess it must have been a difficult time for me. I didn't care much for the new school at first - though that was probably due to Mother's death, rather than anything else. Apart from a few tears at Beatrice's house, I remember feeling that I needed to be strong, and that the only way to get through it was for the two of us - my Father and I - to unite somehow. I could see he had taken it hard, and for a while he was a shadow of his normal self. Facing such a situation, I knew I couldn't let myself go to pieces."

Beatrice's role became crucial over the following few weeks, as the male members of the Packard family went through the painful - and uncommunicated - process of adjusting to their new life. She would often spend time at the Hampstead house helping with the domestic chores; a contribution that continued until she arranged for a Domestic to help out on a part-time basis.

> "It was strange. I'd come home late in the afternoon sometimes and find that the house had been cleaned, that there were freshly ironed shirts, that the beds had been changed. Sometimes it turned out that Beatrice had been in; at other times, Mrs. Hazeldene. On and off, she was with us for about five years - but she seemed so much like a domestic fairy, I guess I saw her no more than a couple of dozen times."

> (Interview with Michael Parkinson, 1984)

After a difficult first month, Mark began to settle down in his new school. He was an above average pupil, though not an outstanding one; in consequence, he found himself located in the top sets for all of his subjects though with unremarkable expectations. His first report at the end of that autumn term would remark on a quiet, studious boy; beyond that his teachers struggled for comment. His passion for history came later.

His Father spent much of that same period out of the house. There were low key meetings with Healey - who was, as yet, refraining from applying any pressure on Packard to begin thinking about his next book - and rather absent minded visits to renowned London institutions. For a while Packard gave a solid impression of being a tourist on an extended visit.

Between Packard and his son, a bond began to grow; an alliance forced upon them by necessity as their one natural link had been removed. With Beatrice still very much on the scene during the weekdays, it was at weekends that the relationship began to develop. Often they would take the tube into Central London, pick one of the main line stations, and jump on a train to see where it would take them. As the weather became less pleasant, their small adventures saw them in Southampton, Ramsgate, Norwich, Birmingham and Bristol. Once they even managed to "Do" York in a day.

A visit to Cambridge was to prove especially significant for Mark.

"I had never seen a place like it before: those imposing buildings; the aura of learning; the sense of history. We picked up a guide book and walked around the very same streets that had been trodden by famous men too numerous to mention. I found myself touching the very doors and walls of the colleges where people I had only heard of in books and classes had actually studied. The idea that I had placed my hands on the exact spot where they had placed their own - perhaps that was the beginning."

For Packard, these day trips were difficult at first. As he had so clearly recognised, he knew little about his Son. Apart from the occasional game in the park or family day out, Mary had been his interpreter as far as the boy was concerned.

> "At first conversation was difficult, if not impossible. More than that; I suddenly realised that I didn't actually know how he behaved, what he was like in public. It was, I suspect, an education for both of us. I remember trying the safe subjects first - like football, school, even girls - and gradually I began to build up a picture of the young man now in my charge. Thankfully, by Christmas, things had moved on."

> (Interview with Michael Parkinson, 1984)

Two other things also happened during that three month period that were of some moment.

Firstly, Packard began - slowly, at first - to write again. Although he had been toying with various ideas earlier in the year, he was as yet unable to carry them through; instead, he found himself facing the need to come to terms with Mary's death.

> "It wasn't an exorcism, don't get me wrong. It was more an attempt to understand. I began to realise that I didn't really know the woman who had been my wife - or, at least, I hadn't known her for some time. My fault, I could see that, but there it was. But

not only had I lost touch with Mary in some profound way, I had also lost the sense and meaning of our relationship, and I knew that was wrong. It seemed I had no choice; the only means at my disposal to counter this lack, this absence was to explore it, and the only tool I had for exploring it was my writing."

(Interview with Michael Parkinson, 1984)

So it was that Packard began to make small notes about Mary and their life together. At first, these took a variety of forms: short prose, poetry, even reportage. As time passed, Packard began to sense that there was something more important about what he was doing, and that it might not be just "occasional" writing. He began to cultivate a sense of debt; that if there was one thing he could do for Mary, even posthumously, it would be to try to understand her and to honour the woman he had fallen in love with in that Midlands' Art class.

The second significant event was Packard's breaking with Prunella. After the funeral, she had tried on several occasions to arrange to see him. There were many phone calls to the house - and many requests for return calls that went unheeded. Occasionally she would find him at home, and there would ensue a stilted and uncomfortable dialogue that normally ended with Packard closing it abruptly.

"I told myself that it was stress, and that he had yet to get over Mary's death. I knew that it couldn't be me; that it couldn't be anything that I had done - because I'd done nothing. So I decided to give him time. I didn't know how much he needed, but it seemed all I could do."

Despite Prunella's intention to be patient, patience was not one of her virtues, and by the end of November she began to be a little more insistent. The two of them had not met for several weeks, and Packard's own instability was beginning to affect her too. Coincident with Prunella's pressure was Packard's beginning to write about Mary, and the preoccupation that was starting to instil in him. The result was inevitable.

> "I didn't see that I had any choice. I had begun to be consumed by a desire to - I don't know - do justice to Mary in some way. What I was beginning to write - and think about, and plot - had meaning, and was something I believed in. At that moment it was the single most important thing I could think of. Pru hadn't done anything, not really. The only thing she was guilty of was being there. But just by being there she was a symbol of something: evidence of my infidelity; proof of the fact that I had not done Mary justice in the past. If this were all about righting wrongs -

and I still can't say exactly if that were so - then I couldn't carry on both the writing and seeing Pru. They just weren't compatible. Under those circumstances, she had to come second."

(Interview with Michael Parkinson, 1984)

On the 5th of December, three months after Mary's death, Packard wrote Prunella a letter in which he tried to explain why he was unable to see her again. There was no immediate response.

-*-

As he wrote this, he remembered Maxine's question in the cafe: had he wanted to end their affair? Mark reconstructed the scene as he paused, taking the opportunity to sip from the coffee brought to him by Simon. She had delivered her question - at least, as far as he could recall - somewhat flatly and without passion; and as he thought about it now, he recognised that he had been taken aback by the very presence of the question rather than the manner of its delivery - and it was this latter attribute that caught him up now.

Perhaps it was inevitable that there would come a time when their liaison would come to an end, and Mark wondered if Maxine might be so calm and dispassionate then. Perhaps she had been able to make her offer in such a manner because she was certain of his response; but if that were not the case, if she knew that there was a danger that it was indeed all over between them, how much more might she have invested in the dialogue? There was an assumption on his part that it would be Maxine asking the question, and considering his present location in his Father's biography, Mark knew that there were multiple potential scenarios on offer to him here. It felt very much like attempting to foretell the future - to recall events before they had become history - but despite this, Mark found himself trying to construct a situation where, like his Father, he would be forced to give Maxine up.

The direct parallel - the death of Julia - was the obvious place for him to start. Mark tried to envisage a sudden and tragic demise; how would he respond? Perhaps in death many things that are unknown become clear; but even having allowed for that, he failed to see how he could be consumed by sufficient compassion or guilt - or any such associated emotion - which would have the result of forcing him to relinquish Maxine. Indeed, might it not be the case that he would find himself freed to enjoy their relationship in the open, rather than in its present closet and secretive fashion? Mark tried another tack. Perhaps Claire might suddenly declare undying love for him, forsaking Peter and throwing herself at his mercy. Under such a happy circumstance, Mark knew that the problem would be duplicated in that he would have to resolve the situation with both Maxine and Julia. Prudence told him that it would be wise to surrender on only one front.

What his Father had done, Mark concluded (though whether out of respect for his Mother or due to his own visionary musings he could not say) was truly laudable. Forsaking Pru, perhaps in his hour of greatest need, stood out as a sacrifice worthy of any romantic title one might wish to pin upon it - providing one was prepared to accept the somewhat duplicitous nature of affairs as they existed in the first place.

-*-

Although living a considerable number of miles away, George Walker continued to offer Charles what little practical assistance he could. The two men had spoken little at Mary's funeral, which was an indication as to the distance that was growing between them. The removal of the Packards from Walker's general proximity was without doubt the major factor in this weakening of the links, but he had already begun to feel marginalised by a man who was growing ever-more successful.

"I didn't really know what was going on any more. Charles' life was becoming more a mystery to me than ever before, and he managed to find other, more professionally sympathetic ears to listen to him."

When Walker and Healey met at St. Matthew's, they had taken an immediate dislike to each other.

Although she was beginning to blend a little more into the background, Beatrice continued to provide Packard with his main support throughout the remainder of the year. Having discovered Mrs. Hazeldene and attended to other various matters of day-to-day practicality - such as finding back-up arrangements for getting Mark to and from school - she gave the appearance of gradually withdrawing from the scene and attempting to revert to the standard role of Sister/Aunt.

One person who, on the contrary, was making more of an effort to be accepted as someone for Packard to lean on, was Prunella. After receiving his letter, she had left England for a short holiday in Italy. The break - a combined walking and painting holiday in Tuscany - had been arranged even before she had met Packard, so a temporary interruption in their affair was bound to have occurred. She had refrained from telling Charles of her holiday until the last minute - and his letter prevented her saying anything at all.

"While I was away I thought a great deal about Charles, and whether or not he meant the things he said in his letter. I was sure he was upset, blaming himself even, and that if he was doing that, then he would be blaming me too. I could see that I had put some pressure on him, I could see that; but I felt - before I went to Italy - that I had a right to know where I stood. And he had told me. Oh, yes. So while I was away I tried to decide what to do: I could either forget him, or I could try again and hope that he hadn't really meant to end things."

When she returned to England, Prunella rang the house and spoke to Packard. Having not heard from her for three weeks, Charles had accustomed himself to the notion that their affair was over; he was finding himself free to write about Mary, and, in general, his life was beginning to become more ordered and productive. Prunella's call might have re-kindled his earlier anxieties, but having managed to re-establish some degree of equilibrium, he felt able to confront and deal with almost any situation. They agreed to meet.

> "I knew there was no way back. Even when we met and I saw again Pru's striking good looks and that assured manner of hers, I knew that there was no way I could go back to her. I wasn't ready for Pru yet - or for anyone else, come to that. There was something - still indefinable, of course - that had to be done, and that I was about to be doing; and that thing could not be compromised. I think she saw that almost immediately. She offered to help, to be around, to be my "friend"; she wanted, she said, to be "inside", not "outside". She said she would give me time, but I didn't want time - not her kind of time anyway. Oh I could have asked her to wait for me, but that would have been too tacky, too contrived. And it would have been dishonest too, and I was beginning to develop a strange notion about honesty. Not necessarily to others mind, but certainly to myself."

> (Interview with Michael Parkinson, 1984)

Packard and Prunella were never to meet again.

-*-

Mark knew that, at the very least, Pru felt his Father had been dishonest with her. He recalled their three short meetings where they had discussed the book and its subject. At each of the first two she had been reticent to talk, nervous, she said, about the light in which she would be cast. She had accused Mark of being biased and that, no matter what she said, he would tell the story from his Father's side.

"I've no intention of doing that," he had responded, "but if I can't get your side of things clear, then I really don't have any option."

She had filibustered, asking him about the style and content of the book; he recalled rather vague questions about his intention, the audience the book was to be targeted at - even his own relationship with his Father. It wasn't until their third - and longest - session that she had opened up a little.

Twenty years had aged her, but even so, Mark could see the remnants of her former hypnotic qualities. She had stayed, she told him (during something of a monologue, much of which was of no use for the book), for another year in London. Someone she had met on the painting holiday in Tuscany had kept in touch with her, and, when they found themselves in need of an editorial assistant on a Northern-focused arts magazine, had offered her a job in Newcastle. Mark noted the strain of regret in her voice when she told him about how difficult it had been for her to leave London - obviously intending that he infer how difficult it had been for her to leave Charles.

He had found, through all his research, that almost everyone had an angle they were intent on pursuing; even George Walker had wanted to get his slant on Charles Packard across. Perhaps, Mark thought, that this was inevitable; that his real job was to put on show all these different views of the same subject - like a set of distorting mirrors in a fairground - and allow the true picture of the man to show through. If so - and if his view of his Father were just another element in the amalgam - then this would neatly fit one popular definition of what a Historian was meant to do and would, almost certainly, satisfy Beatrice's demand for equilibrium.

Prunella had been no exception to this theory. Despite her attempts at being even-handed - dispassionate, even - Mark could see that behind her words lurked her own interpretation of events, and her own history.

In the end, only one of his questions truly unnerved her.

"Do you think he felt guilty?" he had asked towards the end of their final meeting.

"Guilty?" The concept seemed foreign to her.

"About the way he treated you, after Mary died."

"Should he have felt guilty?" She had paused. "Of course he should!"

"That wasn't my question."

"No?"

"At your last meeting, after you came back from Italy, did you get any sense that he felt guilty about what had happened? That there was in any way a feeling on his part that what he had done - ending your relationship - was unfair?"

She had looked away from him at that point. Across the park - they had met near the Mall - two policemen were riding towards Buckingham Palace, and the sound of their horses' hooves carried faintly to them. Mark recalled looking from the riders to his notes just as she spoke.

"No."

He could understand her answer; even sitting at his desk working Prunella in - and out - of his Father's life all over again, the reply was easy to comprehend. But it was not the answer Mark had expected.

-*-

For all his denials that his writing in relation to Mary was neither an exorcism nor the only process by which he could expunge some internal disquiet, Packard did feel an over-riding sense of guilt in terms of the way he had treated his late wife. He had described the process as a means of 'doing her justice' and the only way he could 'understand' their relationship. Exploration it was, of course, but as much in the context of his own feelings in relation to their partnership as about the partnership itself.

The signs that Packard was undergoing some kind of penance driven by remorse manifested itself in physical form too.

"He spent a great deal of time with me; talking mainly, and in a grown-up way. I guess as he had missed out on my being a child, he knew no other. He became - for a short while, at least - a responsible individual, a responsible parent. He still drank, but only in very moderate amounts; often he would only drink wine with meals if I took a glass with him - which of course to a thirteen-year-old was tremendously exciting!"

If this rebuilding of Packard's relationship with his son was another example of his guilt, it was, in many respects, one of his few available means of making an emotional repayment.

By the middle of 1971 the new pattern had been established. With Mark now settled in his school, a routine had built up revolving around domestic necessities and work. What had also built up was a considerable volume of words written in various forms, all with an anonymous - though obvious - subject.

"Perhaps I always knew that what I was doing would turn itself into another book, but when the idea came to me - early one morning as I lay in bed trying to sleep - it came more as a shock than a revelation. I knew that I couldn't give Mary any of her time back or undo any of the things I had done - or do the things I hadn't, come to that. But I knew that the one thing I *could* do was to re-live her life for her. Or at least a part of it. And if I managed to achieve something of this nature, then maybe, in that semi-profound literary sense, she would live forever."

(Interview with Melvyn Bragg, 1986)

In August of that year, the notion of <u>If Time Was A Book</u> was born. Packard began to re-thread all his recent work into a story about a woman who, discovering she has an incurable disease, is given an approximate life expectancy. The woman - 'Elizabeth' - decides that she needs something more definite, and chooses a date upon which she will, one way or another, die. Having made that decision, she then looks at the remainder of her life as if it were an empty book, one blank page for each outstanding day; her aim is a simple one: to fill the book with stimulating and interesting things.

It was, of course, something of a departure for Packard. He had never written as a woman before, though some of his sketches since Mary's death had allowed him to experiment. Healey was nervous.

"It seemed such a gamble. I even considered blackmailing Charles into not writing it. After all, if it were a disaster then although he was beginning to be well-known, he wasn't so indispensable that a flop wouldn't ruin him forever. Early on, however, I saw that he wasn't for moving, and the more he talked about the project, the more I became enthusiastic. I even came round to considering the positive view: if the book was a success, then he would attain a pedestal from which he probably would never be moved!"

There was little doubt that Packard regarded <u>If Time Was A Book</u> as significantly more important than anything he had written thus far; and it was an importance that was intensely personal, not just professional.

"I listened to Peter's arguments. They were powerful, I don't deny it; but the more he argued against it, the more I became convinced that this was the only thing I could possibly do. How could I even consider going on and writing something else - some sham thing - knowing all along that I had this book burning my guts out?"

(Interview with Melvyn Bragg, 1986)

For the next year, Packard toiled at his new book. It proved to be harder than he had anticipated, finding that passion and some indescribable inner drive was not enough to get it written. For the first time in his career, he found himself producing draft after draft of the same scenes and the same speeches. He was later to describe it as his 'apprenticeship', and remark how unusual it was to undertake such a task having already become a professional.

The soft-drinking, celibate routine that was ushered in after Mary's death, continued throughout 1971, 1972 and into 1973. The stability of those years allowed Mark to begin to establish himself at school too, and in September 1972 he began his first O-level year with good prospects in all his subjects, especially History.

On February 14th, 1973, at around nine fifteen in the evening, Packard walked into the lounge of his Hampstead house from his study. From the drinks cabinet - which had seen so little activity for such a long while - he withdrew a bottle of malt whisky. It was half-full. By the time he fell asleep on the settee some two hours later, the bottle was empty. He had completed his first draft of <u>If Time Was A Book</u>.

Chapter Twenty Nine

Day One

I am going to die. Almost as if it is something I have never known. I know it now. Doctor Hillman has told me, and there is, he says, no mistake. Perhaps Doctor Hillman doesn't make mistakes. And I wonder what Michael will say when I tell him. I will need to be brave, to prepare myself.

The Good Doctor - for all his charts and diagnoses, his stethoscope and his stiff white coat - is unable to be more specific. He listened to my question - 'How long?' - with the detached passivity of someone who has heard it all before; who has said it all before. He is not affected. He stands looking out of the window at the gardens below, and allows Death to brush past him. It has not touched him yet. His smile - professional, apologetic, offered as if it were the answer to my question, any question - is not enough. Oh once it might have been, in different circumstances. Perhaps it still stands him in good stead; I have noticed the way Kellie, the Australian Nurse, watches him as he sails through the ward. She was there, standing at the foot of the bed, when I asked him. And she looked his way too, awaiting his answer. Perhaps the smile was for her and not for me. Michael will arrive later bearing his own smile like a gift. It will be a nervous affair; full of hope, full of dread. He will probably just look at me and know. However hard I try to dissemble, he will know. And then I shall break down and cry in his arms. I hope he remembers to close the door.

Of course the Good Doctor had closed the door, as if he knew what was coming; he is the doctor, after all. 'How long?' he said through his frozen smile. It was difficult to say. It was not a precise science, after all. Much depended on me. Would I fight? How hard would I fight? How much did I want to live?

I nearly lost it then, my calmness. How much? How much did I want to take the holiday to Tuscany Michael and I had planned? How much did I want to try one more time for a child? How much did I want to see Michael make a success of his business? How much did I want to outlive him?

How do you measure such things?

And if I did fight, how much difference would it make? It was, the Good Doctor corrected, more a question of not giving in; giving in was the killer. Would I give in?

How long, Doctor, how long?

Not that long ago Mother had died suddenly in similar circumstances. Perhaps she had chosen not to fight; after all Father was not there any more and at sixty two perhaps there is little to prevent you giving in. Knowing her, she would not even have asked the question. The last time I saw her she seemed almost as if she were making an inventory, taking stock of her life and packing it away in some invisible cupboard - which would, no doubt, have been as neat and tidy as those in her kitchen. It was all that was left. It became the only thing she wanted to do - even to the extent of ignoring me when I spoke to her, pretending I didn't exist. There was no persuading her; she had decided.

For a second that's what I thought of doing; making my own list, a little catalogue of existence. But it would be too short - and it was because it was so short, because there was so much I wanted to do, that I knew it wasn't right. Not for me. It would be untidy and half empty, and full of regrets and longings. I didn't want to face those - nor leave them behind me. It wouldn't be fair. Not to Michael.

I watched the doctor - the Good Doctor - as he paused, trying to conjure up some suitable answer (for he knew I wanted an answer now), and thought of Michael and what he might do after. 'After'; it was a strange notion. He would, I knew, go to Harrogate and visit his Mother, and she would try and console him with her extensive range of pithy anecdotes that always annoyed him because they were a generation out of date. She would tell him to 'remember the good times', to 'keep his chin up', that it was 'all part of God's will'. He once told me that she had used that phrase when, as a child, his dog has been run over in the road. 'Bugger God!' he had thought.

I had been staring at my feet when the sound of Doctor Hillman's voice pulled me back. 'Bugger God!' I had echoed to myself and suddenly knew exactly what Michael had meant.

'At least a year.' The Good Doctor's voice was professionally syrupy. If he chose to whisper like that into Kellie's ear I am sure she would have just feinted away. 'I think I can say that, yes; a least a year. Which is good news, really; isn't it?' It was the kind of conversation that requires no other participant. You see women in supermarkets doing it all the time. 'Could be as long as two, maybe two and a half.' His face clouded at that point and I knew he had gone beyond where he was comfortable. Inside me a little voice said 'Expect a year' and then went quiet. 'And you can stay at home, of course. We'll need to give you a course of medicines naturally, and at the end, well, things may become a little less comfortable.' I looked at Kellie as she watched him; part of her dreaming,

I'm sure, of getting into a comfortable situation with the Good Doctor. And inside me the little voice said 'It's a year then'. And I thought, 'It's a deal.'

In the end it was Michael who took it worse than me. Perhaps because I'd had time to prepare. After Doctor Hillman left my room - and Kellie had puffed up my pillows, trying to make me as much at ease as she possibly could (including all sorts of inane chatter) - I just sat for a while, looking towards the window and the blue sky beyond. I cried a bit too, I'll admit that. The Good Doctor told me that I'd probably be able to go home the next day, so at least I had some positive news for when Michael arrived. It would be little comfort to him, I knew that.

Kellie came back a while later to check my pulse and things, and I asked her if Doctor Hillman was popular with the nurses. It must have been the way I asked it, because she blushed right up and gave a short giggly kind of laugh. So I knew that he was, even without her saying anything. Didn't I think he was handsome, she wanted to know; but I told her that I was just a patient and hardly qualified to comment. She told me to stop pulling her leg, and asked if I'd like any tea.

On the dot of seven, Michael arrived. It was a funny sort of hospital, clinging to traditional old routines alongside all the new innovation for which it had become famous. Apparently some of my treatment was quite ground-breaking; Kellie told me that Doctor Hillman was famous for his radical thinking. I said that I bet he was. Visiting hours was one of the old habits they couldn't get out of - even down to a clangy old bell they rang once five minutes before the end of the hour as a warning, and then twice on the stroke of eight to force the visitors out. Maybe if any were caught in the hospital after curfew they admitted them and carried out some kind of operation on them, just to teach them a lesson. Michael would never be late - or early, come to that. It wasn't his way. His time-keeping was as tidy as Mother's kitchen cupboards.

Neither of us broke down immediately, which was some kind of relief. It turned out, of course, that we'd both been preparing for the worst - me in my bed all day, and Michael as he tried to concentrate at work. That made it easier. Not easy mind; it could never be that. He sat down and we got through the normal stuff quickly enough, about how was I feeling and how had his work been. I knew that I couldn't put off what needed to be said - and so did Michael, because his first real question was 'What did the Doctor say?'. I don't recall there being any promise of news that day, but he had obviously expected some.

I tried to be as calm as I could. It had occurred to me that I might have asked Michael to close the door, but that would only have made the whole thing more melodramatic and difficult. At least with a kind of open invitation for anyone else to pop in (I mean, if they chose to) we were forced to maintain some degree of decorum. There was, I told him, some good news. I had decided to start with that. During the afternoon I had rehearsed both scenarios: good followed by bad; bad followed by good. Strangely enough I wanted to start with the bad news. That's where I had begun, and how I had managed to begin to sort things out; but I guessed that it wasn't right for Michael, and for this single hour at least, that was the most important thing. So anyway, I told him that I would be allowed home within the next couple of days, probably once the Doctor had sorted out my medication. I was unreliable taking pills, and told Michael that he had my permission to chide me severely if I failed to do so. That made him smile a little, which was something. Then I let him know that the Doctor thought that I would be fine for about a year, but after that he wasn't sure. I guess I didn't deliver that bit too well, because Michael - the smile long gone, of course - asked me straight out 'Did he say you were going to die?' I wanted to pat his hand and say 'We all die sometime', but that would have been too much like his Mother. So I said yes, but that it wasn't going to happen tomorrow, or the day after that. I was going to be at home, and I would be fine for a long while; I told him that we would be able to do things together - even the holiday to Tuscany, if we could bring the dates forward a little bit.

That had been the moment I let everything slip, and I buried my face in his chest and cried. That was the worst part; the only time I ever felt like giving up. I didn't want to go through the agony. I didn't want him to go through the agony. In my moment of weakness I wished I was going to die the next day, just to get it over and done with; to free Michael from his share of the pain. A bit later we tried to be more upbeat. The Doctor could be wrong, and I might live for years yet; and who could say what they'd find out in that time? There might be new drugs, new treatments. Michael's Uncle Bernie had been given three months to live and had finally died seven and a half years later when he had a heart attack at an Arsenal football match. The family folklore said that it was because Arsenal had scored. I had hated Bernie, but at that precise moment I was grateful to him; he was some kind of beacon for Michael to cling on to.

I say for Michael because I didn't need anything, you see. The one thing I hadn't told Michael about was my decision - and the fact that I knew exactly how long I had to live. Sitting alone in a hospital room, you do a lot of thinking. Especially when you know you're going to die. I had heard stories about people's 'last days', and I knew that it could be very unpleasant. I didn't want that. And I didn't want to wake up every morning asking myself 'And how do we feel today? A little worse, perhaps? Is this the beginning of the end?'. That would kill me. I knew that I'd manufacture a decline, just to get things moving. And I didn't want to spend the rest of my life with a shadow on my shoulder, nagging away at me. I wanted to be in control.

This wasn't easy; after all, I'm not a strong woman. It's just that - I don't know; work it out for yourself.

Doctor Hillman said I had at least a year. That sounded to me like it was going to be a reasonably good year; that beyond that things could get dicey. I could do a lot in a year - even get to Tuscany, maybe. And I decided that that's what I'd do. I'd have another year - exactly. And then I'd go. My choice; my time. And Michael would be spared the painful decline. We both would. And a year would give me a chance to get my inventory sorted - maybe to get enough things on it. Which is why there's this record I suppose.

-*-

Day Six

...And though it took me some time, I did finally persuade Michael that I was well enough to go out on my own. Just to the shops, I told him, and no further. They were, when all's said and done, just down the bottom of the road - well, down to the bottom, then across at the lights, round the edge of the Park, and then over a second crossing - and it was a journey I had made hundreds of times. And yes, I told him, if I don't feel too well then I'll get a taxi back; they're always skulking around outside Woolworth's waiting to take advantage of young Mums with too much shopping and too many children.

Strange, but I have felt increasingly better since my return home. Doctor Hillman suggested that this might happen, something to do with the new pills I was - so far - regularly popping. There had been no need for Michael to nag just yet. I know Michael has been alarmed at my zest. When we went out yesterday - even though it was only as far as the Park - I swear he was more nervous than me. Like that short walk, today's was an adventure; something else for my little log book. Michael used to watch 'Star Trek' all the time: Captain's log, Star Date 6.

I took my time getting to the shops, though there seemed no need really. I mean, I was never out of breath, or faint; but it was a nice warm day, and the lake was busy with ducks and swans, and holidaying school children feeding them. The Lake? Yes; well, I went round the Park the long way.

It was strange being in the shops on my own. Oh, I had nothing to buy, which was odd in itself. Michael had been an angel and seen to all of that. Poor Love bought all sorts of things we never ate - and forgot all sorts we did. I didn't tell him, of course; and I decided that I wasn't going to return from my little expedition with anything that might have suggested his failure. So I just wandered, really. Odd.

You do see some strange people though, shopping. Perhaps they'd always been there, but I'd never set eyes on them because, like them, I was too busy shopping myself. In Boots I came across this woman who would pick things off the shelves and then read aloud to herself what was written on the front of the box, or the bottle, or whatever it was. She wasn't noisy or crazy; at least, I don't think so. Perhaps that was just the way she shopped: "Hair Spray; Super Firm Hold. Essential 12-hour Moisturiser (Normal/Oily Skin)". Some times she struggled; hypo-allergenic became hyper-allergic. I followed her for a little while then let her go between the Shampoos and Bubble Bath...

-*-

Day One Hundred and Ninety Seven

Today I didn't feel so well. For the first time really. There have been odd days when I've felt a little under the weather - like that time when I caught cold and had to spend a few days in bed - but today was different. And it wasn't as if I woken up with it either. That's how I'd imagined feeling poorly again; waking up to it, as if it had stolen upon me in the night. But it hadn't.

I'd gone to the shops to pick up the photographs of the holiday. The woman remembered me because I'd needed so many rolls of film to be processed. 'Looks like you had a nice time', she said as she took my money. Perhaps I might have minded once; you know, been upset that she had looked at them. They have to check them I know, and it's gratifying in a way - the fact that she remembered me and said how nice the holiday looked.

I managed to get as far as the lake. It was warm, but not sunny. I began to feel a little hot, even though I'd only a light blouse on and a skirt. But it was nothing unusual, not immediately. But then it hit me. I'd stopped to look at a little boy sailing his boat. He was a bonny chap, and the boat was a fine one; it seemed almost too big for him until I noticed his Dad watching from a little way away. The boat sailed out towards the centre of the lake, making a graceful turn on the breeze, and the little boy got up from his knees and began to run over to his Father. That was when I wanted to turn and walk on but found I couldn't move.

Oh, it only lasted a second, I know. A fraction where I was suddenly immobile. Maybe the moment was so short that it would have been impossible to measure it. Perhaps it would have been imperceptible to anyone watching. But I knew.

I thought about sitting down for a rest, but I was on my way again and decided that I didn't need a rest. I just wanted to get home.

After I'd made some tea I went up into the bedroom and sat on the edge of the bed. From the back of my bedside table drawer I took the box that contained the bottle of pills I would soon be taking. I checked the date again and knew how long I had to wait.

It's strange how time creeps up on you; doesn't matter whether you expect it or not. There's a kind of relentlessness about it; a plodding inevitability. Oh, we always look back and say 'Where did March go?!' or 'What happened to last week?!' as if someone had whisked them away while we weren't looking. But of course no-one has whisked them away. They were around just as long as usual...

_-*-_

Day Three Hundred and Twenty Seven

...I've stepped up a gear on my medication. Michael doesn't know, but I've already moved on to a higher dose once. It appears the Good Doctor's initial guess was a pretty good one: I'm glad I didn't put any faith - or hope - in anything other than that.

My other bottle of pills has become almost like a friend to me now, something I turn to when I'm in need of comfort. It's a bit like having a magic wand that will make all the nasty things go away.

I was a little late taking my pills at lunchtime today. Well actually I forgot them until near three. It was having another bad turn that reminded me. And being sick. It's the first time I've been sick. Afterwards I looked at myself in the bathroom mirror. I know I'm right; I couldn't face a future that looked like that...

_-*-_

Day Three Hundred & Sixty Five

I made Michael a cooked breakfast this morning. A special treat. He was amused; what's the special occasion, he wanted to know. I told him that there was none; that I just felt like making him a cooked breakfast. He kissed me on the back of the neck as I was frying his bacon and asked me if I'd taken my tablets. Not yet, I told him.

That was a couple of hours ago. He went off to work bright and cheery. Things have been going well for him, and his firm has just landed a big new order; he's going to see if he can give his staff a small bonus to thank them for their hard work. I expect he's quite a nice man to work for, my Michael.

I didn't take my pills. Not my Good Doctor's pills. I'm beginning to feel it now, which is what I'd hoped really. I decided in bed last night that I needed to be feeling rough at the end. If I felt well - or at least fit - then I might lose my nerve, and I didn't want to do that. Not now. So I'm sitting on my bed writing this. On the bedside table is a nearly empty glass of water - and an empty bottle. I wasn't sure, so I took them all.

And now I don't know what to expect I feel scared. Very scared.

After breakfast I tidied a few things up - you know: did the washing up; ironed a couple of Michael's shirts; even dusted a little bit. I don't want him coming home to a dirty house. He's not going to want to worry about that is he?

I've put the Will I made a few days ago on the bedside table by the empty bottle. I thought about leaving him a note, but that didn't seem right. Not when I've written all this down. He'll read this and then he'll understand.

Outside it's sunny again. I shall miss my little walks to the Park. I shall miss a lot of things I suppose. I took the chance to read some of this yesterday, just to remind myself, you know? I thought all the stuff about Michael's Mother's inventory was funny, but it got me thinking. I still don't know how mine's shaping up to be honest. Is it tidy? I suppose so. And I wonder if I've done what I wanted to do. I mean, here in this little book of mine.

My hand has started to shake a little bit. Those last words seem a bit scrawly. And my legs feel a little bit cold. Perhaps I should just have a little lie down; just for a minute.

Chapter Thirty

Mark lay on his back, his eyes fixed on the white ceiling above his head. To his right he could hear Maxine's slow even breathing: history told him that this was a sure and certain sign she would soon be asleep. He turned his head to check the clock on the bedside table. It was a little after three. Julia would be expecting him home soon after four, so unlike Maxine - who had arranged to take the afternoon off work - Mark was unable to allow himself the luxury of falling asleep.

He would, he knew (eyes fixed, once again, on the plain white space above his head) stir around three fifteen having decided in advance whether or not he should disturb Maxine. Then after a quick shower, he would dress and - his hair undried - leave to make the journey from Marylebone to Hampstead. He would arrive home bearing all the outward manifestations of someone who had just enjoyed a hard game of squash; this premeditation - especially in the confidence of the outcome - also gave him a sense of security, a feeling born from a certainty of the future.

It was a little disturbing to him - if only from the point of view that it represented a deviation from the norm - that neither word, 'hard' nor 'squash', managed to allude (however remotely) to their recent love-making. Maxine, normally so overtly physical - if not downright aggressive - had seemed to him to be particularly passive on this occasion, and their coupling had been unusually perfunctory. Mark had developed something of a passion for her demanding and quirkily assertive style, and this had translated itself on at least one occasion to him pursuing Julia with something akin to that same 'hard squash' philosophy. Given that Maxine had fallen asleep so readily - and that there had been so little foreplay or post-coital activity - he concluded, without any need to significantly question his reasoning, that she had simply been tired.

The light shade (now the focus of his attention as he endeavoured to resist the hypnotic rhythm of Maxine's breathing) hung motionless overhead, undisturbed by recent events. Mark, wondering abstractly whether or not the light had ever been disturbed, allowed his eyes to trace an imaginary line across the ceiling to the window, attempting to gauge the force of wind that might be needed to generate motion had the window been open. It was, he knew, a frivolous kind of estimation, but (as he returned to the shade's bright yellow) one which at least prevented him from closing his eyes.

He felt her fingers move slightly within the palm of his hand, and turned his head to look at her. Immediately he looked upwards again however, disturbed into an overwhelming need to searching out the certainty and safety of the plain white ceiling.

But the canopy was different. He closed then opened his eyes, struggling to come to terms with the very real sense of displacement he now felt. Indeed, there was something in the way the sunlight filtered through the leaves of the trees, dappling the area beneath with an ever-shifting pattern of light and shade, that seemed idyllic. The image, he knew, conformed to a certain romantic stereo-type and, if he were prepared to ignore the intrusive sounds that now surrounded him - the vigorous game of football, the noisy children's picnic, the excited shouts of Frisbee players - Mark imagined that he must have reached the frontier of some kind of unworldly satisfaction. This was especially so in the unquestionable and irrefutable knowledge that, were he to turn his head slightly to the right again and forsake his study of the leafed blanket above, the sight of Lydia laying alongside him offered an undeniable reinforcement.

He felt her fingers move again. She was laying on her back, face towards the sun, and - being less in the shadow than he - with her eyes closed. He allowed his own eyes to linger on her body for a moment, watching the gentle rise and fall of her chest that accompanied her slow, relaxed breathing. Beneath her white T-shirt were the breasts he had kissed for the first time just the previous evening. It had been a moment - amidst an evening of moments - that came back to him now; the smell and taste of her skin returning to him as if borne on the wind.

He turned his eyes to the sky again. It was strange how suddenly things seemed to have happened. Despite the fact that it had been nearly three weeks since they had met in the Tate gallery - a recollection that demanded the dismissal of the five or six encounters since then - the momentous events of the previous night seemed to have come upon him in a rush; a helter-skelter ride from one chapter to another - almost from one age to another. There had been the tentative kiss after the cinema; the invitation back for coffee (knowing her parents were away for the weekend); the holding of hands; that first real embrace (in the kitchen, as they waited for the kettle to boil). Mark ran through the evening again, replaying it all as if on some internal video. He felt his pulse rise as once more he saw Lydia remove her skirt; he shivered when he recalled her hand on the belt of his trousers. There was a sequence here that he had already determined not to lose; a step-by-step process that he could detail, even physically record if he should want to. But having done so, having replayed this fragment of his past so hot off the press, he already found himself unable to re-assemble some aspects of the scene. Could he, for example, remember exactly how he felt? - for now it was his emotional response that was suddenly key (despite the physical arousal), and it was this which, in defiance of the vivid recall of Lydia's skin or smell, was already betraying him.

Mark shivered. A gust of wind blew across them and he felt cold, immediately sensitive to the dampness of his own t-shirt which, despite the heat, had yet to completely dry after his rowing exertions on the lake.

He looked upwards once more, aiming to define the direction of the breeze from the movement of the trees - only to rediscover the plain white ceiling. In the far wall he realised that the window he had earlier fixed upon was indeed a little open, and its consequent draft was causing the shade to maintain an almost imperceptible rhythm of its own. A sensation in his hand caused him to turn his head once more.

"Hello."

"I... I thought you were asleep."

"Me? Nearly. And you too." Maxine's voice was calm, carrying a sense of quiet satisfaction about it. Despite that, she still managed to convey - even in the most intimate of moments - an air of self-knowledge and certainty. "But you've got to go soon haven't you?"

"Yes."

"Pity."

Mark allowed the word to float upwards, his eyes following it as it dispersed invisibly, perhaps adding its own momentum to the rocking of the light. He felt Maxine's hand move across his thigh. As her fingers reached it, he realised that his penis was once more erect.

"I thought you were tired?" she said, an undercurrent of playfulness in her voice.

"Me?" Mark reached down and lifted her hand to his mouth and kissed it. "A little. Like you."

There was, he could tell, no real desire on Maxine's part to make love again. An offer were there - he knew her well enough by now to understand that - but, despite apparent evidence to the contrary, he was confident that she sensed his own tiredness too. What he hoped she did not sense was that - for all he knew - his current state of excitement had been generated not by her presence or his desire for her, but by an ancient memory which had suddenly come unbidden and invaded his thoughts.

Mark showered vigorously, as if using the soap as a weapon with which to banish unwanted memory from the surface of his body. But it was not there that the memories were resident; they defied physical incarnation. Had they been available in such a vulnerable form, then (and this as he drove towards Hampstead) their removal would have been a simple and clinical process.

"Good game?"

"Yes, fine." Despite his present preoccupation, Mark had rehearsed his entrance. "Mike Duxford. Remember him?"

Julia paused, walking away from the hallway and back towards the kitchen.

"I don't think so."

Mark followed her.

"Was a member a couple of years ago, then left to go and work in South Africa? Anyway, he's back."

"Did you win?"

Mark affected a laugh.

"No-one wins against Mike Duxford!"

Julia returned to where she had been chopping vegetables. There was already a warm and comfortable smell about the place.

"Smells good," Mark offered.

"Stew. Or boeuf bourguignonne. whichever you prefer." She looked at him. "You ok?"

"Absolutely."

Mark walked to where they kept the tea things and switched on the kettle.

"Coffee?"

"No thanks; I've just had one."

"I'm going to go and do a bit of work. I've had a couple of ideas that I need to get down."

"Fine."

There was no way that he felt able to share his present feelings with Julia. The suddenly recurrent memory of Lydia - first at the Tate and now, of all places, as he lay next to Maxine - was, Mark knew, something that he would have to reconcile for himself. The notion that open communication between partners helped to resolve all sorts of personal difficulties was not one he subscribed to, and though Julia did not openly espouse it, he felt certain that she - unlike him - believed in it.

The delicate issue of how to handle uncomfortable situations had not arisen between himself and Maxine, this - amongst other things - leading Mark to feel that their relationship was driven more by flow than theory. They bowled along without the need to intersperse any navel gazing; perhaps there were secrets between them (as he held his secrets from Julia; especially his past) but they were of little moment. In any event, they had never made their presence felt, not until now.

It was uncomfortable - to say the least! - that Lydia had returned to him twice, and both times in Maxine's presence. Sitting at his desk staring at a blank sheet of paper, his fingers playing with a pen, he could only wonder why that had been. If there were a connection he was struggling to find it. They shared, after all, nothing that might be regarded as being common. In terms of temperament, Maxine and Lydia could have been installed at opposite ends of the Fiery-Timid personality scale. And physically they were different too. Lydia's physique, her dark hair and olive skin - her almost Mediterranean appearance - was totally dissimilar to Maxine's short, lithe stature; factors from which, when coupled with their respective temperaments, was derived an entirely different physical relationship too.

He stared out of the window. From downstairs he could hear the occasional rattle and clink as Julia continued her work in the kitchen, embellishing the attractive cooking smells that had managed to reach him even here. Outside it was beginning to darken a little. They were on the run-in of the summer and, perceptibly, the evenings were now beginning earlier each day.

From somewhere Mark thought of his Father. And thinking of his Father reminded him of his Mother. Mark had, in dealing with her death, managed to exorcise something from his past. It was not, he told himself, anything like the absolution of guilt or the ridding oneself of a troublesome memory; rather, he chose to think of it as over-coming some kind of obstacle. Perhaps - and here he allowed himself to slip into the theoretical - in accepting the challenge his Father's biography presented him, he had also accepted that in doing so he would have to deal with certain events that were very much intrinsic in his own past. If this were so, the death of his Mother would certainly be one such milestone.

Staring back at the paper, he considered (but only for a fraction of a second) that he might make a list of these events in order to be better prepared. Two things stopped him: firstly, that it would ultimately be an empty and a futile action, and secondly that, as far as he could see, the only other event of any personal import was the death of his Father.

It was, after all, not his story but his Father's, and Mark had decided that he should intrude upon it as little as possible. The relationship between himself and the text - even though it was his creation - could only be one-way, and he argued that it was only at such major happenings his presence was merited at all.

Suddenly he shivered - and in shivering he remembered his shiver in Hyde park. It had been a foolhardy expedition, but he had been spurred on by an inner sense of occasion. Oblivious to the strength of the wind, they had approach the lake from shelter, arm in arm, chatting quietly, engaged in the newness of their relationship like two strangers who had chosen to thrust themselves together. It had not been as random as that of course. Mark had, probably within minutes of their first rendezvous - if not before he had left Lydia at the Millbank bus stop - decided to pursue her. It was never wooing in any traditional sense of the word; indeed, struggling to find the correct description, it appeared to him that the passage of time - history itself - had consigned such notions to the ever bulging dustbin of language, words destined to be replaced by nothing but the actions themselves. It wasn't wooing, he recognised that; but then any other notion of pursuit also failed to offer him a sufficiently accurate framework.

Not that any of this had been troubling him as they came upon the boathouse. There was no queue - which should have been a warning in itself - and only six or seven boats were out on the water. Before he knew it, money had exchanged hands and they were faced with the hasty choice over pedalo or rowing boat. Obscure and unspoken rituals centring around masculine virtue demanded they take the rowing boat and that he should do all the work.

The first few minutes were pleasant enough. They made for the centre of the lake then turned to face the Knightsbridge end. The wind - for now they had both made an unspoken note of its presence - pushed them on easily in the choppy water. The island passed on their right, and away on Rotten Row they could see two Policemen on horseback. Reaching the bridge, he dropped the oars back into the water and turned the boat around. Having done so, he pulled the blades against the water. It was as if the wind had taken on the persona of a spiteful and slighted suitor, and the more Mark tried to row back towards the boathouse, the more determined his invisible adversary seemed in preventing their passage. After five minutes they appeared to have gone no distance at all. Mark redoubled his efforts and slowly, stroke by stroke, they drew level with the island. Another ten minutes saw them pass it, and ten more witnessed the bump of the boat against the jetty.

It was not, of course, how he had wanted it to be. His arms felt weak from the effort, and his shivering - that present reminder of his struggle - had been sudden and considerable. Mark had tried to laugh it off; indeed, they had both made a joke of it, and his condition - less than robust, it has to be said - had given them an excuse to relax beneath the tree.

Shivering again - though this time to retrieve him from the captivity of his memory - Mark stood up and closed the study window. He resumed his seat and looked down at the paper. Unconsciously, he had made a rough sketch of a boat on a lake. It was a childish affair, barely enough beyond doodle to stray into representation. Indeed the lines offered so little in terms of depth or accurate form that they possessed a kind of naive abstraction - so much so that Mark felt one could be forgiven for taking the drawing to be some form of rudimentary map. A vague smile crossed his lips. If it were a map, then it was unlike any map he had ever seen. There were, Mark knew, certain assumptions one could make about maps: more often than not they were extremely accurate (as befitted their purpose); occasionally they bore a degree of artistic licence or mystery about them; some - and especially those he had seen on the back of cereal packets designed for the interpretation of children - bore no resemblance to any physical reality at all, instead aiming to depict some desert island upon which was hidden the secret treasure. If this feeble drawing were to be interpreted as a map then, as far as Mark could see, it fell into none of these categories, lacking as it did accuracy, mystery and the promise of a rainbow's end.

He remembered those old boxes of cornflakes and sugar puffs emblazoned with banners inviting him to 'find the hidden treasure!'. Mark wondered if he had ever taken them seriously; if, having absorbed the notion as a child, he had carried it around with him as he moved inexorably towards adulthood. Had there been any sense in which he had wished to find such a treasure? The smile slipped slowly away. If so, then such a discovery would surely have had more to do with mapping out the future than anything else, for a real chest of gold would allow its finder to chart their life ahead; as such, the map would both lead towards something, and then subsequently offer the route away from it too. It was,

Mark knew, a notion that he could never have entertained as a minor; indeed, floating it as he did now, he felt uncomfortable, dissatisfied with its inherent distance from reality. A fairy story perhaps.

A couple of weeks later, walking through Green Park - pausing on the bridge to look at a small lake bereft of boats - Mark had recalled the unpleasant experience on the Serpentine. He turned to Lydia; she was smiling.

"What's funny?" he asked, inquisitively.

"Oh nothing. I was just thinking about the other week."

"In the boat?"

She nodded, her eyes - somehow darker now than he remembered them - focused hard upon his own. They were deep but not lifeless nor unfeeling. She pressed his hand, forcing him to smile too.

"I know. I was just thinking the same thing."

"It was stupid wasn't it?"

"Stupid?"

"Going out in that wind. Trying to row."

Mark moved away from the balustrade, pulling Lydia gently along with him. Her use of the word 'stupid' worried him. Their decision - and it had been their decision, after all - had not been particularly wise; fool-hardy even: but he would not have called it 'stupid'. He wondered if Lydia had actually meant what she had said, as if there had been an unwitting misapplication of the word.

Looking down, he noticed that his shoelace was undone, and, stopping, loosed Lydia's hand. He knelt to re-tie the knot. There had been, it seemed to him, one or two moments when Lydia's choice of phrase had veered towards the peculiar. Mark did not consider himself to be particularly correct with his own manipulation of the Queen's English, but he did pride himself on a certain degree of correctness; indeed, his studies - if he were to be historically accurate - demanded as much of him. Neither did he regard himself as fussy or pernickety on the subject; it was just that, at such moments - such as her use of the word 'stupid' - Lydia seemed to be toiling with her Mother Tongue as much as if she were a foreigner.

Standing up again, Mark saw her waiting at the far end of the bridge. She was a handsome young woman without doubt. Her white dress - made whiter still about the shoulders where her dark hair fell upon it -

seemed cut to make the most of her figure, and its hem, billowing a little in the breeze, added to the sensuous image she now cast. As he walked towards her, Mark found himself - carrying forward his immediate theme - being able to imagine her as a Foreign Princess lost in a strange world where he were her Champion.

She began to smile.

"Not reading my mind again?" he called towards her.

"No," she replied playfully. "Why?"

He stopped - and then made a rush towards her. Lydia let out a small scream and tried to dash away from him, but he caught her within a few strides, the two of them falling onto the grass. Before she could protest, he took her hands and held them above her head, gently pressing his mouth to hers.

He looked again at his sketch of the boat. It was, he decided, just a sad little picture, and hearing Julia's footfall on the stair gave him the impetus he needed to rip the page from the pad and throw it, scrunched up, into the waste bin.

Chapter Thirty One

In a life that seemed by now to have established a pattern of peaks and troughs, the publication of <u>If Time Was A Book</u> came to represent another major milestone for Charles Packard. Peter Healey, who had been completely overwhelmed by the first draft of Packard's 'soul-cleansing' novel (as it later became known), had pressed Charles hard to complete his revisions in time to rush the first hardback copies of the book into the shops by Christmas. He also swung Macmillan's publicity machine into overdrive and November saw Packard in great demand for interviews and readings.

> "It had been hard enough to get to the end of that first draft, but when Peter suddenly put the pressure on, well - I don't think I ever worked so hard. And it *was* work too. Just finishing that final sentence seemed to take all the emotion out of what I was doing, as if by reaching the end I had completed my side of an undocumented contract. From that moment (or at least that moment the next morning when I awoke on the front room sofa!) it was back to work. It felt like work again; like I remembered it."

> (Interview with Melvyn Bragg, 1986)

Healey had not expected <u>If Time Was A Book</u> would sell out instantly, which was just as well. Of the five thousand printed, a little under half were sold in the two weeks prior to Christmas.

"The numbers - for once - weren't the important thing. I don't know if Charles realised it at the time, but 'Time' was not about making money; not in the first instance anyway. It had become for us - for him, me, even Macmillan - the vehicle that would prove, finally, whether or not we had someone special, a Class Act, on our books. So it wasn't the numbers, it were the reviews that really counted."

The verdict was, for the first time in Packard's career, unanimous and full of approbation. It was, said one reviewer, 'a tour de force'; another, somewhat peculiarly, likened the achievement to Dickens' triumph when writing as a woman in 'Bleak House'. For once Healey found himself doing the unthinkable: scanning the papers for a bad review. He found none. The result was that Macmillan decided, immediately after Christmas, they would prepare a large paperback run of <u>If Time Was A Book</u>. Healey phoned Packard on the day before Christmas Eve to tell him the good news.

In the Packard household it was a strange Christmas. The second without Mary, it was the first which saw the remaining members of the Packard clan on anything akin to a normal footing. Charles had never been particularly adept at Christmas, always seeming to be too much of one thing or another: too generous with the presents; too liberal with the whisky. With nearly a year and a half of solitude behind them, the male Packard's - their routine now established - found themselves taking Yuletide in their stride. Charles, his festive excesses curbed, played host to Beatrice and Simon on Boxing Day with all the accomplishment of a man who had been born to the task.

"The house was tidy and well-ordered. They both appeared neat and clean. Things seemed so very much in their place. At one moment (when they were out of the room) I confess I even suggested to Simon that, at any moment, we could expect Charles' secret woman to emerge from somewhere, for it seemed plain to me that such order could not have been achieved by Charles alone!"

It was a sense of harmony, peace and organisation that reached a peak over those few Christmas weeks - and that was destined never to be seen again.

Packard had spent much of the year being troubled: he had fought with the book and the demands he placed on himself with respect to Mary's memory; he had struggled to grow a decent and proper relationship with his son; and he had battled to remain balanced and sober, fighting off the invisible whispering that attempted to drag him down. Now, at New Year's Eve, Packard found himself staring at 1974 with an overwhelming sense of opportunity. <u>If Time Was A Book</u> had already been - and would continue to be - a major success, and he needed to face the fact that, as Healey kept telling him, "he had arrived".

> "It was, quite frankly, vaguely surreal. I felt as if someone had - with an amazing sleight of hand! - banished my past. Almost as if I had been born again. And it was like that, a rebirth. Oh, don't worry! The irony that I should feel this way having actually used Mary's death to put me in such a marvellous position (and it was a marvellous position) wasn't lost on me. Not at all. I kind of floated through Christmas, gradually breaking into the New Year with the awesome sensation that I could do just whatever I wanted. I had never felt that before. It gave me a kind of power I suppose.

"I remember that Mark wanted to stay up with me to see in the New Year, but I wouldn't let him. (I'd already turned down an invitation to go over to Belsize Park.) I wanted it to be my New Year, just as it was my future. Don't ask me if I had any inkling of just how selfish I was in danger of becoming. That night I was only able to make it from one chime of the midnight clock to the next."

(Interview with Melvyn Bragg, 1986)

Derek Shutts was another man who had begun to see an opportunity to make 1974 his year. Attempting to steal a march on his rivals, Shutts had followed up his own positive review of <u>If Time Was A Book</u> with systematic wining and dining those of his associates who professed to have influence in the world of television. Shutts knew that Packard's earlier work had already roused a general sense of interest in that media (despite the lamentable translation of <u>No Easy Fight</u>). He also knew that there was a very real possibility that Packard's latest offering was likely to stimulate even more enthusiasm. The proposal he touted around London's fashionable bars and restaurants early in January was that he could secure Packard's services to pen something exclusive for any TV company prepared to pay his price.

Shutts, who moved from Huddersfield to London as an idealistic young man, had begun his career at the foot of the lowliest ladder Fleet Street had to offer. At first he rose rapidly, but all too soon he found that his ambition outstripped his abilities by far. As if in consolation for those journalistic limitations, Shutts attempted to develop the more entrepreneurial side of his career, working within a profession he had come to understand more as a promoter than a publisher. The regular reviews he managed to hang on to gave him an entree to the bigger fish.

Neither Packard nor Healey had any idea what Shutts was up to. Healey began 1974 as he began every year; skiing in Switzerland. It would be several weeks before he would hear of Shutts' back-door approach to his Client. For Packard, despite the remarkable weight of his New Year resolution, January passed with little momentous to record against it.

-*-

Mark tried to remember the beginning of 1974 and the transition from one era to another. He had always found something exciting about being able to write - for the first time - the digits of a new year. The sight of '1/1/19..' had filled him with a kind of expectation that was now merely a thing of memory. In those days, of course, years were significant tracts of time; they seemed to last an age in themselves, punctuated with predestined events like markers on a map. Much of his life as a child revolved around the recognition of such signposts - not because they showed you where you were, but because they indicated where you had been and where you were going. For Mark at that age they were not temporal icons, but spatial ones. On Sunday evenings (when he was much younger admittedly) the sound of 'The Saint's' signature tune didn't merely herald the beginning of a television programme; it told him that he had probably just finished supper, and that in an hour's time he would be going to bed. Perhaps it was for this reason that repetitive mileposts - such as the coming of a new year - actually began to blur into a pile of beginnings and endings: having never been important in themselves, they retained significance only in relation to other things.

It was, Mark recalled, his second Christmas alone with his Father; and it was the Christmas of his Mother's book. This didn't seem to help. He knew there would be no photographs to place him at the scene of those Yuletide festivities, so was forced to attempt a trawl of his memory to locate himself there. It was likely that his Father had been able to buy him something significant as a present. By the time he moved into the school's Sixth Form he was a well-equipped young man, prepared for the academic rigours ahead with calculator, typewriter, and quality pens of various flavours. All, he was sure, had arrived in his possession as gifts: perhaps the Christmas of 1973 had brought one or more of them; perhaps the first stamp of '1/1/1974' had come from the carriage of his new typewriter or the barrel of a fountain pen. It was impossible to say.

This absence of certainty about his own past failed to disturb him, however. These were merely missing details that amounted - even all together - to nothing more than a collection of trivia; a mass of flotsam that served no real purpose apart from clogging up that which was more important. Mark was confident that where things were critical, his memory was solid. The book, a retelling of significance unencumbered by jetsam, was surely evidence of his mastery of the past. He knew how 1974 had begun for his Father, and that was the critical thing; as for himself, a vague certainty that he had written '1/1/1974' somewhere and loaded it with import - and the knowledge that, in doing so, he would have been foretelling the first half of his new school term (if not the entire year) - was enough for him.

-*-

After that Christmas, the Packards began to see significantly less of Beatrice and Simon. It was as if the revelation that they were actually managing had severed the only remaining thread of support that Beatrice was still maintaining.

"I knew they weren't doing it all themselves; after all, there was still the domestic who did for them. But it was obvious, however one looked at it, that they were coping. It was organised. I suppose I ceased to fear for young Mark's well-being."

When Healey returned from his holiday, Packard arranged to meet him for a drink. The sensation that he had regained his life and was now free from his debt to Mary, fired Charles with a need to return to his more reckless ways.

> "Mark seemed well-balanced enough. He was getting on OK at school, and Beatrice had effectively given me the thumbs-up, so I had no concerns there. With the book out of the way I felt as if I deserved to let my hair down, to run a little wild again perhaps. It wasn't as if Mary was gone and forgotten; she could never be that. But now, for the first time, I felt able to do things without the guilt. Someone once told me - I think it might have been Peter - that my problem was that I never wanted to feel guilty ever again. Maybe he was right."

(Interview with Melvyn Bragg, 1986)

The evening with Healey started as many of their previous evening over the previous few months: they met in a restaurant; discussed business; drank a little wine.

"This time it was different, I could see that straight away. Charles was going after the wine like it was going out of fashion. He seemed possessed almost. Oh, he was polite and everything; we discussed how the book was going and what might come next. I asked him if he'd had any thoughts about the future. He said that he'd only managed see himself walking out of the restaurant and getting laid: "That, I'm afraid, is the full extent of my present horizon!". We laughed of course, as if it had been a joke, but I could see the old Charles Packard beginning to rise again."

After they left the restaurant, Packard attempted to persuade Healey to join him for a drink in the Compton Arms. Healey pleaded family commitments and hailed a taxi. Charles entered the pub alone.

By eight the next morning, Packard had still not returned home. Mrs Hazeldene arrived at the house to find Mark making himself ready for school. He had showered and got dressed, and was eating breakfast as she walked into the kitchen. It was the first day of his new school term, but it was not to be the last day that he would wake to find himself alone in the house.

"I grew up fairly quickly, I guess. I don't suppose I'd intended to, but there seemed little choice. I wasn't blind, and I knew what father was like. I was still a kid - but I was old enough to be able to cope. I think I even managed to get some kind of gratification from the knowledge that he was prepared to go out and leave me to fend for myself."

-*-

Once a month, 'The Merlot' held an 'event' dedicated to the recent availability of one particular wine or another. It was an idea that had been born from the annual alarum-filled arrival of Beaujolais Nouveaux which, year-after-year, had proven to be such a money-spinner. Initially these promotional evenings had been well attended, but over time the proprietors had discovered that numbers dwindled to a combination of their hard core regulars and those who just happened to wander in off the street. The Beaujolais evening – something Mark knew to be a mastery of marketing by their French cousins where they sold the British gallons of rubbish with which they would not even deign to clean their floors – continued to be ever-popular.

As he closed the door of his car and began to follow Julia towards the entrance, he found himself wondering if these evenings had undergone any radical change since they last attended one (it must have been three months by now), and whether the prospect of a bright new Alsace – "not really like a German wine" Julia had tried to assure him – would make any tangible difference. His wondering as to the source of her information ceased when he paused on the threshold to glance at the flier posted just beneath 'The Merlot's' menu. 'More French than German' it tried to persuade him, as if character and prejudice associated with nationality were carried over to their domestic products – which (and this as he paused at the door) they surely did. He had taken several steps inside, compiling a list of countries and produce in a league table of desirability, when he heard his name called. He had reached olives (by what route he could not say) and was in the process of deciding if Greece might hold sway over Italy.

In looking up to divine the source of the voice (Peter sitting not fifteen feet from him) Mark became suddenly aware that the bar was throbbing, a realisation that had come upon him as if someone had burst the soundproofed bubble that had been protecting him.

"Busy!" he offered as he reached Peter, his voice several decibels higher than was normal for this environment. It was something he found strangely uncomfortable.

"Isn't it just!"

Mark sat down. The other two chairs were empty.

"They're at the bar", Peter said, responding to Mark's unasked question.

Mark nodded and scanned the room. He wanted to immediately look towards the bar and seek out Claire, his mind travelling back to their last encounter here. He remembered her blouse, and for a moment wanted to know if she were wearing it again – and if so, how many buttons would be undone.

"It's not the wine."

Peter called him back.

"Sorry?"

"It's not the wine that's brought all these people here. Apparently there's some 'do' going on for a company that's just found out that it's closing." Peter indicated the general throng and Mark sensed a degree of commonality about them, as if they belonged together. They might just have well been uniformed.

"Not the lure of the non-German Alsace then?"

Peter laughed.

"I spoke to one of the chaps at the bar. They found out about two hours ago that they're all going to be made redundant, so they just downed tools and came in here. Something to do with the troubles last winter and the government. Poor Bugger started raving on about Edward Heath!"

Neither Mark nor Peter had been particularly affected by the current economic challenges the country was facing, and had carried on through recent months of domestic political turmoil unscathed. In some respects, the situation actually opened up opportunities for a natural entrepreneur like Peter; a skill, turning a difficult situation into a positive opportunity, which Mark envied. For his own part, Mark's interest was little more than perfunctory. He found himself less concerned in the 'historical' here-and-now, knowing that he would only begin to become fascinated once a situation was over and had been factually 'topped and tailed'. Under these circumstances – without the indefinable distraction of loose ends or unanswered questions – he was confident that he could engage; it was, in a way, history on his own terms. He could write about recent events of course; the pieces on Kuwait and Ireland (though now slightly discredited apparently) were entirely possible given a clean, tight and close definition.

His Father's book presented a life without loose ends; or at least this had been his premise at the outset. The protagonist having died, there was no 'unfinished business' relating to his Father about which he needed to concern himself. There was - biologically, at least - quite clearly, an 'end'; and as he sat watching Julia and Claire appear from the crowd and head towards their table, he had, for the first time, the sensation that this was just about in sight.

Claire deposited a bottle of Perrier and another of the promotional Alsace on the table and sat down. Julia had carried the glasses. As Peter picked up the wine to examine the label, Mark waited for Claire's traditional greeting – the peck on the check – but none was forthcoming.

"Busy, isn't it?" She smiled brightly enough, the rouge of her lips – which to Mark's eyes seemed a little subdued for Claire – complemented by the high-necked ribbed sweater she was wearing. The ensemble seemed a little out of character somehow.

"They've all got the sack," Julia said, indicating the general melee.

"So Peter said."

"There was one chap next to us at the bar, already drunk."

"Yes," said Claire, picking up Julia's lead, "right about at that stage where you turn from being jolly to being completely morose. Give him another twenty minutes and he'll be crying into his Chardonnay!"

They all laughed. Peter, having dispensed with the label, poured wine into each of the four glasses – "Let's see how non-German this is then!" – and with that took a large sip. The others waited for his response.

"Definitely French", he said with a flourish, "probably from a little vineyard just outside Berlin!"

Again they laughed. Mark, the moment the pale liquid touched his tongue, was able to confirm his friend's diagnosis.

"Grapes trodden by Herr Fritz himself!"

It was a relaxed enough beginning. Mark, who for a moment (when Julia and Claire walked towards them from the bar) had the briefest sensation that all was not well, found himself comforted by the jollity. Julia had seemed pre-occupied before they had left the house, but he had given it little thought. Seeing the two of them together – her with Claire – he found himself wondering whether or not Julia's friend might have had some difficulty of her own which was weighing on Julia's mind. The notion – which, he knew, was born from a complete and comprehensive absence of fact – remained with him for a few moments more; sufficiently long enough for him to re-scrutinise Claire for any other outward signs of distress.

In spite of her joke – which, after all, might have been delivered for Peter's benefit above all else – Mark thought he sensed an air of imbalance about her. Perhaps the toned-down lipstick (which struck a distinct chord with him) and conservative jumper was indicative of something significant. Certainly Peter appeared to be either unconcerned or unaware of any possible internal disharmony in her – which for Mark began to add weight to his burgeoning idea. Was it physical perhaps? Or emotional? He had not seen her since their squash match – and in realising this, Mark felt a veil lifting. Had that accidental collision meant something to Claire too, perhaps? Was this new-found show of modesty – and in his presence too – indicative of something more significant? She had, he recollected suddenly, failed in her usual greeting. Was this all part of the message?

As the conversation rattled along, buoyed by the positive start they had made – and, a little obtusely perhaps, by the fact that many of their fellow imbibers were facing a less than certain future (the self-confidence such a thing can imbue!) – Mark found himself more expansive than usual, weighing up, as he chivvied and chased their dialogue, the notion that the portents of Claire's behaviour were all in his favour. It was a notion that gathered moment almost exponentially, with each smile, comment, inflection of voice adding to the stock that compiled his evidence.

His behaviour was also helped by the fact that Julia had agreed to drive home, consequently allowing him to indulge more than was normal. Indeed, as he became less inhibited – even the noise of the crowd ceasing to intrude – Mark found Julia becoming more quiet, and any effort he made to bring her round and re-include her seemed only to drive her further under cover. At one stage even Peter seemed beaten into submission as Mark and Claire indulged in a mock argument relating to the nature of pornography.

By the time they stood up to leave – some two-thirds of the way through their third bottle – Mark was convinced that it would only be a matter of time before Claire must declare herself to him. It was a prediction made all the more inevitable by her accepting the challenge of a second squash match later in the week – and by her avoiding, for the second time that evening, any physical contact at their parting.

As they pulled out of the car park – Julia habitually taking more care than he would have – Mark found himself drawing parallels between Claire and Maxine, and attempting to assess the predicament such a situation – having to somehow 'choose' between them – might present him. He found himself drawing a mental list comparing the various competitive attributes of each; a process – had he been in a state to recognise it – not too dissimilar to that relating to Olives and Mediterranean countries.

-*-

> "Shutts' letter – and the invitation to dinner – took me a little by surprise. I knew of the man, of course; if only because he'd written one or two nice things about me. I didn't really think very much about it, to be honest. I accepted – the maxim about any publicity – assuming that he would want to turn the evening into some kind of interview which he could sell. By now it wouldn't have been the first time such a thing had happened."

(Interview with Melvyn Bragg, 1986)

The tack Shutts took with Packard followed exactly the same approach as he had taken with Thames Television's David Bramble. He had told Bramble that he could secure Packard to write a specially commissioned play for Thames; and he told Packard that he could secure him a lucrative contract if he had a mind to turn his hand to television. Effectively, Shutts' idea was to introduce Packard to Bramble and then step away – maximising his "cut" for the minimum of effort. Bramble was interested; the meal was to intended to swing Packard his way too.

A number of things in Shutts' suggestion appealed to Packard. Firstly - and most importantly – it gave him a chance to address the wrong inflicted upon him through the bastardisation of <u>No Easy Fight</u>. He still associated pain with that experience and the opportunity of being able to prove what he could do - and thus restore that portion of his reputation which had suffered - was a powerful magnet. The money was attractive too. Although Shutts made it plain that he was in no position to guarantee any particular level of income, he quoted figures that others had reputedly earned for similar work.

The final prod for Packard was the chance to do something different. Having completed <u>If Time Was A Book</u> and taken the opportunity to close a particular chapter in his life, a new venture – in a year which he had already begun to see as a rebirth, his "marvellous position" – seemed only natural.

> "I must have met with Bramble a couple of days later. He seemed a straight enough chap, and I guessed there was a connection. Although we were both initially cautious, enthusiasm for the project grew in an infectious way. By the time I'd left his office I knew I was going to do it."

(Interview with Melvyn Bragg, 1986)

Initially Packard had no idea what 'it' was, however. On hearing the news, Peter Healey was initially upset. Although he had not broached the subject with Packard, he had been keen to follow <u>If Time Was A Book</u> with another novel; it was, he said later, 'a time of hot irons, and a time to strike'. Packard however – who by this time, Healey knew, held all the aces – protested that he had no idea what his next book might be about, and that a foray into a new media could both freshen his writing while adding another string to his bow.

The subject was the problem. Bramble had given him a couple of weeks to come up with an outline. Thames already had a production date in mind, and if they were to hit their target Packard would need to deliver the finished script by mid-May. Two days before Bramble's synopsis deadline, there was still nothing concrete in Charles' mind.

> "The whole thing crystallised during a lunchtime meeting with Peter. He had heard on the grapevine how Shutts had been bragging to his fellow hacks; he had boasted about the commission he was to receive from Thames, and about how little he'd had to do for it. I felt like I'd been taken for a bit of a ride, even though I wasn't really impacted. Peter filled me in with the little he knew of Shutts' history, and the seed was set.

> "I suppose the other thing that engaged me was the oil crisis of 1973; the notion that entrepreneurs on the extremes – the Arabs – looked like they could bring down the UK government through hiking the price of oil. It was an interesting cause and effect. Perhaps I wanted to explore this kind of power on a smaller scale, I don't know. Or the new sphere I was moving in, that London was giving me. Maybe subconsciously I felt the need to get back to something "Social"."

(Interview with Melvyn Bragg, 1986)

Whatever Packard's inspiration, in September 1974 Thames television screened <u>A Suburban Bandit</u>. The story of a middle-class social climber,

Alexander Le Moins was his first anti-hero. An unscrupulous financial entrepreneur, the play charted Le Moins' irresistible rise – and then his inevitable fall, crushed by the system to which he was wedded. Ten years later when <u>A Suburban Bandit</u> was re-shown it was described – by Shutts – as 'a visionary exposition of Thatcher's Britain'. "It was," said Healey, "one of the few things he was ever right about."

Chapter Thirty Two

A SUBURBAN BANDIT

28.   Int.   Le Moins' Study

Inside Alexander Le Moins' study. Whilst its relatively small size and angular ceiling indicates that it is obviously a loft conversion, the fixtures and fittings are of the highest quality. The desk and bookcases appear to be hand-made and snugly fit the contours of the room. The wood from which they are made is teak rather than pine, and carries a dark but not over-powering stain.

Against the centre of the desk there is a large, high-backed black leather chair. It is in this which Le Moins now sits. He has swung the chair away from the desk to face James Shaw, who sits in the slightly lower arm chair near the study door. Le Moins may be casually dressed, but even so he appears exceedingly well turned out.

On the desk, a small plume of smoke rises from the Gitannes cigarette burning in an ashtray.

Le Moins

You don't think it can be done?

Shaw

I didn't say that.

Le Moins

You didn't – but it's what you're thinking.

Shaw

Maybe.

Le Moins laughs.

Le Moins

And why is that? What is it that makes you think that I can't deliver what I say I can? Eh?

Le Moins laughs again as he picks up his cigarette and takes a long draw. Shaw shifts a little in his chair.

Le Moins

My guess is that you're worried. Not that I can't do it, but rather how I might. Is that it?

Shaw

I don't think I would ever suggest there was anything you couldn't do, Alex.

Le Moins

Very back-handed! But still I'll take it. It's the method isn't it? You're concerned – what? – that it might be illegal; perhaps that's it. Or at the very least somehow dubious. Not the kind of thing James wants to "get messed up in"…

Shaw stands, banging his head slightly on a low portion of the ceiling as he does so. Le Moins, finishing his cigarette, watches him. Then he stubs out the cigarette.

Le Moins

I wonder?

Shaw

You wonder what?

Le Moins

Whether that little bang has knocked the sense in or out.

Shaw

Very funny.

Le Moins

I did warn you.

Shaw walks towards the door. Le Moins swivels slightly in his chair to keep him full in view. Shaw seems uncertain as to whether he should stay or go. He looks at a print that hangs on the wall alongside a bookcase.

Le Moins

Of course it's probably worse.

Shaw turns to face Le Moins.

Shaw

Worse?

Le Moins

It's not illegality or dubiousness that worries you, James. At the end of the day it's more likely to be the fact that there is an absence of ethics.

The notion of restoring equilibrium through entirely pragmatic means you find difficult to swallow.

Shaw

"Restoring equilibrium"? "Pragmatic means"? Fancy words for revenge don't you think?

Le Moins

I'm not sure; after all, "revenge" is such an emotive word. Vengeance. Comeuppance. There are all sort of ways you could phrase it. All I want is to get back something that's been lost. Isn't that restoration?

Shaw

And a bit more.

Le Moins

Well, let's call it "interest" if that makes you feel any better. Someone took something from me – or, more correctly, from us – and all I want to do is to get it back. With a little interest.

Shaw

Let him have it.

Le Moins

Let him have it?!

Shaw puts his hand on the door and pulls it open. He remains standing in the room however, still facing Le Moins.

Shaw

It's gone. Gone! Sure it was a fair amount of money – once you translate it into currency, into what the picture was actually worth – but he's got it now. Maybe it's the fact that he tricked you that galls you so much. Is that it?

Le Moins

Tricked us, James; tricked us. And I don't want the painting back. To be honest, I never really liked it. But it was important, of value. It did belong to me. It was worth a fuck of a lot of money. Balance. That's what I want; to redress the balance.

Shaw

Any you think some swindling little scheme is going to do that?

Le Moins

I don't know. Probably. But if not, I've got insurance.

Shaw

Insurance?

Le Moins

Sit down James.

As Shaw returns to his chair, Le Moins turns his back on him and pulls open the lowest draw in his desk. The draw is on the side towards Shaw's chair, so the contents will be visible to him when he regains his seat. Le Moins pulls out a brown A4 envelope and hands it to Shaw.

Le Moins

Take a look.

Shaw

What is it?

Shaw withdraws some photographs from the envelope. They are in black and white. A man and a woman can be seen in various stages of undress. They are evidently in the process of love-making. Shaw flicks through them as Le Moins talks over.

Le Moins

A little birdie told me that our mutual friend had been "playing away" rather a lot recently. So, I simply spoke to a chap I knew who spoke to a chap he knew... The photos were taken at the Marriott Hotel in Winchester two weeks ago. Clever how small they can make cameras these days. Of course, poor Justine doesn't have a clue! And could you imagine what she'd do if she found out?!

Le Moins laughs, and Shaw looks up from the photos. Le Moins holds out his hand, but Shaw does not return them immediately.

Shaw

Blackmail. Is that how low you'd go Alex?

Le Moins

To right a wrong?

Shaw

To get your own way.

Le Moins

Please.

Le Moins extends his hand a little further. Shaw leans forwards slightly and passes back the photos. As he sees into the drawer, he stops.

Shaw

Or is that as far as you'd go?

Le Moins

What?

Le Moins follows his gaze. He smiles and laughs briefly. Placing the photos in the envelope, he deposits the envelope in the drawer, removing a small revolver with his free hand as he does so.

Le Moins

This? This has nothing to do with Michael. It is, I'll grant you, a little piece of "insurance" in its own way, but only against intruders. Protection – for people who try and take things that don't belong to them. Perfectly legal.

Le Moins suddenly raises the gun and points it at Shaw, pulling the trigger. It clicks harmlessly. Shaw flies up out of the chair, banging his head again as he does so. Le Moins breaks into a laugh.

Le Moins

And perfectly empty!

Shaw heads for the door, pausing momentarily before leaving.

Shaw

You dumb bastard! You frightened the shit out of me! You might have made a mistake! You could have killed me! Fuck you!

Shaw disappears leaving Le Moins laughing in his chair and cradling his gun. He calls after his departed guest.

Le Moins

It's only insurance! Harmless. Just like me!

-*-

A call from somewhere in the lower part of the house forced Mark to stop the video and stand up. At one stage, having a dedicated television and video recorder in his study would have seemed nothing less than the kind of indulgence embraced by those who had become addicted to both technology and the display of their own wealth. However, almost as soon as Julia had moved in, he found monopolisation of the set-up downstairs had become impossible, which, as soon as this had proven inconvenient, led him to make a secondary investment.

It had been surprisingly freeing, particularly in relation to any research work for the articles he wrote. Being able not only to record any programme he choose from the satellite network, but to watch videos again and again without disturbance, provided him with a tool that had surpassed his expectations in all sorts of ways.

The video of 'A Suburban Bandit' had been seeing rather a lot of air time in recent days, yet even so – and now as he descended the stairs to seek out Julia – it was still no closer to helping him solve what for him were a number of key problems. After all (and here he was little removed from some of the more guarded reviews the programme had received all those years ago) it was a somewhat divorced from his Father's usual work; this not only in terms of medium and style, but because it had been analysed by one or two as little more than a "naïve thriller". Mark could see where such critics had been coming from. Undoubtedly there were echoes of 'Dawn' and 'No Easy Fight' in elements of the characters. Indeed, take all the goodness and modesty out of George Maxwell and perhaps Alexander Le Moins would never be far behind. But the presence of the gun (which to Mark seemed a mistake) and then its role in the dénouement, only succeeded in leaving the taste of contrivance in his mouth.

"In here." Julia's voice emanated from the lounge in response to Mark's call. As he walked through the door, his reflections on Le Moins' passage through the story came to an end.

Julia was standing at the far side of the room, looking out of the window onto the garden. At her side, the telephone table. Mark thought he recalled hearing it a few minutes ago (probably around the time Shaw cracked his head for the first time) but could not be sure. For some reason – perhaps her posture, or the fact that she did not turn to greet him – suggested that she had received bad news.

"Is there something wrong?"

"Why did you tell me you had entered the squash boxes?" She spoke without moving.

"What?" Momentarily Mark felt decidedly off-balance. He had expected nothing like this. "What do you mean?"

She turned.

"You didn't enter the squash boxes. Why did you tell me you had?"

Mark allowed a small, involuntary laugh to escape. It only lasted a second or so before he caught it up and chased it away with words.

"Squash boxes? Who's been telling you that I didn't enter the boxes?"

"Claire." She paused.

Again Mark found himself thrown. The connection he made between squash and Claire was entirely different to that Julia was now suggesting. He tried to gauge where Julia's anger was based (it was evident that she was upset); to define if there were more to her words than the simple statement she had made. Luckily Julia immediately clarified for him.

"Well Peter, actually. Peter was talking to some chap and your name came up. He asked how you were getting on in the boxes and this man said he hadn't seen you in them. Swore blind. Peter actually went to check."

"To check?"

"Then Peter told Claire – and Claire has just told me."

"Peter? Told you?"

"Look, it just came up in conversation! Mark, why did you tell me that you had entered the boxes when you hadn't? Why? I don't give a damn about them – but I do care about you lying to me. Why did you do that?"

There was an honest answer, of course; but the impossibility of telling Julia about Maxine meant Mark had no other alternative than to compound the fallacy. He thought about sitting – or at least encouraging Julia to sit – but immediately knew that might be interpreted as an admission of guilt.

"OK, you're right, I didn't enter the boxes." He started with half the truth, which in turn was rewarded by Julia – who had returned her gaze to the garden – looking back at him. "It's just that I've been working so hard on the book..."

"I know you have," she interjected, attempting to shoot down his excuse.

"Yes, but much harder than you realise, I think. What with the time spent in Belsize; tracking down those eye-witnesses; research at the publishers; and all sorts of digging into the kind of things Dad used to get up to" – here he felt himself veer dangerously towards the truth – "I guess I didn't want you to know I was working so hard on it. In case you worried."

He knew it was limp, but it was all he had to offer.

"Worry? Why should I worry? I'd worry more about finding out that you had lied to me, wouldn't I?"

"Maybe I didn't want you to think that I had become – I don't know – obsessive."

The last word had hung in the air for a moment before Julia responded to it. As Mark made his way later that afternoon towards Bruce Congreave's offices from the tube station, he replayed her further protestations: why had he done it? didn't he trust her? why the elaborate charade with packing his sports bag? and the games with Claire, had they been real? At least he had been able to tell her a little more of the truth there.

Bizarrely he had been rescued by another telephone call. Congreave's Secretary – in a voice he failed to recognise – wanted to know if he could make a meeting at 3pm in the Thameside office. Mark had kept her talking long enough on the phone for Julia to give up on him and leave the room. Once he had finished the call, he decided not to seek her out to draw the threads of their conversation together to their logical conclusion.

-*-

75.   Int.   Michael Dyer's study

A large but sparsely furnished room. Along two walls, bookcases which run virtually floor to ceiling hosting not only books, but videos, various filing systems, and odd items of paraphernalia. There is a sense of organised clutter about them. Against one wall, in front of the window, a large, old fashioned desk which is verging on the antique. A typewriter sits in one corner partly obscured by a newspaper apparently neglected. Pulled slightly away from the desk, the upright chair is virtually in the centre of the room facing the door which leads out into the hall. This door is closed. On the chair, Michael Dyer sits. He looks vaguely dishevelled, and it is evident from the dark patches at the armpits of his shirt that he has been sweating. Standing with his back to the door, Alexander Le Moins stands, hands in his pockets, as if on guard. There is a suggestion that he too has recently undergone some form of physical exertion. Against the far wall (that opposite the window and nearest the door) James Shaw sits on a small settee. He looks a little unsettled, echoes of how we have seen him earlier.

Between Le Moins and Dyer, a large rectangle – wrapped in plain brown paper – leans against one of the bookcases. One corner of the wrapping is torn, revealing a portion of the painting underneath. Le Moins glances down at it.

Le Moins

You know Michael, I never really liked it.

Dyer

Why don't you just take it?

Le Moins

You didn't hear what I said. I said, I never really liked it. And if I never really liked it, then why should I want it back? I think you should keep it. After all, you did seem particularly keen to lay your hands on it – didn't he James? Do almost anything, it transpired.

Dyer

But?

Le Moins

But what?

Dyer

If I keep it, then you want something in return.

Le Moins

Well, it seems only fair doesn't it? After all, I'm the one who's been robbed... Ooh, strong word, "robbed"; sorry! But there; it's out now.

Dyer

I didn't steal it. Tell him James; I didn't steal it.

Le Moins

Not exactly, no. I'll grant you that. But then I didn't exactly give it too you did I? Perhaps we should call it the first element of an exchange: I let you have something, and in return...

Dyer

So what do you want? What does he want, James?

Shaw

I'm not sure; not any more.

Dyer

Is it money? Is that what you want? You know I haven't got that kind of money just lying around. It would take months.

Le Moins

Years, probably.

Dyer

Years?

Le Moins

When you consider the interest...

Dyer

Now who's the bandit?

Le Moins

And the insurance. I might just have to cash in on the insurance.

Dyer

Insurance? Peter, what the hell's he talking about?

Shaw

I don't want anything to do with this.

Shaw makes to stand up, but a vaguely threatening action from Le Moins forces him to resume his seat.

Le Moins

I would prefer it if you stayed, James. After all, I want to make sure nothing untoward happens.

Dyer

What the hell are you talking about, Alex!

Le Moins

Who is she Michael?

Dyer

Who's who?

Le Moins

That raven-haired floozy you were shagging in the Marriott hotel?

Dyer

The...

Le Moins

Great boobs! Bet she humps like a rabbit, eh? And those magnificent thighs. Looked great in the photos!

Dyer rises to make a rush at Le Moins who, ready, pulls the revolver from his jacket pocket. Dyer freezes, then takes a step back. Shaw stands.

Dyer

Jesus!

Shaw

Christ, Alex! What's going on?!

Le Moins

Shall we all resume our places? We might get along a little better. As for this? The second half of my insurance – but then James was already aware of both, weren't you James?

Dyer

Why didn't you tell me? Why didn't you warn me?

Le Moins

Because James is on my side – aren't you James? Because you tricked him too, and he wants what's coming to him as much as I do.

-*-

"Mr. Congreave will see you in the Board Room, Mr Packard. You know where that is?" His Secretary smiled benignly.

Mark had never seen her before, and had been thrown slightly in not being able to enter the normal banter he had previously enjoyed with Grace. However, not only was Grace absent, Congreave was waiting for *him* – which felt very unusual – and on territory that was, to all intents and purposes, not entirely his own.

"A couple of doors down, just past the lift on the left?"

"Yes, that's the one. Would you like me to bring you a drink? I think there should be coffee in the room already, but if you'd like something different..."

"Coffee will be fine. Thanks."

The day was beginning to turn out to be unsettling. Firstly there had been the two 'empty' messages left on his answer machine. They had come from a public phone box, so he had no way of being able to identify the caller. Then there had been the episode with Julia. Significant in itself, of course, it had broken into his work on 'A Suburban Bandit' which – being for him, one of his Father's more difficult works – had always caused him a degree of trouble. Having his concentration broken, the conversation with Julia merely succeeded in leaving Le Moins and Dyer rattling around inside his head, their conflict unresolved, and their words bouncing back to him from the screenplay.

'If I never really liked it, then why the hell should I want it?'

'The notion of restoring equilibrium through entirely pragmatic means'.

'All I want is to get back something that's been lost'.

In addition to this mental disruption, his usual walk from the station to Congreave's office was curtailed by driving rain and the necessity of taking a taxi from Waterloo. Thus those valuable few minutes so often used to decipher, analyse or resolve – sometimes all three! – had been stolen from him, and faced with a new Secretary, Mark felt as unprepared as he could be when he walked into the Board Room.

Congreave was sitting at the far end of the table; Michael, one of his editors, and another man Mark did not know, flanking him.

"Mark!" Congreave's usual tone, "Here you are! Take a seat, please."

There was a chair, two seats down from Michael with an empty cup already set there. Michael had risen and was heading for the coffee machine that simmered on a slim table against the far wall.

"Coffee, Mark? White, no sugar?"

"Thanks."

Things felt staged, planned out. Mark took the seat as prompted, nodding to the new man, then glancing out of the window. The rain beat against the window. He looked back along the table.

"How are you, Bruce?"

"Just fine. You didn't get wet?"

"No, I took a taxi from the station. Your message implied that it was urgent."

"Urgent?"

Michael interrupted both Congreave's words and Mark's line-of-sight as he poured Mark's coffee. There was a short silence.

"Thanks."

Mark watched Michael retreat, then return towards the table.

"Important, rather than urgent I think." Congreave returned to the question, forsaking his habitual rapid vocal delivery for something a little more measured. "But difficult ahead of both of those."

To Congreave's left, the new man pulled two envelopes from a folder that he had in front of him, edging them out onto the table but not apparently in any specific direction.

"Coming straight to the point Mark, I'm afraid we've decided to terminate your contract."

"What?"

"Difficult decision for us, of course – particularly after such a long and previously successful association."

"Bruce, I don't understand. 'Previously successful': what does that mean?"

"It's really very simple. We spoke about those pieces on Kuwait and Northern Ireland; about the 'discrepancies' – remember? Well I'm afraid things were a little more serious than we first thought. It's not that I don't respect your work, Mark, but I was already becoming a little concerned as you know. That was before we had the … what's the correct term, Charles?"

"I think 'objection' might be most appropriate," said Charles, keeping his eyes on Mark.

"Objection; yes."

"I don't know what you're talking about?" For the second time that day, Mark felt the ground softening beneath him. He had been able to stabilise things with Julia thanks to a little invention on his part; but here, outnumbered and without all the facts, he began to feel a little sick in his stomach. Le Moins' words about restoring equilibrium came back to him.

"There was the prospect that we might be in some serious difficulty over one of those articles; most likely legally, but not necessarily so. There were meetings. Appeasement was required. In fact, those meetings were only concluded this morning when – how shall I say? – a consensus was reached which has suited all parties. One element of the agreement has resulted in us having to part with…"

"'A consideration'?" Charles' job seemed confined to plugging gaps in Congreave's dictionary.

"A consideration – thank you again, Charles. The other condition – which was, I am almost ashamed to confess, an offer on our side – was to dispense with your services."

Mark's face felt suddenly warm, and the sips of coffee he had taken did nothing but exacerbate the condition. 'Restore equilibrium', 'Restore equilibrium' began to hum through his head like a mantra.

"I can explain. Let me explain. I'm sure it can all be sorted out."

"Mark, it has been sorted out." Congreave leant forward and lifted the two envelopes from the table. He tapped them lightly in his hand. "I'm going to get Jenny to send these on to your home address, rather than give you them now. I think that might be best. One contains the money we owe you for work to-date – plus the appropriate sum in lieu of work that we might have given you over the next few months. The second is a letter explaining everything."

"For reference," Charles offered. "I think you will find them all in order."

Certainly there was now a need to restore equilibrium. Mark knew that something had indeed been lost, and he knew he needed to get back both it and his equilibrium. But there could be no simple lie which he could use to fob Congreave off in the same way he had derailed Julia. And even though the situation had been outlined to him, Mark still knew only a portion of the story. The mist, as it descended, became a red one. He felt suddenly trapped, betrayed. Was this how Le Moins had felt? Or Dyer? And what about James? What was his part in all of this? Mark could see now why Le Moins had wanted revenge. That was the word. And he had had insurance. If only Mark had insurance. His hand moved almost involuntarily to his jacket pocket – the one with the blemish, yes! – to feel for a revolver, but there was none there.

"You bastards!"

It was weak, but it was all he could muster. He rose, his face still aflame.

"Fuck your money! And your shitty little magazine! And you" – Mark rounded on Charles – "you can shove your 'consideration'..."

"Mark, please!" Congreave had risen almost simultaneously. "There's no need for this!"

For a moment Mark remained motionless. The coffee cup on the table, still half-full, was tempting; but in a suddenly lucid moment, Mark knew that dashing it across the room would be totally inadequate either in terms of protest or revenge. If only he had some insurance…

Without speaking, he pushed back his chair (which tottered, but did not fall) and walked to the door. He could feel the three pairs of eyes on his back. As he placed his hand on the handle, he was suddenly George Maxwell and Alexander Le Moins rolled together. He felt suddenly as if he were all his Father's heroes and villains rolled into one. And then he was unnervingly calm.

"Remember that awards ceremony in the West End a few weeks ago, Bruce?" Mark had turned and was coolly staring down his tormentor.

"Yes, I think I know the one you mean. Why?"

"Well I know who that woman was you were with; the one in the red dress. I wonder if your wife does?"

His felt his words leave him like the report from a gun, then saw them hit their target square on. It was not nearly enough in the way of revenge, but it was something, and it helped.

-*-

78   Int.   Michael Dyer's study

As before. Le Moins stands guard over Dyer who remains seated in the chair towards the centre of the room. Shaw is perched on the edge of the small sofa. There is a tense silence.

Le Moins

Well?

Dyer

Well what?

Le Moins

What do you think of my offer? Seems very generous to me, don't you think so James?

Shaw

Leave me out of this, I said.

Le Moins

How can I, James; how can I?

Dyer

You want twenty-five thousand now?

Le Moins

Now-ish. I know it will take you a day or two. And then regular payments of my little premium. In return, you get to keep that thing –

Le Moins waves his gun-carrying hand at the brown oblong leaning against the bookcase. He seems a little more relaxed. There is even a sense of him now becoming a little over-confident and potentially off guard.

- and your wife never need know about the little incident at the Marriott. In fact Michael, I see no reason why you shouldn't continue to enjoy the fruits of that particular labour; after all, your secret will be safe with me!

Le Moins breaks into a little laughter which gradually becomes louder. Then, a second or so later, there is a loud noise from downstairs. Instinctively Le Moins stops laughing and turns his head towards the door. Dyer, evidently prepared, leaps out of the chair and rugby tackles Le Moins before he has time to react. The two fall back against one of the bookcases, Le Moins' head hitting the shelving first and the gun spilling from his hand. As they begin to wrestle, Dyer manages to cry out.

Dyer

James! Go for help! Go!

Shaw, who has already stood up, darts for the door and disappears. Le Moins and Dyer struggle. Having fallen backwards, Le Moins finds himself in the weaker position and attempts to push Dyer off him. There is a flailing kind of fight which shows no signs of being conclusive. It lasts for a few seconds before Le Moins, managing to get some leverage, succeeds to rolling Dyer away from him. However, this is only towards the gun which lays near the door on the floor. Le Moins only sees it as Dyer's hand descends upon it. Le Moins freezes. Dyer rises slowly. They are both breathing hard.

Dyer

Well, well. You seem to have dropped your insurance, Old Boy. Very careless.

Le Moins

James has gone for help remember. You sent him.

Dyer

Yes; I did, didn't I? That's good.

Le Moins

Good?

Dyer

Get up! Stand where you were.

They are both standing, Le Moins in roughly the same position as before; Dyer in front of the chair on which he had been sitting. He has the gun pointed at Le Moins. Without looking, Dyer kicks one leg out behind him to send the chair toppling to the ground.

Dyer

What did you say Alex? Something about me being able to enjoy the fruits of my labour? Oh, I intend to, believe me! And you also suggested that my secret will be safe with you... You know, I really think it will.

Le Moins

What are you going to do?

Dyer

I'm sure we should be able to call it self-defence, don't you? After all, I'm sure that James will see to that.

Dyer pulls the trigger and sends a single shot into Le Moins' chest. He looks surprised then pained. He falls into a heap on the floor. Dyer waits for a few moments then walks over to inspect him. He lifts Le Moins' arm and lets it fall. It hits the mat limply. Taking the gun, he places it in Le Moins' hand, then removes it. Ensuring some of his own finger prints are on the handle, he then tosses the gun across the floor. Walking to the bookcase, he lifts the brown parcel to check for damage, then returns it to its original resting place. With a final glance at Le Moins, Dyer steps over the body and leaves the room.

Chapter Thirty Three

On the river, boats plied their various trades almost in spite of the modernity of the times. Barges with cargoes that remained indiscernible from a distance of over a hundred yards, seemed to pass within inches of each other as they made their way beneath Waterloo bridge, upstream and downstream, to load and unload at anonymous locations. The trippers too – small white craft, whose passengers appeared as less than faces at their windows – bounced along in the hurly-burly of the river, as if there was very much to see.

Although he had yet to visit there, he had a view as to why a similar excursion in Paris, say, or Amsterdam might provide something more in terms of worthwhile entertainment. What was there here: a few concrete bridges and a few concrete buildings? Perhaps Tower Bridge or Westminster was compensation enough for nothing more than a glimpse of the dome of St. Paul's cathedral. Whatever it was – and he had not tried a trip on this river. either (though not because of a lack of opportunity) – he was suddenly struck with the banal sameness of the picture: boats appearing and disappearing from under bridges, then the same boats reappearing elsewhere. Repetition was not to be celebrated. One of the things he was enjoying with History was that its journeys always took you from one place to another, from one state to the next.

A tap on his arm roused him from his reverie. He looked down from the river (rather than up) to see the pigeons still circulating at his feet. There were fewer of them now compared to when they had opened their sandwiches – a whole flock had magic'd themselves suddenly before his eyes! – but the one with the dodgy wing and missing toes was still there, eyeing them hopefully; perhaps pigeons were the bird equivalent to the down-and-outs who slept in the cardboard city just along the embankment.

Lydia had been talking to him and, now that she had stopped and tapped his arm, doing so became a fact of which he was suddenly aware. Where had they got to? What had been on the agenda as he had taken the last bite of his beef and tomato sandwich before raising his eyes to the river?

"Sorry." He tried to raise a smile as he turned his head to look at her. Perhaps he had been successful, it was difficult to say. It certainly felt as if he had failed, but Lydia's response – a bright smile of her own and the renewed pressure on his arm – indicated otherwise. "I was miles away."

Well, perhaps a few hundred yards rather than miles – though he might just have well have been.

"Shall we go?" She asked.

Mark was not aware that they had anywhere to 'go'. His response to her question was to somehow assume that they had finished all their 'going' for the day. Indeed, wasn't his rather vacuous staring at the river an indication that they had – on at least one level – come to a halt? He glanced up again. Still the barges on their endless loop, travelling but going nowhere.

Their trip to the National Gallery had not been that much of a success, at least not for him. It had been too busy (the weather was good and it was the start of the holiday season) and, thanks to a party of Italian school children, much too noisy. They had wandered from room to room, occasionally hand-in-hand, in the semi-reverential way that one was supposed to, but the visit had lacked the naïve excitement he had felt the day he ventured in to the Tate and met Lydia for the first time.

A small number of months had passed since then – this looking at her as she rose before him – during which, if he were honest with himself, he had managed to fulfil all those fantasies that had been instantly generated upon their meeting. As she stood before him now, the bra-less breasts hidden beneath her pale blue tee-shirt were breasts that he had cupped and caressed; her full lips he had kissed; he had run his hands across very inch of the tanned skin, and marvelled in its subtle difference from his own. In his sudden confusion, he wanted to grab her and demand that they go back - physically and in time - to that brief first moment at the Tate so that he might re-generate his embryonic, nervous and exciting desires. *That* was where he wanted to go; he wanted to make history with her again.

"Where?"

"Home, silly!" She laughed and held out her hand. "We said we might go via the park, as it's so nice…"

He remained motionless and stared out at the river. It was suddenly much darker, but at least the rain had stopped. The walk from Congreave's office – undertaken through a blur of emotion – had brought him to this seat and this view of the river. It was too inclement for pleasure boats. One or two had passed by, but they had been largely empty, perhaps not on duty at all but on their way between moorings or boatyards or wherever they were berthed. A few barges, sometimes in chains of two or three, chopped their way through the water.

But things did change, of course. Good and bad. He had just been sacked. He had just threatened – in a juvenile and empty way – to expose a man for his infidelity, not knowing if it was true. He was sitting wrestling with a new and confusing emotion – currently without a name – that might take some time to understand.

He was also sitting where had sat all those years before; where he began to recognise that some things might warrant change because in themselves they had failed to so do. The barges on the river. How often was that a story to be repeated?

He stood up.

Deciding not to go straight home, he got off the tube a stop early and walked to his Aunt's house along Belsize Avenue. There was now no sign of the earlier rain, the warmth generated by the sudden sun already starting to bleach the pavements of any trace of damp except in the most inaccessible places.

Usually he would knock when he arrived, if only out of courtesy or habit, but knowing Beatrice and Simon to be away in Brighton for a few days, Mark simply let himself in. There was a small uneven pile of letters lying on the hall mat which he picked up and deposited, untidied and unsorted, onto the hall table; then, without hesitation, he climbed the stairs.

Pushing open the study door, he paused on its threshold, his eye drawn to the large brown oblong that rested against the bookcase. He imagined Michael Dyer's study as his Father had written it – and then the television translation. Perhaps the parallels were not that strong – only one bookcase and not two; a single chair rather than a small sofa; a desk that was far removed from anything truly antique and solid – but it was a study all the same, and there were echoes.

Mark walked to the desk and withdrew a small pair of scissors from the drawer. In three strides he was alongside the bookcase where, with less violence than he might have anticipated, he made a small cut in the brown paper. Peeling back the wrapping just a little, he stood up.

Perhaps for a moment he had been uncertain as to what he would find - or what he hoped he would find. Perhaps he had expected Dyer's painting to have mysteriously appeared inside the packaging. Perhaps this was what he had wanted to see; anything rather than the mirror.

-*-

At sixteen, Packard sent his son to boarding school. It had been both a selfish and self-less gesture, and one taken with only minimal consultation with either the family's remaining matriarch, Beatrice, or the boy himself. For Charles the separation gave him the space he needed to explore his new-found celebrity, and to indulge in an overtly hedonistic lifestyle which was to become his primary way of living for the next five years or so.

Later, he confessed to Mark that internally he had argued the move with a view to giving his son the best possible start in life. Money from the television production of <u>A Suburban Bandit</u>, coupled with other spin-offs, made the decision a simple one in financial terms at least. For the young man, who had inevitably begun to mature quickly after his Mother's death, such transportation had initially been borne as something of a sentence; the only blessing turning out to be that his Father had chosen a mixed sex school.

For a boy of sixteen, fresh from moderate success at "O" levels and blessed – more or less – with a parent whose fame was beginning to spread, Mark's primary concern was not academic achievement or ambition, but girls. On more than one occasion it seemed cruel to him that, in spite of his Father's undeniable success in this non-academic area, so little of his knowledge and talent appeared to have been passed down in either direct teaching or inherent genealogy.

"The standard masturbatory fumblings had begun two or three years earlier, I suppose, and in the privacy of my own room in my own house, and continued to a kind of pattern or habit stimulated by various untouchable goddesses – and the certainty of not getting caught. Boarding school changed all that. My room was replaced by the dorm – and the untouchable goddesses were usurped by young women who, while still untouchable in one sense, were in fact very real and always on the premises.

"They were very different, the girls at that school. I guess they had made the transition between girl and young women during the summer in between. As an adolescent boy feeling somewhat trapped, the similar scale of transition for me was not to be made for at least another two years.

"So it was that my muses became Cathy who sat opposite me in English, and Bryony from History. Unlike my Father's muses, who could be converted into either physical lovers or characters with whom he could make love in an entirely different way, mine remained painfully and pitifully removed."

Mark's early attempts at courtship were consistently met with physical rebuff. Cathy twice struck him during unwanted and cumbersome advances, and even Linda Forester – whose reputation as the 'school bike' engendered some hope in him – one day lured him into the nearby park simply to hone her humiliation skills.

_*_

Not being tired had been his excuse, leaving the bedroom to go and make himself some coffee. It had seemed reasonable enough. The day had been a relatively hot one and they had each spent much of it, one way or another, out of doors. There were other things he could have added to bolster his defence - his head still spinning from the notions of and need for change he was now suddenly wrestling with - but these allies had not been needed; her own sleepiness had conspired with him. So much so, in fact, that when he returned some ten minutes later – without a drink of any sort – she had already fallen asleep.

Having eschewed the duvet for a single sheet, this now rested half-off the bed, the upper part of it only partially draped around her sleeping form. From the waist up she was naked. Mark, feeling as if he were becoming ever more awake moment by moment – in a complete and absolute reversal of her state – eased himself down onto the floor by the door, his back against the wall, and watched her breathing.

For a few moments he focussed on her right breast which, owing to the way she was lying and his own position and consequent horizon, presented itself in almost perfect profile. As she breathed, a silent, unobtrusive kind of breathing, he watched its gentle and almost imperceptible motion, its rising and falling exaggerated the most at the tip of the breast's nipple – and then only if you looked hard enough.

His concentration, he found, began to remove the focus of his attention from any relationship with reality. Firstly, the breast became anonymous: it ceased to belong to her; it might have been anyone's. And then the flesh itself was not part of a breast but just flesh. And after that… There was something after that, but he felt it difficult to articulate, even to himself: an amalgam of skin and tissue, a blend of tone and texture; and although the combinations (combinations *he* had known) were different, they began to blur. It was as if there were nothing to distinguish them after all. Reward them with names - the names of their owners - but even so the distinction ceased to exist, and perhaps not just for the physical form and flesh, but for everything else too.

Chapter Thirty Four

In the rollercoaster that was Charles Packard's life, the publicity and freedom offered by the success of <u>A Suburban Bandit</u> ensured that the next three or four years continued to maintain the theme of a twisting, turning and sometime unpredictable journey. However, over this period the trajectory was primarily trending towards the downhill. For the first time in a long while - perhaps for the first time in all his mature adult years - Charles was essentially alone. Without Mary, and having packed Mark off to his boarding school, he was a free agent, at liberty to do almost anything he wanted.

Although Packard initially tried to ensure he was on-hand to attempt the role of Father during Mark's school holidays, even this constraint became gradually loosened as his son began his own journey through life.

"It didn't seem to take very long for a distance to begin to grow between my Father and I. This wasn't intentional on either side, of course - or at least I assume not. Boarding school initiated the second part of the metamorphosis that had begun with my Mother's death, and then when I went on to University, the links were loosened even further."

Initially, Charles filled his days with the spin-offs and trappings of his recent literary and public renown. Peter Healy ensured that he was regularly seen at popular cultural events, awards ceremonies, and first nights. He would be occasionally interviewed on the "red carpet" that adorned the entrances of Premiers to which he had been invited or where Healy had wrangled a seat. There were vague conversations about his next book or a screenplay, but when the flashbulbs popped it was often to capture him arm-in-arm with either an up-and-coming actress or one potentially past their sell-by date.

> "All in all, it was a little bit surreal. I mean, I used to be someone who might catch a glimpse of these glamorous affairs on the television or see pictures of the stars in the papers. Now, here I was, actually walking the same red carpets; rubbing shoulders with those same stars; even being interviewed! If I'd thought about it for too long, I simply couldn't have reconciled that with my background, and how someone like me had managed to find his way there. So I took the easy route: I stopped trying to reconcile it. I decided that it was my moment, that I had earned it somehow, and bugger me if I wasn't going to enjoy it!"
>
> (Interview with Michael Parkinson, 1987)

Packard's conscious decision to make the most of his good fortune - and his way of ensuring he did so - was not lost on a media who had neither loyalties nor honour in their pursuit of the next good story. For a while he was good copy. Some of the things that were printed were inaccurate, of course. One story in particular relating to Penny Weston-Hart - a young socialite trying to effect a breakthrough into either modelling or film - was so wide of the mark that Healy, under advisement from the MacMillan legal team, sued the 'News of the World' for libel and defamation of character. The action was settled out of court.

> "I felt sorry for Penny. It was a very brief coming together of two people who were trying to establish themselves, if you like, each of us building our public persona. No. Actually Michael, that's rubbish! It sounds as if we were doing something unbelievably calculating, which certainly wasn't true in my case. I was just trying to enjoy myself! Penny was a bit naive really, and never did understand what she wanted nor how to go about it. She didn't understand how the game worked - not that I did either, of course, but the difference was I didn't care. It didn't matter to me. We spent a few weeks together; there were some photographs, an allegation from a former boyfriend. You know the sorry tale. The allegation that I hit her ex, slapped her sister - all untrue of course."

> (Interview with Michael Parkinson, 1987)

It wasn't just the media who were trying to take advantage of Packard's new celebrity to generate their copy. Derek Shutts - considered by some to be, like the paparazzi, devoid of loyalty or honour - sensed another opportunity.

Although <u>A Suburban Bandit</u> was, in part, a thinly veiled attack on Shutts and his modus operandi, the man himself either failed to see the parallel or simply did not care. Packard had delivered on the promise he had made to LWT, and in doing so had ensured Shutts earned his commission. The new celebrity was, in Shutts' eyes entirely bankable; it had pound notes attached to it, and he could see the opportunity to grab a second slice of it.

This time Shutts' idea was a different one. In his mind, the success of the LWT play was not a vehicle for another screenplay but another book. On and off, Healy had been gently nagging at Packard to consider what he was going to do next. He was convinced that another novel was the right step. Although privately acknowledging <u>A Suburban Bandit</u> had done wonders for his client's overall stock, he was concerned that it had been the wrong thing for Packard to do when viewed at a more "purist" level.

"Of course the books sold better after the LWT thing. How could they not? But this wasn't the Charles I knew; he was so much better than that. Some people - some influential people - thought the play was a little tawdry or cheap, that it lacked depth or imagination. Charles knew that too, and whilst he brushed it off, on some level I'm sure it hurt him. I tried to get him to think about another novel; something serious. He was always too busy; didn't have any ideas yet; proclaimed that the time wasn't right. In a strange kind of way, I think he was also a little vulnerable just then too, trying to work out his new life - so when Shutts made his suggestion… Well, it was an easy option for him."

When Shutts made his approach to Packard, he was initially rebuffed. Packard was still a little sore from the underhand way the agent had gone about his business previously, and on that basis was at first unwilling to entertain him again. Shutts was persistent however, openly playing on the notion that, by following his suggestion, Packard was now established in the big league, and arguing that if he had not been involved then the author would not be enjoying the benefits of minor celebrity: red carpets, interviews, actresses and the like.

It was an argument Packard could not counter. Without <u>A Suburban Bandit</u>, he might have just another minor novelist trying to make ends meet.

> "Derek's idea, when he unveiled it, surprised me a little. I had assumed that he would be pushing for something populist - there was big money in television, of course. So that he should also suggest - as Peter did - another book, well, I wasn't ready for that. Of course what was clever about the whole scheme was that he had wrapped the whole thing up in a box and tied it with ribbons. He had the idea - a sequel (or "prequel" you would call it now) to <u>If Time Was A Book</u> - and the people in place to make it happen. Of course his notion was a little vague, but it answered one key question for me: if I wrote another book, what would it be about? And it gave me an option - if Peter objected - to produce it outside the MacMillan machine."

> (Interview with Michael Parkinson, 1987)

Packard's contract with Peter Healy - one that had evolved over the previous three years - was not an exclusive one. So when Healy did object to the subject matter of the proposed novel, Shutts' back-up publisher - the 'bow' on the box - was waiting in the wings. In the end, this was where Shutts made his killing.

The core tenet of the proposed new work - quickly settled on as being called <u>Uncertain Genesis</u> - was a semi-autobiographical tale of a working class boy made good. All Packard had to do, Shutts argued, was write about himself. It was also a way - so Shutts' persuasion ran - to explore the beginnings of things, and in looking back at how the book's hero meets the love of his live, it was a way to honour Mary again.

"I objected to it on a number of levels once Charles had outlined it to me. My primary concern was that it was a mistake to do anything semi-autobiographical - especially at this stage. Get a few more things under his belt, build up the reputation a little further, get closer to potential he had to be some kind of literary statesman, and *then* write a full autobiography. *That* was the way to go. But the plot felt a little flimsy too, and however well he might have written it, could only reflect badly on Charles in my view. I just couldn't see the point of it. But Charles seemed convinced; Shutts had made his pitch perfectly. For Charles it was going to be easy - and quick. What more could he want?"

In rejecting the proposal on behalf of MacMillan, Healy was attempting to ensure that when people made a Packard-MacMillan connection, they knew they would be looking at a quality product. If something by Packard didn't have the MacMillan 'stamp', then it could only be second rate. To some extent <u>A Suburban Bandit</u> also seemed to fit that landscape.

> "I was disappointed that Peter wouldn't take on the book, but he explained his reasons and I respected them. Of course I did. I trusted him totally. And I knew it wouldn't break our friendship, or our business relationship. On reflection I should probably have listened to him more; taken more of his counsel. I might still have produced the thing anyway, of course."

> (Interview with Michael Parkinson, 1987)

-*-

Sitting at his desk, re-reading the draft material to cover seventy-six through seventy-eight, Mark knew he was reaching a critical point in the depiction of his Father's life. It wasn't so much because of what had actually happened to him during this period, nor because there was suddenly a dearth of material, but because 'Uncertain Genesis', in being the way-mark for the times, had become the symbol for so much that was personal to *him* in a very sharp and meaningful way.

Had he been writing his own life story and covering this period and his University years, Mark wondered how he would have portrayed himself. More acutely perhaps, he wondered how any biographer might have chosen to portray him. For a short while, it had been a time of rebellion and idealism. There was, Mark knew, nothing on a grand scale, but as his Father become more popular and more public - and, in consequence, some of that inevitably having an impact on him through the familial shadow that was being cast - so he, consciously or otherwise, seemed to strive to create an ever greater distance between the two of them. He wanted to avoid being his Father's son, if that were at all possible; he felt the need to be credible and individual in his own right. Looking back now, Mark did so with a little guilt. There was a period during his second year at University where he and his Father were in each other's company just three times over a six month period - much of that as a result of Mark's planning.

Mark looked over his shoulder at the bookcase. 'Uncertain Genesis', in its non-MacMillan livery, stared back at him. It was a book he had never been able to read. He had tried, of course; and more than once. He knew he had to; there was an element of duty about doing so - not as the son of the author, but as his biographer - but it was a duty he had never been able to fulfil.

"I'm not surprised you haven't been able to read it," Beatrice had said to him one day.

"Why?"

"Because it's cheap and shoddy, and not worthy of your Father."

Mark wondered how much of this was uttered from the perspective of literary merit, and how much driven by other factors - such as in defence of his Mother. Mark knew - even from the small part of the book he had managed to get through - that it could be read in such a way as to shine a harsh and unflattering light on the book's main female character, someone who was all too easily seen as a scheming harpy. He felt certain that this could never have been his Father's intention, and may have been one of the reasons why he had been unable to finish reading the book - and perhaps one of the reasons why Beatrice despised it.

"You've read it then?"

"I read everything he ever wrote," Beatrice replied, the phrase noticeably layered with meaning, "even that. Stay clear of it, Dear."

"Really?" Mark had been surprised that she should be so adamant. "Don't you think I need to force myself to? Won't there be a gap if I don't?"

"Perhaps. But I can't think what good you reading it will do; there isn't enough of a gap it could fill."

But it wasn't just the untouched volume on the bookcase, nor memories of his small scale rebellion within the safe precincts of his University that brought Mark up short. Soon enough he would be needing to negotiate the final phase of his Father's life, and the question as to how he would handle the matter of his death had been haunting him from the day he had committed his first words to paper. In many respects - leaving his Mother aside - this was the one thing where he and his Father were truly connected; it was perhaps the one scenario where he would have to intrude in a more direct and personal way into the biography, because his Father's death - unlike his professional publishing career and many human 'adventures' - was an event where *he* was the star witness, the key player. At some point biography might morph into eulogy, and right now Mark had no idea at all how he was going to handle that.

It also loomed as an ending. Whether Mark chose to recognise it or not, working on his Father's life story had given him a purpose and a sense of direction. It was, to some extent, a "north star" by which he could navigate - and one that was all the more important given some of the turbulence that now was beginning to surround him. The affair with Congreave, for example. Because of the book, Mark was able to relegate it in importance; he permitted himself to gloss over it and deny some of its meaning or potential repercussions (in spite of his outburst in the Board Room). Had he not had his Father's book as his staff, then he would have needed to take the situation - what it *meant* - much more seriously than he had thus far. Any potential unravelling that may have caused - in terms of his professional career, of course - was therefore masked, and he was allowing himself to be protected.

Had he given it further thought and explored beyond that concrete example for a moment, he might have extended the notion of this safety net further; but for other instabilities he had his adventure with Maxine as his comfort blanket, something that kept him warm and feeling secure. He didn't need to be told that there was something awry with Julia, but he could make excuses there; certainly she seemed to be piling the pressure on herself with respect to Laura's wedding, and he remained convinced - in spite of these difficulties and the flashbacks of Lydia he had experienced recently - that, by and large, things were fundamentally fine.

If all that were the case - that the book was his shield for now - Mark was wise enough to know that when it was finished (and he suspected he needed another two or three months at most to hone the final article) he would need something else to occupy him going forward. If the ending was worrying him from a purely technical and historical perspective, then it was also causing him concern in that it represented a step into an unknown future; or a future where he would need to proactively decide what happened next. It was perhaps the reversion from unravelling and depicting history to the need to *make* it - and to make his own - that may have been his greatest concern (had he been able to articulate it). Once the book was finished and put to bed, then he would need to *do* something. In some respects he had allowed himself to be swept along by his Father's history, the manner in which he lived his life, and the philosophy that allowed him to lurch sometimes from one crisis to the next. Mark knew this was not his own natural character, but there was something infectious about it - perhaps inevitably so - that bled from this past second-hand life and into his own.

-*-

The contract that Packard signed with Shutts' publisher - Reynard Books - was reminiscent of the first he had signed with Dawson all those years before. It was more straight-jacket than contract, not in financial terms but in the commitments he made relating to the production of <u>Uncertain Genesis</u>. It turned out to be the last contract he signed with anyone other than Peter Healy and MacMillan.

> "As far as the money went, the deal was fine. The split - three ways, of course - was reasonable enough, though Shutts' earnings would, again, be disproportionate to his effort. It was a great deal for him. My problem with it - and I hadn't realised this up front - were the constraints I imposed on myself in terms of getting the damn thing written. Remember, I hadn't tried to write anything for a little while; I was too busy enjoying myself. And I didn't start on it as promptly as I should have done. The consequence was I had precious little time to get a first draft out. And it was really poor. When the Publisher came back suggesting - no, requesting - changes, I had no real room for manoeuvre. I was actually grateful that there was someone there giving me a steer, lighting the way. It meant I didn't have to think too much. The end result was a book that was delivered on time - just. And one that was a million miles away from what I would normally have found acceptable. I hated it. It was poor in terms of quality, and thin in terms of spirit. I knew it would be a disaster."

> (Interview with Michael Parkinson, 1987)

Packard, backed into a corner, called on his old friend Healy to see if he could offer any advice. He knew that there was no way out of the contract and that the book would be published either with or without his blessing.

"Poor Charles was in a bad way on this one. He knew he couldn't get out of it, and there was nothing we could do to help on that score. It was a question of damage limitation, really. As MacMillan, I couldn't afford to get involved with something current from another publisher. All I could do was to give him some ideas in terms of how he might be able to distance himself from it - without being in breach of contract, of course."

In what little time he had available, and where opportunities presented themselves, Packard tried to put some of Healy's advice into practice. Reynard ensured that there were pre-launch interviews that Charles was obliged to attend, and to his credit, he never missed a single one. The subtleties came when he was answering questions such as 'Would you say this will be your best book to-date?', or 'How would you describe your new book?'. For the former, Packard would consistently find a way of ensuring that the questioner knew the answer was 'No'. More than that, without denigrating it, he tried to show that he was dispassionate about it, even detached. In terms of description, he often used words like 'experimental', 'rough', 'immature' - anything he could think of to make sure people knew that it was not going to be the finished article, and that there was more to come.

"Considering the difficult situation he was in, Charles did a really good job - both for him and for us. By the time the thing came out, people knew he wasn't that attached to it. He had managed to get across that it wasn't an important work by any means. Some people, who knew him well enough already, could see through the gloss to get closer to the truth. It was also - as it turned out - good for us. In talking down <u>Uncertain Genesis</u>, Charles would often talk up his other work, things he had published with us. It became clear to many people that the MacMillan stuff was the cream. We even saw a little spike in our sales of his books in the run up to <u>Uncertain Genesis</u>' publication date."

In the end, the book was not a disaster. True, it received some mixed reviews. Most people were neutral, but there were some at either ends of the spectrum - the naysayers always being more vocal. Commercially it sold well enough, though probably not as well as Reynard or Shutts would have liked. Packard continued to honour his contractual commitments in terms of book signings and readings - though in the case of the latter, there were only a few passages he was happy to be caught personally endorsing. Neither Reynard nor Shutts were particularly enamoured with Packard's performance, especially after the publication - though the publishers were the only ones who cared.

> "In the end I guess I got out with my reputation more or less intact - at least publicly. And amazingly my relationship with Peter at MacMillan's seemed stronger than ever. It was a lesson, I suppose - which goes to show that you're never too old to learn! I did what I had to do; the minimum I had to do. Worked through to the last committed signing and reading, and then stopped. Since then I have never read from nor signed another copy of the damned thing, and I never will."

(Interview with Michael Parkinson, 1987)

The public crisis had been averted, but personally <u>Uncertain Genesis</u> hit Packard hard. When his chance to redeem himself next came, he grabbed the opportunity fully and passionately - although there was a little water to pass under the bridge before that time came.

-*-

Uncertain Genesis

'Where the hell did you get that from?!'

'What?'

'You know what!' He could see she was really angry now. Her face looked red raw. 'Come to think of it, where do you get anything from?'

It was a question he had not expected, nor understood.

'What's that supposed to mean, eh? What? I've told you once: I bought the bloody thing off a guy at the pub. Thought you might like it. Wasted my bloody money.'

'Ha!' She said it as if it were a triumph. 'There, see?!'

'See what, exactly?'

'The money. We haven't got any money, have we? And then suddenly we have. And you go splashing it about on crap like this.'

As she picked up the figurine his breath caught. He knew it wasn't rubbish; he knew it. Antique, probably. It hadn't been cheap - and it had been for her. And now her she was waving it about in the kitchen as if it was a cheap chalk trinket from the travelling fair.

'Put it down, Lou. If you hate it, I'll try and get the money back; just don't smash it.'

'Would I?' she said, her arm raising just a fraction higher. 'So where'd you get the money from?'

'Dogs,' there was defeat in his voice. 'I won it on the dogs, didn't I?'

She lowered her arm. The object of the debate landed softly on the kitchen table.

'You promised me, Nat. You promised me that you'd finished with those bloody dogs. As if my life isn't hard enough without you bleeding our money away on those things...'

If truth be told, they were both beaten now. She sat down. He paced.

'I tried. I tried. And then when I did that bit of extra overtime and I had a few quid spare...'

'How long? How long, Nat?'

'Just once or twice.' He stopped his pacing and spread his arms out pleadingly. 'That's all. Honest. And I got a bit lucky.'

She shook her head then looked down at the table. In one corner the cheap veneer was beginning to peel away, revealing the even cheaper wood beneath. It wasn't what she wanted. It had never been what she wanted. She remembered her old Gran who'd had the most marvellous kitchen table, all solid wood with proper grain in it and everything. "One day," she used to say to herself, "one day, I'll have a table like that." And what did she have? Cheap shit from some second-hand place near the indoor market.

'Luck never lasts, does it? It always runs out. Especially on losers like us, Nat; especially on us.'

Chapter Thirty Five

If the study of History was teaching Mark anything, then he suspected that above all it else it was the supremacy of sequence. In many respects, if he wanted to be as abstracted as possible from his subject, then - in its most raw sense - that was all history actually was: the following of one event on from another, usually in a causal fashion. Given that he was, by nature, a structured and methodical individual, such a framework lent itself to his world view (perhaps in part as a direct response of his Father's opposing tendencies), and - more importantly - was perfectly in tune with the way he liked to tackle his assignments. It was a harmonious marriage. The consequence of this was that he could be relied upon to produce accurate and navigationally correct pieces of work that seldom missed - or mis-placed - key links in the historical chain, and allowed his tutors to identify him as a "solid" upper second student relatively early on in his studies.

Where he struggled - and where he would most often fail - would be when interpretations of historical events were needed, or where the links between one event and the next in the same chain were more tangental. Mark, of course, given his analytical nature, was all too aware of this, and he approached such "loose" subjects with some trepidation, often relying on the insight and wisdom of others to hypothesise and fill in the gaps; a tactic which often drew criticism for an over-reliance on third parties rather than his own developing knowledge. The fundamental issue, he knew, was something of a stunted imagination (in direct contrast with his father); one which struggled to generate very much that might be considered novel or innovative.

This paucity of imagination was not just related to the study of History, but was a wider and more fundamental personality trait that, consciously or not, he had to live with. How much it might stop him from doing certain things or exploring particular avenues he was unable to say. He felt - perhaps more so than many twenty year olds - that he was, for example, really pushing the boundaries of rebellion as he strove to establish his individuality. On one level this may have been true - but only in the strict sense that his boundaries were so much narrower, so much closer to him than others' due to his lack of imagination, that he felt as if he were butting up against or even transgressing them very quickly indeed.

For some of his friends at college, this made Mark something of an odd character; a person who was, in their eyes, almost totally conformist, but who, from his own perspective, was so far from home plate that he was living dangerously. Lydia - who was herself a conservative individual, but by choice - would occasionally tease Mark about his inability to see beyond the obvious, immediate and safe.

"I don't understand sometimes," she said one day as they were leaving the British Museum, "how you can be your Father's son."

"What do you mean?" Mark asked, a cross note in his voice. She knew he did not like comparisons with his Father.

"Oh, you know. I can imagine him seeing round things - *through* things - to get to the other side. Sometimes you just see the things themselves and never make it beyond them."

She had said it playfully enough, but it was a criticism, and that was something else Mark struggled with.

"And you do?"

"I try," she said, modestly. "Often I fail - and I nearly always keep my thoughts to myself - but it's something I need to do for parts of my subject."

"Why so?"

"Well, although a chunk of my Classics stuff is history, it's really old history. Mythology really. And so there isn't that much corroboration, or supporting material, or ways of joining the dots together."

"And some times the dots don't join. Or may not even be dots!" Mark's point was that mythology was not history. It was an argument they'd had more than once.

"Yes," she agreed, taking his arm, "and that's my point. If I don't try and see around the little that is there, what have I got?"

"A pile of old statues," Mark suggested, referring to the building they had just left.

"A pile of old stones, yes!"

Mark was glad - this after they had parted and he was sitting on the coach to head back to his University - that they were studying at different colleges. It was great they had found themselves studying close enough to each other (Warwick and Birmingham) to enable them to meet most weekends, and that trips to London were easy to coordinate too - especially as Mark could use the Hampstead house as a base. But he struggled to comprehend how the two of them would have been able to function successfully if they had been at the same university and in each other's pockets all the time.

Whether it had been the episode outside the British Museum or some other trigger - or even the simple accumulation of events, incidents, feelings over the time they had known each other - Mark found himself evaluating their relationship as the coach headed towards the A40. Although they had only been together for a relatively short time (it was their second term), Mark could not escape a growing feeling that they had reached a point of exhaustion. They had bonded incredibly quickly after their accidental meeting and seemed to rush rapidly through the early stages of their liaison with a pace that, on reflection, astonished him - certainly when taken in the context of his previous experience. Their bond became a close one almost immediately, cemented by a strange kind of telepathy that was eerily profound on occasion. It helped, of course, that Lydia was a striking individual; and on those relatively rare occasions when she spent time in Warwick and met some of Mark's friends, they were always impressed by the almost classical beauty of this slim, slightly olive-skinned, striking young woman. She was - they always protested - too good for Mark, and privately he revelled in their approbation and their jealousy of him given that was such a rare flower. And yet, over the drone of the coach tyres on the open road, Mark wondered if that was enough.

Mentally, he could plot their journey together in the same way he might tackle a history assignment, and though the steps and events along the way were presented in a compressed timeline, all were clear enough. And there was a causality and a link that pleased him too. Often it would be a simple phrase or gesture that had taken them from one part to the next, but there it was, and he knew it, could define and articulate it; it was the kind of analysis that made him feel confident. But there had been no such catalyst for a number of weeks now, and Mark was struggling to see what came next. He sensed somehow that there was no logical next step ahead; that, if something was to happen and to move them on again, that it would probably need to be engineered in some way, or require effort - and he did not have the capacity to be able to divine what that might be. It was not only the problem of making history - his own history - but the challenge of being able to see round or through things to the other side, just as Lydia said. For all Mark knew, she was already there; she probably knew what would or should come next; she may have already made some kind of connection that was beyond him.

As the coach rumbled on, Mark found himself increasingly in the dark - both in real terms as evening descended, but also in relation to Lydia. It was not a comfortable place for him to be. His Father, when they had last been together - the three of them - had been at his charming best, and Mark knew that Lydia liked him enormously. They had a simple rapport that Mark envied. He was sure that her background provided something of a connection that was denied him. From the little he knew thus far (it was a part of herself Lydia chose to keep close), her past had been relatively cosmopolitan, and there were things that she and his Father could discuss which proved beyond his sphere somehow. It was as if Boarding School had imprisoned or encased him - as well as protecting him - just at the very time when there were things he should have been learning and experiencing in order to make him a more rounded person. Perhaps that was a talent Lydia had; the ability to tune into others in such a way that made them instant friends. Whatever it was, and however you defined it, it was not a talent that Mark possessed. Indeed, as this new darkness descended on him as he journeyed to Warwick, the fact that he could add it to the growing list of differences between himself and his Father left something of a sour taste in his mouth.

Abandoning himself to logic - his standard fallback when imagination was required - Mark wrestled with the question of "what next?". He had no idea why this should suddenly have come upon him here and now as something that needed to be answered, but now it loomed large before him.

-*-

Uncertain Genesis

Lou knew Nat was a coward. It was a trait he managed to display in so many different ways that she could almost have kept a daily log of his failings. There was a part of her that wished he would stand up to her just once; it would have given her something to push against at least. But she always had the upper hand; always felt in charge. Once upon a time she had tried to fight it, to resist, to bring him out, to make the relationship more even-handed; but the more opportunities he gave her to dominate him, the further any prospect of equivalence retreated into the distance.

She knew, for example, that he would not give up betting on the dogs. Had he done so, it would have demonstrated some spine; it would have taken away part of her excuse to harangue him. If he had made that sacrifice and shown that strength, then she would be forced to respect him - just a little. But he could not, and had not. Lizzie's husband had been talking, and Lizzie had been talking. Lizzie always talked. Lou knew how things were. And if she had a sense of his failing luck with the dogs not simply from the way Nat was behaving, then she would have had her evidence via another route.

If only it had just been the dogs. If only Nat had chosen to leave it there; to have the one vice. If only he had been able to prevent the displaying of his weakness in other ways. If only he had not known Deirdre. That slag.

"Heard some news this morning," she said over tea, her voice flat, hiding emotion.

"Aye, what's that?"

His detachment riled her. The way he tried to give off the sense that, whatever she said, it could hardly be of interest to him; as if he were above her title-tattle.

"You know Deirdre?"

"Deirdre?" he echoed.

"The Barmaid from the 'Lamb and Flag'."

"Right," he said in non-committal acknowledgement.

"Apparently, she's up the duff. So Lizzie says."

"Reg's Lizzie?"

"Who else?"

Nat said nothing.

"Nearly two and bit months gone, Lizzie reckons. She'll have to give up working soon enough. Can't go humping those big barrels down in the cellar when she's got a kid growing inside her, can she?"

Nat said nothing. Lou was fighting to hold on to her emotions. Now was not the time. Now it was just enough for Nat to know that she had her suspicions. Perhaps it was her desire to give him one last chance to be the man she used to want him to be.

"No-one knows who the father is, they reckon. Or at least she's not saying." - then the barb - "Maybe she can't say because she doesn't know, eh? There might be too many runners and riders..."

Nat said nothing, avoiding her eyes as he picked up his mug of tea.

"Lizzie had a go at Reg. Swears its not him. And it couldn't be could it? Reg hasn't got it in him, has he Nat?"

"Doubt it."

"But some have." She lifted her own tea. "If she keeps it - and Lizzie reckons she's already made her mind up - then it's the little Bastard I feel sorry for, maybe never even knowing where he's come from."

Lou took a sip from her drink and then lowered her eyes to her plate. She felt Nat looking at her now.

-*-

As he sat in the conservatory of the Hampstead house, looking out over the back lawn that was so lovingly tended by Mrs Hargreaves' son (and what a find *he* had been!), the recollection of that coach trip returned to Mark with a clarity that seemed improbable. Although it was peaceful here, sitting on the well-padded wicker sofa - the only sounds in the relative stillness being the birds he could hear through the open double doors and somewhere not too far away the buzz of a lawnmower - the thrumming of those tyres on tarmac seemed to have invaded his quiet, pulsing insistently as his memory once again tugged at him. Perhaps the lawnmower's engine echoed that.

The previous day, they had - if his memory was not deceiving him - sat in this very room, the three of them, looking out into the garden and watched the rain falling in a heavy curtain of beads. Perhaps it was his sitting there and making the most of the privacy of the moment, that had encouraged him to slip back those few years and think of Lydia again. He wondered why he should have lighted on that coach journey rather than something else, something more positive; but it was, of course, a pivotal moment for him - and a tipping point in his relationship with her. That it should have occurred in relative isolation (as opposed to the more concrete solitude he now enjoyed) was of little surprise to him; cocooned in his bubble, sitting alone towards the back of the coach, he was able to dissect and analyse without interruption and interference, much as he was now, sitting quietly there drinking his coffee. Julia was out with Laura again, and he would himself be going out soon enough to play squash with Claire.

It was rare, he knew, for him to take decisions on the spur of the moment; he simply was not made that way. He could think of relatively few instances where he allowed fate to take a hand in setting his direction of travel - though his initial meeting of Lydia had been one such. And, perhaps, Maxine. For a moment, he struggled to remember how he had met Julia, then gave it up. It was, he could only assume, his academic discipline that had endorsed a personality trait that showed a preference for calculation and facts. Perhaps it was also his upbringing - the fact that he was his Father's son - that also steered his course: his needing to be practical about getting himself to school after his Mother had died; the regimentation of Boarding; the general day-to-day comfort he got from simply being organised. There was, however, relatively little comfort to be gleaned now about the decision he had taken on that journey back to Warwick. That it was the right thing to do he had no doubt; but he had not been so totally callous as to fail to understand that it would have some unpleasant repercussions, or be difficult for a while.

His logic, and all that by which he chose to navigate, had drawn him to the conclusion that his relationship with Lydia had run its course. During that journey through the darkness of the A40, he had weighed the pros and cons of continuation, and, in spite of the obvious benefits of maintaining their partnership, the correct outcome was in little doubt. He knew, of course, that he would miss her; their trips to London (to sit in this very conservatory!) could be remarkably satisfactory, and she was a very attractive, attentive and physical young woman. But he could not countenance a simple maintenance of the status quo when the future appeared to be little more than a repetition of things disappearing off into the distance.

Mark knew he was a different man now, of course. He had grown and developed; he charted his course in an alternative way now, even if the underlying philosophy remained the same. It was this ability to detach himself that was of benefit to him, that provided clarity; it was this that allowed him to rationalise Maxine, to maintain his equilibrium with Julia, and to take the decision he had already made with regard to Claire. The difference - if he was to accept that difference existed (and he knew he had to) - was in execution. If he were faced with his dilemma with Lydia now, he hoped that he would act in a better way. He had to admit - and this he could only ever do privately and within the security of his own mind - that he had acted poorly, without courage, and had undertaken a course of action that had hurt her. His withdrawal from her - gradual, unannounced, unexplained - had been, on reflection, inappropriate. Mark knew that had he been more mature, he would have handled himself differently; but then, wasn't that what growing up was for? To build wisdom and understanding?

He had allowed himself to become distant. He had claimed pressure of work for not going up to Birmingham the next weekend to see her - and then a family matter that took him alone to London the weekend after. When Lydia came to Warwick next, she found him slightly distracted, aloof. She had challenged him; he had claimed difficulties with one of his subjects (he recalled making one up); he tried to excuse his lack of enthusiasm on a variety of other things. Once the die was cast that next Warwick weekend, there was no going back. It was only later Mark saw that. And at least he could feel some guilt as to the way he behaved, even if at the time he was oblivious to the pain he was inflicting on her. She was - he knew and could see all the more clearly now, with the benefit of hindsight and distance - an intuitive and deeply emotional person, even if she chose to keep some of the latter safely tucked away. He had broken - without warning - that instinctive bond they had established so soon after their Tate meeting, and he had done so in a way in which, here, now, and away from the thrumming of the coach tyres, he knew was inadequate. If he were to try and console himself in any way, it was with the notion that Lydia - with her ability to feel, to see through and round and beyond - might just have sensed something was coming, and perhaps was not therefore taken totally by surprise.

-*-

Uncertain Genesis

Nat had never wondered what it would feel like to be a boxer. Pugilism held no interest or fascination for him. Yet now, here he was, metaphorically on the ropes, punch-drunk from pummelling and staring defeat in the face. He had not appreciated the cumulative effect of the subtle jabs. He had assured himself that he was able to swat them aside like annoying midges on a Summer's evening. The volume of them; he had never truly appreciated the volume of them.

Weakened to a degree he could never have expected, when the first body blow hit him - hard, disguised - he was winded in such a way, his breath taken from him, the pain sudden and sharp, that he was forced to both lean forwards and rock back. The ropes, such as they were, saved him from falling. But he was prone now. His chin prominent, exposed, saying 'come and hit me'. From somewhere in the corner of his eye, the glimpse of a flash of red, moving in his direction; slowed to frame-by-frame animation. The red blur and his fragile chin were destined for each other.

Nat knew he could not take another hit. He knew that would be the end of him. Knowing now what it felt like to be a boxer, he knew he would have to fight.

-*-

Mark had driven to the squash club erratically and absent-mindedly. He had missed the changing of one set of lights and burst through them well after they had turned from amber; at a pedestrian crossing, he had only just seen the lady with the bright red shopping bag at the last minute, but thankfully had time enough to slam on the breaks. The squeal of his tyres had made her jump, and she looked fearful when she summoned up the courage to actually finish crossing in front of him.

There was nothing on which he could immediately blame his lack of attention, other than nerves. He was going to be a little early - of course! - and he had changed into his sports gear and tracksuit before leaving the house. His racket bounced softly on the seat beside him, and he felt ready to perform. He also felt ready for Claire. Perhaps he had been planning tactics for some while now, almost in the same way he might map out the game itself or a chapter from his book. He felt confident and in control. Much of this confidence was born from the logic he chose to apply to recent events, and his interpretation of them. There had been a string of signals for some time now - both from Claire directly and, as a supporting cast, from others - that had all conspired towards a single conclusion. He had never really entertained the possibility that much of his evidence was circumstantial at best, and in his dissection - against historical premise - only one outcome stood up to scrutiny. Some of his confidence stemmed from his relationship with Maxine. For Mark, it was proof - if proof were needed - of a whole range of talents and attributes residing within his compass that he knew he had and knew how to employ. Why should Claire be any different?

He had deliberately chosen one of the two totally enclosed courts at the club. There were no glass walls, no spectator balcony. Normally these were the courts booked by players as a last resort as they were also a little tired, their white walls greying and marked, the red service line chipped, and - in one or two places - the floor just a little uneven.

"Why are we in this one?" Claire asked as soon as she arrived, placing her racket cover in the corner opposite Mark's. He had been on court warming up for a few minutes.

"Aberration on the part of my brain," he smiled. "Apologies."

"I saw one of the glass ones nearer reception was free; do you want to move?"

"I don't think so," said Mark as he launched a ball against the wall and in her general direction, forcing her to react and hit it back. Once a rally had started he knew they would not move.

The first two games were close, partly because Mark was playing at about eighty percent, and partly because he was waiting for his chance. It was an approach that actually generated the opportunity.

"That was close!" Claire panted as she leant against the side wall to get her breath back after the second game. She was wearing a sleeveless but relatively high-necked pale green sports vest and dark shorts. The shorts surprised Mark a little; it wasn't really her style. In fact, he had never seen her play squash in anything other than a white skirt.

He went to the corner with his stuff in it and took a drink from his water bottle.

"Are you not feeling up to it?" Claire asked. "I mean, I get the impression that your heart's not really in it today. If so, we can stop if you like."

Mark put the bottle down and walked towards her.

"There is something on my mind actually." He volunteered it slowly, with the barest of smiles, and in such a way that Claire could only push for an explanation.

"What's that then?"

He stopped when he was about three feet from her.

"You."

She stood slightly more upright, still leaning against the wall, her demeanour essentially unchanged.

"What; that I'm not enough of a challenge for you. Is that it?"

"No. I mean, I've been thinking about *you.*"

At this, Claire took a half-step backwards and let go of the wall. The smile drained from her face.

"What do you mean, Mark?"

He was convinced that she knew exactly what he was talking about; that she was just toying with him, and must have been waiting for him to declare himself. He edged a little closer.

"Mark?"

"You're a beautiful woman, Claire," he continued, missing completely the tone in her voice, "intelligent, sophisticated, lively…"

"Mark, stop this now!"

"I've seen the signs. I'd need to be blind to miss the signs."

"What signs?! What are you talking about?"

"In the wine bar; the last time we played here. Lots of little things. Lots of little things that have brought me on."

"Mark, just stop it - now!" There was a rising note of panic in her voice. "I don't know what you're talking about. There were no signals. Nothing." Mark started to move towards her again. "Come any closer Buster, and I'll hit you with this."

He looked at the slightly raised racket and smiled.

"Don't be silly, Claire."

"Julia warned me."

Her words made him freeze.

"Warned you? About what?"

"About you. She said there was something going on, but didn't know what it was. She said that she was worried about you. That I should" - she hesitated - "be careful."

Mark laughed. It was a sudden laugh that surprised even him. What did Julia know? What could she see? She didn't have a clue about him, not really. About how he felt about her, or his book, or Claire. How could she possibly understand? It was ridiculous.

Simultaneously, Mark took a step forwards and raised his arm. He was gong to place it on Claire's shoulder and squeeze gently. He was going to make her see that there was nothing to be afraid of. He was going to demonstrate what he felt for her, and she - when she saw and understood that - was going to fall into his arms.

Then he felt the crack of her racket on his outstretched arm, hitting him just above the wrist. The pain was sudden and sickening. The surprise of it made him drop to his knees. There was a big red mark already on his skin. He heard movement and looked up, in case she was gong to hit him again. But all he saw was her back as she ran towards the door, pulled it open, and fled the court.

Chapter Thirty Six

During the next three years up until the middle of 1981, Charles Packard began to slip a little from the public consciousness. What little fame he had managed to acquire began to wane slightly, partly because he was gradually seen less in public, and partly because some of that fame began to morph into notoriety - fame of a different flavour. There were still the occasional appearances at premiers, or readings; at the Cheltenham book festival in 1980, Packard was one of the 'star turns', though it was a performance for which he prepared little and enjoyed marginally less. Peter Healy kept in contact religiously, certain that the man he had backed thus far still have more to give.

"It was an awkward time for Charles; we could all see that. Many authors go through a dry patch - after all, we'd seen that with him already. But this? Well, it felt a little more like a slide. I tried to stay upbeat with him; to do what I could to prevent it turning into a nose dive."

Domestically, Packard's life was essentially routine and dull. For the first time in a while his horizon was boring: he was not writing; there was no-one in his life to whom he had any romantic attachment; and he rattled around in the Hampstead house more or less on his own. Mark had graduated from university with the predicted solid upper second, and had taken a variety of part-time jobs in and around the Midlands in order to try and find out what he wanted to do next.

> "Journalism was one of the things. He got a slot on a small local rag providing 'colour' when there was no news - which was most of the time, as far as I could see! I think he may have used his name - my name! - to get through the door, I don't know. Anyway, the work seemed to suit him well enough. I mean, it was probably easy after all the academic work he'd done. I occasionally read things he wrote; they were OK. But that wasn't where his heart really lie. It was a bit like an apprenticeship: it confirmed what skills he had, and he just needed to marry those with his love of history and find a way of making them commercially viable - not that we were struggling for money. It was only after a year or so - probably in mid 1980 - that it occurred to me to introduce him to MacMillan through Peter. He landed a sub-editor job on one of their history series imprints, and he was happy as Larry after that."

> (Interview with CBS, 1987)

Packard himself was far from happy. Whether it had been Mary, something he was writing, or one of his more colourful adventures with the opposite sex, he had always had some kind of focal point around which to navigate. As the decade turned, there was no such anchor.

> "I had stopped doing so many things, it seemed. I'd stopped writing for one. Although I knew it was an aberration and not really me, <u>Uncertain Genesis</u> had knocked my confidence for six. And my motivation. I didn't have a single idea about what to do next - and even if I had, I doubt I would have had the inclination. After the episode with Penny, I'd sworn myself off 'bright young things' too. Suddenly seemed all a bit too dangerous. Or I was getting too old. That was one of the reasons I cut down on the premiers and stuff; wanted to remove temptation. Oh, don't get me wrong, I wasn't entirely celibate! Just a bit more 'careful', I suppose. Or less committed. Callous, even. You choose the phrase. It was a horrible time in many ways, and if you asked me to write down what happened - what happened in any positive or meaningful sense - in 1979 or 1980 I'd probably end up with a blank page."

> (Interview with CBS, 1987)

As 1980 turned to 1981, there was little to suggest much was about to change in the Packard household. In Hampstead, Charles and Mark continued to pass like ships in the night, the latter beginning to make his own name at MacMillan as promising editor material, while his occasional pieces of journalism - now becoming more serious - were seeing some daylight. That New Year's Eve was the first they had spent together since Mark's Boarding School days, primarily because neither of them had a better place to be nor a better person to be with.

The coming of the new year saw Peter Healy still plugging away at his reluctant author, trying to persuade, coerce and cajole him into some kind of creative activity.

"I suggested all sorts of things. Even the idea of going away for some kind of holiday, to get inspiration. I used Charles' experience of going to Greece as an example of what might happen - but I must have hit a nerve, because he almost ripped my head off. I still don't know to this day why it was such a sensitive suggestion."

Healy did manage to persuade Charles to commit to attending a book fair MacMillan was arranging to hold at the Barbican one weekend in May. It was essentially a PR exercise for the company and an opportunity for them to sell books and ensure their brand remained in the public's consciousness. Although Packard had been initially a little reticent about the idea - especially as Healy wanted him to be one of the three writers on an 'Ask the Author' panel - Mark, already showing signs of brand loyalty himself, proved to be a valuable Healy ally.

It was to be a remarkably propitious intervention.

> "I wasn't keen; both Peter and Mark knew that. But Mark played the loyalty card; you know, everything that Peter had done for me, the debt I owed MacMillan - that kind of thing. So I agreed. There were three of us on the stage plus one of the MacMillan PR people in the chair, and essentially we just took questions from the audience. I don't know how stage managed the whole thing was, but they had chosen three very different writers. I mean, I had nothing in common at all with the other two. But that ensured that the answers to questions varied; once or twice we even got a little heated, the three of us, over our responses to the same question. It was actually quite fun. I think it was the best time I'd had in a long while."

> (Interview with CBS, 1987)

In the audience was Simone Dumoulin. Originally from Amiens, Simone had spent much of her professional life commuting from her home on the Normandy coast either north to London, or south to Paris, where she worked as a freelance translator. A committed Anglophile, she variously worked for the National Trust, several London theatres, and a boutique travel company with offices in both capital cities. In Paris, she also taught English. It was not the first time she had seen Packard perform having been at the Cheltenham book festival the previous year. Her attendance then had been accidental; her being in the audience at the Barbican that May certainly was not.

She had been impressed by Packard at Cheltenham and, according to friends, admired his somewhat 'surly authority'. When a tour she was accompanying happened to be in London in the May of 1981 and coincident with the Barbican event, as soon as she found out Charles was appearing, she booked her seat. Subsequently, all Simone would admit was that her attendance had been the extent of her planning; her decision to take advantage of the 'open house' after the formal event was made on the spur of the moment.

> "I think I had been talking to someone about <u>If Time Was A Book</u>; I'm sure I signed their copy, or something. Peter was

hovering, trying to make sure I was okay. As I said, I was actually enjoying myself. Then that conversation finished, I looked up, and there was Simone. There was something about her. She had that kind of simple chic that only European women can muster. I saw her first, of course, and then she stepped forward, offered me her hand, and that gorgeous accent tumbled out of her... I didn't stand a chance really, did I?"

(Interview with Michael Parkinson, 1987)

Although the initial public conversation was, by Packard's own admission, a little stilted, there was enough in it for them both to recognise some kind of connection. Once she had expressed her enjoyment of the evening and her appreciation of his work - though she was, as Charles remembered it, specific about the things she did and did *not* praise - he asked her about herself, if she lived in London, and so forth. Peter Healey remembered the encounter explicitly.

"Simone was certainly striking. I hadn't seen her at first, and then suddenly there was this stylish woman with a marvellously rich French accent talking to Charles. I saw a spark in his eyes that had been missing for such a long time. I'm sure it was because the event had been a success - I could see he had enjoyed himself - but Simone certainly put the cream on that particular cake. When she slipped him her business card before she disappeared into the crowd, I thought he was going to float away!"

The business card contained her name and two telephone numbers, one English, one French. On the reverse side it listed the major organisations she worked for, her role, and a telephone number for each of those. It was both minimal and factual. As far as Packard was concerned, a single phone number with her name would have been enough; the detail that was there only served to pique his interest.

After the event, there was a small, late supper for the panelists and the MacMillan panel Chairman, hosted by Peter Healy. It was always quiet in the City after about nine in the evening, and that evening was no exception. The restaurant was virtually deserted. Healy remembers the dinner as being a calm and slightly subdued affair; all the panellists seemingly exhausted by their endeavours and focus, their energies spent. He also remembers it for one remarkable fact: Charles Packard refused to drink.

Simone Bouvier Dumoulin was born on the outskirts of Amiens in the autumn of 1939. When she first shook hands with Packard at the Barbican she was nearly forty-two, some seven and a half years Packard's junior.

The Bouvier was a surname passed down through her mother's side of the family by tradition. She was related to Eugène Louis Bouvier, a famous entomologist, who she met once as a child before his death in 1944. There was no relationship, however, with the more famous Bouvier; the Jacqueline who married US President Bobby Kennedy. She grew up an unremarkable child with the one exception of an inherent linguistic ability. Although she also learned some German and Italian, it was in English she excelled, and predominately through her love of English literature, became a frequent visitor to the UK.

These visits were initially to London with her parents during school holidays, perhaps once a year; but when she had completed her university studies and became independent, then the frequency of her trips across the channel increased, as did their geographical range. By the time she was twenty-five she had probably seen more of England than the average English native. Teaching the language came easily to her, and was the source of her first income. She established herself at a private college in Amiens and then, by recommendation, began to take occasional assignments in Paris, often crash courses to business executives. It was through these classes that she gained an introduction to the travel company for which she was working by the time she met Packard, as well as endorsements that found their way into the London stage and the National Trust. For the former, she provided a link to cultural events and tours from France; for the latter, she could act as a host at NT events (her German and Italian helped here too), as well as provide some 'colour' around continental connections at NT properties.

By the mid-1970s, with the majority of her work split between Paris and London, she moved to Boulogne-sur-Mer. Not only was this convenient for getting to England - via boat from Calais and Boulogne, as well as plane from Le Touqet - the train to Paris went through Amiens, which allowed her to easily visit her family. In Paris she would stay with her sister, Marie, who had married a Parisian lawyer; in London she initially stayed with friends or in cheap hotels, until her travel company agreed to subsidise a small flat in Ealing. In 1981 the pattern of her work was well set. Given the nature of tourism, during the summer months the larger proportion of her time tended to be spent in London; as autumn turned to winter, the balance would shift again towards Paris. At no point however, did she tend to be exclusively working in either country.

The fact that she was a free agent allowed her flexibility. Unlike her sister, she had no permanent relationship to anchor her anywhere. There had been, over the years, a small number of select partners who had come and gone. A fixed attachment was not something that she had pursued or desired, although some torches still burned brightly for her, none more so that that of Eric La Fosse, and industrialist working in Paris with who Simone had enjoyed a two year affair in the mid-seventies. They remained friends. It was one of her talents, retaining friendships. As she walked in to the Barbican that May, Simone was unattached.

> "I rang her the next day, of course. It was difficult to tell if she was surprised or expecting the call; and she never let on either way. I asked her if she would like to have lunch at some point. In saying no, her counter offer surprised me. My birthday was coming up the following week. Birthdays were something to which I paid little heed, you understand. Anyway, Simone had found out it was my birthday and proposed - if I was free - that we go for an early supper and then on to the National Theatre; she had managed to score some good tickets, perks of the job I suppose. I accepted of course.

> "The next few days were tortuous, if I'm honest. I felt a little bit schoolboy-like, giddy with excitement and anticipation. For once, my birthday couldn't come round fast enough! We'd arranged to meet somewhere along the river - there were relatively few places to eat there at that time - and, unlike me, I was early. That mild spring evening saw me pacing up and down, looking out at the barges on the river, for a good twenty minutes before she arrived. I'm sure I'll never lose that image of her as she walked towards me. She was wearing plain, but wonderfully cut cream trousers, with a white blouse, pale blue cardigan, and a dark blue wool wrap draped around her shoulders. She was slimmer than I seemed to recall, and that, allied to her clothes and her way of walking, carrying herself, reminded me just a little of Audrey Hepburn. Had I been able to look around me I would have noticed that she was a real head-turner - but I wasn't, because I couldn't take my eyes off her!"

> (Interview with Michael Parkinson, 1987)

It was a chaste encounter, something arguably out of character for Packard. The dinner was simple and plain, the play - "Twelfth Night" - adequate rather than inspiring. After the play, they walked across the river to Embankment station where Charles saw Simone on to the tube for Ealing Broadway before taking his own back up to Hampstead. Before they parted, they arranged to meet again two days later on the Saturday.

"I made no advances. Perhaps I was a little bit in awe of her, who knows? She was a confident - *self*-confident - person, perfectly at home with herself, totally in control. It gave her a kind of command really. She knew what she wanted and what she didn't want - perhaps that had come from her upbringing - and I knew, instinctively, that if anything was going to happen between us, then Simone would be the judge and do the driving. Of course I was desperate. She had me hooked from the moment she spoke, from the instant I saw her walking towards me on the South Bank, but for once I was content to be the passive one. It was not really my style - or maybe, not my style any longer. I had grown used to being the aggressor, if you like, and yet not being like that with her was perfectly fine."

(Interview with Michael Parkinson, 1987)

When they met on the Saturday afternoon, at Speakers' Corner in Hyde Park, Simone greeted Packard with a warm kiss and immediately took his hand. She too had made up her mind. It soon became clear, however, that any relationship she and Packard were to embark on would need to be undertaken on her terms.

"I think it was during that very first weekend; Simone made it clear the way she wanted our relationship to work. If I hadn't been besotted, I might have taken offence at the almost contractual nature of it! Essentially she told me that her life was precious and that she had it organised in a way that worked wonderfully well for her; on that basis, if at any point I had any ideas about her coming to live permanently in London, or giving up work, or anything like that, then I should forget such foolishness - unless she initiated it. She also told me - and I saw signs of this a little later on - that part of her reason for being so clear up front was that she had been hurt in the past when she was much younger, and wanted to avoid any possibility of repetition. She was setting out her terms. She wanted us to start with clarity; without any misunderstanding or misconception.

"It was quite remarkable. I mean, I had never known a woman like her in my life. In many ways she behaved almost as a man might. It was an arrangement - yes, that's it; an *arrangement* - that she wrapped around us. It was a framework which - and this bit really surprised me - actually *allowed* us to be passionate, loving. More than that; I think it might have even enhanced and endorsed that passion because we could embark on our affair without any

379

miscommunications, or mixed signals, or different aspirations. It was a 'take it or leave it' offer that was, to be frank, easy to accept. Not only because, perversely, it gave us the freedom to be natural together, it also gave us the freedom to be natural when we were apart. Don't get me wrong. There was no suggestion that it might not be a monogamous relationship; that we were free to 'see other people'. Far from it. It was as complete and open a commitment of equal partners that I had ever experienced."

(Interview with Michael Parkinson, 1987)

During the week that followed, Simone worked most days though, because of what she did, her timetable lacked consistency. Consequently she and Packard would have lunch one day, tea the next. Between the occasions when he would see her, Charles managed to occupy himself well enough but in a slightly more contented and structured way than before. He even paid a visit to the Tate gallery on the Wednesday afternoon after he had Simone had enjoyed lunch together nearby. On the Thursday evening, Simone had dinner in Hampstead and stayed the night in the house. Packard felt that this was some kind of seal on the week. Simone was flying back to France on the Friday, and spending the night, formally and for the first time, both closed out their first week together with a clear statement, as well as confirming what was likely to follow.

For Packard, that first weekend without her was difficult enough; the prospect of not seeing her until late Tuesday was a daunting and uncomfortable one. Allied to that, apart from a call to tell him she had arrived back in Paris safely and one on the Tuesday to confirm what time she was likely to be back in London, there was to be no communication.

"It was all part of her rule-set. I baulked at it at first, of course, but her logic was clear and completely aligned to the way she wanted the relationship to work. From her perspective, she knew - and therefore I should instinctively know - that she was coming back to me. On that basis, where was the need for confirmation in between times? And she didn't want to get into any kind of habit that meant we had to speak every day. Simone felt that generated both obligation and constraint; that only negative things could come of it. I didn't realise it that Friday, but she was right of course. It was all part of the freedom thing."

(Interview with Michael Parkinson, 1987)

He tried to be as calm and detached as possible the next time he saw her; he did not want to demonstrate how much he had missed her. He need not have worried. Simone *was* demonstrative when she saw him next, and made it very plain that *she* had missed *him*. It was proof that her framework did indeed 'enhance and endorse that passion'.

As May bled into June, the pattern of their relationship - built around Simone's work and travels - became clearer to Packard and settled to both of them. After a month, all her arguments for clarity, independence and a self-reliant approach were proven. Everyone noticed a change in him, from his son, through Beatrice his sister, and on to Peter Healy.

"Charles was the happiest I had seen him in a long time. He looked years younger; he was dressing a little more smartly; shaving more often! He even arranged to see *me* once or twice - and I was the one usually doing the pushing. I'm sure he had cut back on the drinking a bit too; I just had a sense of him being fitter within himself. And - the really exciting bit for me - he confessed to thinking about writing again."

Healy knew when Packard said he was thinking about writing, that usually meant he *was* writing. Perhaps some short outline sketches, or thinking about plots or characters. Whatever it was, it meant he had an idea; Charles Packard having an idea was the thing that gave Healy the buzz.

> "At first I didn't know if anything would come of it. Simone gave me the initial spark; not directly, but in the way she went about things. It was this clarity of choice and action she had about her; the range of principles and mores that guided her. It suddenly struck me - don't ask me how or when - that she was a perfect model for someone who had made very clear choices about their life; the way they wanted to live and the rules they were going to live by. It gave her this freedom and power. And then I thought about the other side; about people who did not make such choices; who fell from one thing to another, without any kind of control. On reflection, perhaps I was looking in a mirror at myself to some degree, and the way I had lived some parts of my life. I don't know. Others might be better to comment."

> (Interview with Michael Parkinson, 1987)

Packard came by the embryonic title for his next work very quickly. <u>Beggars and Choosers</u> seemed to sum up exactly what he wanted to talk about, one of the core polarities in the way people live their lives. The story revolves around a lead character - a woman, Scarlet Morrison - and charts her journey from being a 'beggar' to a 'chooser'; someone who is at first completely subject to others and the vagaries of life, and then, through a series of unpleasant and ultimately calamitous incidents, sees the light and makes the transition to a person in control. As he began to sketch it out, each of the characters in the story falls on one side of the line or the other - but Scarlet is the star. She is not like Simone - not French, not cosmopolitan, not linguistic or artistic - but Simone was undoubtedly the inspiration behind her.

-*-

As it turned out, the character models in <u>Beggars and Choosers</u> gave Packard the ideal opportunity to exorcise some ghosts. Although he would never go as far as confessing to undertaking his own analysis of his past behaviours (his 'mirrors' comment to Michael Parkinson in 1987 was as far as he ever went publicly), he used the framework of his new work to examine - tangentially of course - some of the key relationships from his own past. His focus rested most squarely on experiences with Stella and Pru particularly, and many people suggested that in the characters of Paul and Ralph, he had found a way of looking back on the relationship with his son.

Throughout the summer of 1981, Packard's work moved on from idea and sketches towards a full-blown plan and then in to hard drafting. The weekends when Simone was back in France proved to be the most productive times, and often he would write between five or then thousand words a day. He had never been so driven. Later he would refer to himself as being 'possessed'. He would also acknowledge that it was all Simone's doing; that without her inspiration, the book would never have seen the light of day.

As autumn broke, Simone's schedule began to change, and she started to spend slightly less time in London.

> "I knew it was coming of course. She had made her timetable completely transparent to me - of course she had! - but it was still difficult to deal with. Instead of four days a week with her, it was three days a week; and then the pattern of the days changed. Eventually, we arrived at a situation where it was only weekends that she was in London, most of her work then being the language teaching in Paris, mainly to big corporates. It was an adjustment she had tried to prepare me for with plenty of forewarning. We talked about it in advance. The fact that she knew it would be hard told me that she'd been through something similar before - or rather a man she had known had… I remember a really hard conversation one evening where we actually talked about calling it a day; deliberately avoiding any difficulty that might follow by

making a clean break. God knows I didn't want that, even though I could see some logic in it. I held on to knowing that May wasn't that far away. If only I could see it through the winter - because it was, fundamentally, about me."

(Interview with Michael Parkinson, 1987)

As their calendar changed, so did Packard's writing schedule. It became so that he didn't write at weekends any more, but stepped up his efforts during the week. His output increased, the focus on his novel helping him through the darkening weekdays. Peter Healy became more involved.

"Charles started sharing things with me; early drafts. I had never seen him so committed before. Some of the early material was a little weak in places, but as we got closer to Christmas - as he saw less of Simone, I suppose - so the volume and quality increased. It was almost as if the book was his substitute for her. He once told me (I think he might have been a little drunk - which was now a very rare occurrence) that writing the book was his only way of making love to her in her absence. I don't think that one was ever on record anywhere!"

Simone visited over Christmas and spent nearly a week in Hampstead with Charles and Mark (she continued to use her Ealing flat as some kind of base during most winter weekends when she was in London). The book took a back seat during those few precious days.

"I couldn't recall seeing my Father so giddy, ever. He was like a schoolboy! Simone was, of course, exceptional. Beautiful, charismatic, intelligent - French. It was all too plain to see what was so special and attractive about her. But there were times, a few, when I saw him looking at her as they sat quietly on the sofa watching a film or something. There was a profound sadness in his eyes. And once or twice, in hers too."

Packard had realised - and that Christmas had driven it home to him - that he simply could not continue the part-time relationship he and Simone had. During the summer it had worked, but now he saw her so infrequently, it was becoming impossible for him. She saw it too, of course; she had warned him what might happen. The final evening before she left to return to France there was a long conversation that lasted well into the night. Tears were shed on both sides.

> "Perhaps it was inevitable, I don't know. We talked about it for hours. I knew Simone's terms of course; I had always known them. And you know what? I never once resented her nor the position she was taking. I simply couldn't make it work; I missed her too much. And I didn't want to lose her. I didn't want to not

have her in my life, even as a friend. I would sacrifice our affair to keep our friendship. I would probably have sacrificed most things. Afterward, we spoke occasionally on the phone, and I would see her once a month or so when she was in London. When May came and her schedule reverted we saw a little more of each other - but now always as friends. In some deep, profound way, Simone became the best friend I ever had. I miss her terribly."

(Interview with Michael Parkinson, 1987)

In 1984, Simone Bouvier Dumoulin died in Paris from cancer. It had been diagnosed too late to allow any kind of meaningful treatment. Charles Packard attended her funeral in Amiens, the quiet Englishman who wept at the back of her family's local church.

At least she had seen, at the turn of 1983, the publication of <u>Beggars and Choosers</u>. She told Mark Packard that it was 'one of the most beautiful things I have ever read'. When he relayed this to his Father on his return from the funeral, Charles collapsed in a heap. Simone's view was widely shared. So much so that <u>Beggars and Choosers</u> - with its dedication 'to SBD with eternal love' - was nominated for the 1984 Booker Prize, and although it did not win, the critical acclaim that followed assured Charles Packard his permanent place on the literary stage.

Chapter Thirty Seven

Beggars and Choosers

There was hostility in his eyes. Sasha could see that. It was if he were having an internal conversation with himself and it was not going well. Sasha could also see what Belinda was trying to do, how she was wanting to calm Mike down; how she had only been trying to help him; how she was on his side. Sasha wanted to stop their argument and say all of this in a way that would make Mike understand and take that look from his eyes. But Sasha knew his English was too weak, not good enough to say the things he wanted to; and as he struggled, silently, to find the words, the heat increased.

"I didn't *mean* anything!" Belinda could see the look in Mike's eyes too. It was not the first time she had seen it, though never quite like this. In the beginning this passion had been one of the things that had attracted her to him, made him intriguing. It was a clear that there was a price to pay, a fee Mike would extract from her if she was to be associated with him. If Mike was to say, publicly, 'This is Belinda; she's with me', then he would have to be able to do so from a position of supreme confidence - which in his case, meant control. Although she was subjugated to him, she still wanted to be her own person; she still needed to be independent to some degree.

She had tried to help him by speaking to his boss, Richard. There must have been some misunderstanding, surely. Yes, Mike could be a little hot-headed from time-to-time, but he was good at what he did; one of the best. His sales figures were consistently right up there. How could Richard afford to lose him?

"I was only trying to help."

"Yes, Mike. Please." Sasha tried. "I heard some. It was good, what Bel said."

But whatever Belinda had said, Richard had heard something else, or filtered out what he had deemed unnecessary or that which didn't suit his purpose. He had confronted Mike with what appeared to be accusations from Belinda. Mike was irrational, uncontrollable; Mike wanted his own way; he was a Bully. There were no places for Bullies in Richard's team, that was for sure.

"Help? Help?!"

Mike took a step closer.

"Mike."

Even though Sasha could see the look in Mike's eyes, he could not read their intent, and when his arm flashed out from his side and caught Belinda squarely on the side of the head, he was almost as surprised as she was.

The force and the pain combined to tug the carpet from underneath her feet, and suddenly she was down, staring at the worn pile, the dining table's legs, Sasha's shoes with the disembodied voice coming from somewhere above it. "Bel, Bel!" it said, faintly. Then she saw the heels of Mike's shiny black brogues - the ones she had always hated but never had the courage to tell him - disappear through the door. Then Sasha's face, tears in his eyes, up close to hers. "Bastardo!" the face was saying. "Bastardo!"

-*-

Whether it was the incident with Claire or the point he had reached in his Father's history, but Mark suddenly found himself compelled to drive on and attempt to finish the biography as quickly as he could. If he had a sense that this motivation bore some parallel to the feelings his Father had when working on 'Beggars and Choosers' he could not say; if there were a link in terms of effect, then there most certainly was *not* one in terms of causality. Could Claire - if she had not misunderstood, and then as a consequence, rejected him - have come to be his Simone, the irresistible muse that drove some all-consuming force through his Father? He doubted it. Although he had not known Simone that well, he knew she and Claire were poles apart. The fact that what he felt for Claire was on altogether a different, more lowly and less noble plain, did not really register. Yet something had triggered this sudden imperative in him.

Its manifestation was immediate. The day after the squash match, he left the house early and arrived in Belsize Park while Beatrice and Simon were still having breakfast.

"My, you're early Dear!" Beatrice had exclaimed.

"I know. Sorry." He paused only briefly in the kitchen to secure a coffee. "I find myself possessed by an urgent need to crack on and get through this thing."

Beatrice noted the tone.

"You're near the end?"

"Yes. About six years out."

"Simone?" his Aunt prompted.

"Yes, just through that bit. And 'Beggars' has been published."

"I see." She smiled. It was a comment that felt as if it were laden with meaning, but Mark struggled to find any.

He worked all through the day and didn't get back to Hampstead until early evening when Julia was already back from work. They ate together, then Mark shut himself in his study for the last two hours of the day. It was a pattern repeated the next day and the one after that too. When Julia queried what he was doing, he gave her the same answer as he had Beatrice, though slightly embellished.

"I just need to get through it now, that's all. For some reason I just have to get to the end of the draft. Maybe I need a break for a bit - but the only way I'm going to really get that is by making it to the end first."

Julia had nodded. Mark could sense that she was pleased to see him so focused; perhaps she also knew that there was a line he needed to cross and quickly. He had expected her to challenge the dramatic change in approach, or the fact that he was so much out of the house - and would continue to be - until he was done. He wondered whether she might complain about seeing less of him if these most recent days were to be the measure of things for the next few weeks; but she did not. She seemed to him strangely inscrutable on the subject. It was unlike him not to be able to read her.

His shift of tack not only affected his hours and location of work, but also how he was going about the contents of the book. Perhaps it was related to him now being an increasingly valid actor in the scenarios he was painting, but he was beginning to find the words of others - his father especially - as being the most genuine way of telling the story. By utilising more of what had already been said, on record, and historical fact, it allowed him to withdraw a little from the need to interpret. It felt as if such an approach gave him license to tackle the end of the book in a more detached fashion, which was where he felt most comfortable. It also allowed him to pursue multiple threads through the final chapters simultaneously.

For obvious reasons, he had been unable to secure any material from Simone, but Peter Healy's input was now proving more valuable than ever.

"You gave me all the relevant letters you had, didn't you?" he asked Beatrice on the third morning of his new sprint for the line.

"I think so, yes. I assume you've used some of them?"

"Here and there, of course. I'm keen to avoid telling my story at the end - as I've said before - so including as much useful third party material as possible is critical.

"I see," she said, an echo from two days previously. This time Mark felt a shadow pass over her.

"Would you do me a favour and just check again, Aunt?"

"In case I missed any?"

"You don't mind?"

"I'll have another rummage over the weekend."

Up in the study, Mark flicked on his computer and waited. Having moved the mirror further into a corner the previous day, it was less obtrusive if he should swivel in his chair to talk to his Aunt or Uncle when they came in. Even so, he could still feel its presence.

Absent-mindedly, he watched the screen flick into life; an initial glow that was still, somehow, black, then followed by a burst of Microsoft blue before the log-in screen. Although no-one else used his computer (he wasn't even sure if Simon would know how!), he always protected his data. It was a habit he had acquired after he had lost some draft material during his post-University early professional years, only to find his words materialising, rejigged, in a rival publication about a week after they had gone missing. Someone had taken his outline and then played with the text, the final copy positing an argument that was not one he could subscribe to, and with words that were no longer his own. It was only this unwillingness to be associated with something unworthy of him, that prevented him from launching some kind of complaint.

On the desk in front of him was a plain buff folder containing the photos on his 'long list' for inclusion in the book. He had pulled it from the shelf yesterday and opened it again now. It was part of his ritual to regularly sift through the images, his logic being that the ones he became more and more comfortable with would be the ones that he should include; those that, even after many reviews, he was still unsure of, would never see the light of day. The short-list for inclusion was still very small.

As he worked through them, he was brought up short by a picture of Lydia. Not only was this entirely out of place - what did she have to do with his Father's history?! - but he couldn't remember seeing it previously. She was sitting on a low wall outside the Museum and Art Gallery in Birmingham city centre. She looked young and happy. Mark tried to recall when the photo might have been taken, probably during their first few months together, though he struggled to place the event precisely. She did appear *very* young. It was a long time ago, obviously, and Mark knew that the mind played tricks - but even so, he struggled to recall her like this.

Perhaps that was in part because of the last image he had of her - the last real image, captured in the flesh with his own eyes - was of a still young woman, but older, and much less happy. It had been perhaps three months after his decision to move on. They had met in Stratford - he recalled that he had wanted it to be on neutral territory where the final die was cast - near the canal basin outside the theatre. Their contact had dwindled significantly, though there had been no formal closure by either of them. As far as Mark could see, Lydia was still clinging to something; still hopeful that, whatever 'phase' Mark was gong through, he would come out the other side and things would return to normal. His ambition that she would be able to see through the situation, interpret it, and move on without him needing to do anything, had remained unfulfilled. So much so that the only option was for him to be slightly more decisive, and to take the action that he had wished to avoid.

As she walked towards him, he knew that the damage had been done. She looked haunted - though how much was only apparent when she was just a few feet from him - and all the bounce and spark had gone out of her step, her eyes. The complexion that had boasted health, vitality - and almost Mediterranean splendour - now looked sallow, unhealthy, worn out.

"I know why we're here," she had said, her first - and last - words that day, "and yet I still came. I just wanted to see your face when you said it."

"Said what?"

If he had, in any way, hoped for a clean break, to remain friends, then he was to be profoundly disappointed. His actions had already - and quite clearly - left their mark on her. He had tried to be kind (at least that was how he remembered it) and soften the disappointment of telling her he could not see her again. But even as he spoke he could see that the blow had already been struck - and some time ago - and that Lydia was still reeling from it. He had never realised how much affection she had held for him.

He watched her from where he sat when she turned and walked away, back towards the canal basin, and then left in the direction of the town. He lost sight of her once she had reached the bridge and the main road, his last glimpse being of her in profile waiting under a red man at the pedestrian crossing. She hadn't once looked back. For a few seconds longer he allowed his eyes to rest on the traffic lights, the illuminated men switching from red to green and back three times before he stood up. The basin was quiet, a barge just emerging from under the same bridge, its helmsman ducking down as low as they could to avoid decapitation. Slowly the narrow boat emerged into the sunlight and then edged into a mooring space just a few yards in front of him. A young man leapt from the bow with a rope which he then deftly wrapped around a small bollard as the craft cut its engine and edged against its berth.

How had he felt, just at that moment? He could imagine himself to be that young man with the rope, a proficient waterways sailor handling a seventy-two foot craft through the narrowest of channels; but he would have expected something else, just at that precise moment. He had just watched Lydia walk out of his life - in a way, saying goodbye to his first real partner - so surely there must have been something both immediate and residual? As his screen hummed almost inaudibly back at him, Mark thought of his Father - and of his Father with Pru, or Stella, or Constantina. What was there in terms of feeling as an epilogue in those cases? Something? Nothing? Mark believed he knew the answers well enough, after all he had been writing about them! Were any of these parallels with he and Lydia? How would his Father have felt if it had been he who had just closed things off with Lydia? Probably relieved, or overcome with a desire to get drunk. At least Mark knew the latter did not apply to him.

As he tried to return his attention to his work, an email alert flashed on his desktop. He was not normally one to allow intrusions, but as he had yet to start in earnest, he clicked on his email programme. At the top of his Inbox was an item from Maxine. Immediately he felt a little brighter. Opening the missive, he read:

"Hi there! Are you around tomorrow? Need to see you. Can you make 3? Near the bandstand in Hyde Park? I won't have much time, sorry."

He had planned another full day on the book, but her words 'Need to see you' shouted at him. He hadn't seen Maxine for a week now. She had been busy in the final stages of preparing for the launch of a new show, she said, and so her time was precious. Even thirty minutes with her would feel like the injection of a stimulant to him; how could he refuse, even if it meant cutting his working day a little short?

Closing his email, he tried to focus once again. 'Beggars and Choosers' rested on the desk beside his keyboard. In its own way it was a symbol that he was on the last lap.

Beggars and Choosers

She had seen the idea on television. She couldn't remember whose idea it was or which programme it had been on, but it returned to her as she sat that Friday evening nursing both a bruise and a glass of wine, sitting alone in her so small flat staring at nothing in particular.

The idea was a simple one. On a single sheet of paper - A3 had been recommended - you make a collage of your life; pictures of things that represented how you were living: photos of your car, the town you lived in, something to represent your job, your clothes, what you did in your spare time; anything you could think of. It was important, she remembered, that you did this in one go, a single concerted effort to create a snapshot of how you were living. And then, they had said, you put your sheet away for a while - at least overnight - and then come back to it fresh, and see how you felt about it.

"If it's perfect," she recalled the presenter saying with a deep rouge smile and the studio lights glinting off her jewellery, "then that's wonderful. If not, then you do the same thing again. Take a large sheet of paper and make another collage, this time representing all the same things, but how you would *like* your life to be. So, change your car, your clothes, your house. Then you leave that picture aside for 24 hours before you look at it again. See what reaction you have. If it is different - and for most people it will be! - then look at the two images side by side. At that point you have to decide what you are going to do about it."

Of course Belinda couldn't be certain those were the presenter's exact words. In fact she was sure they would not have been. But it was enough to see her, on Saturday morning, in town buying A3 paper, glue, and magazines of various kinds: clothes, cars, property, holidays, lifestyle. When she got back to her flat she made herself some tea and then spent the next two and a half hours bent over her small dining table, flicking through pages, snipping and glueing. Resisting the temptation to study her collage after lunch was difficult, so she took the paper and placed it on the top of her wardrobe, then had lunch and went back into town. It nagged at her all day. The more she thought about it, the more the images seemed to fade from her mind. She couldn't recall which pictures of shoes or clothes she had chosen; which picture of the town square. Was there a picture of the town square?

When she woke in the morning, after an uneven sleep, she wanted to immediately take the picture down, but she fought to be disciplined, and had breakfast, showered, dressed. By the time ten o'clock came (the time she had agreed with herself) she was calmer, ready. She took the sheet, laid it on the table, and stood looking down on it.

The shock was incredible. She hated it. She hated almost everything about it. The nausea was powerful, almost overwhelming. There was almost nothing there she liked. Her car was horrible, the town was horrible; the images of clothes were of clothes that looked like they should belong to someone else. The town looked boring. Even the holiday shots, cut from brochures of the last two places she had been to, were drab and uninspiring. And in the middle, a picture of Mike.

She wanted to tear up the sheet. To cut it. Burn it. She felt angry, violent - towards her collage and towards herself. The page represented failure, defeat. It wasn't a picture of her, the true Belinda; it was a picture of what she had become. And then she cried.

The smiling, rouged, glittering presenter had not warned her of this. But Belinda knew that wasn't what rouged and glittery presenters did. At least she had told her what to do next though. Once she had finished crying and made another cup of tea, she cleared the table, retrieved the same magazines and set about the second collage - the one she wanted to see. It was important, she had been told, to use the same sources; the same magazines and newspapers. It was important to try and keep the balance; so if there had been two photographs of cars on the first sheet, there should be two on the second. Belinda worked to that rule as religiously as she could. The one key difference she knew already: there would be no picture of Mike on the second.

By lunchtime she was done. She placed both sheets back on top of the wardrobe and made herself some lunch. Then, to kill time, she went back into town and spent the afternoon in the cinema. She hadn't cared what she watched. Anything was fine as long as it busied her mind.

She had decided that she wasn't going to wait until Monday morning for the final review. Somehow that would be too late. And she knew what to expect after her early morning shock. Monday was a work day; it would be difficult, too late. She wouldn't have time to compare before she set off, and if she left it until she returned from work, it would trouble her all day. No; she would compare that evening.

Belinda returned from the cinema and made her tea. Then she listened to the 'Top 40' on the radio as she always did on a Sunday evening. After that, she made coffee. And then she went to the wardrobe.

The pictures on the table looked like they belonged to two different people. They were showing two completely different lives. One was a life of dull colours, defeat and boredom; the other, vibrant and colourful and exciting. She wasn't surprised, of course. There was no way she should have been. But the magnitude of the difference staggered her. There was her dull blue Ford; and there the perky little Alfa Romeo she'd always wanted. There, shoes were black and brown; here, they were red and vibrant. There was a cathedral and foreign shops; here a beach and a glorious sunset. She knew they were just things cut out and stuck on a page, but they still made her cry. For the second time.

And then the words of the presenter came back to her. The final step. Having come this far. She had to 'decide what you are going to do about it'. It was simple. Did she want to carry on living in that first life? That was the initial question Belinda asked herself. The answer was obvious, but it was only part of the answer. Did she want the second life? Did she want to strive to achieve that life? Was she prepared to make the changes, the choices, to move from the first page to the second?

There were some easy things to focus on to help. The car was one. She could fix that. She could sell her Ford and go looking for an Alfa. That was simple. Did she want to do that? She could think about her next holiday and go and book something; somewhere with a beach and a sunset. What was stopping her?

The answers were easy. She *did* want to do those things. And there was nothing stopping her. It was her life. She could change the picture into anything she wanted. And the starting place was obvious. She looked at her first sheet. Taking a felt-tipped pen, she drew a line through the photograph of Mike. She would start there.

-*-

When he returned to Hampstead that evening, the house was empty. There was a note on the hall table from Julia saying she had gone to Laura's for an 'emergency session' about wedding arrangements. As she wasn't working the following day, it was likely she would stay over.

It was an absence that failed to trouble him. His head was spinning with the book. Once he had finally managed to get into the groove, he had been able to cover a lot of ground; indeed, he had been so absorbed in sifting and sorting quotations and extracts, that he had failed to register the return of Beatrice and Simon until he found his Aunt standing in the doorway of his room.

"Is that the time?" he said, checking his watch.

"Things going well?" she asked.

"I seem to be getting through it," he confirmed, "though I'm a little bit all over the place just at the minute. You know, collecting stuff for the last chapters simultaneously. Not my normal approach, juggling like this, but that's how it seems to have fallen out."

"No missing pieces?"

It seemed a strange question. Mark looked at her standing in the doorway, the one consistent female role model in his entire life. She had been a rock - continued to be a rock - but, just now, she appeared a little older, a little more fragile. He had, he supposed, taken her fore granted for far too long.

"I don't think so. But then, you don't know what you don't know - I think that's what you're supposed to say, isn't it?"

She smiled at his joke.

"I'm going to have that final rummage I promised you - probably tomorrow evening. Just in case. Will that be all right?"

"Perfect."

Mark found a pizza in the freezer which he threw in the oven, making himself some salad as it cooked. There was a bottle of wine open in the fridge and he poured himself a glass while he was waiting. When everything was ready, he took it into the lounge and sat on the sofa and ate in front of the television. This was a rare treat, and reminded him of those days when it was just he and his Father in the house - mainly when he was on his own, his Father being out at some event or meeting or assignation. It was a feeling of some freedom, and as he bit into the pizza (picking it up with his fingers!), he was reminded of many, many evenings spent alone either here or in Warwick. There was some comfort in it.

If he had intended to do some work in his study after supper he let it slip, becoming engrossed in what was beginning to look like a rather dated James Bond adventure. Sean Connery was not his view of the ideal man in any sense - though he knew his Father had liked the films - but for where he was on this particular evening, sitting alone in his house, drinking wine, it was the perfect accompaniment to, and means of, doing absolutely nothing.

Although he had gone to bed tired and a little earlier than usual, Mark had not slept well, and at breakfast he was still feeling sluggish. Perhaps he had drunk a glass or two of wine too many; that had to be it. Certainly, 007 was not the cause for disturbed slumber as the spy failed to make any appearance at all in his dreams. At least he was not going to work a full day on the book today - which felt good - and he was going to see Maxine later - which felt better.

In spite of himself, he was in Belsize Park early again. He had written Julia a short note and left it on the hall table in exactly the same spot as her own had been; it simply told her when he expected to be back. As he had locked the door and walked to his car he reflected that perhaps he should have called her the previous evening, but then she had not called him either, so that was probably okay. Once again, Mark caught his Aunt and Uncle at the tail-end of their breakfast, and spent a few minutes drinking coffee with them before he retreated to his room. Despite a vague air of freshness suggesting that Beatrice had been in the previous evening hoovering and tidying, everything remained untouched on his desk.

He worked fitfully until lunchtime, harvesting quotes in much the same way as he went about picture selection, drafting these into their likely final resting places in the text. If he were to compare that activity with his usual approach, it occurred to him that he was behaving more like an archeologist than an author; he was uncovering and laying bare, rather than stitching together and weaving something new. It was an interesting sensation - and one which he was comfortable enough with, if only because he knew the weaving and stitching was still to come. After lunch Mark achieved little, his time limited and his mind beginning to stray towards central London.

The weather was bright enough. As he walked from the tube station at Hyde Park Corner into the park and towards the Serpentine, Mark could still see some evidence of the rain that had fallen overnight; the paths were dry except for the occasional small puddle in a dip or in a runnel against the grass verge. Turning off the main path as the bandstand came into view, he cut across the grass, water spots immediately showing on his shoes; it was wetter than he had expected.

Approaching the bandstand, Mark could see that around half the benches nearby were occupied. He was early enough, but rather than just take the nearest one, he started to walk round the stand just to make sure Maxine was not already there. When he saw her, he was surprised. She was sitting, tucked up in a dark green coat, perched on the end of a bench, a bag - larger than a handbag - clutched at her side. She looked somehow alone. As he walked towards her, she glanced in his direction and offered the slightest of waves.

"Hi," he said as he reached her. He had expected her to stand up, to show some animation at his approach, but she just offered him a minimal smile and he was forced to bend and kiss her forehead before he sat next to her. She did not move the bag, so it remained between them.

"You're early," he said brightly and unnecessarily. "That's normally my trick!"

"I don't have much time, I'm afraid. We're over-running on something and I have to get back as soon as I can."

"But you just had to see me," he laughed.

"Yes, I just had to see you. But not in the way you think."

She looked away from him and over to the bandstand. The smile had gone from her face, coincident with a stray cloud that momentarily darkened the park. Mark waited, an uneasy feeling beginning to rise from somewhere.

"Look," she said suddenly and in a rush, her voice lacking the self-confidence it normally carried in spades, "I mean, you've probably been having the same thoughts as me. I'd be a bit surprised if you hadn't, to be honest. But it looks like I'm the one to say it first."

"Say what?"

There was a look of shock and surprise in her eyes as she turned her head towards him again.

"You haven't see it coming have you? Shit!"

"Seen what coming, Max? I haven't seen you for days now; that's all I haven't seen. I don't know what you're on about."

"Us, Mark. Us. It's over; finished. Haven't you seen that coming? Haven't you felt that? Please tell me you have." There was begging in her voice, her eyes; her hands tightened their grip on the bag. She shivered.

"Over? No. I don't know what you mean, 'over'. How can it be? What's gone wrong?"

"Wrong? Nothing's gone wrong, not in one sense. We've gotten on really well. Too well. Maybe its me, I don't know. But we've got to a point - for me anyway - where there's a decision to be made. Where I have to make a decision." She paused. "Help me here, Mark!"

He was stunned and confused. Their relationship had been going so well for him. He could relax with her, enjoy himself. There were no constraints, nothing to bind him.

"Look," she tried again. "I said once that I wasn't going to try and steal you away from Julia, didn't I? Well, we've reached a point - *I've* reached a point - where there *has* to be a next step. I've become too fond of you for there not to be, Mark. Don't you see? Now I either *have* to try and steal you away from Julia, or give you up. I have no other option. I can't carry on in any other way."

"But isn't it going great? I mean, aren't we having fun? Isn't it fun?"

"Yes, we've had fun. But now that's not enough; not for me. I need to protect myself, Mark. If we were to carry on, I'd need you to myself. I'd have to try and take you away from Julia. I'd *have* to. And I might lose. And I can't afford to take that risk. I don't want to take that risk. I hadn't planned for this to happen; hadn't expected it. It was 'fun', at first. And then something more. I wasn't ready for that. I have to get control back. And that means I have to give you up. We have to end it."

"But that's crazy..."

"Crazy to you, maybe," she stood up at this point, anger suddenly in her voice, "but not to me, Mark. Maybe I've changed, who knows, but I'm beyond 'fun' now. And I don't want to get hurt."

There was a pause; his mind was reeling. He had never seen this coming.

"What can I do, Max? Tell me."

"Do? Nothing. You could promise me that you'll give up Julia for me; that's one thing you could do. But I don't know if I could believe you if you did; not because you didn't mean it, but because it wasn't your idea. Because it would be something I'd forced you into. And later; later, you would resent it; resent me." She paused. "Would you give up Julia? Now? This minute?"

"I..."

She started walking away from him. He rose.

"Stop! Stay there. Don't follow me, Mark. Don't shout out. Don't call me tomorrow. Don't come to my house. Do you understand? Don't you see how hard this is for me? How difficult? If you have an ounce of decency and feeling for me, then let me go and be miserable for a while, before I jump on the merry-go-round again. Don't think about it. Don't change your mind. Don't do anything."

Paralysed, he did exactly as Maxine told him; he stood and watched. She walked around the bandstand and then back towards Rotten Row and then in the direction of Apsley House. Her green coat stood out, made her easy to follow. For those first few seconds, Mark expected her to turn, to run back towards him, to say that it had all been a mistake, that she had been wrong, foolish. But she just kept on walking. He lost sight of her after a short while, then sat again and remained fixed, still like a statue. What was he supposed to do now? She had told him all the things that she did not want him to do, but nothing that he should do. Even as the sun broke through the clouds again, Mark felt totally alone. Sooner or later he would need to force himself into motion, and return to Hampstead.

Chapter Thirty Eight

It was two hours later when Mark turned the key and walked into the house. The note he had left was still on the hall table, but unfolded. On the floor, a suitcase; the one she had taken to Laura's, obviously. He couldn't hear Julia, but knew she had been in and sensed she was there still. He had walked slowly through the park after Maxine had left him, a wide circuitous route that eventually saw him regaining the tube at Queensway. It was a walk that, in spite of all his efforts to reevaluate them, brought no further understanding of Maxine's words. It was not that he failed to comprehend them - their literalness - but rather the motivation that lay behind them. He could see no reason why he and Maxine should not carry on as they were. It was, as far as he could tell, an arrangement that was working perfectly well for both of them; after all, he was imposing no constraints upon her, making no demands. She was free to see him as often as she chose. Or as little. He did not impinge on her career, nor she on his. It was, in many ways, perfect.

The need for change; that was what perplexed him. He tried to fit her words into other characters - both real and fictional - to see if he could make any greater sense of them if spoken by someone else; but he failed there too. His range of vision simply deserted him. All he had after his meanderings both through the park and through his mind, was the image of Maxine telling him it was over and to 'do' nothing. Even as he approached the house, his mind was still processing the bare facts of the event - the history of it. As ever, the facts he had no issue with, it was the interpretation that was the problem.

Mark walked along the hall and to the threshold of the kitchen. At the table, Julia sat cradling a mug, steam rising slowly from it. She was staring into space, frozen, mind elsewhere; so much so, that she was clearly unaware of his presence. He stopped and stared at her. Maxine's words echoed back to him. 'Would you give up Julia? Now? This minute?' He knew that it was the biggest question Maxine had ever asked him - and the one he had singularly failed to answer. Why was that? As he stared into the kitchen, he tried to replay the scene yet again, to alter the outcome, to try and predict what his answer should have been. Either 'Yes' or 'No' would have been better than the fumbling hesitation he had managed.

And if she had been standing behind him now, right there in the hallway, and whispered that same question in his ear - 'Would you give up Julia? Now? This minute?' - how would he have answered her? The Julia he saw before him now had been, in many ways, his rock; had supported him when things had been a little difficult - like with Congreave - and had encouraged him when he'd had doubts about the book. She had been his lover, his friend, his companion on holidays, at others' weddings, at funerals, at parties. Mark felt a different question assail him. 'And now?' the question came; 'And now?'. Somehow he was conscious he was using the past tense: she 'had' been his lover. What did that mean? 'Would you give up Julia? Now? This minute?' He wanted to answer the question, desperately so - but not for Maxine (that was too late now), but for himself.

She suddenly shook herself from her reverie and turned to look at him. Her eyes were red.

"What's wrong?" he asked as he stepped into the room, heading towards the kettle. He suddenly needed a drink.

"Why have you been lying to me, Mark?"

He stopped, surprised. This was not something he had expected. More than that, it was not something he was ready for. He was off-guard, weakened.

"What? Sorry?"" His mind tried to sift through mountains of data and reflections to see if he could settle on something relevant. An idea came to him. "Not the squash club again? Not the ladders?"

"Yes. I mean, no." She seemed confused. "That's part of it. But what about Claire, Mark? What about Claire?"

Mark had been certain that Claire would say nothing, convinced that it was not in her interest to make public his advance. Had she done so? He waited.

"She told me what you did. She told me."

So now he knew. The scene on the squash court had, he finally concluded, not reflected well on either of them. Perhaps for his behaviour then, and for her part leading up to it. That assessment had been his default defence against wider publication of the event.

"What did she say, Julia?"

"That you made a pass at her. Yesterday. At the club."

"There was a misunderstanding, that's all." He tried to sound confident, and moved towards the kettle again as if his very action would trivialise Claire's statement and dismiss the whole thing. And part of him was convinced that it had been just that. Mark expected Claire, over time, to reflect on it and - especially contrite over her own violent actions - realise that she had made a terrible mistake. Not keeping quiet destroyed any possibility of reversal from her perspective.

"It didn't sound like a misunderstanding; not the way she told it to me." Julia paused. "How's your arm, by the way? She said she hit you pretty hard."

He had largely forgotten about his arm. He had rubbed ibuprofen gel on it when he had returned home and then bandaged it. This morning it had throbbed a little, but felt better. It had slipped his mind completely since then, but now, on cue, it started to hurt again.

"She didn't mean to. It was an accident."

"She was defending herself! That's what she told me. Defending herself from you!"

He felt cornered. He said nothing, metaphorically trying to cover up and wait for the punches to stop.

"But that's not the half of it, Mark. What about Maxine?"

It was as if he had been set up by a series of weakening jabs - first in the park and now in his own kitchen - but here came the massive body blow. He felt the wind leave him.

"Maxine?" he whispered, breathless.

"Yes, that little tart you left the awards ceremony with and who you've been screwing ever since! You complete bastard!" Still holding the mug fiercely, Julia rested it on the table. Mark, alert now, watched it intently, expecting it to suddenly be launched towards him. "Claire saw you get into a taxi with her after the dinner."

"Claire?" So it had been her with Congreave!

"Simon corroborated the story."

"Simon?!" Mark was stunned. "He was too pissed to know what he saw."

"He saw you, Mark. Just like others have seen you when you think you've been oh so clever and oh so discrete. At the Tate Gallery, maybe? Down by the river?" She was beginning to lose the composure she had fought so hard to hold on to. Tears were coming again. "Why Mark, why? What's happened to us, to you? What's changed? Ever since you've been writing that damned book about your Father you've become a different person..."

"Now wait..." he tried to interject.

"It's almost as if you're trying to be like him. Or like he's infecting you. I don't know you any more Mark. And I don't think I want to."

'Would you give up Julia? Now? This minute?' And Mark knew now that his answer would be 'yes'. Should have been 'yes'. But it was too late. He struggled to know how to defend himself and could think of nothing. She had drawn parallels with his Father. What would Charles Packard have done in this situation? His mind raced. It was clearly his turn. Julia was waiting for him. He had to say something. He thought about when Charles had left Mary and then gone back to her. Was there experience there he could use? He thought of his Father's honesty - especially when he spoke, many years later to Bragg and Parkinson.

"I'm an idiot," he said slowly, trying out the words, the play of being honest, contrite. He wasn't sure if that was how he truly felt, but it was the only gambit he had. "Claire was a misunderstanding, I swear. But Maxine… You're right. I give up. I don't know why. You've been brilliant. I shouldn't have. I mean, I didn't plan to. Or want to. Maybe I was drunk or something? It was a mistake. I'm sorry, Julia. I'm so sorry. But it's over; finished. I swear it is. I'm never going to see her again."

"I don't believe you," she cut in. "I don't fucking believe you! Why should I? You've lied to me for weeks. Weeks! And now you're trying to wriggle out of it."

"I'm not! I won't see her again because she doesn't want to see me any more."

Julia rose, her hands still on the mug.

"And she's not the only one. I'm leaving you, Mark. I talked it through with Laura last night - and Claire too. I have no other option. You've hurt me. Made me feel a fool. Look a fool. You've been using me. You've been so dishonest. I can never trust you again. Never. No second chances. You've used them all up."

It was at that point she launched the mug at him.

He saw it just in time to duck, but it still managed to catch the top of his head before it crashed into the wall and shatter. He watched the pieces fall around him, then turned to see Julia run into the hall and grab the suitcase. Mark knew then that the case was not from the previous night but had been prepared for this sequence of events. The slamming of the front door felt like the knock-out blow.

-*-

Everything fell into place for Charles Packard during the first half of 1984. <u>Beggars and Choosers</u>, a Booker runner-up, sold well and secured his future, both financially and reputationally. Having verged on becoming persona non grata, the book returned him to the fold.

"<u>Beggars</u> did brilliantly well for us at MacMillan. Of course, it wasn't just that it was a wonderfully crafted work, there were other factors. The Booker run was fantastic of course - just a shame <u>Hotel de Lac</u> beat us - but more significant in many ways was that there was a personal story behind it. Although Belinda wasn't Simone, Charles' debt to her was evident. And the public loved that connection, the humanity of it. He handled it all remarkably well; it could have so easily gone wrong."

Peter Healy tried to protect Packard as much as he could during those first six months of the year. Events at which Packard was present were stage-managed as much as possible, interviews carefully controlled. Healy managed to get Packard some meaningful television exposure for the first time, most noticeably Charles' interviews with Melvyn Bragg on 'The South Bank Show', and Michael Parkinson on 'Parkinson'. They were both interviewers Packard could relate to, with a certain northern grit that they never lost. That they had worked hard from unprivileged positions to gain their success resonated with Packard who, because of the connection he felt (real or imagined), was never in awe of either of them.

> "I loved talking to Michael and Melvyn. There was something - I don't know - rudimentary about them. Their interviews were never a chore; never. Oh they were difficult at times; they had a job to do, of course. But they were always gentlemen about it. I knew the questions they would ask - the difficult ones - so I was never taken off-guard, but there was a compassion and understanding about them that made it easy. Although there were cameras and an audience and things, sometimes it felt as if it were just the two of us having a chat in a pub."
>
> (Interview with Russell Harty, 1988)

In spite of the success of 1984, it was still a difficult year for Packard. Simone's death was not only fresh, he was constantly reminded of her. People would talk about her in the context of the book, or about her in the context of his life.

> "It was hard. I still hadn't quite come to terms with losing her - maybe I still haven't. The only way I managed to get through it? I think I tried to create two different versions of her: there was the one I talked about in interviews and things, and the one that

remained private and mine. I guess I managed to keep a distance between the two, and that saved me - and saved my memory of her. When people asked me questions, I tried to stick to historical fact; you know, things that happened. All my feelings - my real feelings - were kept for the second Simone, locked up tight, away from the public."

(Interview with Michael Parkinson, 1987)

Packard still needed some kind of safety valve to protect him, of course; something that would allow him to be open and intimate outside of the public gaze on those rare occasions when he needed to. Peter Healy proved an occasional foil for this, but Packard began to turn more and more to his son, Mark. They would sit - hesitantly at first - and talk about Simone.

> "Initially it was all factual stuff. I mean, that was Mark's profession, after all. But after a while, we'd talk for longer and I'd loosen up a little, I suppose. I'm sure I told him things I'd never tell anyone else. He helped me, not only to order Simone's life from a historical perspective, but if I had any emotional ghosts to exorcise - and I don't think I did - then I would have done so. But it became more than that. We'd never been close, Mark and I. Talking as we did started to bring us back together. Even after she was gone, Simone became a bridge, if you like. It must have worked because Mark began to spend more time back in the house. We are more like an old married couple now than ever before!"

(Interview with Michael Parkinson, 1988)

The other things that these Father and Son conversations began to do was to provide Packard with a means of looking back further than Simone and deeper into his past. They allowed him to be reflective. He had a sounding board, someone with whom he could not only explore his factual history - and who had been close enough on many occasions to actually pass meaningful comment - but also a mechanism that allowed him to be honest with himself about what had happened.

> "It was remarkable really. Another of Simone's legacies; something else she gave me. I found I was able to peel back layers of myself, uncovering things that I knew and felt but hadn't realised that I'd known or felt. You choose the metaphor. But it was as if I was suddenly free to be honest with myself, and for the first time. Having Mark there to listen was a catalyst and

404

enabler, of course, but the key thing for me was that something had been unlocked; something deep inside me."

(Interview with Michael Parkinson, 1988)

Packard's new-found freedom to delve honestly into his past started to bare fruit during the last summer of that year. His conversations with Mark had taken him so far, but not - he realised - as far as he needed or wanted to go. If Simone had inadvertently created a platform for him from which to view his life, then he needed a mechanism with which to do so. He consulted Healy.

"Charles' notion was a simple one. He felt that he had reached a point where he could look back on his life in an open and honest way. He expressed a desire to record what he had done and not done. The medium he should choose was obvious. In August of 1984 he came to me with a few pages of something for my opinion. To be honest, in many ways it was unlike anything he had produced previously, and I struggled to categorise it. Of course, Charles wasn't concerned with that; he just wanted to know if it was any good."

> "I remember Peter wanted to call it something. I suppose that's just the way publishers work. If they can label something then it makes life easier for them in terms of, I don't know, style, format, content, marketing and so forth. But I was adamant that, although this was me looking back, it wasn't an autobiography. And it wasn't going to be written as one. All the characters were fictitious; one step removed from me. Because of that - and because it was too fragmented and incoherent - it was impossible for it to 'fit' there. I didn't want it to be an autobiography either. I'd always felt that was what you did when you didn't have anything else to say, or when you'd run out of ideas. Which I hadn't."

(Interview with Melvyn Bragg, 1986)

Packard was a little tentative and uncertain about how to approach <u>Scenes From A Life</u>. Internally, he knew what he wanted to do and needed to produce, but the mechanism stressed him. He and Mark talked about it during that summer.

"From what I could see, Dad wanted to explore himself, and do so in an intimate way. But he wanted to be outside of it, somehow. Hence his notion that it wasn't an autobiography. He struggled with approach really. I guess when he'd tackled his novels, he had free rein to go where the

405

story took him; but this time he didn't. There were lots of fixed points along the way."

> "Mark helped me in the sense that he provided a way for me to structure the work. He suggested that I tackle it historically, if you like: to take it, in sequence, a year at a time - or, as it turned out, more like a person at a time. There was a link throughout - the absent 'me' - but no single narrator. Does that make sense? It was as if I'd taken the mirror I'd wanted to look into, but broke it before I did so. There were lots of fragmented, diverse images, all pointing in a slightly different directions, yet all within the same frame… Actually, I quite like that; I might use it later!"
>
> (Interview with Melvyn Bragg, 1986)

Packard continued to work on <u>Scenes From A Life</u> during the rest of 1984 and for most of the following year, before delivering what was intended to be his final draft in the early autumn of 1985. He had wanted it to be ready in time for Simone's birthday, but final editing and late changes made him miss his target.

"I know Charles wasn't happy with us for pushing him on one or two things. He'd set himself this deadline which I suppose we made him miss. Yet he never showed his displeasure in the way he might have previously. He knew we were trying to get the best book we could on the shelves. I wanted to suggest to him that doing so would be the best tribute to all those he was writing about, including Simone. Although he never said anything, I'm pretty sure he could see that too."

MacMillan missed their key Christmas deadlines too, and the book was eventually published in February 1986. The sleeve made free with references to Packard's previous works, especially <u>Beggars and Choosers</u>, and was - for the first time - able to add labels like 'Booker Prize nominated', 'renowned', and 'critically acclaimed'. They also put out the paperback edition at the same time as the much more limited run hardback.

> "One of the other reasons we were late was that I wanted one or two people who were essentially *in* the book to be comfortable with it before I went out. Peter said it wasn't necessary, but I felt strongly about it. Some of the most important people - Simone and Mary - couldn't comment obviously, and there were a few I couldn't give a damn about, but one or two others I wanted to be sure were comfortable with the thing before it hit the shops."
>
> (Interview with Melvyn Bragg, 1986)

Neither Packard nor Healy ever disclosed who was on that shortlist. Even Mark, who surprisingly did not get to see a pre-release copy, was not aware who had that privilege.

-*-

Scenes From A Life

I had expected to wake up alone. That is, although I had given it no thought, it had not occurred to me that it would be otherwise. Actually, in some respects, just waking up was in itself some kind of victory to be celebrated. Given a certain combination of history and circumstance, one has to be grateful for 'small mercies' as they say, and waking up at all could quite easily fall into that category.

There had been a song. I remembered that much. There was no tune playing across my mind as I opened my eyes; no lingering echo to give any clue. There had been a meeting; I knew that of course. I could recall the context, the vague too-ing and fro-ing of debate and argument. There had been an unspoken consensus that the six of us had needed to reach agreement, and then, according to convention, success was celebrated in a bar, then in a restaurant, and finally – somehow magically almost – on the private dance floor of the small, intimate, out-of-the-way restaurant that we had managed to stumble upon. Hence the music.

And now, as I tried to force my Betamax memory into rewind, I was unsure that 'stumble' was correct. It might have been planned all along. I was not responsible for any of the organisation; I had just gone along for the ride, offering small dimes of insight where I could, trying to help reach the collective resolution. Thus the meeting had closed with handshakes, beer, wine, good food, and – in my case, at least – sudden, unexpected, involuntary (or voluntary!), passionate, climactic sex.

Convinced, in that small instant between waking and conscious thought, of an absence of solitude, I forced my eyes open to stare at the ceiling above me. And with my eyes, my ears opened too, and I listened, expecting to hear something; breathing, the rustle of sheets, perhaps a sound elsewhere. But there was nothing. I tried closing my eyes but leaving my ears open, in case there had been a synaptic clash somewhere in my brain. I forced all my sensory powers into listening and sought out – something. Perhaps a tap running in the bathroom, china in the kitchen. Anything.

I had expected to wake up alone – and now I had.

'It's me.'

'Whoa! Well what happened to you?!'

'That's what I'd like to know.' I paused. 'I was wondering if you could fill in the blanks for me...'

Jim laughed. Well, who wouldn't have?

'Sorry Pal, I can only tell you what I saw. Can't help you with after you left.'

'OK, well start there. Did I leave alone?'

He laughed again.

'You kidding me?! You two were glued together! There was no way you weren't going to leave that way.'

'But did you see us? I mean, did you actually see me leave?'

'Christ, you are in a bad way! Why do you ask?'

'Jim...'

'OK. You both got into a taxi at the same time as the rest of us. No idea where you asked to go. We assumed your place or hers. Where are you?'

'My place.'

'And?'

'And I'm alone.'

There was a moment's stillness before he spoke again. Still nothing to be heard other than the faintness of Jim's breathing.

'I'm not sure if that's a good thing or a bad thing. And from the sound of your voice, I'm not sure you do too.'

'Jim, who was she...?'

Chapter Thirty Nine

"You know he gave me one of those fabled draft copies to read before it was published?"

Beatrice had appeared in Mark's study to tell him lunch was ready; his copy of 'Scenes From A Life' was open next to his keyboard. He had come to Belsize Park that morning as if nothing had changed, as if the disaster of the previous twenty-four hours of his life had not happened or was a fiction straight out of one of his Father's books. He couldn't really recall in any detail exactly what he had done after Julia had walked out. He knew he hadn't undertaken any meaningful work in the evening, confining himself to eating and drinking; the television had been his sole companion. When his alarm woke him from a fitful sleep, he had showered quickly and eaten a light breakfast before leaving the house. It was, he told himself, the best thing to do: stay occupied and not let his mind wander. Even so, he was struggling this morning - and this was the day he needed to deal with his father's death.

"Really?!"

"Yes, really. Why are you surprised?"

"I don't know." He paused. "Given that I haven't been able to confirm anyone who'd got a copy, maybe I had assumed I never would and just gave up on finding out."

"You had one?"

Mark shook his head as his Aunt sat in the armchair.

"No, I didn't."

"Did you ever ask him why?" She showed no sign of surprise at his revelation.

"I can't remember - but I doubt it. After all, I didn't find out that there were such copies until much later. He and Peter Healy said nothing. Do you know who else got one?"

Now it was her turn to be negative, her eyes fixing on the open book.

"I don't. And he didn't tell me either."

There was a slight pause. This was an unusual gambit for Beatrice, to both open the conversation about his Father and the biography so directly, and then to sit in the chair. Usually she would just deliver her message or fulfil her task, and then retreat. Mark had the sense that there was more of a purpose to her visit. He checked his watch. It was still only just after twelve; a little earlier than usual for lunch to be ready.

"What was it like? The draft version, I mean." Mark picked up his copy of the book, flicked through a few pages, then closed it and put it back on the desk. "Was it very different to this?"

"A little," Beatrice said, returning her gaze to him. "But only in places. Some of it is difficult to recall; it's been a while since I read either."

"But when he gave it to you, what did he say? What was his reasoning? Publicly he said that it was because he wanted some people to be 'comfortable' with it; but what did that mean?"

"Oh it was simple enough," Beatrice replied, then began to glance around the room as if everything in it was somehow involved or implicated. "He was concerned how I was being portrayed. Did I have any issues? Was it fair? That sort of thing. Presumably that's what he mean by being comfortable."

"And that was it?"

"Not quite, I suppose. After all, I was in something of a privileged position; I knew him intimately, I knew Mary. I knew *you*. I had met some of these people or been involved with them, though all on the periphery if you like. In that sense maybe I was the best placed to provide some kind of impartial judgement. He couldn't ask you to do that, could he? You were even more involved - with your Mother, obviously - and so being unbiased wasn't going to be possible. I also think he appreciated how far you had come together."

"You mean during 1984?"

"Yes. There was a new closeness there. I suspect he never said anything, but he really appreciated that. I don't think he wanted to risk it."

Mark could relate to that from his own perspective. It had been a much better year for the two of them together; perhaps the best he could remember. For a moment he was glad he didn't get to see an early copy. And he had come out of the book itself unscathed, even if his part ended up being relatively minor. A thought occurred to him.

"Did you suggest any changes? I mean, did he change anything as a result of your feedback, what you said?"

Beatrice shifted, giving the impression she was just about to get out of the chair.

"As I say, Dear, it's been a long time since I read them both…"

"Come on, Aunt," Mark was not willing to take her evasion, "this was a pretty big deal. I'm sure you would have talked to him about it. If you had a view he would have listened - otherwise why else give you a copy? But did he make changes?"

"Yes; only one or two." Her confession came slowly.

Mark leant forwards in his chair.

"But this is exciting, relevant. It means that the book is not the whole story."

"It's the story that he chose to make public," she said, rising. "Isn't that what counts?"

"Perhaps. But not for *my* book. What was left out, or added, or changed is really significant. Or at the very least, could be significant. If you were to take the view that his final draft was what he *truly* wanted to say, then what was published is sanitised, censored."

She laughed. A laugh intended to lighten the seriousness of the mood.

"You're not suggesting that I was some kind of moral policeman or guardian?!"

"No, of course not. But there might be something there. You do see that?"

Beatrice placed a hand on his shoulder and squeezed gently.

"Of course." She paused. "Look, let's sit down after lunch, shall we?"

A frown passed across her face. It was a look Mark had seen before when she was struggling with something. He had noted it most when they had previously talked about his Mother.

-*-

By the time <u>Scenes From A Life</u> had been out for three months or so, the hullabaloo that had surrounded it was beginning to fade away, and Packard was able to return to a more normal existence. The challenge for him now, however, was a redefinition of what 'normal' actually was. Since he had met Simone some five years earlier, his life had become rather episodic, and although each period flowed from one to the next in a logical sequence, they remained disjointed. They each had their own different epicentre and focus: a period with Simone, then a period without; a period working on the book, then a period when it was being published. Certainly there was overlap and a degree of continuity, but for Charles there was no sense of "normal".

> "I didn't realise until afterwards - probably the late spring of '86 - how bizarre my life had become. Not only that, but <u>Scenes</u> had also allowed me to look back too; a re-examination, a re-investigation. In many ways I was living both in the past and in

the present; but neither of these were real somehow. All the present stuff was too much 'in the moment'; too super-charged with emotion or effort. There was my Simone life, and then my non-Simone life; my writing life, and then everything that went with getting the book 'out there' - including things like this. I remember thinking that I didn't know what 'normal' actually was. Or what it had ever been. Or when I had experienced it last. It was a question I tried to answer but patently failed to do so."

(Interview with Michael Parkinson, 1988)

This complaint was something that Healy was familiar with.

"For lots of successful writers, their lives have a kind of pulse or beat: a period writing, a period promoting, a period reflecting. And then back round again. Charles' life was much more haphazard than that. He was missing some kind of solid base upon which to execute this cycle of activity. He didn't have that. His 'normal' was fairly abnormal by anyone else's standards: the drinking, the affairs, the lack of a stable home life. I think that was one of the reasons he was pleased to be getting closer to Mark; it promised him something."

In many respects, Packard had arrived at a place in his life that demanded further reflection. <u>Scenes From A Life</u> had started the process in many ways; or perhaps, more accurately, it was the continuation of a process that had begun with Simone.

"In spite of the way she lived her life and the way it made our relationship work, the framework it gave it; in spite of that, Simone actually gave me a mirror to consider how life *could* be lived. Of course, I didn't know that at the time. It was only after she had died - which then forced me to consider the way I *had* to live, at least in the short term - I realised that. And in doing so, it gave me a kind of lens to look back on my past. I felt a little bit like the scientist in the white lab coat looking through the microscope; but the thing I was examining on the slide was myself, and at the end of the working day, unlike that guy, I had no home to go to. But that sounds maudlin or a cry for pity, which it isn't meant to be. I guess I came to see where the gaps in my life were, and in doing so, what I needed to do to fill them in."

(Interview with Michael Parkinson, 1988)

And so it was that in the May of 1986, Packard deliberately decided to draw a line under his past and - almost literally - turn to a blank page. He called it his 'birthday present to himself'. Typically for the man, extremes were involved. He stopped drinking, for example: not choosing to cut back, but to stop altogether. Even at readings, interviews, Macmillan events, he refrained from alcohol. He tried to eat more healthily, and started taking daily walks on the Heath to try and improve his fitness.

"He talked about getting a dog. We'd never had a dog as a family - in fact, I don't think we ever had any pets at all. Dad suddenly had this notion that a dog would help him keep fit, and be a companion for him."

Packard began building an image of what he wanted to be, creating an ideal for himself, of where he fitted in the grand scheme of things. Healy was roped in too.

"We started having regular meetings. We'd talk about his sales, about events he might attend or participate in; we'd even talk about other writers in the MacMillan stable. Occasionally he'd float ideas about his next project, and we'd discuss these. It was all theoretical, of course. Some of the ideas were incredibly fanciful and not him at all. Deep down, I think he knew where he was headed, though if he did know he never said. But it was strange to watch him re-invent himself like this. He became 'professional'. I wondered if he was trying to be the person he thought he ought to be, not who he was; trying on someone else's clothes, perhaps. I loved the old rogue Charles, and there were bits of him I missed, naturally."

The outcome - if it can be identified as such - was that for the second half of 1986 and all of the following year, Charles Packard became that one thing he had singularly failed to be for pretty much his entire life: steady, predictable, dependable, reliable, 'normal'.

"We never did get that dog, though I think we came perilously close. But then the notion for his next book came to him, and that was it; he was off on his next cycle of writing - the difference this time was that he had a regular life upon which to build it. He worked at it, I saw him; and it was 'work' in the sense that most of us mere mortals would understand."

Reconciled with himself, and - more importantly - with his past, Packard began writing with a profound sense of purpose and mission. He was, he knew, a mature man now, and in so many ways; it was time to act like one. He was also confident, fulfilled, self-reliant. It gave him a depth of certainty where in the past there had been just fragility.

> "Actually I've started work on something new. Just a few months now. What is it? How can I describe it? Something triggered it, I don't know what. I came to feel that _Scenes_ had allowed me to reflect on the historical episodes in my life and to use them as the

template for that fiction. But then it occurred to me that there was still a question that remained unanswered - or that I hadn't asked myself at all, actually. And that's the 'Why?' question. What in God's name took me down this road in the first place? The writing mainly, but not just that. Was it a fluke, a whim? Was it just luck, driven by a base instinct to impress a girl at a Birmingham art class? And after that, did it take on a life of its own? Was I just a passenger, rather than the driver? I suppose I've always assumed an answer to that question - I guess we all do - but I feel that now is the time to try and answer it. I think I'll never be in a better place to."

(Interview with Melvyn Bragg, 1987)

Packard had said nothing to Healy specifically prior to his interview with Bragg.

"I don't even recall this being one of his ideas, one of the things we talked about. I didn't know, and he didn't warn me. We talked about it the next day, and he told me where he was. Turned out he'd already mapped out quite a lot and the first two chapters were drafted. Even had a title: <u>A Small Enough Impulse</u>."

-*-

"I've made some tea," Beatrice said as Mark was loading his lunch things into the dishwasher. It was a statement heavy with meaning and innuendo; more than an invitation, an instruction. "I thought we could have it in the conservatory."

He sensed her leaving him in the kitchen, certain that he would follow her once he had finished his tidying up. Mark suddenly envied her that aura, the appreciation of certainty she seemed to carry with her. It was only when she was not sure of her ground or how things would turn out that she bore any sign of worry or concern. He recalled the frown she had worn in his study just a little while ago.

The conservatory was a room he visited infrequently. Occasionally he and Julia had tea in there with Beatrice and Simon, but these had been rare occurrences and, he knew, now unlikely to be repeated in the future. But perhaps - this as he walked towards the double doors that led from the kitchen - things would change; Julia would change. She would see that she had made a mistake. Wasn't that the most likely outcome?

He wore the signs of his thinking all too plainly.

"Sit down, Dear," Beatrice said, already established in her favourite spot, the rattan chair positioned in such a way as to give easy access to the small table in front of it and a view along the length of the garden. She used to joke that it was the perfect spot for 'keeping and eye on Simon', and 'making sure he's doing the weeding properly'. That image - of Simon weeding - was one Mark struggled with; the notion of Beatrice keeping an eye on him was, of course, an entirely different matter.

She leant forward to pour tea from the large white china teapot into similarly large cups. As he sat, watching her practiced action, he noticed the folded sheet of paper on the chair by her side.

"There." She edged a cup towards him. The day had brightened, and outside it appeared promising; the sun, when it broke through the white clouds that were chasing across the sky, immediately heated the conservatory. Half-way down the garden, Mark spotted a squirrel scampering across the lawn towards the small silver birch.

"Are you all right, Dear?"

Her question was - although vague and open-ended - traditionally to the point.

"All right? Why do you ask?"

"You seem a little preoccupied. And tired too. Especially this morning."

"I didn't sleep that well."

Although he hoped that would be enough, his experience of his Aunt told him it would not; more must follow. And, intrigued by the paper at her side - which he assumed, was destined for him - he was not so inclined to engineer a quick escape.

"There's a lot going on, I suppose," he offered, loosely.

"With the book, of course," she suggested.

"Yes."

"But not just that. I know it's taking it out of you, but there's more isn't there, Dear?"

"You can tell?"

It was not what he meant to say. He had wanted to offer some kind of non-committal denial, but the words were out of him before he could stop them. It was a 'yes', in any other language. He knew Beatrice would press, so there was no point in postponing. To keep it simple, he settled on the obvious thing she would be interested in and relate to.

"It's Julia, actually."

"Oh. I did wonder."

Mark immediately noted the lack of any outward signs of surprise.

"Why do you say that?"

"I sensed something wasn't quite right, if I'm honest. Perhaps for a little while. You both seemed a bit - I don't know, Dear - distant."

"'Distant'?"

"I assumed it was because you were working so hard, or so involved. Your starting to come here earlier and stay longer - well, that seemed aligned somehow."

"No, it's not the book," Mark corrected her. "We had a bit of a misunderstanding, that's all. She's gone away for a few days. I'm sure it will turn out to be nothing."

"Are you?"

"Am I what?"

"Sure?" She paused. "You don't sound like you're terribly sure, Dear. Quite the opposite for you, actually. Was it a row? Is it possible she might not come back?"

He hadn't wanted the direct question. Although he had given it no conscious thought, he knew - now the question was live and in the ether - that he hadn't wanted it. He chose to avoid it.

"Yes, a row of sorts. As I say, a misunderstanding." He picked up his cup. "Or more a misinterpretation. She's made some assumptions about something that aren't correct, that's all. And one of her friends has been stoking the fire..." He allowed the embellishment to hang there. It gave him both a sense of protection and distance; it enabled the suggestion that he was the injured party - which in the case of his arm, was undoubtedly true.

Beatrice allowed a small pause.

"If there's anything I can do, Mark, please let me know. I do have some experience in this area."

She had paused before the second sentence. Mark was sipping his tea as she delivered it.

"With Simon?!" he asked, incredulously. He could not conceived how he might transpose Beatrice and Simon into the same roles and situation that he and Julia were playing out.

Beatrice laughed at his false assumption.

"No, of course not, Dear! Simon, indeed!" The thought amused her for a moment, and then her face darkened slightly. "With your Father, of course." When Mark did not respond immediately, she looked out into the garden and carried on. "More than once we've sat here like this, he and I, putting the world to rights."

"But since when? I mean, you haven't lived here that long have you?"

"Long enough, Dear. Think about it. Think about when you first came here. It was years and years ago now. Sometimes Charles and I would talk about the past - well, he did most of the talking, of course. It was mostly about the past. Especially when he was working on those last couple of things of his; you know, when he was looking back."

"'Scenes', you mean?"

"Mainly, yes. Particularly as he was drafting it. He wanted to check things, you see. He used me as a bit of a sounding board for dates, ideas, interpretations if you like. I suppose he wanted to try and get it as 'right' as he could - whatever that might mean."

"And then afterwards? After he had given you the draft to read?"

She sighed. It was a heavy and sorrowful sigh.

"Yes, then too."

"What did he change, Aunt? You said he made one or two changes, didn't you. I need to know what they were, don't I? I need to know for the book, but I don't think you want to tell me."

"You're right about one thing: I don't want to tell you. But you're wrong about the other. It's not really about the book; that's not why I have to tell you. It's because you need to know. Oh, it will mean you have to put a little something extra in, or change something, I suppose; but it's not really about the book."

She had looked back at him as she delivered her last assertion, and then allowed her gaze to drift back outside. Mark followed suit. The squirrel had long since gone and the sun, still playing hide-and-seek with the clouds, was throwing shadows and edges across the lawn. He knew he could only wait for her; wait for her to be ready. He finished his tea and replaced the cup on the table.

The breeze that was scudding the clouds rippled through the flower beds causing the crocosmia and golden rod to sway vigorously giving the border a rhythmical motion that was countered by the short, squat shrubs that guarded them. Sitting here, they were close enough to be able to make out the occasional bee as it went about its business, harvesting plant to plant, before it headed back to the hive.

"It was more reductions than changes," Beatrice suddenly said, softly; breaking into the moment as if it were a simple continuation from where she had left off. "There was a little more history in the draft I read than made it into print. Not masses, mind you. In most cases just subtleties: events that added little to the narrative, things that your father wasn't sure whether he should include or not."

"Such as?"

"Oh, evenings spent drinking, mostly. When he was younger. As far as I could see, re-telling such exploits only served to endorse an image that he was keen to let slip away. They didn't add anything at all, you see. I mean, where was the interest in that?"

Mark weighed this up. From a purist perspective, he would have like to see everything included - if not in 'Scenes From A Life', then certainly in his own work.

"So I won't have these in my book?"

"I seriously doubt it, Dear. But then, have you logged every evening your father spent in a bar, or every pint of beer he ever drank? I don't think so." She paused again. "There was one related incident that I suggested he remove."

"Related to drink?"

"Yes. Did you know he'd had a fight with that dreadful Shutts fellow?"

"No. Really!"

"Yes, really. Oh it was something and nothing, like most fights between men. Fists flew, punches were thrown - but I don't think any actually landed. Charles left me that impression."

"So he took it out?"

"He did." She sensed Mark tensing slightly. "I have the draft somewhere. If you want to include it, I can give you the sordid details."

"Thanks."

From his perspective, such colour was relevant and material - especially given Shutts' involvement in his father's publishing career. It was probably a small event, but part of the fabric. He was about to return his gaze to the garden when he noticed Beatrice's hand move to the paper beside her.

"Is that all?" he prompted.

She looked uncomfortable; the most disquieted he could ever recall seeing her.

"Not entirely."

Mark could see the moisture suddenly there in her eyes. It was something he had never previously witnessed. When she spoke next, her voice was fragile and slightly broken.

"Mark, Dear, I have to confess that I have been dishonest with you. And for some time. You kept asking me if there was anything else I had, anything that you needed to know for your book - 'evidence' you might have called it once, I think. And I always said 'no', didn't I? But there was. There is." She picked up the folder piece of paper. "There is only this one thing - but there's the story that goes with it."

"What do you mean?"

"I mean that it wasn't just the fight that Charles left out. He left out a whole person too. Oh, they were there in his draft; only sketched in, because that was all they could be, but there nonetheless. I was stunned when I read it. Not because it was badly written. Nor because I didn't know about it. Well, actually I didn't know, but I had my suspicions. I just didn't know why he had included it." She suddenly sobbed. "Oh, I'm messing this up! I tried to tell you once before, but I couldn't go through with it, not properly. Of course I knew why he had included them. How could he not?! But it just didn't seem right. After all this time. What good could it do? What benefit did it bring?"

There was no gap as far as Mark was concerned. In all the conversations he had ever had with his father, in all the material he had read, the people he had spoken to, there was no-one missing. No-one. How could there be?

"I don't understand. Who is missing?"

Beatrice held out the paper for him. For a split second they both held it, and as they did so, she spoke.

"You have a sister."

"I what?"

The paper was pale blue, thin and lined. Mark recognised his father's handwriting immediately. There was a date: September 1964.

> *Dearest Constantina,*
>
> *Your letter has just reached me this morning. I confess myself stunned by your news. Are you absolutely certain? I assume you*

must be, otherwise why would you say such a thing? Does your family know? What do you plan to do? There are various things going through my spinning head at the moment, some of which are not pleasant.

I know you say that you have made your mind up, but are you certain? In your letter, you ask nothing of me. Is that what you want? Obviously it is impossible for me to leave England, but surely there must be something I can do for you? I have a little money but not much. If I can help, then I will do so.

I will keep this letter short so that I can get it to the post. You know I cannot telephone you. You asked me not to make contact at all. But then your letter. This news. I don't know what to say.

Charles

PS: I am glad your sister is now fully recovered from her illness.

By the time Mark had finished the letter, his hands were shaking. For a moment he seemed to have lost the power to speak, or even think. He looked up at Beatrice wanting more, needing to understand.

"You have a sister, Mark," she repeated. "Constantina gave birth early in 1965. A little girl. But that's all we know. Your father made some enquiries later, discretely. He had to, as she never contacted him again. But then, he never contacted her either."

"What do you mean?"

"Isn't it obvious? You have the original letter in your hand. Your father didn't send it. I asked him if there was another version that he did send, but he always denied it. I have never seen the letter he had from Constantina, but there must have been one mustn't there? When Charles left Hydra, they agreed never to contact each other again. That's what he told me. What was the point? There was nothing either of them could do about it. But she was pregnant before he left the island. Whether breaking their agreement and writing to him had any specific goal or purpose, I don't know. Charles said he didn't know either, and I believed him. Maybe that's why he didn't send that letter."

"No-one knew?"

"Just he and I. And that was the way we agreed it would stay. Once 1964 then 1965 passed, we assumed that somehow Constantina had sorted things out back in Greece. No claim was ever made on him; at least none that I knew of. It tortured him greatly, of course; sometimes more than others, inevitably. But I got the impression that he was learning to live with it. And then he drafted that book of his, and he included the postscript to Hydra. It was only in the draft *I* saw. He was careful about that. I remember we sat here and talked about it. I told him that he had to take it out of the book. He *had* too. He didn't want to. Said it would be dishonest. We argued. But in the end...well."

She stopped, then leant forwards to pour more tea. It was a way to fill the void. Mark re-read the letter twice more.

"And you?" She said, quietly. " Now that you know. How are you?"

Mark tried to assess how he felt, the weight of the paper in his hand. How could something so small and light carry such portent?

"I'm okay, I think." He spoke slowly, measuring his words. "Somehow I'm not as surprised as I might have been, I guess. All those affairs, after all. And because it has never affected me, I guess I can distance myself from it."

"She would be a year to two younger than you."

"Do you know her name?"

"I don't. And if Charles did, then he never said."

A thought struck him.

"There were two people missing."

"Sorry?"

"Two people missing from the history: the baby, and Constantina's sister. I never knew she had a sister. Dad never mentioned her anywhere either. What do you know about her?"

"A little. She was younger. I've no idea what the illness was the letter refers to. Charles seemed to think that she left Greece at some point to study in Europe, though where he got that from I've no idea."

Mark played his father's timelines through in his head.

"This means that he would have written 'Under The Olive Tree' with this hanging over him. Gone through all the rigours of publication, everything, at the same time. That's quite something."

"That had never occurred to me. Perhaps it gave him an incentive," Beatrice suggested.

"Incentive?"

"You know; if it was successful, it would generate more income. Just in case."

Mark smiled. It felt a sad, wearied smile even as he delivered it.

"Does that sound like my father? I don't think he was ever able to join the dots in a practical way like that."

Beatrice leant forwards and placed her hand on his knee.

"Not at that age, Dear; you're probably right." She allowed her thought to float towards him for a moment. "Are you sure you're okay? You seem fine, but it's a bit of a jolt."

He stood up.

"I'm fine. As I said, it's all too far away and too surreal to bother me. Honestly."

"Good." Her relief was evident. "What are you going to do now?"

"Oh, I need to draft a little bit more, then I'll call it day. As I said, didn't sleep that well last night, so I'm a bit tired anyway. Back tomorrow - if that's all right."

-*-

When 1988 came to a close, much of the work for <u>A Small Enough Impulse</u> had been completed. With the bottle of champagne Packard gifted Healy as a New Year's present - a tradition of some five years by this time - there was, as the accompanying note informed him, just 'window dressing' left. Christmas had been a quiet affair, strangely dominated by the new normality in the Packard household.

"It was an understated end to the year. Dad was clearly happy with his new work, though he never did tell me much about it. I just got a sense of satisfaction from him. Maybe it was self-esteem. He clearly felt he was doing something truly worthwhile. He told me his New Year resolution was to have it finished by Easter."

It was a relatively mild January. The month was sunnier and drier than the norm, and there was no snow. To Packard, who was still maintaining the walking regime he had initiated over two years earlier, it was ideal for the Heath. He had, in the course of the previous few months, lost nearly a stone in weight and was leaner and fitter than he had been for years. Although he was nearly sixty-seven, he boasted that he had the figure of a man ten years his junior, and for people who did not know him, that boast might well have rung true.

What the exterior disguised however, was an internal mechanism that had been struggling to keep up for some time. The legacy of years of abuse and hard living, along with associated periods of stress and tension, had taken their invisible toll.

On Sunday 14th January, 1989, he left the house bemoaning - as was now traditional - the absence of a dog to keep him company, and headed to the Heath. Occasionally Mark would accompany him, but not this morning he had arranged to spend time with Julia Walters. Twenty minutes later, as he was heading towards Parliament Hill, Charles Packard was felled by a massive heart attack. The doctors later suggested that he was dead before he hit the ground.

Some people who had been in the park tried to help. An ambulance was called. It arrived fifteen minutes later; traffic had been horrendous.

"I didn't find out until I got back later that afternoon. We had been out in Richmond and there was no way to contact me. I knew something was up as soon as I saw Beatrice and Simon's car outside our house. Simon shook my hand - and Simon rarely shook my hand in those days - and Beatrice was in pieces. Instinctively I knew what it was. I guess you always do. They let me see him when I got to the hospital. I remember he looked entirely peaceful. It was amazing. And it occurred to me that he probably had never been as much at peace with himself as he had those last few months. It was fitting somehow."

Peter Healy helped Mark with the arrangements; Beatrice handled a lot of the invitations for the funeral, the flowers, the caterers.

"I wasn't sure what to expect in terms of turn out. There were some of my colleagues from MacMillan there, plus a few of the authors from our stable - the ones Charles had shared a platform with from time to time. Inevitably there was a smattering of press, but not too many. But overall, my abiding sense of the day was how quiet it was. I know that's because a lot of the people Charles had known had gone before him, but it still seemed quiet. Too quiet. He deserved more."

<u>A Small Enough Impulse</u> would not be published in Charles Packard's lifetime.

Chapter Forty

It was a night not of dreams but of images, flickering before his eyes as if from a rotary slide projector, their sequence jumbled, without order or history. And the images as they came to him were primarily of people; his father, his mother, Julia, Claire, Lydia. Most of these he recognised from photographs he had taken or seen, but some were imagined from days out, events; what the photographs might have looked like if someone had been there with a camera to take them. And there were surreal visions too: pictures of people he had never seen - like Constantina, olive-skinned and statuesque - created from a perception of what they might have looked like, or how their story portrayed them. And some of the images blurred, combined; threw people together in strange and abstract ways, in ways that could never have occurred, either from a historical or a practical perspective. His mother with Stella, for example; Julia with Lydia. And then there were faces he was unable to locate in his memory. Faces painted against a backdrop of London, or Stratford, or Greece. And when he struggled to locate these people, these places, he failed to sleep; and each twist and turn of his body only succeed in generating a new image, a new conundrum for him to solve.

And the face that was missing from this kaleidoscopic collection was his own. Always looking, but never seen. He wanted there to be images of himself *with* people; it was important. He needed to know that he was real; that he related to these others. How was he when this picture was taken? How did he appear, or seem, or feel? There! There was Beatrice and Simon. He recalled that day; he was there. They sat by the fountain and his father had taken a photograph of the three of them. He remembered that; he knew it. But where was he in the image his mind now replayed to him? He had been erased, removed. There had only been one photograph taken, of that he was certain; so where was he? He had exorcised himself.

When the alarm clock finally rang, it roused him not from sleep but from a kind of torture. Mark knew that he must have slept a little, but it did not feel that way. The images - fading now as his day-time consciousness kicked-in - had come at him in a torrent; there had been no time to rest. He had been nagged continuously, mercilessly. At one point he had tried to read, but couldn't concentrate. He had tried a soothing tea infusion, pills, anything - all to no avail. And now the morning found him, grey and dishevelled, like a man returning home from a night on the tiles.

A quick glance in the bathroom mirror told him that he could not afford to let Beatrice see him like this. He needed to shave for one thing, but could not find the energy to do so. He showered at least, though that failed to cleanse anything it seemed, and he ending up sitting at the kitchen table with a black coffee watching the clock. He knew Beatrice and Simon were going out for the day. He would wait, delay his arrival in Belsize Park to ensure that he missed them. The notion of not going there, of not working on the book, did not occur to him, in much the same way as it had not occurred to him just two mornings earlier after Julia's departure. He had just buried his father and there were lose ends to tie up, closures to make. The book had appeared in his over-night panoply of images too, become animated, live, voracious, its cover temporarily a mouth, teeth chomping towards him. But this had been fleeting, replaced by the sight of Julia standing at the bowsprit of an old sailing ship pretending she was in 'Titanic'.

Mark glanced over to the answer phone. The tell-tale light was not flashing. No message from Julia again. Perhaps she was still thinking it over; still trying to reconcile her judgement against the reality of the situation. Once he had finished this draft of the book, then he would have some time again; then he would be free to invest it elsewhere. Perhaps that was all Julia needed.

When he had finished his coffee and knew it was safe to move - safe in that he would arrive at an empty house - Mark roused himself, put his mug in the sink and made for his car. It was a dull day with fine drizzle in the air; the kind of rain that covers the windscreen, yet does not feel heavy enough to warrant putting the wipers on. He drove the short distance distracted, his concentration uneven, his vision obscured by the rain on the window, blurred as it had been for some of the images he had seen during the night. The car seemed foreign to him, almost uncontrollable, and he was almost hit as he made a right turn in the face of on-coming traffic whose speed and proximity he misjudged entirely.

The driveway of his Aunt's house was empty. Mark parked his car untidily, taking up both available spaces, then got out and let himself in through the front door. There was a note waiting for him on the kitchen table: a piece of paper, folded, with his name written on the outside. He left it there, unread. It seemed sufficient that his existence was recognised with that single word. He paused by the kettle. Did he want more coffee? Would that be a good idea? He thought so. He could make it extra strong, to help him get through the morning; that would be the thing to do. He flicked the kettle on without checking the level of water in it, then walked out of the kitchen and up the stairs.

On the threshold of his room, he paused. The door was open, as usual. From where he had stopped, he could see part of the chair, the edge of the desk, some of the bookcase. And the very corner of the brown paper package just edging into view.

It was still here. Somehow Mark had assumed that it would have gone. Had it been there yesterday? If Julia had left him, then why had she not taken the mirror with her? It was nothing to do with him after all. Perhaps its still being there was some kind of sign; a sign that she was intending to come back to him. Or maybe she was taunting him with it. Was that the reason she had left it, deliberately, wilfully? Either way, Mark knew now that it had to go. Perhaps he had known it all along, but now he was certain. Now he could act.

He walked into the room and sat down at his desk, automatically turning on his computer. The same buzz and flicker as usual. After a minute or so, his desktop, and in the top left-hand corner, the icon that would take him to his father's biography. It was still there, where he had left it. He clicked twice and the folder opened, exposing document after document, text upon text, theories and quotes and testimonies. His words - the amalgam of all those things - secure in forty separate files, one Word document for each chapter. And at the end of that list, the final chapter, the one he had been working on yesterday. He opened the document and read the last few words. He read: 'it still seemed quiet. Too quiet. He deserved more.' And even though this was about his father, Mark suddenly felt as if it were true for him too. Wasn't it too quiet? He was alone now; that could not be right. Where had his father gone? Where was Julia? Why wasn't Lydia there?

And then he remembered that he was missing too. Not only missing from all the images he had seen during the night, but from all this material too. He was nowhere. He had spent all his time writing about others, and what was he in all of this? He had allowed himself the odd comment, but was that enough? Didn't *he* deserve more?

But part of him said 'no'. He had not done enough to warrant such recognition. He had been incapable, incompetent, had failed. If that were not the case, then where was Claire, his mother, his Aunt, Lydia? Why had they deserted him, merely to come back and taunt him; to laugh at him like chanting children in a school playground?

Then, he noticed the folder containing the photographs he was planning for the book. Proof of something! He ripped it open and the pictures scattered in front of him. He remembered that one, there! He had imagined it last night; and that one! He flicked through them quickly, haphazardly. And then his hand alighted on the photo of Lydia; the one that should not have been there. And he gasped, involuntarily. Lydia. She looked like… It was just like… He shook his head. What had he seen in the night? Who had he created? Yes, that was it. Constantina. They looked the same. Lydia looked the same as Constantina. How was that possible?! Constantina would have been older, surely. How could she look like Lydia? But what about her daughter? If you ignored the age, then perhaps that might be so. Lydia looked like his sister! But that could not be; history did not allow that. Could history allow for that?! How did Constantina look like Lydia?

He dropped the picture, his mind now reeling in the confusion of people present and absent; of black-and-white and colour images; of smiles and flowers and bright blue skies. It was his night-time become real, here and now. And where was he? Where was he?!

Mark put his head in his hands. He was tired. Perhaps the lack of sleep; the pills he had taken. He was confused, that was all. He just needed to get a grip of himself; to ground himself back in reality. But how could he do that? From over his shoulder a whisper that wasn't there. He turned. The brown package. The mirror. He would look in the mirror; that would confirm he was there! He would be able to look at himself, to be certain!

Getting up, he dragged the package out to the front of the comfortable chair and sat down again. The small tear in one corner was still there, showing a glimpse of the glass beyond. He pulled at the stiff paper, ripping it further, pulling it hard until the width of the mirror was exposed; then he stood, raising the object from its cocoon. He kicked the paper aside, then placed the mirror down on the floor, propping it against the radiator at such an angle that, when he sat down, he could see himself clearly.

In the intense accuracy the mirror seemed to possess, he failed to recognise the face that stared back at him. How could that be Mark Packard? It was a drawn, gaunt face; there were dark rings under the eyes, and the cheeks sagged and held a tint of grey. The hair was dishevelled, as if it had not been combed for days, and there was the beginnings of unruly stubble across the entirety of the chin. This was not the man who had wooed and won Lydia or Julia; not the man in the sharp dinner-jacket that Maxine had found irresistible. If not he, then who was it? There in the eyes; there was something there. He had seen that before, that look, that nuance. And then Mark realised. He had seen it - the tenor and depth of it, the portent and meaning of it - in photographs of his father, the old, grainy, black-and-white photographs. Here was his father's son all right; there could be no denying that.

But how could that be? Mark watched the eyes that stared back at him being to blaze. This was someone different. Just as the mirror had exposed the flaw in his jacket, so it was trying to do the same thing now, but to expose him! He could not allow that to happen. This was not right, not honest. At some profound level the Mark that searched found the Mark that stared back abhorrent; it was an image that had to be destroyed. He rose slowly and saw himself disappear from the frame. Then he leant over to his desk and picked up his heavy stapler. This would suffice surely? Then turning, and without hesitation, Mark hurled the stapler at the mirror's surface. There was a resounding crack, the stapler bouncing off and coming to rest against the wall beside the bookcase. He could see a shard of glass on the floor at the base of the chair; just one. He sat back down. The mirror had fractured but not broken, and now, instead of a single image of the imposter Mark looking back at him, there were three, four, five of them; echoes of himself, all at different angles, each exposing a subtly different view of himself.

They were all this other person, and now there were enough of them to go round: one for Julia, one for Maxine, for Claire, for Lydia. They could share the pressure and responsibility between them; it would not be all on his shoulders. This substitute, this imposter could take it all and leave him free. But would it really be freedom? The rough face challenged him on that. It didn't seem likely that such a face would accept his burden, or would be able to live with his past. And what then? What if there were more than one struggling to understand, to resolve; all trying to redress and smooth and arrive at the perfect outcome? If all these replicants failed, where would the contentment come from? Was it not all to be multiplied many times; the incompetence, the failure, the agony?

Like the mirror, Mark felt suddenly broken. And then it was more than that. He was beaten. He had been defeated; routed by a powerful combination and an enemy he had not been able to acknowledge. Julia was probably the catalyst. The Julia that had bought this mirror, installed it here; the Julia who had turned on him, misunderstood him, and left. He knew at that moment she would not be coming back to him. It was as undeniable a blow as if he could feel the fist in his stomach. And in leaving him, she had triggered the others to attack. They saw him weakened now, and had begun their remorseless assault. Claire would never forgive him. She had hit him for real, bruised him. First she had teased and taunted him, and led him on; and now she too was denying him her presence. Not only would she never understand, but she would make sure Peter would abandon him too. Her alliance with Julia would only be made all stronger by Lydia, who would return from somewhere arriving on the train to be met by them both at the station. And then the three of them would come to him, taunt him, bully him. And he would have no defence.

And who would she bring with her, Lydia? With her perfect Mediterranean skin? Then Mark saw in his mind's eye the plane landing at Heathrow, the taxi to the stand, and the disembarkation of three women from Hydra: Constantina, her daughter, her sister. And they would all look like Lydia; they might all be Lydia! And even though they were nothing to do with him, they would be ranged against him, condemning him. He would become nothing. And all the fragments in the mirror, all the images of this shattered face told him the same story.

Who could he range against them? Who was on his side? And the answer was 'no-one'. His mother had deserted him, and his father - who had not cared for him at all until towards the end - even he had gone too. And what was worse was that these faces that stared back accusing Mark from within the mirror's frame, were all his father's. And the Greek women were his. Even - on some level - Julia, Claire and Lydia were all there because of him, because of what he had given Mark. All of this, all this treachery, in spite of the hours and days and weeks of effort and dedication Mark had shown in preparing his book. Was that not a labour of love that should reap some kind of reward? Didn't he deserve more?

But he had one final gambit. Mark knew that now with a clarity that shocked him. He saw the fear in the many eyes that stared back at him. He still had the power. He could destroy them all. And he could do it here and now. He went back to his desk and looked at the screen. Explorer was still open, all his files laid bare. It didn't matter what he wrote, he knew that now. They were just words on a page, and irrespective of his choice or their order, nothing could change - nor reproduce - exactly what had happened. He was not his father. One by one he clicked on each if the files and pressed 'delete'. It was that easy. They were gone. He felt the burden begin to lift. It was start.

On the desk, the physical, tangible photographs were still spread. These would be next. He gathered them up, trying not to examine them; turning them over in his hand, making a bundle. Mark paused. Now what? From somewhere downstairs - was it the kitchen? - he heard a sound he did not recognise; a cross between a bang and a pop. Nothing probably. He pulled the waste bin from beside his desk and emptied its contents on to the floor. From a drawer in his desk he retrieved the old lighter he had used many years ago when he had experimented with cigarettes and which he had kept since then as some kind of memento. Flicking it into life, he held the first image over the flame and watched it catch; then he let it fall into the waiting receptacle. Then the next and the next. The photographs crackled slightly as they burned. With one flourish, he let the rest fall from his hand into the flames; flames that were now licking a little way up the sides of the bin.

How was that? Better? How did the face look now? He moved back to the chair and sat down. The faces stared back, but Mark could see a slight smile playing on the taut lips. Were they teasing him still, or was this some kind of last minute bravado? He knew he was winning now; all he had to do was to get rid of these faces. He stood again, kicking the brown wrapping further away from him; then he picked up the mirror from the floor, rested it face down across the arms of the chair, and hit the back of it hard with his fist. At the same moment as the fragments of mirror flew from the frame and onto the chair seat, so the mirror's wrapping, now resting against the waste paper bin, caught, unable to resist the heat and flames of the burning photographs.

There was suddenly smoke. If Mark had been able to look into a mirror at that precise moment, he would have seen a different expression on his troubled face; but it was too late now. He watched the flames leaping from the bin, the brown wrapping, and now the rubbish that had previously been in the bin. They were between he and the door. He could smell the carpet singeing too. A flame licked the leg of his desk, begging to join the party. And then from somewhere else, he had a sense of other smoke, rising up the stairs to join him. Even the cough that was suddenly wrenched from his body was not enough to rouse him. All of those things that had dominated him, all those people they had belonged to, all were gone, defeated.

Mark smiled. He had won.

Chapter Forty One

A Small Enough Impulse

How does it start? Perhaps with something inconsequential; with something that excites our emotions, or triggers a memory. Perhaps – in the way that it assaults or caresses us – it begins with our senses; is sensual in the most profound way. The sound of a bird in a tree, the rush of the breeze, or warmth on our skin. The taste of lemons that takes us back to Madeira, or the Brunello that is Tuscany, pure and simple. The reflection of the sun, sparkling and dancing on the lake near the bandstand. Cut grass, fresh bread, pavements after rain; an alarm, a church bell, the cry of a baby deprived of milk; haze on the horizon, the magic of a rainbow, an unexpected reflection in a shop window; spices, the coldest ice-cream; coffee – the smell of, the taste of, the sound of percolation.

And then perhaps it starts with an accidental touch. Fingers brushing, momentarily. A fraction of a second that is a fraction too long; long enough to dwell for more than an instant, but in that moment is sufficient time to scribe volumes greater than anyone could ever imagine; whispers of hope and longing, foretelling of regret, sounds of crying, the most bitter taste, the indescribable tingle that sets forearm hairs to attention, hearts racing – not one, but two! – and pulses quickening, and in the eyes..! A whole lifetime. Or then again, is the trigger the absence of those things. Is it the desire for the accidental touch, the lack of sun, the need for rain, the silence in a church?

But start it does. Quickly or slowly, but inevitably. Painfully or joyously it will assail us, teach us, enliven or depress us, inspire, move, motivate, crush, destroy. And all we need is to be aware and awake, sensible to the certainty of its coming, of that moment when things freeze, the world shifts, and we must move on with a different reality. 'All we need'...? The sensibility and intuition of a poet, the openness of a saint, the naivety of a child, a willingness to discover, an acceptance that we do not know enough – that we cannot know enough. And above all else perhaps, to embrace risk, and change, and the courage to make things different.

Is that it? The undefinable? Is that how we migrate through our lives and take our small steps towards a seemingly unending infinity of steps? If we could trace our lives, backwards through such moments, would we be surprised by what we found or lost, or by how little we knew? Would our ignorance astound us, or our lack of bravery and ambition, our absence of courage, bravado, morality –

immorality! – and surrounding all of this, our inability to describe, articulate and make whole anything that has happened to us?

When he thought of language, as he did now, some of these things might have come to him. Drip-fed or in a rush, he might have attempted to unravel or rearrange them, to create a picture that might make sense of things. Above all things, he wanted to understand, and for him understanding was about articulation, for only then could he manage to grasp the unknowable; yet even as he desired this, clumsily working with the tools of his trade – words, paint, pastel, manufactured 'things' – he somehow became further removed and thus more desperate. It was as if every desire he had ever known had been crystallised into a single, simple goal: to describe, something, to perfection.

-*-

He hesitated over the keyboard, his fingers temporarily paralysed as he decided between words. It was a familiar conundrum. And although the words were similar - as they so often were! - there were subtleties about them he had to acknowledge would drive alternative directions of travel. They had both strengths and weaknesses; connotations that implied other words, other realities not included or intended. He had tried to fight them off, these spawned and tangential children, but it was an impossibility. He had tried to nail things down; to describe in precise detail - including what was not meant. How else could he be successful? How else could he say what he meant?

And yet, even if it were possible to neutralise the spurious, it would only be so in his own mind. Others brought their own inferences, context and meaning; overlaid their individual realities on his words. There was no way that he could protect his words against such interpretation. But that was his goal; the unspoken drive. If he could achieve the perfection he sought, there could be no divergence; there would only be one meaning, his meaning, his view of the world. Was that part of his torment; the achievement of that nirvana, the only prize worth chasing?

Sometimes, often when the drink had hold of him, he felt inclined to give it all up; to put aside this impossible chase of words for something more irreverent. But it was a temporary weakness. He allowed himself to indulge in it for that evening, that week, that month. The timespan was of no consequence because the outcome was always the same. It could only be death that ceased his quest. It was as if he were trapped within an infinite maze, always walking forwards, always turning left or right - such a binary choice! - heading for the centre, a prize taunting him with a momentary glimpse above the tops of the hedges.

Occasionally he managed to get close; very close. He felt as if he were always just one hedge, one turn away. But then the path would veer, force him left when he wanted to go right, and he would inevitably be led away from his goal. Weaker men, he consoled himself, would have thrown in the towel by now; those who were not as possessed as he might admit defeat. And even when he wanted to, even at the darkest hour when he was closer to the beginning than the end, it was impossible for him to do so. At the next bend, the next choice, the next change of direction, just then he might be suddenly led towards the centre again and the impossible victory.

Coverstory
books

Coverstory
books